M000199593

THE SPOTTED OWL:
A DEREK RILEY NOVEL

by

Kyle Hiller

DORRANCE
PUBLISHING CO
EST. 1920
PITTSBURGH, PENNSYLVANIA 15238

Dorrance Publishing Co
585 Alpha Drive
Suite 103
Pittsburgh, PA 15238
Visit our website at *www.dorrancebookstore.com*

ISBN: 978-1-6393-7379-6
eISBN: 978-1-6393-7757-2

ACKNOWLEDGMENTS

For my wife and best friend, Shannon.
She is always encouraging while simultaneously putting up with
my many quirks. The world should be thankful she is in it—
she keeps me in check.

Special thanks to Ryan and Beth for helping develop this book
and putting up with the dripping faucet.

I would also like to acknowledge my friend Steve,
whom I continuously bounce ideas off.

PROLOGUE

"Little Boy," the bomb dropped on Hiroshima that ended World War II was approximately 13-kilotons of destructive power. The detonation marked the beginning of the Cold War arms race and initiated the age of competitive nuclear weapons development. In the early years of the United States atomic testing, many of the nuclear weapons experiments occurred in the Pacific's Marshall Islands.

From 1946 through 1951, a total of sixty-seven nuclear tests were conducted. Bombs, ranging in sizes up to 257 kilotons, were detonated along the Bikini Atoll. Issues concerning both security and logistics made continuing these Pacific tests difficult. In 1950, the Atomic Energy Commission determined that Nellis Air Force Gunnery and Bombing Range in southern Nevada satisfied nearly all of the established criteria for a domestic testing program.

Located just sixty-five miles north of Las Vegas, the Nevada Proving Grounds, later named, the Nevada Test Site (NTS) was the most significant nuclear weapons test site in the United States. For over forty years, the US government conducted over 1,000 nuclear tests, including more than one hundred atmospheric tests at the NTS. These led to the development of bigger atomic bombs and advanced thermonuclear weapons. The largest of these tests was "Castle Bravo" in 1954 when a 15-megaton bomb was detonated.

For better understanding, one kiloton is equal to 1,000 tons of TNT. The bomb that leveled Hiroshima was 13-kilotons. There are 1,000 kilotons to one megaton.

When testing began, meteorologists working for the US government were confident that the weather patterns would contain the spread of radiation to within the nearly 1,400 square miles of the NTS. They were wrong. Recently unclassified documents revealed radioactive fallout from these tests actually drifted across most of North America. Unfortunately, the implications of the secrecy surrounding atomic testing did not end there.

During those same years, US military servicemen, referred to as "Atomic Veterans" were used as guinea pigs during the Cold War. The military wanted to see the effects of a nuclear blast on soldiers and ascertain if they could complete their mission following the explosion. The Atomic Veterans did not volunteer for these assignments that, for many, planted the seeds of cancers and other radiation exposure issues.

At the NTS, entire companies of soldiers, literally hundreds of men, were deliberately placed mere miles away from test detonations. Intentionally, few were told what they could expect as the second part of the government's experiment was to determine the psychological impacts of witnessing these blasts. Government psychiatrists were present before, during, and following the tests to assess, not treat, these servicemen.

The soldiers were not provided protective gear beyond what was standard issue, such as utility jackets, weapons, and helmets. Additionally, they were only given rudimentary instructions, such as to stay low and close their eyes. The brightness of the nuclear explosions temporarily blinded some soldiers. Others would later recall how they could see through their own skin and muscles, viewing their veins and bones as if looking at an x-ray.

Following the nuclear explosions, the soldiers would be ordered to stand and walk through the debris fields. These men did not realize they were operating in a highly radioactive environment. Exposure to radiation was still an unknown concept to most of the world's population.

At times, these soldiers would spend hours in the blast zones, drinking contaminated water or eating contaminated food. Only then would the woefully inadequate decontamination procedures begin. Typically, the extent of decontamination was a radiological safety person from the Army running a Geiger counter over the soldiers while another brushed them off with a standard household broom.

These military members were told that they could not talk about what they witnessed. The government essentially put the fear of God in them. Besides believing they could go to prison or be fined tens of thousands of dollars, many thought they could be tried for treason and shot if they divulged what they knew or witnessed.

Not surprisingly, the health issues for these atomic veterans were vastly greater than those of the general population. Hair loss, boils, spinal problems, schwannoma—which are tumors that develop and cover nerves—were only some of the problems most experienced. Many also suffered from a variety of cancers to include prostate cancer, lung cancer, and leukemia. It was not until much later in life, when these men had nothing left to lose that they began coming forward.

Still, this was not even the tip of the secrecy-spear surrounding atomic testing and nuclear sites.

Unidentified Flying Objects or UFOs, recently referred to by the Pentagon as Unidentified Aerial Phenomenon, have been occurring since before the days of Noah. Some speculate that the Catholic Church and some secret elements within different world governments have always been aware of their existence. However, it was not until World War II that increased activity in the skies brought their presence to the attention of military leaders.

During World War II, US airmen on bombing missions over Europe often reported seeing strange flying lights along the French-German border. Often these lights would buzz their formations. These sightings were so common the pilots named the lights "foo-fighters." During the Korean War, US soldiers claimed a "pulsing ray" emitting from unidentified flying objects made entire battalions sick. Doctors examining these soldiers said their illness resembled radiation poisoning.

In the last few years, high-ranking US military and intelligence personnel have come forward and reported unexplained aerial phenomena near bases associated with nuclear power, weaponry, and technology. During the testing years, UFO activity at the NTS was so commonplace that employees there were assigned to monitor the activity.

Minot Air Force Base (AFB), located in the northwestern part of North Dakota, was part of the Strategic Air Command (SAC), now called the Air Force Global Strike Command. The base was responsible for both the bomber-based and missile-based strategic nuclear arsenal. The 91st Strategic Missile Wing alone was tasked with 150 Minuteman: intercontinental ballistic missiles or ICBMs, housed in underground launch facilities.

In 1968, repeated UFO sightings over this and other bases were cause for concern by senior military officials. However, it was not until October of that year, when one event at Minot, sent highly classified shockwaves throughout the Pentagon.

A UFO seen hovering over one of the ICBM silos was observed projecting a light into the facility. This caused the ICBMs to be mysteriously taken off-line as missiles began going into what is called a "no-go condition," or "unlaunchable." The Air Force's Launch and Targeting Officers could find no cause for the weapons malfunctions. Around the same time, a similar incident occurred at Malmstrom AFB in Montana, when 10 ICBMs suddenly became inoperative upon the appearance of a UFO.

It was however, after an incident in Russia, that caused both governments to begin working together behind the scenes. The Russian Strategic Rocket Forces was the Soviet Union's counterpart to the Air Force's Strategic Air Command. At their underground launch facility in Usovoin, Ukraine, dozens of soldiers, witnessed five UFOs appear over the missile silos.

Reports later reached the Kremlin that the missile control panels spontaneously illuminated as the top-secret access codes, necessary to begin a launch sequence, were inputted initiating a countdown. At first, the Soviet Rocket Officers were not able to shut down the launch sequence. It was not until they literally destroyed the control panels with a fire axe that the launch and subsequent nuclear war that would have followed was averted.

After the fall of the Soviet Union in 1989, this event became public knowledge when Colonel Boris Solokov of the Russian Ministry of Defense came forward describing the incident. There has always been some speculation, that misunderstandings between the United States and Russia may occur as a result of UFO activity. To avoid these types of incidents from escalating, the "Hot Line" Agreement established a direct line between the US President and the Kremlin.

Regardless, both countries agreed their national security and secrecy needed to be maintained while the general public remained blissfully ignorant. ◉

CHAPTER 1
"1987"

After a four-year stint with the United States Army, John Winoski joined the protective forces at the NTS. That was two years ago. Aside from the nearly hour-long commute along Highway 95, there was little for him to complain about. John lived in northern Las Vegas and would frequently stop at Indian Springs for coffee before arriving at the main NTS gate in Mercury.

John was a clean-cut, fit young man who enjoyed his duties at the NTS. His daily activities were very similar to the time he spent as a military policeman back at Fort Hood, Texas. Better still was the Vegas nightlife, where women seemed to flock to John's charisma and boyish good looks.

Early in his career, John attempted to join the newly established Department of Energy's Special Response Team, commonly referred to as the SRT. Unfortunately, the physical rigors of the program proved to be too much. John was not able to make it past the second week of the selection process. Having failed out of the SRT program, John returned to his patrol duties within the borders of the NTS.

Though one of his fundamental tasking's was responding to the Device Assembly Facility or DAF in Area 5, if an alarm occurred, John's primary patrol area was along the northeastern

1

corner of the test site. John preferred this district for a variety of reasons. This was the most isolated area of the already desolate NTS. Secondly, John knew the Groom Lake Facility, a secret government installation, more commonly known as Area 51, which had been named after a simple grid reference on an Atomic Energy Commission map, bordered his patrol area.

John was never allowed to cross the line between the NTS and Area 51. When he did happen to drive his patrol vehicle near their common border, stone-faced men, would appear in vehicles poised to intercept him. Even from his side of the boundary, John would frequently observe strange objects in the night's sky.

In late July of 1987, a convoy of vehicles, including numerous semitrucks and trailers, arrived in John's patrol area near the NTS-Area 51 border. They gathered at a remote warehouse situated between the Yucca Airstrip, the Papoose Mountain range and Cockeyed Ridge just south of the S4 site. The S4 site was part of the Groom Lake Facility. For a couple of days there was a flurry of activity in and around the warehouse.

During the daily shift briefings, John and his fellow officers were told these vehicles were part of the Department of Energy's Transportations Safeguards Division or TSD, later named the Office of Secure Transport. John and the rest of the officers were informed sensitive testing was occurring at the warehouse. As such, they were directed to stay away from both the TSD personnel and especially the warehouse.

None of the NTS protective force cared for the agents that worked for the TSD. Highly trained and SRT qualified, these men were arrogant and frequently seemed to look down their noses at the ordinary protective force officers. Often, they sported long hair and beards, justifying the relaxed grooming standard as needed to remain covert when transporting classified cargo across the country.

Rarely did the TSD agents engage the officers in casual conversation. Even among the senior members of the Department of Energy, the TSD agents were considered modern day cowboys not to be trifled with. This perception was by design and encouraged.

When there is a vacuum of information, the void will always be filled. Rumors about the type of testing spread amongst John's coworkers. For several days, he did as instructed and stayed away from the facility. Eventually, boredom, curiosity, and the innate human need-to-know got the better of John.

"This is my district" and "I am the law here; I can go where I want." These were just some of the justifications John told himself as he gathered the courage to disregard his orders.

One evening, John was sitting in his patrol vehicle, observing the warehouse from a hillside. Whitesnake's new song "Here I Go Again" was playing softly over the vehicle's AM/FM radio. Looking through his binoculars, he noticed there was no activity at the warehouse and there were no vehicles present. It almost appeared as if the warehouse had been abandoned. John decided this was the perfect opportunity to explore what the TSD was involved in. He clicked the radio off and put his vehicle in gear.

About a quarter mile from the warehouse, John turned off the headlights to his Jeep Cherokee. Though he knew the roads well enough to drive them blindfolded, he slowed as he grew closer.

He decided to park near a large trash dumpster on the far side of the warehouse. At any significant distance or even relatively close, neither approaching cars nor a casual observer could see where he had positioned his vehicle. If he needed to sneak away, John knew the four-wheel drive of his Jeep could easily go off-road onto the Yucca Flats.

Though these flats had been the site for over 700 nuclear tests, which was evident by the hundreds of craters pockmarking the desert, John was not overly concerned about radiation exposure. Everyone assigned to work at the NTS undergoes radiation awareness training. Known as ALARA, this training taught John that time, distance, and shielding was all that was needed to keep an exposure as low as reasonably achievable. A quick excursion through a "rad-zone" to avoid potential discipline or worse, seemed worth the risk.

John exited his Jeep. Instead of slamming the vehicle's door, John slowly pushed the driver's door shut until the latch clicked. He did not think anyone was in the warehouse, but just in case, he was not going to alert them with the unnecessary noise of a car door slamming.

A single light, protruding from the center of the warehouse was all that illuminated the parking lot. John pulled his large, three-cell Maglite-flashlight out and held it at the ready, though he did not turn it on.

As he approached the side entrance, John was surprised to discover the TSD had constructed a small manmade pond near the warehouse main door. The pond was a square twenty-by-twenty feet and only a few feet deep. Stranger still was that it had been filled with hundreds of goldfish. John knew from his childhood that goldfish are extremely low maintenance and probably the easiest fish to keep alive. He could not find any obvious reason for the pond so John surmised the fish must be part of the experiment.

The warehouse door was locked. Instead of having to carry a bundle of keys for every structure on the site, each member of the protective force maintains a master key. This key provided officers access to all facilities in case of emergency. John used his master key on the door's lock.

Initially, John was concerned the TSD agents would have changed the lock. This would have ended his exploration right there. They had not. As is common, when in an isolated area even security personnel become complacent. This is especially true when that area is surrounded by desert, inside a secured facility such as the NTS and situated near a radiation zone.

Upon entering the warehouse, John raised the Maglite to his shoulder and turned it on. For the most part, John was underwhelmed, as nearly the entire building was empty. However, in the immediate center, a cluster of equipment seemed to designate the area of experimentation. Situated on top of a couple of industrial metal desks, two cheap, black, government-issued desk lamps had been left on. They provided only minimal illumination.

To the left of each lamp sat two computers. This surprised John, as computers were not yet commonplace within the federal government. The Computer Security Act, intended to enhance the security and privacy of sensitive information would not even become law for several more months. These off-white, IBM PS/2 computers had also been left on. The bulky, eleven-inch monitors sat on top of the large boxy base station. A square greenish curser blinked in the top left corner of the monitors. John knew these two computers were top of the line as they had even been set up for using the new 3.5-inch floppy disk drives and an operating system that allowed for the use of a mouse.

Opposite the computers, were a couple gray metal counters with large industrial metal cabinets underneath. The numerous drawers below these cabinets allowed for excess storage. Set on the tops of the counters were a number of beakers, microscopes, and other glass tubing. John thought this contributed to the appearance of some mad scientist's laboratory from most any horror movie he had ever seen. Situated adjacent to the computer desks and counters were two large blackboards on rollers. Written in chalk were a number of mathematical and other equations that meant no more to John than Egyptian hieroglyphs.

What was most impressive however, was the large metal cylindrical tank. John estimated it was about forty-feet in length and twelve feet in height. Three portholes were evenly spaced along one side. A large oval-shaped hatch, similar to what a person would find on a naval vessel was affixed to one end. This hatch was battened down and appeared to be locked from the outside.

As John shined his flashlight across the tank, he observed a couple of hoses and other apparatus. These reminded him of a supersized aquarium air pump. They were attached to the exterior of the cylinder. The hum of a motor seemed to signify they were running and pumping either liquid or oxygen into the cylinder. Silver corrugated aluminum steps had been situated below the portholes. These seemed to have been placed to allow for viewing inside the cylinder.

As John approached the steps, he noticed a soft glow emanating from within the tank illuminating the portholes. Clicking the flashlight off, John replaced it onto his duty belt. The warehouse echoed the sound of his boots as he advanced up the aluminum steps. While standing on the top step, as if he were holding a set of invisible binoculars to his eyes, John leaned forward, placing his hands against the portholes. His eyes were merely six inches away from the glass.

For several moments, John saw nothing as his eyes adjusted to the light reflecting through the water within the tank. As he blinked, John thought he saw something swimming along the far side of the cylinder. Getting as close as he could to the porthole, John strained to see what was in the tank.

It happened abruptly. From within the tank, a hand slapped the porthole John was looking through. The hand was roughly the same size as his own. However, webbing between the fingers, thick dark nails, and the different shades of green scales were unmistakable differences. Perplexed, John stared in shock and bewilderment at the scaly hand. Then slowly, a face rose up in the water opposite his own.

It was an aquatic face that peered back at John. Oval in appearance, the black eyes were the creature's most prominent feature. Teardrop shaped slits were situated where the nose should have been. John observed rows of small jagged teeth, similar to those of a piranha in the creature's partially open mouth. However, it was the row of gills, slowly opening and closing, along the neck that became the focus of John's vision.

Upon seeing this aquatic humanoid in the tank before him, panic was the emotion that gripped John. What he was witnessing betrayed all his spiritual beliefs and knowledge of the natural world. Nearly tumbling off the stairs, John stumbled as he stepped backwards. Never taking his eyes off the tank, he backpedaled several paces. The creature's face filled the porthole. Its black eyes followed John as he turned and dashed from the warehouse.

John was nearly hyperventilating as he reached his Jeep and started it up. Gravel spun from under his tires as he peeled away from the warehouse. All thought of stealth left his mind. He grabbed the hand mic of the Motorola radio affixed to his dashboard.

"Patrol 7! Patrol 7!" John tried to remain calm as he half yelled into the radio's transmitter.

"Dispatch Patrol 7. Repeat your traffic?" came the calm voice of the NTS dispatcher.

"There's something out here! It's a goddamn Gill-Man!" John yelled as his vehicle fishtailed around a corner he had taken too quickly.

"Please repeat Patrol 7?" queried the dispatcher unsure she had heard John correctly.

"It has fuckin' gills!" John yelled.

A long single-note tone came over the vehicle's radio speaker. Typically, these tones indicate a pending alert is about to be broadcast. All officers know that when the tone in broadcast they are to remain silent until the information is passed. They did.

Following the alert tone, a voice neither John nor the other officers had heard before came over the radio.

"Patrol 7. You are directed to report to headquarters immediately. All other units do not repeat anything you have heard until you have been contacted by your immediate supervisor. All other communication is restricted to emergency traffic only." Then the radio went silent.

It took John twenty minutes to drive to the headquarters facility. The entire drive, the face of the creature staring at him through the porthole became seared into John's memory.

The shift sergeant met John at the door upon his arrival.

"Take your duty belt off and hand it to me," the sergeant directed.

Without a word, John removed his pistol belt and handed it to the sergeant. Taking the belt, he turned and led John through the building. The other officers present parted and turned away as they walked past. It appeared that if they actually acknowledged John, they might contract some contagious disease.

"Sit down and wait," the sergeant said as he held open the door to the interrogation room.

The interrogation room was similar to any other. It was small, merely ten-by-ten foot. A small table and two chairs were positioned in the direct center. As John sat, he glanced at his reflection in the one-way mirror. He began to wonder who may be on the other side.

More than an hour passed as John sat in silence alone. He knew he had to come up with a justification as to why he had entered the warehouse. He just could not think of anything that did not come off as pure, unadulterated bullshit. Finally, he decided his best course of action was to simply come clean and ask for forgiveness.

As the door to the interrogation room finally opened, John stood.

"Sergeant, I'm sorry. It was totally my—" John stopped talking as the strangers entered.

The first two who strolled in wore matching black suits, though they looked more like uniforms. Their thick necks and muscled physiques stretched the fabric of their clothing. It was however, their military-style haircuts that confirmed to John these were not members of the TSD.

They reminded John of Schwarzenegger's character *The Terminator* in a movie he had seen a couple years earlier. The men walked to opposite sides of the room, flanking him. Neither spoke. John recognized the bulges under their jackets as weapons.

A few seconds later, a third man strolled into the room. He appeared to be in his late sixties. Though he was tall, at least six foot six, he was incredibly thin, almost unhealthily so. The skin on his face was stretched tight. Combined with his sunken eyes, his head looked more like a skull. His hair was completely white but impeccably trimmed. The gray suit he wore hung ill-fittingly on his skinny frame. The man's hands were long and slender. Each finger seemed to be several inches in length. John's body shook involuntarily as the man seemed to glide across the room taking the seat opposite him.

With a Cheshire Cat smile on his face, the thin man stared at John for several long moments. John could not maintain his gaze and panic began to overwhelm him.

"Mr. Winoski, my name is Smith," the thin man finally said, "and we're about to have a very frank conversation about your future." ◉

CHAPTER 2
"THE ICE CUBE TRAY"

Derek Riley had been in the Marine Corps for just three years. During the first two, he was attached to the Fleet Anti-Terrorism and Security Teams, often called FAST. Derek was planning to go Recon after his stint with FAST Company. He had even obtained a slot to the Marine Corps Basic Reconnaissance Course and was about to depart to the Reconnaissance Selection and Indoctrination platoon known in the Marines as RIP.

Basic Reconnaissance is the Marine Corps version of the Navy's UDT/SEAL Team training and selection process. Unfortunately, Derek's plans were placed on hold in August of 1990. That is when Saddam Hussein's battle-hardened army invaded the small Middle Eastern country of Kuwait.

The entire Marine Corps, including Derek, had been mobilized. Derek was quickly assigned to the storied 1st Battalion 8th Marine Regiment, typically referred to as One-Eight. The "Beirut Battalion" was the nickname of the One-Eight Marines. This was due to the 1983 barracks attack. That was when 241 Marines, about twenty-five percent of the battalion, were killed in the span of mere seconds when a suicide truck bomb was driven into their barracks and exploded while they slept.

The One-Eight Marine Regiment was established in 1917, during the buildup for World War I. For the next hundred years, they would be involved in every large-scale struggle the United States became entangled. From Guadalcanal and throughout the Pacific during World War II, to Korea, the Cuban Missile Crisis, Vietnam, the Dominican Republic, and Kosovo, the One-Eight Marines had taken the brunt of every major conflict from around the world. They were about to once again.

In December 1990, the One-Eight Marines, along with most of the 2nd Marine Division was deployed to Saudi Arabia as part of Desert Shield. Once in-country, every few weeks the Marines would be repositioned somewhere along the Kuwaiti border.

During this time, Derek and his squad lived and slept on the ground. When they moved to a new location, the Marines would dig new fighting positions into the hot desert sand. Both day and night, they would continuously rehearse different aspects of trench warfare or how to navigate through a minefield. Any downtime was spent performing weapons maintenance, writing letters, or betting on scorpion fights.

Saddam had a well-established history of willingness to use chemical weapons dating back to the Iran-Iraq War a decade earlier. To quell an internal uprising, Saddam even used these weapons against his own people. As such, each US service member was issued a brand-new chemical protective suit.

These suits were sealed inside airtight bags. 'Mission Orientated Protective Posture' or MOPP gear was the military designation or name given these suits. When worn, the heavy, charcoal-lined protective suits were designed to filter both chemical and biological agents.

There were four specific MOPP levels depending on the threat level. At the initiation of the ground war, every Marine was to be in MOPP Level-Two. This meant they were to be wearing the protective suit, plus the large rubber shoes that slipped over the top of their combat boots. Wearing these one-size-fits-all rubber shoes made moving in the desert sand similar to walking on a beach while wearing scuba fins. MOPP Level-Three and Four included adding rubber gloves and the gas mask.

Finally, if the suits failed, to counteract the effects of possible exposure to nerve agents, each Marine was issued a Mark One Kit. This kit combined atropine and pralidoxime chloride injectors. Upon initial exposure, Marines were to inject themselves by stabbing through their clothing with the atropine's large needle. Then repeat the procedure with the pralidoxime chloride. These needles were thick enough to puncture through several layers of clothing as well as the charcoal lined MOPP suit.

It was in early January, prior to the coming air campaign, when Derek experienced his first loss of trust towards his leadership. The battalion's medical officer approached each platoon and provided every Marine little white pills. These were contained in small, plain white boxes not much larger than a book of matches. The medical officer told the Marines these were "pre-nerve agent" pills and they were to take one every eight-hours.

Following the second dose, Derek along with half his men, began experiencing debilitating stomach cramps. After questioning the medical officer, Derek learned this was the first time these pills were tested on human beings. Against orders to the contrary, and threats of court martial and violations of the UCMJ, Derek discarded the remainder of his pills into the desert sand and recommended his men do the same.

Derek's second experience with poor planning and leadership came a few weeks later. When the US military deployed to the Middle East, every member had been issued brand-new desert camouflage uniforms. Additionally, all the vehicles were painted a desert sand color. This made complete tactical sense.

Then Derek and his men were instructed to come to MOPP Level-Two. Upon breaking the seals of the airtight bags, the Marines discovered all the MOPP suits were a dark green, woodland camouflage, thus making the need for any other camouflage pointless. They would now stand out like a fly sitting on a white sheet of paper.

"The Green Weenie strikes again!" one of Derek's men said as they begrudgingly came to MOPP Level-Two.

It was hard to understand why this was not a consideration. Given the history of Saddam and his use of chemical weapons dating back a decade or more, someone at the Pentagon should have considered the possible need for desert camouflage MOPP Gear.

On February 24th, 1991, the coalition launched Desert Storm's ground offensive. The Marines of One-Eight were identified as one of the three assault battalions tasked with leading the way through the middle of the heavily laden Iraqi minefields consisting of more than one-million land mines and other defenses.

These defenses were described as "impenetrable" in earlier intelligence reports. US Central Command's own estimates predicted the Marines would take up to 40 percent casualties on the first day. These projections filtered their way down to Derek's level. Assuming it was likely he would become part of that statistic, Derek decided it no longer mattered what happened to him. His only goal was to do all that he could to get his men through the war.

By 10:20 that first morning, all three of the lead Marine Corps assault battalions reported they were in contact with and engaging the enemy. Derek and his battalion had initially been bogged down when the engineers attached to One-Eight struck a chemical mine.

Some of the Marines closer to the explosion had to don their full chemical protective suits coming to MOPP Level-Four. Two Marines, slow to mask-up, received chemical burns from a mustard-type blister agent.

By nightfall, the Marines of One-Eight were moving forward as the eastern most battalion, protecting the flank of the entire 2nd Marine Division. Committing the largest act of ecological terrorism the world had ever seen, Saddam Hussein's Republican Guard set approximately 700 oil wells on fire at Al Burqan, in Kuwait.

Like something out of Dante's Inferno, these fires filled the skies with a thick black oil-riddled smoke while the wells below blazed white-hot. The smoke became so thick, that breathing often became difficult. The Marines' forward progress came to a standstill.

Early that next morning, the One-Eight Marines were confronted by a massive Iraqi column moving towards their position. Known as the "Reveille Counterattack," the Iraqi 7th Infantry and 3rd Armored Division consisting of tanks and mechanized infantry, collided with the Marines.

For the next few hours, the largest mechanized battle in Marine Corps history raged. Battling back the Iraqis, the One-Eight Marines advanced while the Iraqis retreated into fortified fighting positions.

As the wind shifted, the heavy oil-fire smoke restricted both visibility and air support. Again, advancement towards the objectives was temporarily halted.

In an attempt to further secure their eastern flank, commanding officer of the One-Eight Marines, Lieutenant Colonel Bruce Gombar, positioned his battalion into an L-shaped defensive position. Derek and the other Marines dug into two-person fighting holes along the main north-south road leading from Kuwait City. Derek's squad was on-line. Their Assault-Amphibious-Tracked-Vehicle or "Amtrac" was centered about twenty yards behind them.

At 02:30 in the morning, Derek and the Marines were again struck by a two-pronged attack of Armored Personnel Carriers (APCs) and dismounted infantry. Very accurate artillery fire also began to rain down on the Marines. The artillery fire inflicted half a dozen casualties.

Throughout the night, illumination flares lit up the sky. As the flares blazed bright, Derek and his men observed the silhouettes of Iraqi soldiers moving towards their positions. Over and over again, Derek aimed his rifle and fired. The silhouettes fell, disappearing into the darkness and smoke. For the next four hours, the Marines continued engaging the enemy.

That morning, when this battle ended and the smoke cleared of the Iraqi regiment that collided with the One-Eight Marines, only thirteen survived. The rest had been killed. Derek personally emptied six of his seven, thirty-round rifle magazines. He and many other Marines had to seek resupply before anything else. For years to follow, Derek often wondered, of the rounds he fired, how many found their mark. It was probably best he did not know.

The orders came down for Lieutenant Colonel Gombar to advance the battalion to a Dairy Farm, located in a heavily urbanized area east of Al Ahmadi. Due to its appearance on aerial maps, it was code-named the "Ice-Cube Tray." Upon receiving the orders, Derek and his men crawled out of their fighting holes and loaded back into their Amtrac. They pressed forward.

Shoulder to shoulder, they sat like sardines inside the amphibious tracked vehicle. Their faces and the charcoal lined MOPP suits were covered in oil from the thick black smoke that still filled the air around them. None had slept in nearly seventy-two hours and hunger had not been much of a thought.

Exhaust fumes from the massive Cummins VT400 diesel engine filled the interior of the Amtrac. Inside each of these rolling coffins, was a small speaker placed in the far corner. As they advanced towards their objectives, the battalion's radio chatter was broadcast over these speakers. The Marines sat in silence as they listened to the war unfolding before them.

An hour passed as Derek and his men sat in quiet anticipation. Then the Amtrac's commander, Corporal Andrew Miller, began yelling over the intercom.

"Contact Front! Contact Front!"

The Marines inside braced as the Amtrac began a sharp turn, Corporal Miller yelled again.

"RPG!"

Derek closed his eyes and waited.

The entire Amtrac shook as the Rocket Propelled Grenade struck. Jostled around from the impact, Derek and his men fell onto one another. Their Amtrac had stopped moving.

Slowly the back ramp of the Amtrac began to open. Inch by inch it dropped towards the ground. Derek and his men stood, clutching their rifles, prepared to charge into the unknown. The Amtrac's ramp was only halfway down when Derek followed by his men rushed out.

Making a quick assessment, Derek saw they were on a single-lane road. To his left was a small ditch running the entire span of the road. A crumbling, short, three-foot mud and brick wall ran the length of the ditch. To his right, a number of homes, also made of mud-bricks and stones, lined the opposite side of the road. The rest of the battalion was nowhere to be seen.

Then Derek saw him. The Iraqi soldier, less than fifty yards away, was standing between two of the small Kuwaiti homes. Panic filled the Iraqi's eyes as he frantically tried to load another rocket into the tube of his RPG. Quickly Derek raised his rifle and fired a three-round burst ending the soldier's life. To confirm the

Iraqi was alone, members of Derek's squad advanced swiftly on the two houses.

As the Marines of Derek's squad approached the houses, a second Iraqi soldier stepped into the open, his hands raised. The Marines abruptly stopped in their tracks. They began pointing their rifles and yelling at him.

"Get down! Get down!" one Marine yelled while simultaneously waving his arm down to try to demonstrate what he wanted the Iraqi soldier to do.

The Iraqi began advancing and screaming back at them in Arabic. None of the Marines understood.

When the military deployed, most units were allotted one translator per company. This translator usually remained with the command element. As such, Derek's squad did not have anyone who spoke Arabic attached to them. Screaming loudly, the Iraqi soldier kept advancing on the group of Marines.

"I think he's wearing an S-vest!" one of Derek's men yelled.

Concerned the Iraqi had a suicide explosive vest strapped to his body another Marine fired two bursts from his rifle before Derek could intercede. The Iraqi was killed instantly. Derek watched as the Marines advanced.

As a couple Marines searched the dead Iraqis for explosives, others quickly cleared the houses. No other Iraqis were present and no S-vest was discovered. Derek turned away.

Glancing at the Amtrac, Derek saw the damaged caused by the RPG's impact. The right front quarter panel was destroyed and the track itself had come off. Had the RPG struck almost anywhere else, Derek and all the men inside would have been killed. The Amtrac was not going anywhere soon.

Walking over to the Amtrac, Derek began to unstrap his "ALICE" pack, the backpack the Marine Corps issued him. To make room inside the Amtrac, all of the squad's backpacks had been strapped to the exterior of the vehicle.

"We're on foot!" Derek yelled to his men. "Grab what you need."

Quickly the men began grabbing their own ALICE Packs along with additional ammunition, water, and some essential equipment.

"King!" Derek called.

Private First Class Mike King was a tall, skinny, nineteen-year-old African American from Atlanta. He came running up to Derek. Derek had come to love this kid for his extreme enthusiasm and the incredible humor he brought to all situations.

Before the ground war began, Mike would frequently entertain Derek and the other Marines by singing; often taking specific song requests. Periodically, the men tried to pick increasingly more difficult or obscure songs in an attempt to test Mike's abilities. More often than not, he would take the challenge. astonishing everyone with the depth of his musical library and natural ability.

"Let me guess, another SNAFU?" Mike asked.

"Of course. Situation Normal All Fucked Up," Derek replied with a smile. He slapped Mike lightly on the helmet, as a football player might to a teammate who just scored a touchdown.

"Take the point. We are about two miles from where we need to be." Derek turned to Lance Corporal Ernesto Rios, his radio operator. "Rios, call the old man and give him our SITREP."

Rios knew the term *old man* meant their platoon commander, the twenty-five-year-old 1st Lieutenant Wetmore. As he stepped away from Derek, Rios pulled a hand mic off his shoulder. It was attached to the AN/PRC-77 radio he wore. To the Marines, the radio was called a "prick-seventy-seven." Rios began talking into it.

With that, Derek and his team began advancing on foot through the built-up structures. Pointed in all directions, they held their rifles at the ready. Typically, to avoid having a single fragmentation grenade take out an entire squad, patrolling units would keep five to ten meters of separation between themselves. However, to maintain better control of his men, Derek cut the distance in half. Still, his squad was spread-out over nearly fifty meters. To better communicate and control his men, Derek remained in the center of the formation.

It was exceptionally quiet. For over six months following the initial invasion, the Kuwaiti people hid from Saddam's army. When the ground war began, they remained hidden. Though nearly four-million people lived in Kuwait City, it appeared to be a ghost town as Derek and his men patrolled along the outskirts. Only a stray dog, skinny from hunger but too fearful to approach, was seen scurrying across the dirt road in front of them.

They had traveled about a mile from their disabled Amtrac when the first shot rang out. Within seconds, Derek and his team began receiving accurate machine gun and small arms fire from a hillside and structures overlooking the road.

Marines are taught that when caught in a near-ambush, when the enemy is less than fifty meters away, they need to aggressively charge through the threat. For far-ambushes, the standard operating procedure is to lay down suppressive fire and maneuver on the enemy's position. Those currently engaging Derek's men were over two hundred meters away on the top of a hill.

"Contact left!" Derek yelled without having too. His men had been well trained and were already moving.

Running and diving into the shallow ditch, the Marines took cover as bullets impacted the small stone wall and the earth around them. Lance Corporal Jeremy Skiers, a black kid from Jamaica and Private First Class John Deis from Nebraska, opened up simultaneously with their FN-249-SAWs. Together, they began returning a massive amount of fire with their belt fed automatic machine guns. Within seconds, Derek's entire Squad was returning fire on the hill above.

As the firefight raged, Rios crawled up to Derek and grabbed him by the arm. Derek turned and looked at his radio operator.

"It's Charlie Company!" Rios had to yell to be heard over the massive volume of weapons fire going back and forth.

"What!" Derek exclaimed needing to be sure he understood Rios correctly.

"On the hillside above us," Rios yelled and pointed. "It's Charlie Company! Lt. Wetmore didn't tell them we were moving in on foot. They think we're an Iraqi unit!"

Derek did not need to hear anything else. "Cease Fire! Cease Fire!" he yelled while simultaneously waving his hand in front of his face giving a redundant arm signal to stop shooting.

The Marines of Derek's squad repeated both the command and arm signal until all his men had stopped firing.

"That's Charlie Company! Keep your heads down! Keep down!" Derek yelled as the Charlie Company Marines continued to fire on them from the hillside above.

"Rios!" Derek grabbed his radio operator by the collar. "Get on the radio and tell those stupid sons-a-bitches to cease fire!"

Rios held up the hand mic attached to the AN/PRC-77 radio, showing it to Derek. It was shattered.

"It must have taken a round. I can hear them transmitting, but I can't reach them!" Rios apologized. They both ducked when a bullet struck the ground between them.

In 1991, when the Gulf War began, blue-force trackers and other IFF devices were not yet readily available. When one unit commits friendly fire on another, it is called fratricide. Since the start of the air campaign over a month earlier, more than two-dozen Marines had been killed in fratricide incidents.

The single worst incident of fratricide occurred on January 29th, when a missile fired from an Air Force A-10 Warthog, destroyed an Amtrac, killing all the Marines inside. Derek was not about to let that happen to his men.

"Fuck!" Derek exclaimed as he scanned up and down the line of his men hiding in the ditch protected only by a short crumbling wall. Then he saw Corporal Shawn Jackson, one of his fire team leaders.

"Jackson! Get over here!" Derek yelled.

Corporal Jackson began crawling along the inside of the wall towards Derek. Several times Jackson had to stop as shots fired from the hillside landed nearby. Less than a minute later Jackson was lying in the ditch next to Derek.

"Do you still have that American flag on you?" Derek asked as Jackson nodded in understanding.

"Well, get it out and start waving it!" Derek ordered as Jackson began digging through his pack.

"Riley!" Rios yelled in almost a panic. "They're calling a mortar strike in on us!"

Derek looked from his men to the buildings forty to fifty yards away. If they broke cover and ran towards the structures, half his men could get cut down by the small-arms fire. The other half would be killed by the mortars when they tried to save their wounded brothers. He made the decision instantly.

"Dig in! Dig in!" Derek yelled as the Marines tried to get as small as they could in the shallow ditch.

They all understood that unless a mortar landed directly in the ditch the explosion and fragmentation would most likely blow up and away. Derek looked at Jackson. He had gotten the flag out of his pack just as the whistle of the first mortar round could be heard flying through the air towards them.

"Incoming!" Derek screamed. He curled into a tight ball as several mortar rounds exploded near their positions throwing dirt and other debris over them.

"Jackson!" Derek commanded without further explanation following the first volley.

"I'm working it, boss," Jackson replied while he began frantically fastening the flag to the barrel of his rifle. The second volley of mortar rounds began to whistle their arrival.

"Incoming!" Derek repeated and he again ducked low.

As the first round impacted, Derek saw PFC Michael King thrown into the air, landing outside of the ditch. He was thirty yards from Derek's position. Derek was on his feet and running towards King before the last mortar exploded.

As he drew closer to King, Derek was only slightly aware of the bullets striking the dirt near his feet. Instead, he focused on King's injuries. King's right leg was missing from the knee down and his left leg had been turned into Swiss cheese from the shrapnel.

After a quick assessment of the battlefield, Derek returned his gaze to King who lay unmoving, face down near the ditch. Derek yelled, "Corpsman!"

Unlike the Army, the Marine Corps does not have medical personnel. Instead, Navy corpsmen, who are all called "Doc" by their Marine brothers, are assigned to each rifle squad. These corpsmen eat, sleep, train live, and die alongside *their* Marines. This closeness develops the tightest of bonds. Many of these corpsmen have won the highest awards for valor risking their lives to save injured Marines.

Doc Comfort, a country boy from Wyoming, had been Derek's corpsman since he was first assigned to the One-Eight Marines. Upon hearing his squad leaders cry for assistance, Doc Comfort leaped from the ditch, oblivious to the small arms fire striking around him. He sprinted towards Derek's position.

Derek grabbed King by the collar and pulled him back into the ditch. He looked over at Jackson who was leaning against the short wall. Having gotten the flag attached to his rifle, Jackson was holding it over his head as high as he could. Without exposing himself he began waving the flag back and forth. Doc Comfort arrived and knelt next to them. Derek grabbed King by the shoulder and began to roll him over.

As King's body turned towards Derek, it began to change and morph into a hellish creature. King's shoulders grew large and became covered in thick black hair. The body armor he wore became an enormous barrel chest. Finally, the youthful face of the young PFC grew large and covered in hair as the dark eyes of a gigantic Sasquatch stared up at Derek.

"Holy fuck!" Derek exclaimed as he sat up in bed, dripping wet in his own sweat.

As the intensity of the dream faded, thirty years had suddenly passed. The events he had experienced on the Kuwaiti road was the theme of an occasional reoccurring nightmare. The appearance of the Sasquatch, however, was a new, disturbing element.

As he wiped the sweat from his brow, his phone began to ring. Derek snatched it up.

"This is Riley," Derek stated after pressing the talk button.

"Major Riley, this is the TOC. Your team is being activated" came the voice on the other end of the telephone. ☉

CHAPTER 3
"TERMINATION"

Night had fallen. They were clad in black tactical uniforms and wearing ballistic, load-bearing vests or LBVs. Night vision devices were affixed to their dark helmets. The infrared lasers attached to their suppressed Heckler and Koch MP5SD 9mm submachine guns, guided their movements. These officers were the sharpest arrow in the quiver of last resort.

Like shadows of a tree rustling in a breeze, they moved through the parking lot of the building complex. Even those watching, who knew what to look for, had difficulty seeing them. Each movement was synchronized and choreographed into a lethal dance. The outcome was predetermined the moment they were called.

Randy Gallagher had taken hostages. After seven hours, negotiations had broken down. Randy had been a twenty-two-year employee and a member of the teamsters union. His drinking issues began even before his wife had divorced him.

Over the last several months, his problems with alcohol began manifesting at work on an ever-more-increasing frequency. Most recently, he was in an accident involving a forklift. This had caused an injury to another employee. The final straw and been reached. As a result, he was losing the only thing he had left, his job. Randy was being terminated.

Randy had been directed to meet with his manager Justin Mackey. Justin, typically a man with an easygoing personality and good humor had put up with enough of Randy's shenanigans. Shelia Luttman, a representative from Human Resources, was also going to be present. This meeting was to be held at 3:00 p.m., in a conference room near the main lobby of the 2430 Stevens Center.

The Stevens Center complex consists of four similarly constructed multistory buildings. They are situated around what can best be described as a stylish traffic circle. Nearly one hundred employees occupy each of these buildings.

After he arrived, Justin and Shelia began providing Randy his termination paperwork. Never one for accepting responsibility and decades of blaming others for his troubles had come to a peak. Randy drew the handgun he had previously concealed in the small of his back. After threating to kill both of them, Randy pistol-whipped Justin across the mouth. That is when everything truly spun out of control.

An alert receptionist, aware of the termination occurring not far from her workstation, heard the commotion. She immediately dialed 9-1-1. Within minutes of the emergency notification, the first two officers from the Richland Police Department arrived. As their vehicles entered the parking lot, Randy fired a warning shot out the window of the conference room. This initiated the standoff, launched a flurry of activity, phone calls, and radio traffic as the building employees went into lockdown.

The Stevens Center complex is occupied by the Department of Energy and the workers within are either employees of or contracted to the federal government; however, the buildings reside in the City of Richland yet the main access road borders Benton County. This jurisdictional geography rapidly added to the confusion of the response.

Command elements of the Richland Police Department and members of the FBI's local field office arrived. Almost immediately, squabbles concerning legal responsibilities and fears of liability crept into their decision-making process. The Benton County Regional SWAT Team was capable but their authority to operate on federal property was in question. The FBI could gather a part-time tactical team out of Seattle, though it could take several hours for them to arrive. Unfortunately, as a part-time team, their ability to bring this hostage crisis to a successful conclusion was in doubt.

That was when Colonel Harris of the Department of Energy's Hanford Special Response Team provided an acceptable compromise.

The Hanford Special Response Team was the only full-time, highly trained unit within three hundred miles. They would perform the Hostage Rescue. Harris further explained to the gathered leaders, if the SRT failed, the other agencies could point the finger of blame at them; whereas they could take full credit for any successful outcome. The senior managers for both the Richland Police Department and FBI enthusiastically jumped on board.

At the height of World War II, because of Hanford's general location and isolation, covert elements of the United States Government took notice and determined the area was ideal for a special project. In 1942, the US Army purchased nearly 650 square miles of land and evicted the residents. The Hanford Site was created solely for one reason, the top-secret Manhattan Project.

During this time all the land and buildings were owned by the US government. The Army Corps of Engineers began working on the additional foundation needed to house and support the nearly 25,000 men and women brought in to work on the ultra-secret Nuclear Weapons Program.

The project was so compartmentalized, other than the small piece they were assigned too, most of these people knew little or nothing of the extent of the project that they were working on. In fact, the Manhattan Project was so secret not even Vice President Harry Truman was "read into" the program until after the death of President Roosevelt.

Though bombings of Hiroshima and Nagasaki brought an end to the war, the production of special nuclear material expanded. Fear of the Soviet Union's own nuclear weapons program began the Cold War era. In 1954, Congressional concerns about the military having complete control over the nation's nuclear weapons program and stockpiles led to the creation of the Atomic Energy Commission and the Atomic Energy Act.

This Congressional Act allowed for very specific enforcement powers for the officers employed by the Atomic Energy Commission. These officers were given "Q" Level Clearances, the highest clearance in the US government. Additionally, they were given authority and jurisdiction other law enforcement officers did not possess. These officers were and remain a truly paramilitary organization. Equipped and trained to fight as a military unit, yet authorized to enforce laws as a police agency.

It was from these beginnings that Hanford Patrol was formed. At that time, the Patrol consisted of mostly former members of Army Intelligence. Their primarily responsibility was to protect certain categories of special nuclear material and other classified National Security assets.

During the 1980s concerns grew about the ever-increasing terrorist threat. It was determined a highly disciplined team of operators, men trained in specialized military and police tactics, were needed to protect the US National Security interests. Hanford Patrol was the first DOE site to develop this Special Response Team, commonly referred to as the SRT.

Though some law enforcement personnel with particular skill sets were brought on board, recruitment for the SRT came almost exclusively from branches of the military's Special Operations community. Even though those recruited to join the SRT already had prior experience and most brought extraordinary tactical skills, they were still put through one of the most rigorous training programs ever developed. A quarter of these candidates, already proven and tested with other units, were not able to complete the SRT program.

By design, rarely does DOE's SRT make the news, but in the April 1991 edition of *Soldier of Fortune Magazine*, one such article was written. In this article it said:

> *"The DOE Central Training Academy is the American response to terrorism. Those fortunate enough to graduate from the SRT Basic Class are the beneficiaries of the most advanced antiterrorism training currently available—anywhere. Purposefully low profile and unheralded, CTA-trained SRTs can match acts with any of the world's more highly publicized snake eaters."*

Alpha Team, Hanford Patrol's on-duty SRT unit was the first element to arrive at the Stevens Center. They immediately assumed tactical command of the crisis, cordoning off the area and setting up an inner perimeter.

Half of Alpha Team began to systematically evacuate the Stevens Center complex as well as the surrounding buildings. The remainder of the team positioned themselves near the double-doors of the conference room where Randy had barricaded himself with the hostages. There they prepared to conduct a hasty assault if it became necessary.

Quickly, a problem with performing any standard assault was identified. After locking the doors, Randy used Justin's shoelaces to tie the door handles together. Additionally, he blocked the doors and the only entrance with the conference room table and numerous chairs. Randy's makeshift barricade would not stop Alpha Team, but might delay them a few precious moments from gaining immediate access. This impediment could allow Randy just enough time to execute the hostages during the tactical assault if he chose to.

In an attempt to keep Randy segregated, Alpha Team placed a couple of low-level cellular telephone disruptors near the exterior walls of the conference room. These effectively shut down all incoming and outgoing cell phone calls.

Randy's only form of communication to the outside world became the conference room's landline. This telephone was completely isolated and under the control of the SRT. Regardless of who Randy tried to telephone, if he attempted to dial out, the call would be diverted to the Tactical Operations Center or TOC.

Alpha was now fully occupied, staged, and prepared to conduct a hasty assault. They were no longer in a position to conduct additional planning or rehearsals. As such, Bravo Team was activated just as the negotiators began to arrive.

Negotiators depend on time to help defuse any hostage situations. Hanford Patrol's negotiators are amongst the best in the federal government. Trained by the FBI's Crisis Negotiation Team, these men and women are experts in psychology and use their skills to build a rapport with the hostage taker. Once empathy has been established, negotiators are typically able to bring the hostage taker around to rational thinking and eventually surrender. Not so in Randy's case.

When Randy began asking to speak with a priest, the negotiators realized he had become fatalistic. They immediately switched into tactical negotiations. Their job now was to delay

Randy long enough until Bravo Team had developed a deliberate assault plan. Once Bravo was ready, the negotiators were to assist as best they could when the hostage rescue commenced.

Alpha Team's snipers, call-sign Sierra, had deployed to a building across from the conference room's large picture window. This window had been designated "opening six" as it was the sixth possible entry point along the front of the Stevens Center building. Such designations were used to reduce confusion in planning and communications.

Unfortunately, Randy had closed the vertical Levolor-shades. Though the snipers had thermal optics available, unlike the movies, thermals, which work well through light brush and smoke cannot penetrate walls and reflect off glass. Unless Randy opened the shades, the snipers were essentially blind.

"Sierra-One, this is Bravo-One. Status?" Derek Riley whispered into the throat mic of his radio.

Maj. Derek Riley was the team commander of the SRT's Bravo element. After a career in the military special operations community, he had come to join Hanford's SRT.

"Bravo-One, this is Sierra-One. There has been no change on side-one, level-one, opening six," replied Sergeant Gutierrez.

Even though the sniper element could not provide any on-sight intelligence, Alpha team had been able to slip a fiber-optic camera into the conference room through the HVAC vent in the ceiling. This provided the one critical piece of information they needed. Specifically, where in the room the hostages were located.

"Copy that Sierra-One. Go to 'weapons hold.' Bravo-Two is approaching from side-four," Derek commanded.

"Copy 'weapons hold,'" Gutierrez acknowledged the command to hold fire.

"Alpha-One, Bravo-One. Be advised we are entering the building through side-two and will be approaching your location from the north."

"Copy Bravo-One," Alpha's team leader said over the radio, responding to Derek's transmission.

Derek Riley, Bravo-One, led his four-person element into the Stevens building through the north employee entrance. This was designated "side-two" in the tactical plan. Though the building had supposedly been evacuated, they moved cautiously. Together, Derek and his team advanced quietly down the hallway as they carried their weapons at the ready.

Outside the building, Bravo-Two, led by Captain David Hammond, a former Army Green Beret, advanced towards the conference room window. His element carried a large ballistic shield as well as a metal pole about seven feet in length. The pole looked more like a battering ram. A Combined Tactical Systems flash-bang distraction device was fastened one end.

"Bravo-Two, set. Side-one, opening-six," Captain Hammond transmitted as they arrived a few feet short of the conference room window.

Hammond and his element hugged tight against the wall. Due to the angle, they had positioned themselves, even if the blinds were opened, Randy would not be able to see them. Regardless, the sniper element across the street would have a clear shot.

Derek and his Bravo element arrived in the lobby and linked up with Alpha Team just outside the conference room. Utilizing hand and arm signals, Bravo Team replaced Alpha who fell into a supporting tactical role.

"Bravo-Four. Breacher up," Derek whispered into his throat mic. Simultaneously he tapped the top of his helmet with the closed fist of his left hand. This arm signal gave the team a redundant visual que for the same command.

Sergeant Jacob Hernandez stepped around Derek. Hernandez could have easily passed as an NFL linebacker. With the additional sixty pounds of tactical gear he was wearing, moving silently in these tight quarters became a difficult task.

Hernandez was Bravo Team's designated breacher. In a specially designed backpack, he carried the standard law enforcement breaching tools such as rams, crowbars, and a ballistic shotgun; however, early in his career the SRT sent Hernandez to the CIA's Clandestine Services explosive breaching course at Harvey Point. There he learned the art of using explosives to open doors or cut holes in walls without killing everyone in the vicinity of the blast.

Since Randy had barricaded the door to the conference room, Hernandez proceeded to a sidewall several feet from the door. Quietly he reached into a small pack attached to his LBV and removed a pre-made breacher-strip. This was an explosive charge made of detonating cord. With deliberate movements, using the explosive charge's adhesive tape, Hernandez applied the cord along the wall in roughly the same dimensions as a door. He then attached the detonator assembly.

With the explosive-breaching charge affixed to the wall, Hernandez moved back behind Derek as the team backed a short distance away around a corner. Corporal Brian Hall passed Derek a ballistic shield. As best they could, Bravo team crouched behind Derek and the shield. The shield would absorb most of the explosives concussion.

"TOC, this is Bravo-One," Derek transmitted. "The teams are set. Have the negotiators initiate contact."

"Copy Bravo-One. Initiating Contact," the Tactical Operations Center replied.

Almost immediately, they could hear the telephone ringing inside the conference room. Within a few seconds, the ringing ended as Randy picked up the receiver.

"Did you find me that priest?" Randy could be heard yelling at the negotiators.

"All teams stand by," Derek whispered and began the countdown. "5, 4, 3..."

On the count of three two things happened simultaneously. First, the TOC cut the power to the building, bathing everyone in darkness. Though Randy was now blinded by this sudden lack of light, Bravo team's night vision allowed them the ability to see clearly.

Secondly, Captain Hammond and the rest of Bravo-Two's element had moved the last couple of feet towards the corner of the window. Using the pole, they smashed through the glass. While raking the broken glass out, they detonated the 175-decibel flash-bang causing the initial shock to everyone inside the conference room.

"...2, 1," Derek's count continued. "Execute! Execute! Execute!"

Hernandez activated the detonator to the explosive-breaching charge. As designed and planned for, the conference room's telephone was located directly across from where the breaching charge had been set.

Randy, already disorientated from the flash-bang, was taken by complete surprise as the breaching charge exploded. Drywall, plaster, and fragments of wood peppered Randy as the concussive force threw him against the opposite wall. He was rendered unconscious almost immediately.

Instantly following the explosion, Derek dropped the shield and entered the conference room through the large hole created by the breaching charge. The rest of the team was right on his heels.

With his MP5 held at the ready, Derek scanned the room from left to right then back. He located the hostages quickly. They were huddled in the corner. A look of bewilderment on both their faces. In direct contrast to where Randy had been standing, Justin and Shelia were at the far end of the conference room, perpendicular to the explosion. Other than a slight ringing in their ears and being covered in dust, they were unharmed.

"Clear!" Derek announced.

As Alpha Team secured Randy, the remainder of Derek's Bravo Team ushered the hostages from the room. As Justin Mackey was being escorted past Derek, he paused.

"Would you mind doing that again? That was a little fast for me the first time," Justin said with a half smile. Relieved to be alive his good humor had begun to return.

"Sorry. They only allow me to blow up one building per day," Derek replied, meeting Justin's smile.

As Justin departed, Derek glanced at his watch. With mission success, his mind was already shifting away from the rescue. The lecture he was planning on attending was not for another eleven hours. Derek looked over at Corporal Brian Hall. Brian was grinning broadly. Derek made a fist and presented it to him. Without hesitation Brian made his own fist and lightly punched Derek's.

"Easy day, boss!" Brian said.

"Easy day," Derek replied. ◉

CHAPTER 4

"REVELATIONS"

The marked police cruiser pulled off Carbon River Road onto Manley-Moore Road. As the vehicle left the smooth asphalt, the crunching sound of gravel could be heard under the tires. It had stopped raining a few hours earlier and the mild September evening allowed Deputy Aaron Sullivan to keep his driver's window down. He had been with the Pierce County Sheriff's Office for nearly thirty-one years and was now a sergeant with the Mountain Detachment.

During his career, Arron had worked in nearly all elements of the Sheriff's Office. SWAT, Search and Rescue, and the Special Investigations Unit were his most memorable. He had even had a short stint in the County's Gang unit until a complaint had him removed, temporarily sidelining his career.

The bottom line was he had been banished to the Mountain Detachment, which most would have considered the beginning of the end in his occupation. That had been nearly a decade ago.

For Aaron, this had truly been a blessing. Of all the jobs he worked, Aaron preferred the Mountain Detachment. Located on the Eastern side of the County, the Mountain Detachment consisted of two sergeants and eighteen deputies with the main office located in the Town of Eatonville. This detachment had a certain level of isolation and autonomy other positions in the department did not offer. For the most part, those that worked the Mountain detail had to be self-reliant.

Aaron liked that.

At six foot three inches and nearly 240 pounds, Aaron was an imposing figure. His red hair, handlebar mustache and a deep baritone voice, only added to the intimidation factor he presented. In another time, he could have easily passed as a Viking.

This night, the sky had cleared from the earlier rain and the moon was beginning to appear over the top of Mount Rainier. There were virtually no streetlights in this wooded and remote area of the county. Although the moon was nearly three quarters full, the only real light came from the cruiser's headlights. Aaron flicked on the vehicle's side-mounted spotlight and began searching for the driveway.

The dispatch center had received a 9-1-1 hang-up call from 27001 Kolisch Road East. During his time with the Mountain Detachment, this was one of the few addresses he had not been too. He did not know exactly where it was located. The GPS device in his car had been a new addition five years ago when they had been installed in all county vehicles.

Unfortunately, the mapping software was rarely, if ever, updated. The software it did have showed barely half the addresses in the more rural areas of the county. Many of the younger deputies who joined the force had a hard time using a paper map over the readily available technology and frequently complained when they came to the Mountain Detachment about the difficulty finding addresses.

It did not matter; Aaron preferred his old Thomas Guide. It was reliable, did not require batteries or a power source and when he discovered a new road or address, he would simply pencil it in. You could not do that with the GPS. This was a new address.

Aaron came to a "Y" intersection and turned onto Kolisch. The earlier rain mixed with the drop in temperature had created a shallow layer of ground mist. As he drew closer to where he thought the address might be, he slowed his cruiser. The spotlight fell across a black mailbox half-hidden by blackberry bushes. The house numbers he was looking for were stenciled across the side. "McCarley" was the name of the property owner. Aaron reached for the cruiser's radio and initiated the broadcast with his badge number.

"49: County. Show me out at the location."

"County: 49. Copy out at the location. 2137," Judy, the dispatcher, replied in her clear, professional tone.

She had been working at the 9-1-1 Center nearly as long as Aaron had been on the street.

"212: 49. Be advised, I'm still almost twenty minutes out" came the second voice of Deputy Frank Aldrich over the radio.

Aldrich was several years younger than Aaron. For officer safety, as was protocol, both had been dispatched to the unknown 9-1-1 call. *Twenty minutes is not bad,* Aaron thought. This area of the county it would not be unheard of for backup to be forty-five minutes or more away. He was not concerned. Most 9-1-1 hang-ups turned out to be kids playing with the telephone.

"Copy that 212. I'll advise," Aaron said. Internally he was planning to cancel Deputy Aldrich as soon as he determined this was another bogus 9-1-1 call. There was no reason to make him drive all this distance unnecessarily.

Aaron turned onto the private lane. Just wide enough for one vehicle, the dirt road banked sharply right and disappeared into a heavily brushed area. About fifty yards after turning onto the road,

Aaron came upon an open, twelve-foot stock tube metal gate. A NO TRESPASSING sign was firmly affixed to the gatepost.

As he drove the cruiser through the gate, Aaron slowly panned the spotlight from left to right and back. The spotlight did little to illuminate the dense forest. Instead, the light bounced off the abundance of Douglas fir trees, creating numerous black shadows that seemed to dance across the low-lying ground fog.

Following the driveway through the woods, Aaron drove for nearly a quarter mile until he came to an opening in the trees. The house sat in the center of a clearing. It was your standard Dutch Colonial complete with front porch and brick fireplace. Though there were a couple of lights on downstairs, the upstairs appeared completely dark.

Initially Aaron thought he caught movement in an open window on the second floor. On closer inspection, this turned out to be just a curtain moving slightly from the breeze coming off Mount Rainier.

Behind the main house, Aaron saw what appeared to be a two-story barn. The barn's large sliding double doors were standing wide open. Immediately adjacent to the barn stood a four-foot tall livestock fence. This fence encircled about a half acre of the property. He did not see any animals inside the fence. The entire property appeared to be surrounded by the dense forest.

Aaron pulled his cruiser to a stop about thirty feet from the front porch. He shut the engine off and stepped from the vehicle. As he stood, Aaron adjusted the duty belt around his waist. It was the same heavy-duty, black leather "Sam Browne" belt he had been issued as a rookie. This was what he preferred over the nylon belts most officers were now wearing. His sidearm, a .357 Smith and Wesson revolver, which he kept in a cross draw holster, was also in many opinions, antiquated.

Younger officers frequently teased Aaron about his choice of sidearm. That was until they saw him shoot. Consistently, throughout his career, Aaron had been one of the Department's top pistol shooters. This served him well as he twice had to use his weapon in the line of duty.

Out of habit more than anything else, Aaron slowly pushed the driver's door shut until he heard the soft click of the latch. He then stood silently and acclimated his senses to the surroundings.

"You don't reach thirty-one years on the Pierce County Sheriff's Office without developing instincts or by rushing in," Aaron would often tell rookies he was assigned to teach.

For some reason, right now Aaron instincts were telling him to get back in his car and leave. That was not what he was paid for, he thought.

As he listened intently, all Aaron could hear were the leaves rustling in the trees as the breeze cascaded through them. Then, slowly, another sound began to drift towards him.

"What is that?" Aaron whispered to himself. Then he realized. It was someone intensely speaking.

Ignoring the hair rising on the back of his neck, Aaron stepped around the vehicle. In a deliberate manner, he approached the house. As Aaron stepped onto the wooden porch, it creaked under his weight. He walked to the front door and pulled out his flashlight. Keeping his shooting hand free, Aaron used the flashlight to rap on the door while he peered inside through the glass of the door's half-moon window.

"Sheriff's Office!" Aaron's voice boomed like a cannon in the night. He received no response. Aaron knocked and announced a second time and still there was no answer. Nothing within stirred.

Through the window, Aaron could see a light wavering in an adjoining room. Who is speaking?

Aaron's right hand drifted towards his revolver, but he refrained from pulling it. In his left hand, he held the flashlight up near his shoulder. He used the light to lead his movement around the side of the house.

At the corner, he paused briefly. Years of training and experience kicked in. He sensed more than thought, "Something isn't right here." Cautiously, Aaron peered around the corner before completely exposing himself to the potential threat beyond. The speaking grew louder and more energetic. He thought he recognized the pastoral quality but could not yet make out the words.

When he reached a half-open window near the middle of the residence, Aaron gazed inside. The interior light was on and he immediately understood where the voice was coming from. Aaron was looking into what appeared to be the family room. A lamp was laying on the floor, apparently it had fallen over. The bulb was flickering as if damaged. The television in the center had been tuned to a local Christian station. On the screen, a preacher was standing at a podium providing a passionate lecture to the crowd. Aaron finally recognized the sermon as coming from the Book of Revelations.

"And the first beast was like a lion, and the second beast like a calf, and the third beast had a face as a man, and the fourth beast was like a flying eagle. And when they shall have finished their testimony, the beast that ascendeth out of the bottomless pit shall make war against them, and shall overcome them, and kill them."

Still he saw no movement from inside. As the sermon continued, Aaron slowly began to push towards the back of the house.

As he reached the back edge of the residence, he again paused. This time the corner presented two possible threats. First was whoever could be hiding immediately around the other side, but what seemed to concern Aaron most was the barn's open doors and the darkness emerging within. The barn was now only about fifteen yards away. However, there was something else.

The stench that was not present moments earlier, had hit him squarely in the face. The combination of wet dog, garbage, feces, and decay made Aaron gag. Unconsciously, he brought his hand to his nose in an attempt to block the foul smell. The sermon continued.

"And there appeared another wonder in heaven; and behold a great red dragon, having seven heads and ten horns, and seven crowns upon his heads."

Aaron eased forward, breathing through his teeth. To maximize his view while minimizing his exposure, he began taking a small section at a time, slowly "piing" around the corner of the home. Aaron did not remember drawing his gun but feeling the familiar weight of the .357 magnum in his hand gave him some comfort.

The glass sliding back door appeared open and he shined his flashlight on it. The light showed the truth. The door had not been opened, it was smashed in.

"And there was war in heaven: Michael and his angels fought against the dragon; and the dragon fought and his angels,"

Again, it was not so much he heard it but rather felt it. The sound had come from the barn. Aaron spun and shined the light towards the barn's open doors. The light was useless against impenetrable darkness beyond the doors. Except now, there was something different. Two large, glowing amber orbs appeared in the center of the darkness. They seemed to rock ever so slightly back and forth, back and forth.

No, not orbs ... eyes! *They couldn't be,* Aaron thought, *they're too high to be eyes.* Aaron blinked. So did the eyes.

"And when the thousand years are expired, Satan shall be loosed out of his prison."

It came rushing out of the shadows. Aaron froze. He did not notice the warmth traveling down his legs. ◉

CHAPTER 5
"SUSAN"

Susan felt nauseated. She had been giving lectures since obtaining her second doctorate, this one in anthropology, nearly fourteen years ago. She had never quite gotten used to it. To help get over her phobia of public speaking, Susan had taken private speech classes and even tried hypnotherapy. The last few years she had gotten better, but the butterflies in her stomach always felt like bald eagles. That was until she started talking.

When she first began her professorship, the university had fully funded her research trips. Then a few years ago, there had been an anonymous telephone call to a local television new channel. This created a minor scandal. She was certain the call had come from her ex-fiancé, Eric. Regardless, the media began asking the university, which received public funding, what "research" it supported with that money.

To quell the negative media campaign, all direct support from the university for Susan's research projects were cancelled. The school's administrators were apologetic, and promised to assist in other ways. Of course, these promises never came to fruition.

For Susan, this sudden lack of funding created the need for her to raise the money in other ways. She loathed giving lectures and attending similar paid, speaking events. Unfortunately, these seemed to be one of the easiest avenues to help raise enough money for Susan to continue her field research.

Just off West Deschutes Avenue, Susan pulled her Subaru into the parking lot of the Three Rivers Conference Center. She had been asked to give a lecture during the International Sasquatch Conference, which was being held there.

This was another paying gig. Nearly two thousand people attended the conference over the three-day weekend. However, she was only scheduled for one, two-hour lecture. Still, at twenty-five dollars per person, she could not pass up the money even though she had to share her earning with the event organizers and other guest speakers.

Susan briskly walked through the parking lot. She smiled and exchanged pleasantries with an older couple who greeted her. They were well dressed and, judging by their age, probably retired. Obviously, they knew who she was as they addressed her by name as they walked directly up to her. However, Susan could not for the life of her remember where she had met them. She had become accustomed to the over familiarity of "the community" as she had begun to refer to those entrenched in the cryptozoology world.

Following a brief conversation about her upcoming lecture, the older woman asked, "What got you first interested in this topic?" The couple leaned in. Anticipation of her answer obvious on their faces.

Susan knew, but never discussed, why her life, her career path, even her very existence had been laser focused. The vivid memory of when she was merely five years old still haunted her dreams.

She was in the car sitting between her parents. It was night and the snow was falling. Susan could not remember where they were going, but that was not important. What had been important was what they all saw. The headlights of her father's sedan illuminated the empty road. The rhythmic sound of the tires crunching through the snow and the wiper blades on the windshield seemed almost in unison. Her parents were having a conversation about some boring adult topic while she held her doll, softly brushing its hair. That is when it happened.

As the large dark shape stepped onto the road, it was fully illuminated by the headlights. Susan looked up as her mother yelled. Her father, startled, pressed his foot down hard on the break pedal. The car began to slide on the compact snow and ice. The monster stepped to one side of the road and stared at them as their vehicle slid past.

Susan locked eyes with the beast as it bent forward looking in the vehicle. She was in shock. It was not so much what she had seen but instead her parents' reaction to it. At five, a child's parents are the superheroes of their protected reality.

To see this shattered on a snowy evening while simultaneously coming face-to-face with a real-life monster is not easily forgettable.

"Drive! Drive! Drive!" Susan remembered her mother's screams as well as the silent fear that filled the cab of the vehicle for the rest of their drive.

Over the years, Susan learned not to talk about the incident. On a few occasions she had tried bringing it up to her parents. Their response had always been the same. Telling her either not to talk about it with anyone or to say she had been dreaming. Her father passed away several years earlier without ever truly discussing the event with her.

Susan's mother, aware of her field of study, only once brought up the incident.

"Don't go looking for them," her mother said. "They're not natural. After we saw it, your father was never the same." Susan and her mother never spoke again of it.

Susan made a noncommittal statement to the older couple and wished them well. Then continued through the parking lot. Her mind wandered to Eric and the call she was sure he had made.

After Susan obtained her second doctorate, she was hired by the university to teach anthropology. It was there she had first met Eric Foster. He was a political science professor with the university. Though Susan always thought he was a little soft physically, she had to admit Eric was handsome, charismatic, and an incredible flirt.

Nearly every day Eric would show up at her office, chatting her up. Eventually, he wore her down and they began dating. This turned into a three-year relationship.

Susan tried several times to bring him into her life. She even took him on one of her field expeditions. Though she had spent a considerable amount of time and energy researching the area, not to mention the money she had used to setup the expedition, he did not seem to appreciate any of it.

Almost immediately, Susan had to end this outing. Early on the second day, her research assistants were threatening to quit due to Eric's snide comments and constant complaining. When Susan pulled him aside, Eric went off about everything from the lack of toilets to the mosquitos. He even made derogatory comments about, "Hunting fables in the woods." To save the relationship, Susan never asked him along again.

It was not that Eric never understood Susan's obsession. Instead, since that time in the woods, he began to constantly ridicule and disrespect Susan and her staff. Initially Susan felt his attitude was due, in part, to the embarrassment he must have felt for the less than manly behavior he displayed in front of everyone during the expedition. She tried to ignore his comments as simply hurt pride, figuring they would eventually subside. She was wrong as his belittling only increased.

"Why don't you focus your expertise on real studies instead of unicorns and fairies?" Eric once said.

Susan had lost her patience with him following this statement, which led to a tremendous fight. Nevertheless, it was at a cocktail party with a bunch of their mutual friends and colleagues that the final straw in their broken relationship occurred.

During the party, Eric made himself the center of attention by making fun of Susan and her chosen career path. They all laughed when he called her, "His little Bigfoot lady." She ended their relationship that evening.

Eric, not accustomed to rejection, began ridiculing her around the campus. Susan began to see a steady decline in attendance in the courses she taught. It was not until Susan threatened him with a harassment suit that the overt ridicule ended. That was, however, when the anonymous telephone call was made to the local news channel.

As Susan reflected, she was relieved to be rid of Eric. Still, she felt a little worried for the starry-eyed coed he had been seen parading around with recently.

"Hey, Professor! I thought you were going to be late." Josh met her at the door to the convention center and handed her a lanyard with an "All Access Pass" attached. She slipped the lanyard around her neck.

Though a little on the thin side, Josh Williams was a pleasant young man with an infectious smile. Josh was a member of the Swinomish Nation. He always portrayed a professional manner while proudly displaying his Native American heritage both in his accessorizing and long ponytail.

Josh had been Susan's assistant for the last eleven months. He was a graduate student in Washington State University's Anthropology Department. Susan's department. Josh knew how she felt about public speaking but also realized she had a flare for it once she got on a roll.

As Josh escorted her through the convention center, they passed numerous vendor tables and even a mascot strolling around in a fury ape suit. Parents and children were constantly stopping the mascot for a photograph. Though Susan appreciated the enthusiasm the people brought to the topic, she quietly wished a more serious approach were taken. Mainstream academia already thought they were a joke without adding cartoon mascots.

"Hey, Doc! I almost forgot. Someone just dropped this off for you!" Josh said, removing the small box he had in his jacket pocket.

"Who?" she asked, a little surprised.

"I don't know; they just left it for you at the main desk. When I checked us in, they gave it to me," Josh remarked, handing her the package.

They stopped walking as Susan took the package and opened the card attached. Though it was not signed, it read: *Keep up the good work!* She unwrapped the small box and opened it. Inside was an Audemars Piguet Royal Oak Chronographic watch.

Susan exhaled audibly while Josh whistled.

"Holy shit!" Josh exclaimed. "Someone must really like you! You know how expensive that thing is?"

Josh, overly eager to see her wearing it, took the package from Susan's hands and removed the watch. She unconsciously brushed some nonexistent lint off her dark blue pantsuit and smiled sheepishly at Josh as he put the watch on her wrist.

"I'm not sure I should even be wearing something like this," Susan commented as she admired the watch. Smiling, she quietly vowed to never take it off. Susan realized it was probably the nicest piece of jewelry she ever owned.

"After all the crap you've had to go through the last few months, you definitely deserve it," Josh said caringly. He had become very protective of Susan, in the way a younger brother may watch out for his sister.

"Are you ready, Doctor?" Josh said after a pause. He looked at her encouragingly.

"Just a minute. I need to use the restroom," she replied. Josh nodded, turned, and pointed her in the direction of the public toilets.

A few moments later, Susan was alone in the bathroom. Still feeling a little nervous, she lightly splashed a little cold water on her cheeks, then dried them with a paper towel.

Taking one last confidence-building look in the mirror, Susan was not unhappy with what she saw. She was in her early forties but could easily pass for much younger. Many colleagues often did not take her as seriously as they did her male counterparts. Not just because of her area of study but rather because of how attractive she was. She often tried to hide her looks by not wearing makeup and choosing clothing that was not flattering; however, that seemed to only enhance her natural beauty.

Susan was exceptionally fit, which was mostly due to the lifetime she had spent hiking around the wilderness. She was just about to look away when she noticed the first gray hair in her otherwise brown mane.

"Ah, fuck," she whispered and turned from the mirror. ◉

CHAPTER 6
"KOKO"

Josh awkwardly stepped onto the stage. The large auditorium was located on the east side of the Convention Center. Though the room's fire permit was for a maximum capacity of approximately 2,500, there were just over 300 people attending her lecture. The more well-known speakers would draw the bigger audiences.

Josh knew these lectures and speeches were needed to drum up financial support for Susan's field research. He hoped this would get them over their recent financial hurdles. He believed as she did, and maybe even more so. When they first met, Josh realized they were kindred spirits in their conviction and he wanted to help Susan prove her theories.

He tapped lightly on the microphone affixed to the podium. The thumping sound, followed by a mild electronic feedback filled the auditorium. Josh took a half step back from the microphone.

"Ladies and gentlemen," Josh began, "I'd like to thank you all for coming to today's lecture. Would you all please welcome Washington State University's very own Professor of Anthropology, Dr. Susan Parker? Dr. Parker holds doctorates in both Anthropology and Linguistics as well as master's degrees in both Microbiology and Quantitative Biology."

Polite claps began as Susan strolled onto the stage towards Josh. As she reached the podium she patted Josh lightly on his forearm and smiled as he walked off the stage. Susan turned towards the crowd.

The auditorium was well lit. The crowd, though only about 300 was still larger than some previous lectures she had given. The people in the audience had not clustered together. Instead, they had spread out among the 2,500 available seats. This made scanning those in attendance easy for Susan.

As she looked around the rectangular auditorium, Susan took inventory of those present. Many she had begun to recognize, such as the older couple who had stopped her in the parking lot earlier that morning. Then there were your typical three groups of attendees.

The first fell into the students and undergraduates wanting credit or information for their areas of study. The second group was those who had nothing better to do on a Saturday morning and attended these types of lectures purely for the entertainment value. The final group was the true believers, either agreeing with or totally opposing everything she said.

Near the laptop on the podium was the bottle of water Josh always left for her. She picked it up and just as she was about to take a drink, Susan glanced around the auditorium.

There he is again, Susan thought.

Just three rows back from her podium, Derek Riley sat alone looking up at her. She had seen him several times before at previous lectures. He always seemed to be alone. Susan did not know his name but a couple lectures prior she began referring to him as "Ed." She had chosen Ed mainly because he reminded her a little of the actor Ed Harris, just a younger version.

Susan did not think he was exceptionally tall, maybe 5'8" or 5'9". Though she did not think others would ever underestimate him. Derek had taken his leather jacket off and laid it across his lap partially covering his khaki trousers. The dark polo shirt he was wearing did nothing to hide his muscles. These were not the useless muscles of a body builder but more those of a professional athlete. His blond hair was closely cropped tight in a military-style haircut.

Susan could not quite make out his age but based on the crow's feet around his eyes, she estimated him to be about ten years older than herself.

As she was looking at him, Derek briefly locked eyes with her. Susan noticed his were a bluish gray, seemed highly intelligent and... dangerous. She quickly looked away.

Clearing her throat Susan began her lecture.

"Occam's Razor! This is both a philosophical and scientific principle. Essentially, if there exist two explanations for an occurrence, one being highly complex and complicated and the other quite simple, the simpler one is usually correct."

Susan picked up a remote clicker and the large screen behind her was lit up with an iconic black and white photograph of an enormous, Sasquatch in full-profile.

"There are two basic groups of people. Those who believe and those that do not. For those who believe in the existence of Sasquatch or consider the possibility, there seems to be a couple primary schools of thought when it comes to Sasquatch, or what I will call the North American Primate.

"First there is the mainstream idea. Specifically, the assumption that Sasquatch is nothing more than a forest hippy: a gentle creature living alone and in harmony with nature. Occasionally helping lost hikers find their way back to their campsite. These mainstreamers believe that Sasquatch is a peaceful giant guardian of the forest, eating berries and smelling flowers. To put it simply they have bought into the *Harry and the Hendersons* Bigfoot image.

"Unfortunately, there is absolutely nothing, including anthropological science, to support their hypothesis. It is wishful thinking that can and probably has gotten people hurt.

"The second theory is where I have been focusing my research. It is based purely on hundreds of eyewitness accounts and applying them to what we already know about animal behavior in nature."

"When this is done, the conclusion of Sasquatch being a North American Primate is not difficult to reach. As such it should be considered a large predator which, at best, views humans as a competitor of resources; at worst, their food. For now, let us forget the fact hundreds of people go missing without a trace in the wilderness every year. Instead, we will apply what we already know about other primates."

A young woman in the audience, wearing a crimson WSU sweatshirt, raised her hand. Susan pointed at the young lady.

"Dr. Parker, hasn't Bigfoot been shown to be nothing more than a few folks running around the woods in ape costumes?"

"As in any field of research a good scientist should look at all possibilities. Before anything else, we should address the hoax questions that surround the North American Primate," Susan responded.

"Stories of Sasquatch date back centuries. Sightings, not all of which can be considered hoaxes or misidentification, continue almost daily. The list of people who claim to have seen a Sasquatch includes doctors, politicians, policemen, and scientists. Their very careers are hinged on a foundation of their integrity. As such, they could not afford to be involved in hoaxing. Although many of these sightings have been reported in the last few decades, the legend of the Sasquatch actually predates the arrival of the white man to North America.

"However, let's ignore the centuries of global sightings, reports and encounters and merely look at what has transpired since the Patterson-Gimlin film. Additionally, let's begin by assuming the Patterson film itself is a hoax. If you look at 'Patty,'" Susan said, motioning to the screen behind her, "the Sasquatch in the Patterson film, the men who filmed it, would have had to create the greatest 'costume' of that era."

"Remember, there was no Velcro, no spandex; and costumes back in the 1960s were made of cheap materials. All anyone needs to make this statement is look at any large budget Hollywood movie monster from the 1960s and 1970s. No monster created by a Hollywood special effects department, at that time, comes even remotely close to the image of Patty.

"Now consider the circumstances around the film. Yes, Patterson was trying to make a documentary about Sasquatch. Many people believe because of this, the film is not credible; however, the reason they were even there was due to a third party report of Sasquatch. That fact is almost never mentioned. Additionally, they had spent nearly a week exploring the wilderness where this report was made. Finally, they were doing something, most researchers even today do not do."

"What was that?" the woman is the WSU sweatshirt asked.

"They were on horseback," Susan replied as if the answer was obvious. "It is my opinon the sounds and smells those horses made, allowed them to get closer to the Sasquatch than they would have had they just been hiking through the woods alone.

"Patterson went to his grave saying the film was authentic. In the 1970s Bob Gimlin, who did not profit from the film and was a struggling farmer and rancher was offered a million dollars, a lot of money in the 1970s, to recant his story. He never did. The Patterson film is one of the most studied and scrutinized pieces of film in all of history and yet no one has been able to disprove its authenticity. Patterson and Gimlin were just a couple of poor cowboys, yet if their film was a hoax, it has proven to be the greatest hoax of all time."

Susan removed the microphone and began to walk around the stage. Glancing at Derek from the corner of her eye, she saw he was smiling slightly.

"To continue the hoax theory, from the 1967 Patterson film until the late 1990s, before the accessibility of digital cameras, every image, and video taken and footprint discovered would have to be considered an elaborate global hoax.

"Additionally, for many of these prints, the hoaxers would have needed a good deal of knowledge of anatomy as some prints were deformed showing possible disabilities, and others actually showed dermal ridges. For those who believe Sasquatch is just a hoax, then it would require everything to have been hoaxed, globally.

"There have been literally thousands of eyewitnesses, photographs, and physical evidence collected over the years. With that, if even one print, one photograph, or one witness testimony was real, then the possible existence of a North American Primate would need to be considered real as well.

"I absolutely believe there is a fair amount of hoaxing occurring. However, that cannot account for every piece of information, video or eyewitness testimony. In the Native American traditions, the history of Sasquatch is far older than the arrival of the white man. This is especially true in the Pacific Northwest, where stories of alleged 'hairy wildmen' that inhabit the region date back hundreds of years."

Susan pressed a button on the clicker in her hand. The screen image changed to what was obviously an ancient cave depiction of a hairy-looking humanoid with its arms spread wide. She continued her lecture.

"The very word Sasquatch is Native American. However, this is only the most popular term. Each tribe across the continent has a different name, though all mean virtually the same thing."

"Here we have cave paintings." She pointed at the screen. "Estimated to have been painted around 500 A.D. by the Yokuts Tribe. It shows their depiction of a 'hairy man.' This painting was discovered alongside life-sized cave representations of coyotes, bears, eagles, and humans. There were no other mythical creatures represented with these cave paintings. So why would we consider this single cave depiction a fabrication? The Yokuts portrayal of this hairy man was 8.5 feet tall.

"In the year 986 AD," Susan continued, "about 500 years before Columbus arrived in America, Viking Explorer Leif Erickson described in detailed accounts, his party coming across wild manlike creatures which were horribly ugly, hairy, with big black eyes.

"The earliest record of large mysterious footprints in North America dates back to 1811 when a well-known explorer and trader was attempting to reach the mouth of the Columbia River. Then in 1846, a Hudson's Bay Company employee referred, in official correspondence, to 'the wild giants of the mountains.'

"In 1918, a story appeared in the *Seattle Times* concerning the 'mountain devils' who attacked a prospector's shack at Mount St. Lawrence, near Kelso, Washington.

"There are literally thousands of stories that occurred prior to the Patterson-Gimlin film. These occurred around the country from people who did not know one another, nor did they have access to the internet. They could not compare notes and yet their accounts are virtually identical. None of these should be considered hoaxes as there was nothing to be gained." Susan paused and took a sip from her water bottle.

"So, if we consider past Native American traditions and historical stories occurring prior to the Patterson film as potentially real, why would 'everything' following the Patterson film be a hoax? The answer is: they wouldn't be."

A young man, who looked as if he spent too many hours playing video games and not enough time performing physical activity, raised his hand. Susan pointed at him.

"Wouldn't we have discovered them by now? I mean, what about finding a skeleton or something?" he asked.

"Let's address that in two parts," Susan began. "First, it wasn't until about 1907 that gorillas were discovered. Prior to their discovery stories surrounding them were very similar to the stories we hear about our own North American Primate. That, however, isn't even the most recent discovery."

With a click of the button she held, the screen changed again. This time a slight gasp could be heard from somewhere in the audience. A huge, muscular chimpanzee appeared on the screen. Susan let everyone absorb the image before continuing.

"For approximately thirty years, stories of a lion-killing ape in an isolated region of Africa were told. However, it was not until 2003, that this species of chimpanzee was discovered. Known as the Bili ape, this is the largest known primate in existence. Estimates have the Bili ape standing upwards of 6 feet, 6 inches in height and weighing over 300 pounds. They have been observed killing and eating leopards and other large cats.

"Now let's consider the possibility of a North American primate and the intelligence they may possess. Humans and chimpanzees evolved in Africa from a common ancestor millions of years ago. Chimpanzees are the closest species to human beings that we currently can confirm. Fossil and genetic evidence show that human and chimpanzee DNA are approximately 96 to 98 percent identical. Chimpanzees are more closely related to humans than to gorillas. As a result, chimpanzees and humans share physiological, emotional, and behavioral traits."

"Human beings are obviously the most intelligence animals on the planet. We are also very aggressive and for the most part the apex-predator. This is mostly due to our technology. Once you remove our technology, we are no longer the top of the food chain. As for intelligence, after human beings, we look at chimpanzees and gorillas, and the intelligence they obviously possess."

The screen changes again. Now a video began to play. In the video, a large western lowland gorilla was casually sitting next to a young blond female. After a few moments it became obvious the two appear to be communicating in sign language.

"For example," Susan began again after everyone had thoroughly absorbed the video, "here we have Koko the Gorilla. In 1972, Dr. Penny Patterson began raising Koko and teaching her sign language. It has been confirmed Koko has developed over a thousand-word vocabulary of sign language. It has been further demonstrated that Koko has an ability to create complex sentences and thoughts. Koko is self-aware and has tremendous emotional depth. More importantly, she has also taught other gorillas and passed on her ability to sign.

"Chimpanzees and gorillas have been known to solve complex problems and have been documented to utilize rudimentary tools.

"If a North American Primate existed, could it be reasonably assumed that its intelligence fell somewhere between that of a chimpanzee and a human? This would make it the second most intelligent animal on the planet! Then, let's take into account the North American Primate has survived in the wilderness for several millennia. It is completely at home in the forest. It would not be too difficult to imagine an intelligent primate being able to avoid humans except for the occasional happenstance.

"Or, let's look at this problem from a different point of view. If a stranger entered your home and you turned all the lights out. You could probably move around easily and remain hidden; whereas the stranger would be stumbling around tripping over furniture. You would have a significant advantage over this stranger.

"Once human beings entered the forest, which would be the Sasquatch's natural territory or their home, not ours, for all intents would they not be more intelligent about their own environment? They would have the advantage. The bottom line being, when humans enter the forest they would fall to number two on the intelligence ladder, making Sasquatch number one!

"As for discovering skeletal remains. Nature cleans up after itself. By a show of hands how many of you have gone camping or hiking?" Susan paused and waited. Everyone in the crowd had their hand raised. She continued, "Now, by a show of hands, how many of you have come across the skeletal remains of a predator such as a bear or cougar?" No one raised their hands.

"In fact," she continued, "most people haven't even come across the remains of a deer or other animal unless it was a recent kill. These animals are extremely common yet within a very short period of time, their remains vanish. Now let's add one more possible element, that being Sasquatch may bury their dead. There are witness accounts of chimpanzees, even elephants burying their dead. It would be completely within the realm of possibility that an intelligent primate such as a Sasquatch might also bury their own.

"Additionally when you consider the 'body discovery theory' there is another possible explanation. Most people only go camping in public campgrounds or hiking on established hiking trails. The Gifford Pinchot National Forest alone accounts for nearly 1.4 million acres of forest and only about 10 percent of that is accessible to most people. If you take a moderately intelligent animal with cognitive abilities, it will avoid places where humans congregate. Why then would they fall dead in the middle of a hiking trail for some human to stumble across? Again, the answer is they wouldn't. Even domesticated dogs, near death often wander off to find isolation before they die.

"As for fossil evidence. If you view Gigantopithecus, which I do, as a possible explanation for Sasquatch, then there has been fossil evidence discovered. If so, the body discovery has already occurred and a reclassification or reevaluation of the species being extinct should occur."

"What do they eat?" a middle-aged female with spaghetti-straight hair asked. Susan noticed the "Harris 2024" button sported on her hemp vest.

"Good question," Susan responded. "Numerous eyewitness encounters with Sasquatch described patterns of behavior. These behavior patterns closely resemble similar behaviors exhibited by chimpanzees. Nearly all primates, humans, chimpanzees, gorillas, etcetera, are omnivores capable of surviving on both plants and animals. Why then would a North American Primate be strictly a vegetarian, as some people mistakenly believe? If you take into account their large body mass, they would need an enormous quantity of protein.

"Forest chimpanzees intentionally hunt in larger groups and with a more elaborate cooperative level than some might believe. They also tend to share meat more actively and more frequently. Male chimpanzees often hunt when accompanied by other males. Research of chimpanzee hunting behavior shows it is as much a social activity as it is a necessity for food.

"There is a tremendous amount of research and documented footage," Susan explained. "Much of it can now even be seen on YouTube. This footage shows groups of chimps hunting in complex and organized fashions. Some working as drivers, others blockers, and finally the ambushers. These chimps work together to funnel monkeys into the arms of the ambushers.

"Some encounters with Sasquatch described ambush hunting behaviors similar to those of the chimpanzee. Theories about Sasquatch include their use of wood knocking and hoots to communicate. This wood knocking and hooting associated with Sasquatch is possibly how they alert one another when funneling prey, such as deer, into an ambush just like their chimpanzee relatives."

"That's awful violent! Only people premeditate their violence!" the woman with the hemp vest said. She appeared agitated.

"Yes, of course we've all heard the stories of Sasquatch being just a giant, peaceful teddy bear," Susan said with a hint more sarcasm than she intended. She walked over to the podium and hit a few keys on the laptop. A video began to play.

Within a few moments, the audience observed a troop of chimpanzees conducting a coordinated and violent attack on a neighboring group of chimpanzees. Once the attack ends, the chimps begin to cannibalize infant chimps killed during the attack. Susan saw the middle-aged woman had slouched a little in her seat.

"Many Native American tribes avoid areas where Sasquatch was known to be. Some tell stories of attacks and violence coming from the Sasquatch. Many stories include the abduction and eating of children. Some Native American tribes refer to Sasquatch as being a cannibal."

"Why would they attack and eat children? They wouldn't eat humans!" Hemp vest asked not quite as confident. Susan felt a little sympathy for her.

"Again, look at what is common in nature. When lions or any predator hunt, they frequently target both the young and very old.

Not only are the young and elderly easier prey, but also, if the predatory animal has to expend less energy and is less likely to be injured, of course they would seek the easiest kill. There is no reason why a North American Primate would be any different.

"Additionally, wolves and dogs are both from the canine family, but a wolf wouldn't hesitate to eat a dog. Chimpanzees eat other primates and cannibalize other chimps. Even human beings eat apes and have cannibalized other humans. It would not be logical to assume a Sasquatch would manifest a behavior that was different from any other animal on the planet. There is also a precedent for stealing children. During times of famine in Africa, chimpanzees have been known to raid human villages, steal human babies and eat them."

Some in the audience had begun to look a little ill. Susan decided to change the topic.

"Most primates, including human beings, spend their lives in large social groups or communities. If there were a North American Primate, why would they, unlike other primates, live in isolation? Again, they wouldn't. Most, not all, photographs and videos of Sasquatch only 'show' a single animal. That is all that was seen, but may not necessarily mean that was all that were present. Many accounts of contact and sightings involve larger social groups or a troop of four or more members.

"If a person has contact with any primate they should consider the presence of multiple members in close proximity, but not necessarily in view."

A young man wearing a football jersey who obviously spent too much time on his hair rudely blurted out. "But where's the evidence? After all these years why haven't they found any proof?"

Susan was not bothered by his interruption, the criticism was common and as a professor, she was used to the rudeness of many of her younger students. She glanced back at where Derek sat. He looked as if he wanted to rip the young man's head off.

"Actually, there has been a tremendous amount of evidence. Ignoring the thousands upon thousands of casted prints, photographs, videos, and eyewitness testimonies, there has been DNA evidence collected. Unfortunately, the DNA was collected by hunters and amateur investigators who have not been trained in scientific evidence collection protocols. Because of this, the samples' chain of custody cannot be verified or the samples themselves are contaminated. As such they do not meet the threshold for scientific proof and are discounted entirely.

"However, that is changing." Susan saw several in the audience perk up and sit a little more erect. She noticed Ed was now intently watching her. "Just a few years ago, a colleague of mine, Prof. Michael Wainwright, discovered a pile of deer bones on the side of Mount Adams. These bones were stacked up and located near some large 16-inch footprints. Two similar piles were subsequently discovered approximately one year later on the opposite slopes of the Mountain.

"The finds themselves were unusual since most predators typically disperse remains rather quickly and do not pile them up. However, when Professor Wainwright conducted further inspection, he noticed large human-like teeth imprints in the bones. Evidence from both piles, including the footprints and DNA, was meticulously collected.

"Bone stacking is a technique that is specific to humanoids and was cited as human type behavior. Just think about the last time any of you ate some Kentucky Fried Chicken. I imagine as you finished one piece, you began piling the remains in one specific area. This is what was occurring on Mount Adams. Professor Wainwright consulted with the Department of Fish and Wildlife, and all known natural predators in the area were ruled out." She had everyone's attention.

"Professor Wainwright studied these gnawed bones for months. The teeth marks in the bones show impressions of incisors and canines closely related to that of a Neanderthal. However, ninety-percent of the teeth were beyond the range of human possibility. As for the mouth size, the bite ratio was calculated at 2 1/2 times wider than that of a normal person.

"Once it was all added up," Susan continued, "the bite radius, footprints, etcetera, you have a bipedal humanoid standing approximately 9-feet tall. This creature is killing animals with its bare hands, at different areas around Mount Adams and eating them, literally skin and bones.

"Professor Wainwright told me he is working on publishing the information in a research paper, later this year. Additionally, Professor Wainwright has begun sending this evidence to include his research to other top scientists so they can begin the peer review process. The four years he has spent on this project will help solve the mystery because the focus was based on forensic evidence. Professor Wainwright said he will be challenging the scientific community to disprove his research."

The back door of the auditorium opened and a lean, professional-looking man entered. He, too, had a closely cropped haircut. Walking quickly up to Derek, he began to whisper in his ear. Without a word, Derek stood and both men walked out. Susan watched them leave; temporarily forgetting she was in the middle of a lecture.

As the door shut behind them Susan continued, "Ah... there are 160,000 square miles in the Pacific Northwest alone which are not inhabited or explored. I believe, if you take both past and present accounts as well as Professor Wainwright's research, it is highly possible, a North American Primate exists. If so, this primate would be related to both chimpanzees and humans, making it highly intelligent.

"It would want to avoid contact with humans and would easily be able to do so. Like all primates, it would have a short temper, and be aggressive. Later this month Professor Wainwright and I will be collaborating on a field research project. Specifically we will be looking at nesting patterns...."

Susan was no longer thinking about her lecture, but instead her mind drifted to the two men who quickly left the auditorium. ◉

CHAPTER 7
"DEREK"

Derek Riley threw on his leather jacket as he and Brian exited the building. The two men walked quickly through the parking lot of the Convention Center. Corporal Brian Hall had been with the SRT program for just under five years.

Recently he had been assigned to be Maj. Derek Riley's assistant. Aside from the occasional deployment where he had to be away from his wife, Amy, Brian thought Major Riley was a very easy man to work for. This assignment also allowed Brian greatly enhanced flexibility in the hours he worked.

While Derek was inside attending the lecture, Brian had been waiting outside in the unmarked Dodge Charger. He was thinking about Amy and making plans for remodeling their guest room into a nursery. Brian and Amy had been trying to have a child for a couple of years. When she became pregnant several months back, Brian immediately asked to be assigned to Bravo Team under Derek's command.

Not only did the major have a great reputation for taking care of the people who worked for him, but the position had provided Brian a number of perks. He had been listening to his favorite podcast while planning the nursery, when the alert came over his issued smartphone. He knew two things—first, Derek would want to know immediately and second, the major had probably turned his phone off.

"So how'd the lecture go today?" Brian queried as they approached the Charger. Headlights flashed as Brian unlocked the doors with his remote key fob.

"Actually, she is starting to really step up her presentations," Derek stated as he opened the front passenger door. Brian walked around to the driver's side and began to get in.

"Do you want me to have Marcus initiate an RDD on her?" Brian asked.

Eager to please his boss, Brian was referring to Marcus Pettiford, the head of the SRT's cyber unit. The cyber unit is the Counter Intelligence and Psychological Operation Section of the SRT, referred to as PsyOps. RDD was the acronym they used for Research, Disinformation, and Destruction.

When a member of the public, or the occasional government official, began to cause issues by asking questions or developing information, which could harm National Security, the SRT would be alerted. The PsyOps unit would then be tasked with initiating an RDD.

Phase-One was conducting detailed "research" on the individual to include data-mining their social media, obtaining the target's credit and banking information as well as all past history. The research included reviewing emails, text messages, and other privileged information such as medical records not readily available to traditional law enforcement agencies. This was done without the need for a warrant through a National Security Clause only a handful in the government were aware of. Primarily the PsyOps unit was looking for areas of vulnerability or where pressure on the individual could be placed.

If the information the individual was disseminating became too credible, the PsyOps section would begin Phase-Two. This was a "Disinformation" campaign designed to make the information look like every other crazy internet theory.

Just a handful of people in PsyOps could create thousands of fake accounts and postings on social media. They could also manipulate original images or videos and then repost those images through multiple links making it appear as if the manipulated image was actually the original. The PsyOps unit had become exceptionally skilled at the "bait and switch" of disinformation. They did this by inserting small elements of the truth into the material to make the disinformation appear credible.

If however, the individual persisted, the PsyOps unit would go to Phase-Three. They would "Discredit or Destroy" the person's credibility. This could involve a variety of options, including changing photographs on their social media network, writing blogs purporting to be one of the subject's "victims," and dismantling the person's credit or their career.

When the National Security of the United States was threatened and these lesser means had proven to be inadequate, planting evidence of a criminal or perverse nature for others to find was not off the table. This had only been necessary a few times, as the disinformation seemed to remedy most issues.

If discrediting and destroying the person's credibility failed, there were rumors of a Phase-Four. This level involved a more direct approach. Not everyone was aware or believed this option existed. Derek was unsure himself, believing Phase-Four was more theoretical than anything else. He had not been informed of anything this extreme even remotely being implemented.

"No, we aren't there yet," Derek replied. "It was handled pretty well a few years ago with a telephone call." Derek knew this was true because he had been the one to make the anonymous call to KNDU Channel 23. That call had gotten Dr. Parker's university funding pulled.

Although he would not admit it, Derek felt a little guilty about the telephone call. It was, after all, part of his job. He had never personally met Dr. Parker though he respected her efforts. That was one of the reasons he attended her speaking engagements. Repaying Dr. Parker, one twenty-five-dollar lecture at a time.

"I do want you to have Marcus begin Research into a Prof. Michael Wainwright however," Derek directed.

"Copy that, boss," Brian acknowledged, as he glanced over his right shoulder and pulled away from the curb.

As Brian accelerated onto Columbia Center Boulevard, Derek removed the iPhone from his pocket and powered it up. He did not like always being on the end of someone's leash. He never had. Occasionally, he would rebel and shut his phone off. It did not really matter, though. He knew Brian would come get him as he had.

Derek had spent nearly his entire life in the service of others. He once described his life as, "One man's quest for a higher purpose." The last nine years he had been with the SRT, where he quickly moved up the ranks. However; recently, Derek had begun to question certain aspects of the job.

Prior to joining, he had spent a career in the Marine Corps. The last several years, Derek was a Team Leader with the 3rd Raider Battalion in the Marine Corps Special Operations Command, commonly referred to as MARSOC. While in the Marines, Derek was deployed to nearly fifty different countries on five separate continents.

In addition to a fair amount of direct action missions, he had fought in three different wars. Derek sometimes mused how all the wars had basically been in the same place.

His career in the Marines ended abruptly when, while with the Raider's, an incident occurred with his team in Afghanistan. Derek was not present at the time, as he was conducting an operation in another area but the entire team became dragged into a politically motivated witch hunt. Though eventually cleared of any wrongdoing, Derek and the rest of his team were encouraged to retire and essentially forced out of the Corps.

Following his time in the Marines, for a short period, Derek joined the Defense Intelligence Agency. While with DIA, he found himself conducting foreign counter intelligence operations. Derek's main task had been to track the movements of known foreign intelligence officers and similar investigations.

This became increasingly frustrating as State Department bureaucrats and career politicians frequently became entangled in the investigation. Strings would be routinely pulled to "look the other way" or investigations would be shutdown entirely.

Derek was about to resign from the DIA when a friend recruited him into the SRT. Once he joined SRT, Derek became hooked. The comradery he had once known in the Corps had returned. Initially the primary mission seemed incredible. During the last few years, wasteful spending, and incompetent leadership at the regional level was beginning to sour him. Loyalty to his people and the mission was all that remained.

His government-issued phone powered up and Derek typed in the ten-character security access code. He scrolled through the missed messages until he found it. The recall message had been sent to everyone both on and off duty and directing them to respond to the "Bunker."

"What can you tell me?" he asked Brian.

"Not much, boss," Brian said as he glanced over his left shoulder and switched lanes. "All the recall message said was

'Type-1, Class-A. Full recall required.'" Derek had read the same message on his phone.

In 1973, the Atomic Energy Commission became the Department of Energy. During the early years of the Energy Department, and continuing today, funding of scientific research surpassed all other federal agencies combined. Sandia, Lawrence Livermore, and Pacific Northwest National Laboratories, known as PNNL and located adjacent to the Hanford Site, evolved into some of the United States top scientific research facilities. These research laboratories became entrenched within DOE's sphere of influence.

Of all the laboratories, PNNL became the nation's leading experimentation laboratory. The best and brightest scientists flocked there to be a part of the innovative research being conducted. Areas of study and exploration included Biological Sciences, the Human Genome Project, the Strategic Defense Initiative (SDI), the anti-ballistic missile defense system (also known as Star Wars) as well as other advanced weapons research and development projects.

Quietly, the different intelligence and investigative agencies of the federal government moved small elements of specialized people into PNNL and began working on the more clandestine scientific projects.

Just a short time after leaving the Convention Center, Brian drove the Charger onto George Washington Way in Richland. This road cut through the heart of the PNNL campus. The numerous buildings of this national laboratory occupied both sides of the roadway. The PNNL campus was designed to give even a casual observer the impression they were looking at a college university. Brian turned the vehicle north onto Stevens Drive and pushed down on the accelerator.

Twenty-five minutes earlier, Derek was sitting in the auditorium listening to Susan's lecture. Now they were approaching the "Wye" Barricade, the southeastern boundary of the Hanford Site. The Charger closed on the hardened barricade. Numerous signs could be seen posted along the route. Most of these signs were mere warnings to the public that they were about to enter a government installation and that trespassing was prohibited.

As this was a weekend, the gate was closed. Brian brought the Charger to a full stop just outside the barricade's main entrance. He pressed a button on the Charger's door and the driver's window came down.

An officer in full uniform with a handgun strapped to his hip stepped out from behind the bullet resistant door of the Barricade. Derek and Brian both produced official government identification and presented them for inspection.

The uniformed officer gave them a quick once-over then said, "Good morning, Major!"

Derek smiled. "Good morning, Randy. Are you staying out of trouble?"

"Absolutely, sir, though my wife might not always agree!" Randy said as he handed the identification back.

"You guys did a great job on that hostage rescue event last night," Randy stated.

"Nothing like blowing holes in walls!" Brian countered with a laugh.

"Just remember, you two," Derek replied with a smile, "that wasn't our doing but rather the tremendous efforts of the brave men and women of the FBI in cooperation with the Richland Police Department."

"Of course. I forgot!" Randy acknowledged with an overexaggerated wink. "Anyway, we had another elk commit suicide this morning. It ran into a maintenance vehicle on 4-South. They've seen a lot of elk around mile post 19, so drive careful in that area."

Giving a half salute, half wave, Randy reached inside the guard shack and pressed a button. The gate began to slide open.

Looming in the distance, Gable Mountain is located in the center of Hanford's 650 square miles. During the Cold War, there had been great apprehension of Soviet Spy planes and satellites collecting data on the US Nuclear Weapons program. To keep the classified research out of the eye of surveillance aircraft and satellites, several DOE Sites to include Hanford created a number of underground tunnels and complexes. "N" and "B" reactors, situated along the Columbia River, had an extensive underground complex running between them.

Worry continued to grow about Soviet Bombers attacking government facilities and strategically important complexes. Defenses were created to counteract this possibility. Some of the Cold War defenses included Nike Missile Bases. Four of these missile silos were officially put into operation at the Hanford Site.

Missile bases were placed on Rattlesnake Mountain, in Othello, as well as Saddle Mountain, and at Priest Rapids. At the time, these underground bunker and missile silos contained the Nike Ajax. The Ajax was an anti-bomber missile designed to take down high-altitude planes. Each silo held approximately twenty to thirty missiles.

Due to the strategic significance of the Hanford nuclear research and weapons complex, it was decided one of the four Nike Sites would be converted from Nike Ajax to Nike Hercules.

The Hercules was an improved model, first installed at Hanford in 1958. This missile contained a nuclear warhead. The theory behind the nuclear warhead was that the missile, when fired, could destroy entire formations of Soviet aircraft with a single air detonation. The Hercules nuclear missile had a 50-mile range, and could reach altitudes of 100,000 feet.

Plans for the Continuity of Government, also known as COG, were put into place to counter a Soviet nuclear strike. During the 1960s across the United States, several massive underground bunker complexes were constructed. This included a COG Bunker and an additional missile silo built into and under Hanford's Gable Mountain.

The theory behind the bunkers was that select government officials, and their families, who considered themselves more important than the general population, could be moved into them in case of a nuclear disaster.

Maintaining control of the country was the "official explanation" to the taxpayers for the need and considerable expense. These complexes were built out of sight of the general population and much of this remains secret even to those who worked on them. In essence, members of the government became the first "preppers."

By 1974, the Nike missile silos were, for the most part, deemed obsolete and the vast majority of the sites were shut down. The COG facilities remained operational, though some were converted into other uses.

Following the collapse of the Soviet Union, production of Special Nuclear Material stopped and the Department of Energy was divided into two elements. One was the National Nuclear Security Administration (NNSA) and the other being Environmental Management (EM). Hanford's designation fell under the "Environmental Management" umbrella. Hanford's SRT program grew.

In order to practice and hone their skills, the SRT routinely competed at tactical competitions. These competitions, usually called SWAT Rodeos, were where police and military tactical teams from around the world would compete against one another to determine which team was the best.

It was in these competitions where Hanford's SRT frequently went nose to nose against Navy Seals, Army Delta, German GSG9, British SAS, and police SWAT Teams such as the LAPD. More often than not, the SRT took the top position. Once again, covert elements of the government began to take notice. Funding and support for the SRT program slowly increased.

In 2006, the last of the Special Nuclear Material, specifically the weapons grade plutonium, was shipped off the Hanford Site. What remained was mostly spent nuclear waste. Other than some environmental protest groups, few people cared about this material. Many considered this to be the end of Hanford's history. They were very wrong.

Quietly, the mission of the SRT program underwent a dramatic change.

Access to Gable Mountain became strictly controlled and limited to specific locations for Native American religious purposes. The COG Bunker under Gable Mountain underwent a covert utilization upgrade. Then, in 2007, the SRT moved in.

Derek dialed the number for the Operations Center on his phone. The line was answered on the first ring. The voice was crisp and clear.

"Patrol Operations. How can I help you?"

"This is Riley. Put me through to the colonel," Derek directed.

"Yes, sir. One moment" came the voice on the other end of the line.

A few moments later, Colonel Stephen Harris came on the line. Derek got right to it. "What do we have, Colonel?"

"Sorry to do this to you again on short notice, Derek, but we have to redeploy your team," Colonel Harris began. "We've been monitoring the situation since the call originated last night about the same time your team was assisting Alpha at the Stevens Center. Short answer is there have been a number of casualties and the locals are on scene. I dispatched two of your team members, Hammond and Hernandez, about two hours ago to recon the situation. They'll be using their standard cover story and should be arriving shortly. How long until you get here?" Colonel Harris asked.

"We're about fifteen minutes out," Derek replied, quickly glancing at his watch.

"Okay. I've had a couple Blackhawks tasked to us from the 2nd 75th Rangers out of Fort Lewis," Harris announced. "They should arrive shortly after you do. We'll have their crews sign the 312s when they get here."

Colonel Harris was referring to the government's Standard Form 312. This is the government's nondisclosure agreement regarding the release of classified information. Once signed, it subjected the person to criminal prosecution for any information they divulge.

"Understood," Derek said and disconnected the call.

Derek and Brian had been traveling north on Route 4. If they continued straight, eventually they would arrive at the retired "B" Reactor. Instead, Brian took a sudden turn onto an unnamed road.

They followed this route as it snaked around the north side of Gable Mountain. At another unobtrusive corner, Brian drove the Charger off the hardtop and onto a gravel road uniquely concealed by some purposeful planting of sagebrush and other foliage. This dirt road suddenly dipped into a narrow ravine. Their vehicle became immediately concealed from any casual onlooker.

Within a few minutes, aside from the dust of the dirt road, even under direct observation, no one would be able to see where they had gone. In the Operations Center however, a handful of key personnel had been tracking their progress.

Along the route, carefully placed and concealed thermal-capable security cameras were tracking their progress. These cameras were designed to identify anything approaching SRT headquarters. When Brian pulled the Charger off the hardtop, their movement had been detected by a variety of ground sensors. These sensors set off an alert in the command center. Immediately, personnel assigned to the center began viewing the Charger on numerous monitors.

A few minutes after turning off the hardtop, the road widen, then abruptly stopped at the base of the mountain. About 100 yards from where the road ended, an extremely sturdy aircraft cable affixed to a couple of metal bollards blocked further progress. Near the bollards, off to the side of the gravel road, stood a small raggedy shack. This shack appeared as if it had been there since the turn of the century.

As the Charger came to a full stop in front of the bollards, the door to the shack opened revealing the truth. The shack was only designed to appear old and raggedy. In actuality, it was a high-tech marvel.

The interior walls were a combination of high carbon steel and a composite fiber designed to take a direct hit from a rocket-propelled grenade. High-definition camera monitors displayed twenty separate images. These images were of different avenues of approach around Gable Mountain. Computer access and an array of communications equipment completed the interior.

As the heavy armored door opened, it exposed a gunport on the inside. Two serious-looking men stepped from the shack. They wore full battle fatigues and load-bearing vests jammed full of equipment. Assault rifles were strapped across their chests. Again, Brian and Derek presented their identification. Although recognizing the Charger's occupants, these men acquired the government identification and compared them to an access list before returning them.

"Major. Everyone is gathering in the Trophy Room. They're just waiting for you before starting the briefing." The operator then glanced at Brian, "Your chauffer needs some more training on the EVOC course, though. He drives like a little ol' woman!"

"Bite me," Brian said with a smile.

One of the men entered the shack and a moment later two things happened. First, the aircraft cable and bollards began to lower into the ground. Then the side of the mountain began to lift upwards similar to what a remote garage door might do.

The side of the mountain had actually been converted into a large hangar door. It was covered in a sand texture as well as other natural camouflage, which had been affixed in place. At fifty feet, most people would never even see this door. The SRT bunker's camouflage was a technique that had been perfected decades earlier at the S4 Site on the slope of the Papoose Mountains just south of Area 51.

The Charger pulled away from the gate and was immediately swallowed up by the mountain. The interior of this complex was huge. Initially after pulling in, they entered what looked like a large hangar bay. More than a couple of Military C5 transport planes could have easily fit with plenty of room to spare.

Several vehicles were parked along one side. A couple were from the government van pool. Others varied from up-armored military HUMVEEs to blacked-out, unmarked government SUVs. Numerous specially equipped Polaris ATVs and rugged-looking off-road motorcycles occupied one corner of the hangar.

Along the north wall, a member of the SRT was performing maintenance on one of the two parked "Global Hawk" UAVs. The south side of the hangar was designed for a variety of training. A rock-climbing wall and rappel tower, which would have been the envy of any extreme sports enthusiast, were obviously visible. Some portable walls and doors, which could be configured to simulate a plethora of structures, were stored up against the far side of the complex.

There were several hallways and adjoining doors. One was labeled "Cafeteria," another, "Dormitory." A red light flashed over yet another door that was labeled "Range 9." Derek knew the flashing light meant the range was in use. Off to one isolated corner loomed a large, heavy industrial-looking elevator. Its label read "Restricted / Holding Area."

Derek did not wait for Brian. He immediately headed towards the main area of the complex, walking quickly towards a secured door. After swiping his identification through a card reader, he punched a series of numbers into a keypad. A light on the reader turned green as the doors swung open.

Walking down the main hall, Derek passed the open door to the gymnasium. Several fit men were inside. Derek paused at the door and looked in. Members of "C" Team were lifting weights or performing pull-ups. One was jogging on a treadmill while a couple others were on the wrestling mat attempting to outmaneuver each other in a complex chess match of Brazilian jiu-jitsu and other martial art techniques.

As Derek turned away from the gym, almost as if they materialized from nowhere, SRT members Mike Davis and Patrick Bennett stepped in front of him, blocking his path. Both had come to the SRT program from the SEALs, though Derek did not know who had originally recommended them. Their fellow SRT members frequently referred to them as the "Huge-Brothers" as both stood six foot four and were each a solid 230 pounds.

Derek had his apprehensions about them. These former SEALs stayed to themselves and their aggressive actions sometimes concerned him. His impression was both seemed a little too eager to pull the trigger. Until recently, Derek had kept this opinion to himself since they were not directly tied to his team. Unfortunately, just a few days earlier, Derek had denied their transfer request to Bravo Team.

"I'm kind of in a rush, boys. Is there something you need?" Derek said as he turned in the hallway to fully face the duo.

"Yeah!" Bennett announced without further explanation.

"What my friend means, Major, is we'd like to know why you turned down our request to join your team?" Davis said with a smile that portrayed little warmth.

"I think you both know why," Derek retorted as Brian caught up to the trio, stepping alongside Derek.

"We have more experience than this little prick you have here," Bennett stated, motioning with his thumb towards Brian. Out of the corner of his eye, Derek saw Brian's jaw clench tightly.

"Experience can be achieved. What I am looking for with my team is something neither of you possess," Derek replied, looking squarely at both of them. Catching the hardened expression on Derek's face, both Bennett and Davis took an unconscious step backwards.

"And what is that?" Davis asked hesitantly, having lost some of his earlier confidence.

"Character," Derek answered as he stepped around the two giants. Brian smiled at the look of shock that had crossed their faces. He then quickly fell in behind Derek.

Marching down the hallway, Derek quickly forgot about the Huge Brothers as he began to focus on the upcoming recall. After passing the armory and several offices, Derek entered the "Trophy Room."

This was a large rectangular conference room. A heavy blue industrial carpet covered the floor. Lengthwise along both walls were floor-to-ceiling glass cases. Not only were these cases filled with the hundreds of trophies from every shooting competition won by the SRT since the early 1980s, but they also contained news clippings and other memorabilia. Many of the news articles reported stories that were intentionally misleading, describing events in the media as something other than what had truly occurred. Derek knew a new article concerning last night's hostage rescue would soon be joining the growing collection.

A twenty-foot oak table ran down the center of the Trophy Room. The men of Bravo Team filled the plush leather seats situated along both sides. The several conversations quickly ended when Derek walked in. Everyone turned and faced their team leader.

"Okay, people," Colonel Harris barked from the back of the room, "let's get started." ◉

CHAPTER 8
"VOYEUR"

Jimmy Russo had always been socially awkward. He grew up without his father, and his mother, Francesca, was mentally unbalanced. Throughout his childhood she kept him isolated, not allowing him access to the outside world. This included no television or radios. Jimmy became Francesca's sole emotional and physical support. She personally bathed Jimmy until he was nine years old. Jimmy, who had been left in complete solitude had never known anything else.

When Francesca left for work, performing janitorial services for a manufacturing company, she would frequently lock Jimmy in his room until her return. She would leave a bucket in the corner if he had to relieve himself. Often, while sitting alone, Jimmy would hear a voice in his head, whispering in his ear: *"You want more."*

On his twelfth birthday, things began to change for Jimmy. That was when an alert neighbor observed the comings and goings of his mother and notified Child Protective Services. Upon checking, they discovered Jimmy's living conditions were not much different than that of a caged animal. Immediately Jimmy was placed in a foster home while Francesca was arrested. She was deemed incompetent to stand trial and began bouncing in and out of mental health facilities.

Jimmy's foster parents tried hard. He found himself fascinated with their electronics. Jimmy would spend hours watching the television or playing video games. His foster father took him outside to play catch once, but Jimmy hated the physical aspects of it.

Child Protective Services believed the best thing was for Jimmy to become socialized with children his own age. Though he was enrolled in public school, Jimmy was placed in the special learning programs. Sheltered nearly his entire life, many, including his foster parents, were surprised to discover Jimmy was highly intelligent.

Jimmy could not hide his awkwardness. Coupled with his consistently greasy hair and hooked nose, the other children teased him relentlessly. This did not help his confidence. By his sophomore year in high school, Jimmy found a part-time job, mostly on the weekends, stocking shelves in a local grocery store. There he earned enough money to buy his first iPhone.

That introduced him to a completely different world of the internet, especially pornography. Jimmy found himself spending hours on his smartphone. Still, that was not enough and the whispering in his head continued.

One day, prior to gym class, Jimmy concealed his iPhone in the girls' locker room. He left the camera recording. After his classmates finished changing, he retrieved the phone. Jimmy still had those recordings.

After graduating high school, Jimmy, began working at a Radio Shack while taking night classes at a technical college. He became exceptionally skilled with all things electronic, especially computers and cameras. He was never able to stop thinking about the images he captured in the girls locker room and voyeurism became his new obsession.

One day Francesca arrived at the door to his apartment. Unable to hold-down a job, she was now homeless. In addition to her mental instability, she had become addicted to heroin. Years of psychological torture combined with an overpowering guilt. Jimmy was no match for Francesca's controlling personality. The woman who bathed him until nearly his tenth birthday was invited to move in with him.

A few years later, while attending community college, Jimmy saw a job posting on the FBI website for surveillance technicians. Though not official agents, these surveillance professionals were employees of the FBI and worked directly under the command of a Supervisory Special Agent. Often, they would be tasked with performing long-term surveillance operations. Jimmy wanted more.

The application process went smoothly for Jimmy. He impressed the FBI's human resource personnel during the interview and his superior knowledge of current electronic surveillance equipment made him a shoe-in. It was not until he underwent a polygraph that his application faltered. The polygraph examiner was relentless.

"I am surprised your deviant lifestyle hasn't gotten you incarcerated yet," he told Jimmy at the conclusion of the examination. Jimmy was escorted from the federal building.

Following the failed polygraph, Jimmy became depressed. He did not return to school for more than a week. He felt a foreboding of things to come weighing heavily on him. The voices kept nagging at him. Like through his childhood, Jimmy sat alone, in the dark of his apartment.

Nearly two weeks after his washout at the FBI, there was a knock on his door, which begrudgingly Jimmy answered. The tall man strolled past him without being invited inside. As the man smiled, Jimmy thought he looked like a skeleton. His impeccably trimmed white hair seemed to glow in the darkness of Jimmy's apartment.

"Mr. Russo, my name is Smith. I work for a branch of the government tasked with, 'special projects.' I believe we could use men like yourself. Men with your special talents." As Smith said this, Russo must have looked a little dubious. Detecting Jimmy's skepticism, Smith added with a sly smile, "We're not as uptight about your extracurricular activities as the FBI."

"More," the voice whispered in Jimmy's ear. Smith, who seemed to know a great deal about Jimmy, did not mention the hundreds of pine tree automobile fresheners hanging from the apartment's ceiling. Nor did Smith convey the impression he had any concerns about the fact that Francesca had not been seen for several months.

Smith's visit had been three years ago. Jimmy loved his job. His paycheck showed he worked for Homeland Security, but he reported directly to Smith. Early in his career, Smith sent Jimmy to a number of schools such as covert lock picking and video editing. Many of these were taught by the clandestine services of the CIA.

Over the last couple of years, Jimmy had gotten so good at conducting surveillance, Smith had begun to task him with training new recruits on surveillance techniques. These junior agents would eventually work directly for Smith in other aspects. However, when they were assigned to Jimmy, they were strictly learning the art of surveillance and he was in charge.

Smith had once told Jimmy that he had a number of surveillance specialists like himself on the payroll. Each had their own specific area of responsibility. Jimmy's current area was the Pacific Northwest. Having taken care of the "issues" with his apartment, JimmyH had recently put in a transfer request to fill a vacancy in southern Nevada. He had nothing left tying him to the Pacific Northwest, including Francesca.

Aside from training new agents in the art of surveillance, Jimmy's primary task was to monitor recent retirees from Smith's special programs as well as any person Smith considered a potential security risk. Jimmy was very busy.

Today, Smith had sent Jimmy on a rush surveillance operation. Some professor Smith had very recently become concerned about. ◉

CHAPTER 9
"ZEIGLER"

The moment he received the telephone call Zeigler was instantly irritated. He did not show his annoyance, though. He had played the game long enough that he knew just the right amount of concern and empathy he needed to display. He was after all the County Sheriff and theoretically responsible for the several hundred deputies that worked for him.

James Davis Zeigler had been the sheriff for almost three years. At five-feet three-inches tall and a plump 250 pounds, he was disliked by most of the deputies on the department. This dislike primarily evolved because they knew he was nothing more than a bureaucrat and as such, Zeigler did not have their backs. More than once he had shown the troublesome ability to throw them under the theoretical bus, especially if it would further his career.

In 1991, after graduating from Evergreen State College, Zeigler had joined the sheriff's office with the specific intent of one day becoming the sheriff. Unlike most sheriff departments where the top-cop position is elected, at that time the Pierce County Sheriff was an appointed position.

This was due to the fact that in 1978, the then-elected Sheriff George Janovich was arrested for running a criminal enterprise, which included racketeering, extortion, bribery, arson, and attempted murder. Following that arrest, the office of sheriff became a position appointed by the County Executive. Zeigler knew all he had to do was look good to the commissioner and one day he would be the sheriff. This removed any need for campaigning, spending his own money or even getting the backing of the department's deputies.

He did not like working the streets. In the early days of his career, often when a serious call came in, then-Deputy Zeigler, would circle the block until other deputies arrived and handled the incident. Two years after he graduated the academy he was able to set his career path in a direction that kept him from having to deal with the derelicts of society.

First, he joined the DARE Program. There he hung around elementary schools and made friends with the many school superintendents from around the county. From DARE he moved into the Civil Affairs division of the sherriff's office where he rubbed elbows with the district and superior court judges.

After that, he volunteered for Internal Affairs. This was where Zeigler's career truly blossomed. Once in Internal Affairs, Zeigler was able to routinely get his name in the paper going after and running roughshod over deputies for perceived wrongs.

For Zeigler, it did not matter what the deputy had been accused of or even the evidence against them, just the profile of the case. The higher the profile the more energy he put into it.

A few years back, he took over the administrator's position at the county jail. Then, finally, when the top spot opened up, his name was on the County Executive's short list.

Earlier this year the Pierce County reestablished the Chief Law Enforcement seat as an elected position. Zeigler knew he was possibly facing a challenge for the office and that the deputies who worked for him would most likely back his opponent regardless of who that might be.

Now that he was the Sheriff, Zeigler felt he had established himself well enough that if he could hold on for another year or two he would be able to make a run at a state democratic congressional seat. He just needed to keep his press positive.

When the call came in at this inconvenient hour, Zeigler was not happy. First, his position forced him, for political reasons, to get up and travel to the scene. Second, it was because of the deputy involved.

In his opinion, Sergeant Sullivan was a cowboy. His first dealings with Sullivan came when Zeigler was a rookie and Deputy Sullivan was assigned as his training officer. During this appraisal process, Sullivan officially criticized Zeigler for being too timid when dealing with suspects. He did not show it then, but Zeigler bitterly disliked Sullivan.

Zeigler smiled to himself as he thought about how he had been able to get even with Sullivan. He had been instrumental in getting Sullivan kicked off the Gang Unit. This was after a local hoodlum made a complaint about Sullivan to *his* Internal Affairs Division concerning a possible excessive use of force. Though there was no evidence to support the claim, Zeigler was able to find enough "witnesses," members of the same gang, willing to testify against Deputy Sullivan.

Although he wanted to get Sullivan fired, the sheriff at the time refused to do so. Instead, Zeigler was able to get him transferred. Having Sullivan banished to the Mountain Detachment was nearly as good as being fired.

Now this rogue deputy had gone and gotten himself killed. Zeigler spent his two-hour drive to the incident command post strategizing how he could spin this event to his benefit.

Due to the narrow roads and lack of infrastructure, the command post had been established at the Carbon River Ranger Station, about two miles from the actual crime scene. Situated at an elevation of 1,700 feet, the ranger station stood about twenty yards off the main road.

At first glance, it appeared to be nothing more than a rural two-story residence. Other than the American flag and standard wooden park ranger plaque affixed out front, there was nothing to distinguish the station. A moderate-sized visitor parking lot was situated to the east. Opposite the parking area was a small well-kept grass field.

The interior of the ranger station was barebones. The main entrance opened into the visitor greeting area where a counter ran the length of the station. A couple of old computers sat on the counter. Restrooms and a few offices completed the lower level. The second floor housed the temporary living quarters for use by the park rangers.

The normally empty visitor parking area was now filled with numerous law enforcement vehicles as well as media vans from every local station. Those vehicles that were unable to fit into the parking area had pulled off onto the shoulder of Carbon River Road. Numerous antennas and satellite dishes pointed skyward.

In direct contrast to the ranger station, the plush Pierce County Sheriff's Mobile Command Vehicle had been brought to the location. It filled the space between the main road and ranger station. Though the command vehicle was made by a specialty company under a federal grant, it truly was nothing more than a large recreational motorhome. It was painted sheriff's green and Pierce County logos decorated its exterior. The extravagant interior had been converted to accommodate a wide array of computer systems and communications equipment. The back had additional sleeping quarters for prolonged events. Now it was in full crisis mode.

The Pierce County SWAT team arrived a few hours earlier and had immediately gotten to work. After clearing the house, structures and surrounding property, they declared the scene secure. While the SWAT team established a perimeter around the property, the team's medic quickly confirmed Sergeant Sullivan and the others were deceased. Once this had been accomplished, the detectives and county coroner were allowed access.

Roadblocks were established on Manley-Moore Road and all traffic into and out of the area had to be cleared through the command post.

Once Zeigler arrived at the command post and had been briefed on the crime scene, he knew a gold mine had been dropped in his lap. The sensationalism of the scene itself was guaranteed to garner national coverage. The local media had already arrived and was staged near the ranger's station. It would not be long before CNN or some other national media began to turn up.

His detectives had informed him that Sergeant Sullivan had not just been killed but that his body had literally been crushed. Worse still was that his head had been twisted around 180 degrees. Zeigler smiled internally and thought it a fitting end.

In addition to Sullivan, two other bodies had been discovered in the barn. The detectives believed these were the bodies of Mr. and Mrs. McCarley, though they had yet to be positively identified. Mr. Mccarley had been not so much decapitated as his head had been ripped off. They had yet to find his head. Mrs. Mccarley had been disemboweled and it appeared as if someone or something had been eating her entrails.

Never letting a crisis go to waste, Zeigler began formulating his press briefing and how he might spin the event for the most sensational coverage. Terrorists, Satanists, and mentally deranged individuals where some of the ideas he might "unofficially" leak to the media. It was around noon when the first Feds began showing up and disrupting his plans.

SRT members Captain David Hammond and Sergeant Jacob Hernandez arrived in a black unmarked SUV. Zeigler instantly disliked the two of them. Not because they were Feds, but instead, they reminded him of those high school jocks who used to pick on him when he was a teenager.

They were big athletic men and sported credentials that identified them as White and Jones, Special Agents with the US Forest Service. This was their official cover story. They immediately claimed jurisdiction and began instructing Zeigler's men on what they could and could not do.

Zeigler was going to have none of it. He was not going to let these knuckle draggers steal his spotlight.

This conflict between Zeigler and who he believed were Forest Service Agents brought all law enforcement activity to a screeching halt. For at least forty minutes, Zeigler tried to work around agents Jones and White. When that had not worked, he decided he would directly challenge their authority.

Zeigler was in the middle of confronting the agents when his voice was drowned out by the sound of approaching helicopters. Everyone stopped and watched as two Blackhawks appeared over the tree line. The media immediately focused their cameras on these new arrivals. The two large helicopters hovered briefly, before the first one flared and expertly landed in the small grass field.

Several men wearing camouflage fatigues jumped from the helicopter and began removing large, square, robust containers. Zeigler then noticed an incredibly fit man with a blond military style haircut also leaped from the Blackhawk. He was wearing a green windbreaker, the words *Federal Agent* stenciled across the back. Derek Riley immediately began directing the others.

Within a few minutes, both helicopters had dropped their payloads and departed. No one from the sheriff's office had said a word. More than a dozen men had gotten off the Blackhawks and they began moving the containers into the ranger station. Zeigler saw that the one wearing the windbreaker was walking over to them. A younger-looking man followed him.

When they were about a dozen feet away, Zeigler watched as the man in the windbreaker turned to Agent Jones and began giving directions.

"Keep the media corralled to the eastside of the ranger station. Let them know there will be a press briefing shortly," Derek commanded. "Also, have the locals pull away from the house and return here. I saw where the roadblocks were set on my way in. They are in a good spot so have them remain there. No one enters or leaves without my being made aware."

As Derek stepped farther away from Zeigler, he began giving additional directions. Zeigler had enough.

"Now wait one goddamned minute!" Zeigler said in his most assertive voice, which, sadly, was a little higher pitched than he had wanted. "I don't know who you think you are. But this is my crime scene!"

Slowly Derek turned and considered Zeigler for several moments. Then without a word, Derek stepped around Zeigler and began briskly marching towards the Mobile Command Vehicle.

"Hey wait. I'm talking to you!" Zeigler began sputtering as he immediately began to follow.

Derek ignored him and kept walking.

Just an hour earlier, following the mission briefing, while the men were loading the equipment onto the helicopters, Derek had received an update from Captain Hammond. He and Sergeant Hernandez had arrived at the scene. Not only was it becoming a circus, but also in the Captain's words, "The sheriff is being a colossal prick." Before departing, Derek asked Marcus to expedite the cyber research on the sheriff. It had not taken Marcus long.

During the flight over, Marcus had radioed Derek with the information. Across the helicopter's internally mounted headset, Marcus told Derek he was able to remotely access the sheriff's personal home computer. Like so many in the government, the sheriff believed he was beyond touchable.

Marcus laughed as he informed Derek that the sheriff's computer password was indeed "PASSWORD." What Derek heard next was a little surprising. Marcus emailed Derek the specifics. As Derek reviewed the file on his smartphone, he realized the Cyber Ops Unit would not even need to fabricate anything to destroy this man.

Zeigler entered the mobile command post on Derek's heels. He had not stopped protesting. Derek saw there were four other occupants in the command vehicle. These deputies had previously been involved in conversation, but they all stopped and looked at the new arrivals.

"Everyone get out," Derek said. Though he did not raise his voice, Derek's tone was clear; there would be no argument.

There was a momentary pause as the four deputies looked from Derek to their sheriff and back to Derek. Realizing who was obviously in charge, the four deputies quickly shuffled outside.

Zeigler hated them for it and thought about how he would make their lives miserable when this was over. He was not, however, going to let this *Fed* get the better of him.

"You may not know who I am, but I am the Sheriff of this County!" Zeigler sputtered.

Ignoring him, Derek walked over to where the coffee was brewing. Taking a coffee mug, which prominently featured a Pierce County logo, Derek slowly poured himself a cup. Then deliberately took a seat across from Zeigler.

"Listen here," Zeigler began, raising his voice one whole octave, "I do not like this one bit! You Feds think you can just show up and take over! I'm in charge here!" Zeigler's face was now turning red as spittle began to spew from his lips. "This is my county! We do all the work and you Feds swoop in and steal all the publicity! When the governor hears about this, I'm going to have your jobs!"

Derek casually held up one hand essentially stopping Zeigler's tirade in its tracks. While Zeigler stared openmouthed, Derek nonchalantly took a sip of coffee.

"Are you through?" Derek calmly asked, as he gradually lowered his hand. Zeigler just nodded.

"So to answer your question, yes, James, I know *exactly* who you are. I also know you are planning on running for a congressional seat in the near future," Derek began.

Zeigler's mouth dropped farther open. Only a handful of his closest allies were even aware of this.

"So one of two things is about to happen," Derek continued. "One is you are going to go out and read this press release to the media." Derek removed a piece of paper from his jacket and unfolded it. He handed it to Zeigler.

"Then, once you've done that, you're going to turn over whatever assets we need to my control." Derek paused. "For your cooperation, your campaign for congress will receive an anonymous $25,000 donation."

Zeigler stared at him for a moment, and then read the press release. After reading it, he looked up and was a little more composed.

"This is bullshit," Zeigler said, holding the paper. Not wanting, but rather needing to know the alternative, he asked. "And if I don't?"

"Well, James," Derek said as he took another sip of coffee, "first you will be receiving a call from the Justice Department directing you to do exactly what I just told you to."

Derek fixed Zeigler with an icy stare. The look made Zeigler shudder.

"Then the FBI will be made aware of those 'other files' on your home computer. Which we have obtained possession of, by the way. After that, I believe not only will your career be ended, but you will most likely serve some time in a federal prison." Derek's tone left no room for doubt.

A good twenty seconds passed before Zeigler spoke. Then in a low whisper he asked, "Who are you?"

Derek only smiled in response. Privately he hoped this piece of shit would refuse to cooperate. ◉

CHAPTER 10
"BELLA"

With an overdramatic mastery, apparently written in the DNA of teenaged girls, Stephanie often told her friends how terrible her life was. She sat on the wide, oak sill of the large six-foot by four-foot picture window located in the living room. She had been texting with her friend Amanda for nearly an hour. Most of her texts were nothing more than complaints about her parents. Particularly about how "weak-sauce" and "lame" they were.

Until just a few months ago, she and her parents had lived in northern Tacoma where Stephanie attended Truman Middle School. However, shortly into her seventh-grade year her parents bought a home a little south of Buckley, in a remote area of Pierce County. As she often described it to Amanda: "Her hell on earth."

As most teens often do, Stephanie did not recognize her own culpability in her parent's decision to move. Ray and Patricia, Stephanie's parents, were well-established professionals. Ray was a senior pilot for Alaska Airlines while Patricia was a quality control manager for Intel Corporation out of Dupont. Their jobs often found them working long hours, away from the home.

They initially developed concern when Stephanie dyed her natural sandy blond hair and painted her nails jet-black. Ray and Patricia became even more worried when she began hanging around some teenaged, wannabe, anarchists who had a tendency for causing minor problems in the area. This group of young people displayed their antisocial behavior by wearing black clothing while listening to deathrock and apparently revolting against anything, they considered part of the establishment culture.

Unlike some fads, the anarchist subculture, had over the last few years been absorbed by Antifa. This had only gotten Stephanie more embedded with the local teens.

Ray and Patricia tried to ignore Stephanie's defiant attitude and at first rationalized it as normal rebellious teenage behavior. Nevertheless, when she and several friends were caught smoking marijuana in the boy's locker room during the school's lunch break, Ray and Patricia decided they needed to get her into a new environment. Ray maintained his position with Alaska Airlines while Patricia took a temporary leave of absence.

They purchased a home and several acres of land in rural southeastern area of the county. The original owner appeared especially eager to sell. Located on Prairie Creek Road just outside of the Town of Wilkeson, the property bordered the Mount Rainier National Park. They began paying for a private tutor who, with Patricia's help, began to home school Stephanie.

Stephanie would never openly admit it, but she did enjoy walking around the small orchard of apple trees in the backyard. Often she would take their dog Bella, a German Shepard-Rottweiler crossbreed, through the trees and down to the little creek just a few hundred yards from their back porch. Without the influence of her "friends," she had started to let her hair return to its natural color.

Though it was only a little after 6:00 p.m., this time of year the sun set early. The darkness outside was making it difficult to see more than a few yards off the front porch. Her father would be home late as he was on a return flight from Anchorage. That flight was not to arrive at the SeaTac International Airport until shortly after 10:00 p.m. As Stephanie waited for Amanda's response to the most recent text, she glanced over at her mother.

Patricia was sitting on the living room sofa intently watching the news. Bella was laying at her feet, her paws twitching as often happens with dogs when they are dreaming.

Stephanie noticed the news feed was coming from a Pierce County Ranger Station and became slightly more interested. Then as she paid closer attention, her interest became mild concern.

A short, fat police officer, who she remembered often seeing on the news, was again on the television. He stood in front of several microphones. Below the officer the television news ticker read, "Breaking News."

"Ladies and Gentlemen," Sheriff Zeigler began, "this is a hard day for all of us. Not only have we lost a couple members of our community, but also a sergeant with the sheriff's office. At approximately 9:30 last night, our office received a 9-1-1 hang-up from 27001 Kolisch Road East. A thirty-year veteran of the sheriff's office responded. Upon arriving, he discovered an animal had attacked the occupants. While investigating the scene the sergeant was also attacked and killed." Zeigler paused and rubbed his eyes, though Stephanie did not see any tears.

"These attacks appear to have been from a large grizzly bear," Zeigler continued. "Due to the nature of these attacks, the sheriff's office has requested the assistance of the United States Forest Service. They will use their expertise in tracking down, and, if necessary, euthanizing the grizzly.

"The names of the deceased will be released after we have ensured the families have been notified." Zeigler paused and cleared his throat. "At this time, I will be turning the podium over to the representative from the US Forest Service."

Stephanie watched as a fit-looking man stepped up to the microphones. She thought he was cute. At first, it appeared as if the fat sheriff was not going to leave the podium, then he reluctantly turned away.

"Ladies and gentlemen, I am Agent Mike White with the US Forest Service." David Hammond paused. He had played the role of "Agent White" so often he knew the script by heart.

"We want to thank Sheriff Zeigler and the Pierce County Sheriff's Office for calling us in. The men and women of the Forest Service understand the sadness this incident has caused the people of Pierce County and our hearts go out to the families that have been affected.

"Due to the tracks and other evidence at the scene," Hammond continued, "our preliminary investigation leads us to believe a large, male grizzly bear is responsible for these attacks. It is believed the forest fires that occurred along the Oregon-Washington border last August displaced this bear. The Forest Service has brought in some of our most experienced rangers, and we are actively engaged in tracking this animal."

From somewhere off camera a female reporter asked, "The forest fires occurred almost 300 miles from here. Isn't that a long way for a bear to travel?"

"It is not unheard of for male grizzly bears to travel 300 to 500 miles simply in search of food. A large fire, similar to what occurred in August, could easily force a bear to travel even greater distances," Hammond answered.

"Are the residents of the county in danger of another bear attack?" asked another reporter.

"Bear attacks are rare; however, everyone should utilize extreme caution over the next several days while our rangers track this animal. If anyone does happen to suspect a bear is near their residence we have established a hotline at (509) 373-2800." The number Hammond provided was a direct line into the SRT operations center.

Stephanie had stopped listening, movement in her peripheral vision caught her eye and she looked through the picture window into the darkness outside. Although the light above the main door was on, it did little to illuminate much of the night beyond the front porch.

Straining to see into the darkness, Stephanie did not really expect to see a bear. After a few moments, she assumed the movement was either a barn owl or simply her imagination brought on by the news briefing. She turned back to the television where Zeigler was again at the microphones.

"I have been your sheriff for nearly three years now. The safety of this community has always been my primary concern...." As Zeigler continued, Stephanie's phone chimed indicating a new text had arrived. She forgot the news and began reading the screen.

While formulating her response to Amanda, for reasons unknown, Stephanie suddenly felt uneasy. Goose bumps had risen on her arms and a feeling of being watched started to overwhelm her.

Slowly, Stephanie's eyes rose from the phone as her head turned towards the picture window. At first, her brain did not register what she was seeing. Then, as Stephanie realized what she was looking at, her unease became overwhelming fear as the panic that seized her, froze her in place.

The creature completely filled the window. In order to peer inside it had bent forward at the waist in what looked like a bizarre angle. This made it appear even more unnatural and grotesque. Both of the monster's massive arms were extended and reached up above the gutters resting its unseen hands on the top of the roof.

Its entire body was covered with thick black hair that did nothing to hide the mass of muscles beneath.

It was not the creature's massive body that had frozen Stephanie in place but instead its gigantic head. The creature's face was on the other side of the glass, a mere six inches away from her own. With large black eyes, it glared at her. As it exhaled, the window steamed just below the creature's nostrils.

Initially Stephanie thought she was looking at a gorilla but quickly recognized the differences. Except for the face, most of the oval shaped head was covered in black hair. The ears appeared proportionally smaller than they should have been. The monstrosity's nose was wide and flat. This reminded Stephanie of a boxer who had been punched in the face one too many times. Its skin was a leathery pale gray.

While Stephanie tried to breathe, the upper and lower lips of the creature rolled back in a huge, gruesome smile. To Stephanie, the stained yellow teeth looked like large piano keys. Though it had only been a second or two, for Stephanie it felt like an eternity. She did not feel herself falling backwards away from the window.

When she hit the floor, Stephanie snapped out of her paralysis and began screaming. Patricia came off the couch and spun towards her daughter. The creature was no longer visible in the window. Bella had also awoken and was standing at full attention in the middle of the living room.

"What happened?" Patricia asked excitedly.

On her hands and feet, Stephanie pedaled back away from the window. When she bumped into her mother's legs, she almost crawled behind Patricia. For several seconds Stephanie took in large gasps of air nearly hyperventilating.

"Monster!" Was the only word Stephanie was finally able to utter.

"No such thing as monsters," Patricia said, trying to calm her daughter.

While doing this, Patricia realized Stephanie had not taken her eyes from the window. Slowly Patricia eased towards the window. With each step, she felt Stephanie pulling her arm in the opposite direction.

The news story was now fully on Patricia's mind. As Patricia reached the window, she placed both hands on her forehead shielding her eyes from the interior light. Patricia leaned forward onto the glass and strained to see into the darkness. Nothing in their front yard moved.

Patricia nearly leaped out of her skin when Bella began barking. She turned to look at their dog. Bella was facing the kitchen in a half crouch, the hackles on her back completely raised. A low, fearful growl emanating from deep within her. Stephanie was still clutching her arm.

"It's okay honey, we're safe. Nothing can get in," Patricia said, though suddenly she did not quite believe that herself.

The loud bang that sounded from outside the kitchen caused both to scream. To Patricia it seemed as if something had struck the exterior wall. The entire house appeared to shake. With foam coming from her mouth, Bella began barking violently towards the kitchen. Patricia grabbed her daughter and almost carried her to the entryway.

Yanking open the door to the coat closet Patricia immediately began shoving jackets around in a frenzied search. Since his job often kept him away, for security, Ray had decided to keep a 12-gage shotgun in the closet. He had taught Patricia the basics on how to use it, such as loading and general safety.

"All you will really ever need to do is rack the pump action. The noise itself will scare away most burglars," Ray would often say this during these lessons.

While frantically digging through the closet, trying to find where Ray had left the shotgun, Patricia doubted her husband's advice would work on a grizzly bear, or worse.

After what seemed like forever, she discovered the shotgun resting against the back wall hidden behind Ray's golf bag. It momentarily snagged on the sleeve of her North Face jacket before she was able to completely remove it. Patricia pointed the shotgun at the front door and opened the chamber. It was empty.

Remembering Ray had left some shells on the top shelf of the closet she began pushing boxes and other items around trying to find them. She saw them in the back corner and strained to reach them.

Standing on her toes, Patricia was able to get the tips of her fingers on the box of shells. She pulled it from the closet. The small box, not much larger than her hand, had a picture of a flying pheasant prominently displayed on the cover. It read "Bird Shot." Patricia intuitively knew these probably were not the correct shells for the situation.

"Mom!" Stephanie yelled. Patricia spun.

Stephanie and Bella were facing the front door. Both had gone silent. Patricia also froze, as she stared at the door. None of them moved. A low, barely auditable growl came from the other side. To Patricia the growl sounded more human than what she thought should have come from a bear. Her eyes widened when she saw the doorknob begin to move. Slowly it turned in one direction then the other. Bears do not use doorknobs, she thought! Instinctively Patricia glanced at the dead bolt. It was locked.

The growling grew louder and the doorframe began to creak. All three, Patricia, Stephanie and Bella, began backing into the closet. Patricia ripped open the box of shells and several fell to the floor. She was able to grasp a couple and slammed them into the shotgun's loading tube.

Immediately Patricia racked the action and stepped between the front door and her daughter. Bella, too, stepped around her legs and stood just to her right. Though shaking violently, the dog also seemed to have decided to stand her ground.

The doors wooden frame cracked.

"Go away!" Patricia yelled. The shotgun boomed loudly in the entryway as she fired one round into the wall just above the door. Quickly she racked the action, chambering another round.

A thumping roar began at a distance and quickly grew louder. Within a few seconds, the entire house seemed to shake from the thunderous noise. The living room was bathed in a brilliant light. In the back of her mind Patricia thought she heard her daughter screaming; however, she was focused on the noises coming from outside.

"Stay here and hide!" she told Stephanie. Patricia pushed Bella into the closet with Stephanie and closed the door. Slowly, with the barrel of the shotgun in front of her, Patricia stepped to the door and unlocked the dead bolt.

Patricia swung the door open and instantly had to shield her eyes from the spotlight shining on her from a hovering helicopter. For decades, her husband, the pilot, had bombarded her with all things aviation. As a result, Patricia knew the helicopter, less than 50 feet above their front lawn, was a Blackhawk.

Men wearing military type clothing with rifles strapped across their backs were emerging from within the helicopter. Patricia watched as these men grabbed onto a two-inch thick rope that seemed to dangle from the helicopter. They began to slide down it. Patricia thought this looked like what a firefighter might do when sliding down a pole in a firehouse.

As the last of the men landed on the ground, in unison they took a knee forming a half-circle. Facing the forest just thirty yards from them, they held their rifles at the ready. The rope they used to descend, fell loose. It landed on the ground as the helicopter banked away. Patricia gawked at the bizzare scene unfolding in front of their secluded home. Several other men, also wearing military fatigues, carrying rifles and equipment she did not recognize, emerged from the opposite tree line. After linking up with the first unit, they began to move together in formation across her impeccably mowed grass. One man seemed to take notice of her and stepped away from the group.

With his rifle hanging loosely across his chest, the man extended his arms submissively towards the ground. Patricia saw that his hands were empty. He held his palms towards her as he slowly approached.

The rest of the men had advanced across the yard and entered the forest on the opposite side just as he stepped up to her. Patricia watched as he reached up and removed a device that looked like some type of binocular from in front of his eyes. Patricia immediately observed his short, blond military style haircut.

"It's okay now, miss," Derek stated in his calmest voice.

Derek did not know this woman but anyone who was scared enough and holding a shotgun could be dangerous.

"Everything is fine. We are with the Forest Service. We chased it away. You can lower the rifle." Derek knew he needed to calm her quickly.

"What the fuck was that?!" Patricia half screamed, half cried as she lowered her shotgun.

"It was a bear, ma'am. A large grizzly bear," Derek stated.

Patricia preferred this explanation rather than calling it a "monster." Though she knew it was the latter. ◉

CHAPTER 11

"MICHAEL"

A few days following her lecture, Susan and Josh met with Prof. Michael Wainwright at Anthony's, a seafood restaurant in Richland. Over the last several months, Susan had been emailing back and forth with Michael.

Those emails were followed by a number of telephone conversations and a few Zoom video confrences on their computers. This dialogue began shortly after Susan became aware of his discovery of the teeth impressions found on the bone piles. It was during one of their conversations Michael mentioned his upcoming field research project. He then suggested Susan collaborate with him on the project. She enthusiastically agreed.

They both had tremendous outdoor experience. Susan participated in numerous expeditions over the years, whereas Michael seemed to be an avid outdoorsman. While determining what equipment they should bring, it became abundantly clear to both they had more gear than anyone could ever hope to carry. However, as they would be heading out shortly, both thought it would be a good idea to meet in advance to finalize the plan and their equipment list.

Additionally, they wanted to establish clear objectives for the research project. Though both hoped for an encounter, they knew this was most likely not going to happen. Instead, their stated goals was to collect enough evidence of nesting patterns to be able to document that evidence into a cohesive and persuasive paper.

Michael and Susan both agreed that the field research team should be small. They decided the team would only consist of Michael, Susan, and Josh. Larger teams often become bogged down with too many supplies and were not agile. Additionally, the activity associated with a large group would most likely scare off any wildlife in the area. All of which would be counterproductive to their established goals.

Josh and Susan arrived at the restaurant early. Since most of the lunch crowd had not yet shown up and current restrictions on occupancy, they were seated outside on the deck overlooking the Columbia River.

A number of boats filled the nearby marina, giving them a picturesque view on a relatively sunny day. Susan ordered herself a Diet Pepsi while Josh asked for a Raspberry Ice Tea. As the waitress stepped away from the table with their drink orders, Professor Wainwright walked onto the restaurant's patio. He raised his hand in greeting as he approached.

"Professor Wainwright!" Susan exclaimed. "So nice to finally meet you in person!"

"Please, call me Michael," he replied and briskly shook her hand, a large smile on his face. "And you must be Josh?" Michael said as he turned and took Josh's hand in both of his.

Michael was wearing a blue blazer and jeans. On his sockless feet, he wore an old pair of gray canvas boat shoes. As he sat down, Michael removed the well-worn, white fedora from his head. The hat was adorned with a thick black band. He set the fedora on the table.

This was the first time they had met face-to-face. Michael was in his early sixties and his receding hairline became apparent the moment he removed his hat. His round spectacles sat on the bridge of his nose. In direct contrast to Susan, who was incredibly fit, Michael appeared as if he would be more comfortable barbequing steaks and drinking beer in his backyard. Susan immediately liked him.

After ordering, they made casual conversation for about fifteen minutes. As they waited for their lunches to be served, Josh—always the student and eager to learn—began asking Michael questions about the bone piles and the professor's interest.

"Obviously, growing up in the Pacific Northwest, I had heard stories of Sasquatch," Michael answered. "I've been fascinated about this topic ever since I was a child. But honestly, I only stumbled into the science of cryptozoological investigations.

"When I first came upon the original bone pile on the western slopes of Mount Adams, I was just on a nature hike with some of my students," Michael explained. "We were not looking for anything in particular, especially not Bigfoot. There was a small lake not far from the trail and we sat down to eat a snack. That's when the pile was discovered. It was immediately interesting as the bones were neatly stacked on top of one another." Michael paused as their food arrived. Susan had ordered a chicken Caesar, whereas Michael had gotten the seafood fettucine. Josh on the other hand had ordered a cheeseburger. As they began eating Michael continued.

"Well, if all we were talking about was a single pile of bones we would probably not even be having this conversation. Though interesting, I would have just brushed it off as an oddity as some of my academic colleagues have."

Michael pushed his glasses up a little on his nose then took a sip of water.

"These scientists"—while holding his fork, Michael made air quotes with both his hands as he said the word *scientists*—"well, they looked at this single piece of evidence and stated that a conclusion cannot be reached. Of course, like any single piece of information, taken alone or out of context, it is hard to come to any conclusion. Or worse, the truth may be discounted entirely.

"In this case, my colleagues were being intellectually dishonest. When you add several other similar bone piles that were discovered less than a mile away as the crow flies, that's more than a coincidence. Then add in the large 17-inch humanoid tracks found within close proximity of the piles, coupled with the numerous teeth impressions, then not forgetting the many historical regional accounts. Well, the evidence begins to compound, does it not?" Michael explained.

"Has anyone else gone down a similar road?" Josh queried.

"Actually, Josh, have you heard of Dr. Melissa Frazier?" Michael asked.

"No," Josh said while Susan nodded her head that she had.

"Well, here you have a respected forensic scientist. She performed a three-year study that concluded in 2017. Her research utilized a similar process as the previously conducted human genome project. Dr. Frazier performed DNA analysis on hundreds of reported Sasquatch samples consisting of blood, hair, tissue, and such from all around the country." As Michael spoke, Josh's eyes widened. "Her results pointed to a Novel North American Hominins that she theorizes is a hybrid hominid."

"Oh my God!" Josh exclaimed, not noticing the look of disappointment on Susan's face. "Why has this not gotten world-wide attention?"

"That's the problem, Josh," Michael began. "Inexplicably, shortly after Dr. Frazier published her works, her credibility was completely trashed, her samples were tainted and her published research paper on the topic was publically crucified. No one would touch the paper or back her findings for fear of a similar occurrence."

"Won't that happen to anything we produce?" Josh asked sincerely.

"I don't think so, Josh," Michael said. "I've taken a number of steps to protect any evidence I have currently collected and am being very selective on who I work with. You are the first two I will be venturing out into the wilderness with."

It was Susan's turn to ask a question.

"Michael, I know I asked you this before, but how did you discover this location we're going to?"

"Well, actually, I didn't," Michael responded as he took a piece of bread from the loaf the waitress had left on the table. "A close, personal friend of mine is an avid hunter and aware of my interest. He was out scouting possible hunting sites when he stumbled across this location. He took several photos and emailed them along with the coordinates to me. He and I then spoke on the telephone several times."

Chewing on a bite, Michael pushed his plate to the side and pulled out the photographs the hunter had sent him. They studied the photos with fascination, discussing the terrain and relevant features for several minutes.

"Funny thing is, after giving me the information; he seemed to have second thoughts and suggested we shouldn't go there. Though he couldn't say anything specific happened, he told me he had a peculiar unease while he was taking the pictures and that he wouldn't go back," Michael said.

Finishing their meals, their table was cleared and Michael brought out a "Green Trails" map of the area they would be going. Together they planned their hike in. Susan agreed the trek in from the north was probably their best approach. All three brought out their packing lists and compared notes as to the gear and equipment they would bring. Josh, the least experienced of the group, added a few items to his list that he had not thought of.

As the waitress arrived with the bill, Susan immediately reached for her handbag.

"No. I insist!" Michael exclaimed as he passed his credit card to the server.

A few minutes later as Michael was signing the bill, they agreed to meet in the following morning outside of Susan's office on the University Campus. They would be taking Michael's truck, as it was the best vehicle they had amongst the three of them.

Standing, the three shook hands again. The excitement they felt for their upcoming adventure was evident on the smiles they wore as they walked out of the restaurant.

None of them had noticed the intense man with greased hair and a ferret nose. Most people never gave him a second glance. Jimmy Russo had been sitting alone just a few tables away. Though appearing to be just another customer, Jimmy had been paying particularly close attention to them throughout their meal. He knew Smith would be extremely interested in the conversation he had just recorded. ◉

CHAPTER 12

"OSS"

The small convoy came to a brief pause near the guard shack at the base of Gable Mountain. They waited just long enough for the mountain's hangar door to open before the vehicles pulled in. When they came to a stop along the east wall, the men began to pile out of the SUVs.

All had several days' growth of beard. Though their uniforms were soiled and the men looked dirty and weary, years of training kept them moving with a purpose. Before they could shower and go home for some much-needed rest, they still had to clean and stow their equipment as well as sit through an extensive after-action debrief.

Derek stepped from his SUV. He paused and placed both hands on the back of his hips then leaned back as far as he could, stretching his lower back. After a week of hiking and sleeping on the ground of the forest, that concluded with a six-hour car ride back to the bunker, his body was incredibly stiff. Brian Hall gingerly followed Derek out of the rear passenger's seat. He was clearly favoring his right leg.

They both reached into the vehicle and retrieved their backpacks and rifles. With gear in hand, Derek and Brian began walking towards the armory. Brian was limping more than he had previously. Derek was proud of him. On the third day of their search, he had slipped on a wet, moss-covered rock, severely straining his ankle. Not once had he complained or slowed down. When Derek asked if he wanted to be evacuated back to headquarters all Brian said was "Bugger that idea, boss!" Derek did not bring it up again.

They had not been successful in the hunt or capture. Initially Derek thought they were on a good track. They had a few visual sightings on their thermals during their second day and had closed the distance. That is when they once again received orders from the command element. These orders completely redirected their efforts. After that, the creature had completely eluded them.

Realizing the effort was futile, on the fifth day the mission changed from capture to one of purely disinformation. This took less than twelve hours.

Two years earlier, a 500-pound grizzly bear in Yellowstone National Park had been identified. One of the SRT members who initially located the grizzly kept calling it "Binky" after a polar bear he once saw at the Alaska Zoo. The name stuck. At that time, the bear was tagged with a GPS tracker to make finding it easier. When it was decided to shift to a disinformation campaign, members of the SRT flew to Yellowstone where they tracked Binky's movements.

Once Binky was found, the SRT tranquilized and caged the animal. Covertly they moved the beast to the Carbon River Ranger Station in Pierce County. There Captain Hammond, again posing as a Forest Service Agent, along with Sheriff Zeigler held another press conference. The media was paraded past the animal's cage and encouraged to take photographs.

They both told the gathered press that the bear "suspected" in the killings had been captured. To keep the animal rights groups from protesting, which would only cause additional negative media coverage, Hammond told the press that the bear would be relocated into a remote area of Montana. In actuality, Binky would be brought back to Yellowstone where it would remain until the next time a similar need was determined.

Within hours, the story of the captured bear, complete with pictures, was all over the news. Even if an alternative story eventually came out, it would be chalked up to just another conspiracy theory.

As Derek and Brian entered the armory, Sergeant Shawn Perry, the SRT's primary armorer, stood up from behind his desk. Shawn had been on the SRT for nearly twenty years. The last seventeen he had been the lead armorer. Shawn had been sent to nearly every armorer's school imaginable. He was capable of not only fixing most weapons but also constructing unique specialty weapons.

"Everything go okay, Major?" Shawn asked as Derek laid his rifle on the counter.

"Other than coming back with a giant goose egg, the operation went perfectly," Derek said as Shawn picked the rifle up. He pulled the bolt to the rear and checked its chamber ensuring it was empty.

"Yeah, I can't imagine it would be easy. Any equipment issues?" Shawn asked as he began placing the rifle in a metal storage rack.

As Derek began to answer, the door to the armory opened and Marcus Pettiford quickly entered.

"Hey, boss!" Marcus began, "I know you just got back, but the colonel needs to see us in the SCIF pronto!"

Derek eyeballed Marcus. "Can't it wait until I shower and have a bite to eat?"

"Ah, he said immediately. He's there now waiting for us." Marcus seemed genuinely apologetic.

"Let me drop this off, and I'll come with you," Brian said as he began passing his equipment to Shawn.

"Sorry, Brian," Marcus stated, "the colonel only wants to see us." He pointed his index finger at Derek then back to himself.

"It doesn't matter anyways, Brian," Derek started. "You are going to clean up then report to medical and have that ankle checked out," he commanded. "As soon as you're done at medical I want you to take a couple days off and spend it with Amy!"

Brian came quickly to attention and gave a sarcastic British military styled salute, "Aye aye, sir!"

Derek smiled. "After you Marcus."

They left the armory and crossed the hangar. After entering a narrow hallway and traveling a short distance, they came to a secured door. Marcus removed his identification card and swiped it past a proximity reader. A red light near the door's lock turned green and a soft click could be heard from within the mechanism. They entered the outer room. The sign on the heavy metal door read "Sensitive Compartmented Information Facility" referred to as a SCIF by everyone in the government.

Government agencies wishing to communicate highly classified information utilized SCIFs. These specially constructed rooms, feature soundproof walls, and other enhanced security features that are designed to prevent the unauthorized disclosure of classified information. On a routine basis, technicians trained in counter surveillance swept the room for listening, recording, transmitting, and other types of similar devices.

Marcus removed his smart watch as Derek took his cellular telephone out of his pocket. Together they set them on a small table outside the main door to the SCIF. The table had been placed there specifically for the purpose of keeping personal electronic transmitting devices from accidentally entering the SCIF. Anyone caught doing so could receive a Security Infraction and face potential employment termination.

As Derek watched, Marcus typed a 10-digit passcode in the keypad next to the door. After another internal click, Derek pulled the arm of the heavy vault-type door, opening it. They stepped into the SCIF.

The lights in the SCIF where dimmed. As Marcus moved to the secured computer terminal Derek stepped towards the room's table. On the table was a logbook that documented who entered the SCIF, the date and their clearance level. Derek reached for the book.

"Leave it be," Colonel Harris stated. "There isn't going to be any record of this meeting."

Derek looked up. The colonel was directly across from him. He was wearing civilian attire and though he had not been on the most recent operation, he appeared as tired as Derek was. Then Derek noticed the other man sitting in the corner staring at him intently.

Derek estimated he was in his late sixties. Though he was tall, at least a foot taller than himself, he was incredibly thin. Derek thought he appeared unhealthy and guessed he outweighed this man by at least ten pounds.

The skin on his face was stretched tight and his sunken eyes made his head look like a skull. His hair was completely white but cut to a flawless perfection. Though the gray suit he wore probably cost more than Derek made in a month, it hung loosely on his incredibly thin body. The man's hands were long and slender almost spiderlike. Derek estimated each skinny finger was several inches long.

"And who's this?" Derek asked, nodding at the gentlemen in the corner. The man's head turned slightly in the colonel's direction but other than blinking, he said nothing.

"We will get to that in a moment," Colonel Harris stated. "Go ahead, Marcus. Get the major caught up."

The projector attached to Marcus's secured computer powered up and the screen to the left of Colonel Harris lit up with an image of a frumpy, short, balding, middle-aged man with glasses. Below the image, a caption read "Professor Michael Wainwright."

"Before you and Bravo Team left," Marcus began, "you had Brian ask me to do a deep-dive into Professor Wainwright. Apparently, what I discovered sent up some red-flags which—"

"Don't worry about that, Marcus," Colonel Harris interrupted. "Just give the major the preliminaries."

"In a nutshell, Derek, the professor is the real deal." Derek saw the colonel wince slightly at the informal way Marcus was speaking. Normally this was not an issue, but apparently doing so in front of this stranger concerned the colonel.

"He lives in Winlock and is tenured at Centralia College. He has impeccable credentials from the University of Puget Sound and Pepperdine, pays his taxes and even gives a good chunk of money to charity. Basically, he's a Boy Scout with no skeletons in his closet that can be exploited. If we need to attack his character we will need to fabricate it." Marcus was already preplanning the RDD.

"So now we get into the interesting part. How he kept this off the radar is a complete mystery but a few months back while he and some of his students were researching in the area of Mount Adams, they discovered the mother lode!" Marcus was becoming animated.

"I could find no trace of his research on any official site, so instead I hacked into his personal computer at his residence. Once I got in, I used our bypass on the rather simple FireVault Mac encryption program and was able to review his transcribed notes and some other files. If even part of what he describes is true, he has the trifecta of evidence. Hair, prints with dermal ridges, humanoid teeth impressions on bones that, when examined could only come from a nine foot tall humanoid, and, he even has properly collected DNA!"

Marcus clicked through some images on the computer, which appeared to have come from the professor's research files.

"Everything the professor had, underwent a very scientific method of collection. After being properly collected, stored, and transported. It will hold up to any scientific scrutiny and his methodology is repeatable. Then the professor got tricky," Marcus continued to explain.

"After reading his notes, he appeared very concerned about security and 'losing' the evidence. He did not want it located and studied at one single facility where it could 'walk away' or be tainted. So instead, he split the evidence into numerous separate collections and either sent them off to be studied or is having them stored at different locations.

"In his notes," Marcus said, looking at his computer screen as he spoke, "he only refers to these locations by numbers so we don't know where to begin looking if we wanted to do a retrieval. He's kinda paranoid, boss! I was able to determine via a receipt of delivery, he sent some of the evidence to the University of Washington's DNA Sequencing and Gene analysis Center to be independently verified and if we don't act quickly it will stand on its own. Additionally—"

"That's enough, young man," the stranger said as he stood, stopping Marcus misentence. Derek reassessed this newcomer. Though tall and thin and a number of years older, Derek felt as if even he might have his hands full if they got into a physical altercation.

"Marcus, I need you to step out," Colonel Harris stated. Marcus immediately obeyed. Just as he began to open the door to the SCIF, the colonel said, "And Marcus, it goes without saying, not a word of this meeting."

"Yes, sir," Marcus said as he shut the door.

The three men stood, looking at one another for nearly a minute before Derek broke the silence.

"Listen, Colonel, I've had a long couple of days, so if you aren't going to tell me what's going on, I'm going to go hit the shower!"

Colonel Harris was about to speak but the thin man beat him to it.

"Major Riley, you can call me Mr. Smith or John Smith if you must, and, no, that is not my real name." Derek did not need to ask. "In essence, I am the Operational Director of all your programs; however, my actual authority and which agency I work for is much more complicated and frankly beyond your need-to-know."

Smith paused and looked at Derek as a lion might look at an antelope. It was rare when this happened, but Smith's gaze made Derek a little uncomfortable. *I'm supposed to be the lion,* Derek thought to himself.

"Derek Riley," the thin man began, he smiled while he spoke, though Derek saw no humor in his eyes. "You've been with the SRT Program since 2011, worked counterterrorism for the DIA and were with a Marine Unit in Afghanistan in 2007, 'Task Force Violent,' I believe." Smith paused briefly before continuing. "What a colorful name. While there, an unfortunate incident occurred where you and all your men were accused of war crimes."

Derek immediately became defensive. Absolutely everything the thin man, John Smith stated had been highly classified including the code name "Task Force Violent."

On March 4, 2007, less than a month after arriving in Afghanistan, while Derek and his radio operator were conducting a reconnaissance of a neighboring village, the rest of his team, highly trained Marine Commandos, were riding in a six-vehicle convoy when they entered the Bati Kot district of Afghanistan's Nangarhar province. There they became caught in a complex ambush. What made it worse; the attackers consisted of extremists and suicide bombers who had hidden themselves among crowds of civilians.

When the attack ended, reports from locals claimed scores of civilian casualties also littered the battlefield. The investigating agents with NCIS, the Naval Criminal Investigation Service, either in a rush to judgment or wanting to make a name for themselves, stated the Marines had gone on a 'wild rampage.' Some even stated this was equivalent to a modern-day My Lai massacre.

These accusations were all later proven false. Many of the witnesses recanted or were merely attempting to elicit money from the United States. However, it was too late; the damage had been done.

The truth eventually came out. The court of inquiry not only acquitted all the Marines but also stated their actions, to include the use of force, was warranted and restrained. As everything surrounding the event had been classified, the media was left with reporting only the sensational, false details and rumors.

"Listen, I don't know who the fuck you are and don't really give a good goddamn, but if you are who you say, then you know damn well my brothers and I were completely absolved of any wrongdoing!"

The thin man held up his hand.

"You misunderstand; this is not a criticism, merely an expression of admiration for your team's aggressive actions and ability to make tough decisions during an obviously difficult situation." Derek was not sure if Smith was being sarcastic or speaking truthfully. Either way he did not like it.

"To date, Major, your career has been very successful," Smith admitted.

"Yeah, well the thing about success is, its kind of like being pregnant," Derek said. "Everyone says 'congratulations,' but nobody knows how many times you got fucked before you got there!"

Though Smith did not appear even slightly phased by the sarcasm, Derek watched as Colonel Harris visibly flinched at his statement.

"Tell me, Major, do you know what your mission is?" Smith asked.

"Of course," Derek replied.

"And during the nine years you've been here, how many captures have you successfully brought in?"

The answer was none. Derek and his men had been deployed multiple times and had even come close once or twice, but they were never successful. Just like this last situation, whenever they seemed to get close, an order would come down from command that made no sense and disrupted their efforts.

"You need to understand," Derek began, feeling as if he had to justify his team's lack of success, "these creatures are capable of feats that are extremely difficult to track. Once they enter the forests, our drones can't see them. Our people can't keep up with them on foot or even in a vehicle. Physically they are capable of—"

"Oh, I understand, more than you realize," Smith interrupted. "I am here to tell you, what you have been told, including your mission, is all smoke and mirrors. You have no actual clue as to the depths of the program and what is really going on. This began even before my time with the OSS."

Derek's eyes raised at the mention of the Office of Strategic Services. The OSS was the precursor to the Central Intelligence Agency, originally formed at the beginning of World War II. Its agents were trained in espionage, sabotage, assassination, and elimination. Most were trained at Camp X near Ontario. Camp X had been dubbed, "The school of Mayhem and Murder."

What shocked Derek the most was, if Smith truly worked in the OSS, today he would be in his nineties, much older than Derek had originally estimated his age to be. That had to be impossible.

Derek realized Smith had stopped talking and was staring at him with a crooked grin.

"Yes, I was with the OSS," Smith stated matter-of-factly, apparently, guessing what Derek was thinking.

"You and your men are doing exactly what we want you to do," Smith continued, getting back on topic. "When one of these abominations wander too close to civilization or otherwise compromises themselves, your task is to divert the public's attention and chase them back to where they belong, the deepest areas of the forest."

Derek thought his use of the biblical term *abomination* was odd.

"Once you're team is deployed, we are notified and begin monitoring your efforts. When it appears, you may become successful, we, or more specifically I, mandate your TOC alter your mission profile. At times, I send my team in to mop up. If you ever did happen to capture one," Smith continued, "within a matter of hours, we would come and take possession of it."

"Did you know about any of this?" Derek a accusingly as he scrutinized Colonel Harris.

"I've seen the orders come down, but I've only just learned about their actual purpose myself," Harris replied, not meeting Derek's gaze.

These revelations from Smith should have been more of a shock to Derek, but a few months back he'd begun questioning the purpose and direction of the SRT program; however, he had not outwardly expressed any concerns.

"So what does any of this have to do with Professor Wainwright?" Derek asked, turning back to Smith.

Smith looked at Colonel Harris. Without a word, Colonel Harris quietly left the room. ◉

CHAPTER 13

"SMITH"

Derek was not sure what he was going to do. He needed to get clean, not from the week spent hiking around the woods but instead from the meeting he had just left. Smith made his skin crawl.

Derek turned the shower on as hot as he could stand it and stepped in. Leaning forward he let the water cascade down the back of his neck while he considered everything Smith had told him thirty minutes earlier. After Colonel Harris exited the SCIF, Smith made his purpose clear.

"Professor Wainwright's research is about to expose elements of the project we are not ready for the public to know," Smith explained. "Usually, when information is about to come out, we can perform a disinformation campaign and if that doesn't work, discrediting the individual will typically end any further inquiries. Your Mr. Pettiford has gotten quite good at this."

As Smith spoke, Derek suddenly realized where this was going. He forced his expression to remain neutral.

"What I am about to ask you to do is in defense of national security," Smith said, looking squarely in Derek's eyes. "If you perform this task, once completed, we will be bringing you into the bigger elements of the program. Exposing you to all the dark truths about these Nephilim, so to speak."

Derek's mind had begun racing trying to remember where he had heard the term Nephilim before.

"Over the years we have had to perform a handful of direct actions against certain individuals," he stated matter-offactly. "Thirteen, to be precise. All of whom were about to expose some aspect of the program. Admiral Forrestal in 1949 and a rather prominent politician in 1963 were the most notable figures."

As Derek turned in the shower, he could think of only one politician in 1963 who had been assassinated. He could not believe what Smith had been telling him and wondered if this was all more disinformation and misdirection.

"These types of things are always regrettable, but sometimes necessary for the greater good and the security of our great country." Derek felt that Smith's proclamation and concern for national security was a little too well rehearsed.

"We have placed a GPS tracking device on Professor Wainwright. He is in the field doing research in an area we absolutely want to keep off the radar. I am asking you to locate Professor Wainwright and make sure neither he, nor anyone that is with him returns from that trip. How it is done is up to you." Smith had paused to let Derek absorb everything he had just said.

"Eliminating Wainwright might not prevent the evidence from being examined," Derek stated.

"No it may not," Smith acknowledged. "However, with Wainwright gone, even if my people cannot locate and dispose of all the evidence, there will be no one left able to corroborate his collection methods or present the material as a whole in a scientific paper. It will simply become one more conspiracy theory in an internet full of them."

Neither spoke for a several minutes. Smith seemed content with Derek's silence. Derek, however, felt an internal need to move away from Smith. Continuing to keep his expression neutral Derek walked to the opposite side of the SCIF, turning his back to Smith. Internally, Derek wanted to know the truth. Hearing the "mission" he had come to believe in was simply a cover story and being told he was just another outsider ate at his soul.

"And if I decline?" Derek asked, turning back towards Smith.

"Well, the professor will be dealt with regardless." Smith's eyes grew a little darker and narrowed when he spoke. "And like the colonel said, 'this conversation never happened.' You should realize at this moment, any attempt to disclose this conversation or anything else...." Smith paused and smiled, "...will be dealt with swiftly."

Derek recognized the obvious threat and wondered if Sheriff Zeigler had felt the same way.

"I'll do it. I just wanted to know my options," Derek stated. "Can I ask a question?"

"Of course." Smith seemed a little more relaxed now that Derek agreed to be his "killer."

"Why me?" Derek asked in all honesty. "Surely you have others tasked to you that you could call upon."

"That is simple, Major." As Smith spoke Derek thought this was the most honest he had been. "First, both your parents passed away when you were a child. Your brother was killed by a drunk driver when you were in the Marines and you had one failed attempt at a relationship. In essence, you are alone. Second, you have the background, skills, and mindset we like. We are always looking for and recruiting new talent. So think of this as your audition."

For the next fifteen minutes, Smith had given Derek the particulars. Basically, the when and where, so to speak. As he stepped from the shower, Derek grabbed a towel and began to dry off.

He was boxed in.

If he did as Smith asked he would be brought into the inner circle of... whatever the hell this was, he thought. He had to admit, getting answers to the questions did appeal to him.

Derek had killed people, but they were enemy combatants, not innocent American citizens. He was not a murderer.

The problem though, if he did not do as Smith asked, the professor would be eliminated anyways. Then he would most likely find himself a target of Mr. Smith's negative attention. The danger of upsetting Smith did not concern Derek. He had lived with danger his entire life. Allowing an innocent person to be killed without intervening, in Derek's mind would be not much different than pulling the trigger himself.

As Derek began considering his options, he did not believe he could come clean on his own and expose what he knew. Who would believe him? Derek decided to pretend to play the hand he had been dealt and make the final decision on how to proceed once he got his eyes on the professor.

After cleaning up, Derek reorganized his backpack, planning for a week's rations. He then acquired the necessary weapons and equipment from the armory. He placed everything on the ground in the hangar near the SUV he was planning on using. Then Derek moved to the ready room.

Derek was reviewing the map and comparing it to the GPS device Smith had given him. The blue dot in the center of the GPS screen was supposedly the professor. As Derek determined his best avenues of approach, Marcus walked in.

"Holy crap, boss, that Smith dude was intense," Marcus stated as he approached Derek. They were alone in the ready room. Derek stopped and looked at Marcus a long moment considering what he should say.

"Marcus, I need to ask you to do something for me." Derek paused. "Completely off the books."

"Hell, yeah!" Marcus said with a grin. "You know I'm always down for some shady shit!"

"Wait, hear me out first." Derek had decided to bring Marcus along but wanted to make sure he knew what was being asked of him. "If you do this, there can be absolutely no fingerprints! None!" Derek's tone grew firm. "Marcus this is serious: no trace. We both would be in deep waters if you mess up. Understand?"

"Yes," Marcus said just as seriously.

Without realizing he was doing it, Derek looked over his shoulder for people that were not there, listening in. This caused Marcus to do the same.

After taking in a deep breath, Derek stated, "I need you to find out everything you can about an Admiral Forrestall. Once you do that, I need anything you can come up with on our Mr. Smith." Then, almost as an afterthought Derek said, "Also find out what you can about the term Nephilim."

"I'm on it!" Marcus stated and began to walk out the door.

"Marcus!" Derek said. Marcus stopped and looked at him. "Keep this just between us. Absolutely no fingerprints!"

"I got it, boss. Trust me." Marcus winked and quickly stepped through the door. Derek was uneasy about what he just asked Marcus to do, but it was too late to take it back.

After he finished reviewing the maps and determining how best he could maneuver to the professor's location, Derek went to see if Brian was still at headquarters.

Unable to locate him, Derek was told that after Brian went to medical, the doctors had determined he had a severely strained ankle. Before going home, Brian had been placed on restricted duty for the next several days.

There was no putting it off. After going to the cafeteria and throwing together a quick peanut butter and jelly sandwich, Derek entered the hangar. As he approached his vehicle, Derek saw the Huge brothers, standing close to his backpack having a conversation.

Patrick Bennett noticed Derek and motioned towards him with his head. Mike Davis turned and both men faced Derek as he drew near. Derek stopped a few paces away.

"What's up, boys?" Derek asked more than a little cautiously. He took a casual bite from his sandwich.

"We see you're all packed up. You going back out again, Major?" Bennett asked.

"Yes, they have me doing some low-level recon. No big deal." Derek deflected the question.

"If it's a low-level recon, why all the hardware?" Davis pointed at the gun cases and equipment as he spoke.

Derek thought this was more of an accusation than a question but did not want to raise any more attention than was already focused on him.

"You know me! I've always liked the Boy Scout motto: Be Prepared," Derek said as he stepped past the two big men and grabbed his gear. He threw everything in the back of the SUV, then climbed into the driver's seat.

As he pulled out of the hangar, he looked in the rearview mirror at the Huge brothers. They were standing where he had left them watching him drive out. The hair on the back of his neck was standing up.

I'm missing something, Derek thought. He took another bite from his sandwich as he pressed down on the SUV's accelerator. ◉

CHAPTER 14

"NESTS"

People who hear the term *rainforest* immediately think of the tropical jungles in South America or Africa. In reality, there are seven temperate rainforest ecosystems around the world. The Pacific Northwest rainforest is the world's largest ecoregion.

This cool, wet climate has led to the growth of some of the largest trees in the world. The understory of vegetation, with moss-covered fallen logs, large ferns, decaying plant life, and spiderwebs of sprouting mushrooms all help retain the moisture along the forest floor.

The Pacific Northwest is also home to many species of animal life, including the largest subspecies of elk on the continent. There is plenty for anyone working in the field of environmental science to study without having to venture away from the mainstream into the world of cryptozoology. That, however, is not what they were here to do.

They had traveled to the Snoqualmie National Forest the day before. Stopping at Marblemount Ranger Station, Susan obtained a backcountry permit while Michael discussed the condition of the trails with one of the rangers.

About an hour after leaving the Ranger Station, they came to the end of the road, literally. The old Forest Service road simply ended.

Michael pulled his truck as far off the road as he could, then the three unloaded. After adjusting their packs, they began their long hike, heading to where they would be setting up their base camp.

Their initial hike in had taken nearly four hours. Occasionally, Michael would stop and remove his fedora. Pulling a handkerchief from his pocket, he used it to wipe the sweat from his forehead. It was during one such stop that Michael exclaimed, "Hey look!"

Susan and Josh froze, looking in the direction Michael was pointing. The large dark shape stepped from the brush no more than seventy-five yards from them. Having spent the summer packing on its winter weight, the black bear was a healthy 300 pounds. Its black fur shone in the afternoon sun.

The bear, sensing their presence, stopped. Then, to get a better look at the humans it was sharing the forest with, the bear stood up on its hind feet. The bear's round ears and prominent snout turned in their direction. The silhouette, from its head through its shoulders, was obvious. Then, abruptly as it had appeared, the bear dropped to all fours and sprinted away. The entire encounter lasted less than ten seconds.

"Wow! That was cool!" Josh excitedly exclaimed. A huge smile covered his face. Though they had all brought bear spray, none of them had even considered pulling it out. "That alone was worth the price of admission."

"Okay, so let's discuss what just occurred," Michael began, turning into teaching mode. "Susan, what were you feeling when you first saw the bear?"

"Excitement, maybe a little adrenaline," she answered. Josh concurred.

"Okay, aside from the digital cameras we are carrying, all three of us have cell phones in our pockets. My question to you, Josh, is why didn't you take a photo of the bear?"

"Honestly, professor," Josh began, "I was so amazed at what I was looking at, I completely forgot I even had a camera on me. Even if I had remembered, the bear would have been gone before I could have fished it out. At best I may have gotten a photo of the bear's butt running away."

"Exactly my point," Michael explained. "Skeptics are always complaining about how, with all the cameras available to people in today's society, there isn't a good photo of a Sasquatch. When a witness stumbles across a Sasquatch, compound the adrenaline and fascination you both just felt with fear, and increase those feelings about a hundred percent. I am amazed we ever get a photo. It makes sense those photographs we do get are usually taken at a great distance where the adrenaline and fear are substantially less."

"And when a clear image is obtained, the skeptics always call it CGI," Susan added. They turned and continued their journey.

Arriving at their destination, they set up their base camp near an open sandbar where the Nooksack River and Walnut Creek intersect. Due to the potential for scavenging bears, Michael collected their food and placed it in a "bear can" specifically designed to keep the food's scent from the bears.

As dusk turned to night, the three gathered around the fire. They discussed their plans for the following day. Tired from the day's travels all three decided to turn in. Susan crawled into her tent and turned on the solar-powered lamp she had brought with her.

While she unrolled her sleeping bag, somewhere in the distance an owl began to hoot in the trees. As Susan drifted off to sleep, she thought the owl must have been incredibly large.

Rising early the next morning, the three of them, Susan, Josh, and Michael Wainwright, made a quick breakfast and drank some instant coffee. As the water for the coffee began boiling, Michael unpacked his drone, a Mavic-2 Pro Quadcopter, he had brought with him. Almost immediately, he began cursing.

"Well, damn it!" Michael obviously irritated, began rummaging in his pack.

"What's wrong, Michael?" Susan asked as she poured the hot water into her tin cup and began stirring in the instant coffee. As the steam from the coffee began to rise, Susan held the tin cup under her nose with both hands.

"Well, I just don't understand this," Michael explained. "I brought this drone up hoping to maybe fly it over our target before we stepped off this morning or at least take some aerial video of the site when we arrived. Before leaving I made sure the batteries were charged.

"Not only are the batteries dead, but so are the spares I brought along as well." Looking at Josh and Susan, Michael raised both his hands showing them the batteries. Continuing to grumble about technology and the high price he paid, Michael stowed the drone away.

After breakfast, they began the long trek up the southern slope of Loomis Mountain. Just as she had been the previous day, Susan was surprised at how nimble Michael was. Though he looked like the typical bookworm academic, he had been hiking nearly nonstop for several hours.

It was not so much the distance that made the hike long; instead, the issue was the rise in the elevation. This coupled with the thick undergrowth of vegetation, their progress was slow. Josh on the other hand had never stopped peppering Professor Wainwright with questions concerning their quest.

"I understand their importance to my Native heritage, but what is it about Bigfoot that speaks to the general population?" Josh questioned.

Michael considered the query for a few moments before answering.

"Well, there are different levels to that question. First, I believe it is simply the mystery of something undiscovered or unresolved. We as human beings have always pursued the answers to unknown questions. Then there is the added mystique because they are so human-like. Finally, humanity's history and our earliest stories have been filled with tales of giants, wild men, and forest monsters. These stories are similar through many cultures, from around the world, during a time when these people had no way to communicate with one another."

"I think it is arrogant to assume we have a fully detailed understanding of the fossil record," Michael continued. "Especially when some in the archeology community claim we haven't even discovered 5 percent of that record. Take the nineteenth century anthropologist Franz Boas. He believed in recording not only the daily activities of tribal members but their stories as well. Boas's opinion was that folklore was as much a part of anthropology as any other aspect. Behind every legend there's some level of truth.

"For example, take the stories of the hobbit," Michael explained. "These stories described tiny humanoids living in the woods. For hundreds of years, long before the Tolkien books were ever written, these stories were simply considered fables or myths. But ask yourself, where did these fables originate?" Michael paused only long enough to allow Josh to ponder the question.

"In 2004, the fossils of Homo Floresiensis were discovered. This was an extinct species of the genus Homo. They stood no more than three and a half feet tall. However, these were not an early form of modern humans but an entirely different species! Could this extinct species have led to the creation of the hobbit myth? The obvious answer is, 'of course.' Which leads to another question, what other fables and myths have a basis in reality?" Michael asked.

They stopped. Their path was blocked by a large old-growth tree-fall. Though they all carried small machetes, the thick ground foliage would have made bushwhacking around the fallen tree time-consuming. Instead, they helped one another as they crawled and climbed, scrambling over the moss-covered log.

Once on the other side, Michael continued.

"So, when discussing the fossil record, I want you to consider chimpanzees. Were you aware, Josh, if modern chimpanzees had not survived, the only proof we would have of them is one partial fragment of a mandible from about a million years ago. There is litterally nothing else in the fossil record that would show they ever existed.

"The tree of hominid gets much bushier than most people realize. The notion that we are the only hominid on the planet is a misnomer, as the record shows we previously shared the planet with a number of other relic-hominoids."

"Why are scientists reluctant to investigate the subject?" Josh asked honestly.

"Unfortunately, the topic attracts large quantities of the lunatic fringe," Michael said with a little contempt. He stumbled slightly while stepping on a rock made slick by the moss. This caused his glasses to shift slightly on his face. While steadying himself on a tree with his right hand, Michael adjusted the glasses with his left.

"This craziness scares off many PhDs and fellow colleagues. Coming out of the proverbial Bigfoot closet, so to speak, has consequences. Even admitting to the interest of participating in a true academic study has the potential to stall careers."

"I can attest to that!" Susan admitted, thinking of her own fall from grace. "When most begin their scientific careers they aren't planning on going down the cryptozoology road, but after all the discoveries, evidence, historical accounts, what true academic could not pursue the science? When you eliminate the likely scenarios, what you are left with is the probable."

"There are however, a few brave academics bold enough to step into the fray, so to speak. Such as your Ms. Parker here." Michael spoke with admiration as he gestured towards Susan.

Susan blushed at the compliment. "Oh, I'm not that heroic. There are many more noteworthy people deserving of your praise, Michael. Obviously, everyone has heard of the professor of anthropology from Idaho State University. He's done tremendous work in the field.

"However," Susan said, looking directly at Josh, "did you know that legendary primatologist Jane Goodall, who continues to be an authority in the world of primatology, has come out and stated unequivocally that she believes in the existence of Sasquatch? That is a huge leap forward. I have also spoken with many others who are working closely behind the scenes in the study."

Stepping over a small stream, Josh used his machete on some ferns and blackberry vines blocking their way. Rays from the midday sun, glimmering through the canopy of the forest, warmed the morning moisture. This created the illusion of steam pillars rising from the forest floor. The trio hiked for several minutes in quiet reflection before Josh again broke the silence.

"What do you think Sasquatch is, Professor?"

Michael stopped walking and turned to look at his companions.

"Well, that's the real question, and why we are here, isn't it? So let's go back to the question of fables. Every single continent has stories of a Sasquatch-type creature; there is the Yeti in the Himalayas, the Yowie in Australia, the Chinese Yeren or wild man, and on, and on, and on.

"These stories began thousands of years ago and are virtually identical to one another. Moreover, we must remember this was before there was the mass global communication we have today, so there must be some foundation of truth. These stories or witness accounts continue to this day from all parts of the world.

"For most," Michael continued. "there are three primary theories. These are the relic-hominid, the hybrid-hominid, and the great-ape theory. With the great-ape theory, the belief is Sasquatch is a decedent of Gigantopithecus. Here you have a bipedal primate that is the right size, between eight to ten feet tall, in the right place, during the right time.

"It makes sense that Gigantopithecus would have expanded its range coming across the Bering land bridge. What many people don't know is that there was once a time when that bridge was a lush forest and not a frozen arctic tundra. Once the Gigantopithecus had crossed the land bridge, it could have traversed to the lower states. At the time this would have been the ideal habitat for a large primate. This all could have easily preceded the human migration.

"I believe Susan here leans towards the great-ape theory," Michael stated.

"I do," Susan acknowledged while adding a slight nod of her head and a smile for emphasis.

"Personally," Michael said, "I am inclined to fall into the hybrid-hominid camp. Based on the evidence we have seen and behaviors described in hundreds of witness accounts, Sasquatch displays both hominid and great ape behaviors. In addition, numerous DNA samples collected by amateur investigators indicated the DNA came from an unknown primate.

"Unfortunately, these samples have been completely discounted by mainstream science because they were 'contaminated' with human DNA. What if the samples weren't contaminated?" Michael asked. "I am hoping the samples I currently have and will be sending off will answer that question. Hopefully we will get some more on this trip.

"Regardless of which theory a person believes, all of this would have occurred at least several millennia ago, if not much longer. Over time all creatures evolve into... something more," Michael said, the last nearly in a whisper.

"Are you saying these creatures have evolved?" Josh asked.

"Well, yes, Josh."

This time it was Susan who answered. "Every animal on the planet evolves and adapts to the environment and conditions they find themselves. In some cases, this may take thousands of years, but on rare occasions, this evolution occurs rapidly. With intelligent animals, this evolution or adaptation can occur much quicker. Did you know there are recent reports of orangutans, considered one of the most intelligent of the primates, using spears to catch fish! This tool use is a huge leap forward on the evolutionary ladder! As you know, Josh, orangutans are the closest living relative to Gigantopithecus.

"If the Sasquatch species is more intelligent than orangutans," Susan continued. "and they have had many millenniums to evolve and adapt, there is no telling where they are currently at on the evolution ladder."

It was Josh's turn to stop.

"But if they are such an intelligent species doesn't that bring about all sorts of ethical questions. I mean what happens to them if we do prove their existence?"

"Josh," Michael said, smiling, "even if tomorrow we are able to prove to the world that they exist, it doesn't change anything. People will not have any easier time finding them or invading their habitat. In fact it may help establish them as an endangered species giving them added protections."

Their trek continued in silence for a while as they considered all the possibilities. Then Susan spoke up.

"I saw one once."

This was the first time she had spoken of her childhood incident with anyone other than with her parents. Even after dating and becoming engaged to Eric, Susan never told him of her childhood encounter.

Josh and Michael stopped in their tracks and looked at Susan, silently encouraging her to continue. She did. For the next ten minutes, Susan talked about what she had seen as a child, and how her parents made her feel every time she brought it up. She did not even realize tears were coming down her face until Josh came up and hugged her.

"I envy you," Michael said as he put his hand on her shoulder. "To think, you have seen and actually know they exist whereas others like me can only hope to believe and speculate. Thank you for telling us." Susan felt as if decades of weight holding her down had been lifted.

As he used a low-hanging tree branch to pull himself over a small log, Michael glanced at the handheld GPS he was carrying.

"We're almost there," he said, spurring them on.

They walked for a few more minutes before the forest slowly began to thin out until eventually the three of them stepped into a large clearing. For nearly seventy-five meters in all directions, the large trees had been replaced by a gently sloping meadow of tallgrass and ferns. The entire meadow was completely blanketed by the warmth of the sun.

Cautiously, they ventured several paces into the clearing. Michael turned and faced the direction they had come.

"This place is perfect!" he proclaimed. "Look around. If we were to stay here, we would have the sun to keep us warm throughout the day. We would have access to water from the many creeks. Food would be in abundance. The Nooksack River has several species of salmon during the fall runs this time of year. As well as relative security. Anyone encamped here could easily see or hear the approach of others."

A few more paces into the meadow they came across a large depression initially hidden by the tallgrass and ferns.

"Look!" Michael said excitedly. Then as he walked around it, he began to narrate what he wanted them to see. "All the great apes build nests on the ground, especially because the trees may not be able to support their weight. Usually, ground nests such as these use branches and leaves as their bedding materials."

"Couldn't this be just where an elk may have lay down, Professor?" Josh asked.

"We can discount that outright, Josh," Michael explained. "See how the grass and ferns are woven together, not crushed as an elk would have just laying down. That woven pattern took time, and look at this." Michael pointed to some small leafy branches. These branches also appeared interwoven into the other vegetation.

"Look around, Josh. There are no trees in the immediate area that match those branches. Those branches were brought here with a specific purpose. That is not something an elk or bear would do.

"After my friend sent me the original photographs," Michael began, "I did a tremendous amount of study on primate nest building. What we see before us is very typical, though considerably larger, to the types of nests I've seen built by the great apes."

Over the next several minutes, they discovered a dozen more similar nests in the glade. Some very close in proximity to one another while others remained along the edges of the clearing. After each new discovery, Michael would remove a small plastic number, similar to what a detective might use at a crime scene and place it by the discovery. He would then jot down a quick note in his notebook correlating the number with a brief description of the discovery. At each nest, Michael pointed out characteristics similar to what other primates do.

"Just like your bed at home, a primate nest provides warmth and protection," Michael explained. "Now gorillas rarely sleep in the same nest twice while chimpanzees frequently reuse their old nests. Some primatologists and evolutionary biologists consider nest building to be a form of behavioral adaptation. This is where the primate troops would socialize, groom one another, even mate."

"Also, Josh," Susan added, "since this nest-building behavior is shared by all the great apes, gorillas, chimpanzees, orangutans, it is probable that the behavior evolved from a common ancestor rather than developed independently in the individual species."

While closely examining one nest, Susan pointed out a large pile of scat or animal feces, not far from the nest.

"Wow! That is one giant pile of shit!" Josh exclaimed

"Yes," Susan agreed. "Much larger than anything a bear or cougar might leave behind."

"Okay, people. It is time to get to work," Michael announced. "Abandoned, nests can hold an abundance of information. From the size of the population to the health of the individuals. Let's divide and conquer. Susan, can you digitally record and photograph the entire site. Be sure to obtain good measurements of each nest."

"Absolutely," Susan stated, having already removed her camera and her own note pad from her backpack.

"I will collect any trace evidence, hairs and such, from each nest as well as samples of environmental DNA. And, Josh, I want you to collect samples from every pile of feces you can find."

"So, as usual, the undergrad gets the shit job!" Josh joked.

"Of course." Michael smiled. "However, we cannot leave out the importance of the feces. First, these samples will indicate the type and abundance of food that is being consumed. Then there is the olfactory distinctions between the different species. This will help in precise identification."

"It's still a shit job!" Josh laughed as he removed some latex gloves and evidence bags from his pack.

For the next forty-five minutes, the three worked on their individual tasks. Occasionally, when one of them noticed something new or unusual, they would call the other two over. They briefly would hypothesize the meaning of the new discovery before returning to their original assignments.

While Josh was walking the perimeter of the meadow, he located another pile of scat. After writing a quick note in his notebook concerning the location of the discovery, he removed a fresh evidence bag and used it to pick up a sample. While holding the sample, Josh paused.

"Hey, Professor!" Josh raised his voice so Michael and Susan could hear him on the other side of the clearing.

"What is it?" Michael asked as he stood up from within the nest he was currently examining.

"These feces are still warm!" Josh stated as he held the bag of scat above his head.

Michael and Susan immediately looked at one another. Josh, realizing the implication of what he just said, slowly lowered his arm. He turned, looking into the forest.

As if on cue, what sounded like a baseball bat striking a tree's trunk could be distinctly heard a distance away from the clearing.

Whack!

Without a word, the three of them began quickly walking towards the center of the meadow. Josh glanced over his shoulder every few steps. As they drew closer, to one another, two more strikes occurred from a position different than the first.

Whack! Whack!

"Many witness accounts include hearing tree knocking," Michael stated. "It is believed this is a form of communication." They stood motionless, listening intently.

Whack! This one sounded closer.

"Michael," Susan said a little uneasily. "In my lectures I discuss how chimpanzees use similar behaviors to conduct ambush hunting."

Whack! Whack! These two knocks were definitely closer.

"Hey, guys, maybe we overstayed our welcome," Josh, also becoming a little more nervous, said as he scanned the forest.

"Yes, I believe you two are correct," Michael said. "We definitely do not want to upset them. Every animal can become protective of his or her home when a stranger enters. Let's quickly collect our things and head back to camp."

It took them less than five minutes to gather all their markers. The last couple of minutes, Josh was running between the nests, grabbing handfuls of items and shoving them into his pack.

As they began to step onto the trail to start the long trek back to their base camp, another tree knock occurred. This one from the opposite side of the clearing.

Whack! ◉

CHAPTER 15
"THERMAL"

Since leaving Gable Mountain, Derek had been driving for several hours lost in his own thoughts. Mostly Derek was formulating a plan on how he should deal with Smith. He was fairly settled on his course of action but was not sure of the particulars on how best he would implement it.

A little more than an hour north of Seattle, Derek turned off Interstate 5 onto Highway 20. The farther east he traveled on Highway 20, the more obvious the term *highway* was, at best, an exaggeration.

This two-lane country road ran through a number of small communities, each one a little more desolate than the last. Twenty minutes past the small town of Sedro-Woolley, Derek observed fewer and fewer residences until only the occasional small farm would appear under the looming mountains and ever-thickening forest.

The United States Forest Service, primarily to aid in firefighting efforts, is tasked with maintaining a system of roads or FSRs, throughout the nation's vast wilderness. These primitive roads are given numerical designations by the Forest Service. Unfortunately, over the last several years, the funding for maintaining these roads had been nearly nonexistent. Nature was taking them back as these FSRs were showing the signs of neglect.

Shortly after turning onto Baker Lake Road, Derek pulled onto the poorly marked Forest Service Road 2400.

This old, roughly graveled FSR, wound its way back and forth, as the road snaked through the thick-forested lands belonging to the Department of Natural Resources. Derek had to drop the speed of the SUV to just over twenty miles per hour. Every hundred yards or so, Derek had to navigate around or drive through clusters of large potholes. These had developed from years of inattention, and they bounced his equipment around the inside of the government vehicle.

In many places, the road was so narrow, unkempt, and nearly overgrown, tree branches scraped along the exterior of his vehicle. The sound of tree limbs rubbing along the SUV's doors sounded like fingernails on a blackboard.

Though the SRT was an elite unit, they could not escape much of the government bureaucracy. The Government Service Agency provides vehicles to all federal agencies. Derek knew when he returned to headquarters, there would be mountains of paperwork to fill out explaining how the paint on the GSA-vehicle he was driving had been damaged.

As he traveled, a labyrinth of unidentified side roads appeared at unexpected times. This forced Derek to occasionally stop and refer to both the map and GPS Smith had provided him. Eventually, FSR 2400 became FSR 1867 as it snaked around Mount Josephine. The road initially rose to nearly 3,000 feet in elevation before again descending into the valley below. At the base, Derek came across a sturdy, secured gate installed by the Department of Natural Resources.

This gate would have prevented most backwoods travelers from proceeding further. Members of the SRT, however, were very aware of these barriers. As such, they were all equipped with a universal skeleton key that allowed them access when on missions. Derek did just that. After unlocking the gate, he pulled his SUV through before re-securing it. He could see no reason to permit some hikers to come up behind him.

Derek was not far from his final destination and had to slow even more. The potholes from the road he now traveled had gotten worse and continued to jostle him around the inside of the SUV. As he navigated around one particularly deep pothole, Derek passed what appeared to be a small abandoned cabin about thirty yards off the side of the road. This shack was not identified on either his map or the GPS.

Typically, Park Rangers and forest workers would build small cabins like this when prolonged work on hiking trails or performing other similar forest maintenance activities kept them in one specific area for any length of time.

Wooden shutters covered the single window. An old wooden picnic table and small pile of firewood lay stacked off to the side of the cabin. Both were covered in moss. With just a quick glance, Derek estimated the cabin had not been used by any visitors for several years.

A quarter mile past the cabin, as Derek drove around a blind corner, he suddenly had to slam on the SUVs breaks. This FSR, like many others, had not been maintained. As such, it had become completely blocked by large boulders and other debris. This natural barricade had probably been introduced by a heavy rain that caused part of the hillside to wash away and onto the road. Even in four-wheel drive, he could go no farther.

Had Derek come across this blockage twenty minutes earlier it would have been a problem. As it was, however, he was not overly concerned. Derek was only a half mile from his final target. He pulled the SUV as far off the roadside as he could.

Derek, tired of thinking about the mission Smith had sent him on, had begun operating on autopilot. Before grabbing his weapons, pack and equipment, Derek spent the next several minutes camouflaging himself. Using a camouflage paint tube, he covered his face in a dark shade of green. He then tied a green and black scarf, called a shemagh, around his neck. Finally, Derek donned his ghillie suit.

This was the same suit he handmade more than a decade earlier during his time in the Marine Corps. By adding local vegetation into the perfectly woven strands of colored burlap and fabrics, Derek looked like a walking bush. However, when he remained motionless Derek could all but disappear.

Years of training could not be forgotten and forced him to proceed cautiously. Any possibility of being discovered did not actually trouble Derek. He was not operating in a foreign land full of enemy combatants. Instead, he was merely approaching some unaware academics. However, he still moved slowly, pausing every few minutes.

While stationary, he would slow his breathing and occasionally, out of habit, close his eyes, heightening his other senses. Derek would listen to the forest, attempting to make out any sound that did not belong. Satisfied, he would advance forward again, only to repeat this process a few minutes later.

It took just over one hour to move the half mile before finally arriving at his destination. Derek crawled the last three hundred feet. The spot he had chosen was on a hill that overlooked a small encampment less than five hundred yards from his location. Though no people were present, three tents and a small fire-pit were visible from his elevated position.

From where he lay, Derek realized almost immediately even a novice shooter could easily engage any target in the camp below.

Even the slight breeze that was blowing towards him would have had little effect on the external ballistics if he decided to shoot. His position was perfect for an assassination. Though he had already decided against that option.

Derek confirmed the campsite on his GPS. This was definitely Professor Wainwright's camp. He surmised Smith's people must have concealed the transmitter in some of Wainwright's gear.

To listen in on any conversation below, Derek initially considered focusing a parabolic microphone toward the camp. After a few minutes, he realized the noise created by the running waters of the Nooksack River and Walnut Creek flowing past the camp would overwhelm any conversations the microphone might pick up.

Instead, Derek improved the camouflage of his position and made himself comfortable behind the scope of his rifle. He settled in to await Wainwright's eventual return.

About half an hour before dusk, three people emerged from the forest. Derek peered at them through the riflescope. At first, he focused on the professor. Just as the dossier Smith had provided stated, he was easily identifiable by the white fedora he was wearing. Then Derek scrutinized the professor's two companions.

"Aw, shit!" Derek whispered to himself as he realized who the people accompanying the professor were. It was Susan and her student aide Josh. Their addition would seriously complicate his plan.

As Derek watched the trio, he realized they appeared a little tired or frazzled. After walking into the camp, they dropped their packs near the largest of the tents. Then, while Josh began to start the fire, Susan and the professor became locked in an intense conversation. Occasionally they pointed back in the direction they had come.

When dusk turned to night, Derek removed the Insight Technologies Thermal vision device from his pack and attached it to the front of his scope. By detecting subtle temperature differences, the thermal instantly turned the black of the night into a plethora of blues yellows and reds.

In the lens of the thermal, the colder the object the deeper shade of blue it appeared. The water of the creek and Nooksack River was the deepest of blue. In contrast, the hotter an item was, the brighter the color in the lens. Yellow and red were the hottest colors. Derek watched as the trio gathered around the fire, their silhouettes appearing as a brilliant shade of red within his scope.

A game trail, probably used by deer or elk to access the creek below, was not far from his position. Derek had decided he would use this trail to quietly move into their camp at first light. Then he would explain to them the situation. He had determined the only way they would survive their mutual dilemma stemmed from their combined ability to convince the media of what was occurring. Derek was ready for the fight, but was not sure how that fight would eventually manifest itself.

While considering his options, Derek observed an incredibly large heat source through the thermal. The silhouette at first appeared to be another person standing behind a tree about fifty yards from the camp. Comparing this silhouette to those sitting by the fire, he quickly concluded the figure was far too large to be a human. Derek instantly realized what he was looking at. The enormous creature was watching the camp.

Moving his head away from the scope, Derek scanned the forest with his naked eyes. The light of the fire illuminated about fifteen feet around the three scientists, but did nothing to penetrate the black of the forest. Derek brought the scope back to his face and scanned the woods around the camp. He counted two additional immense heat sources on the opposite side of the camp. Susan and her companions appeared oblivious to the presence of the giants surrounding them.

Derek knew he would be able to shoot the creatures if he wanted to. Unfortunately, in his rush to leave SRT headquarters, he had not prepared to deal with them; as such, the rifle and more specifically the ammunition he had brought might not have the desired terminal ballistic effects.

If Derek was unable to drop them on the first shot, they could tear through the camp with impunity. He also was not sure if there were more creatures than the three he could see. The sudden realization that there could be more, forced Derek to use the thermal again. Quickly he scanned the area around his own position for other possible threats attempting to sneak up on his own position.

Satisfied he was not in any immediate danger, Derek refocused on the first silhouette. For several minutes, Derek studied the creature. Though he had seen many photographs and videos and had the occasional glimpse while tracking them in the past, this was the longest duration Derek had been able to observe one. He estimated it stood close to nine feet in height. Its wide shoulders, thick torso and oddly long arms were its most prominent features.

While watching the creature, it suddenly dropped into a prone position. To Derek, it almost looked as if it had melted or folded itself onto the ground. Then slowly the creature began crawling towards Susan and the others. Its movements in the thermal seemed unnatural. It reminded him of a cross between a soldier low-crawling through a battlefield and a spider climbing on a wall. As it moved, the creature's opposite side arms and legs seemed to dislocate at the joint as it slowly crept forward.

As Derek watched, the other two silhouettes also began to move. They were circling the camp in opposite directions. Something must have caught the attention of Susan, Josh, and the professor, as they were now standing and facing away from the fire. Without thinking, Derek leaped to his feet and began to running towards Susan and the others. ◉

CHAPTER 16

"PEBBLES"

After leaving the meadow, the return to the basecamp took less than half the time of their initial climb. Not only were they now going downhill, but also they all felt an unspoken urgency to vacate the clearing. They talked very little during their decent. Occasionally, when they slowed, a knocking sound similar to what had driven them from the meadow could be heard in the distance.

Josh had fallen into step at the rear of their little group. Partly due to his instinctual desire to protect Susan and the professor. However, Josh also knew if he was in the front, his fear might override everything else and he would begin running.

Josh found himself looking in all directions. He began to wonder if the shadows moving in the trees, appearing to pace them, were simply his imagination. Once, after having an intense and uneasy feeling, he turned to look back in the direction where they had come. From around the trunk of a large tree, he thought a face was looking back at him. Josh blinked and the face was gone. He did not say anything to the others.

The previous day, when they first set up their basecamp, Josh and Susan had made a large circular firepit using rocks collected from along the river. They then spent the next hour collecting driftwood and branches for burning. For the final touch, they dragged a few large logs over to use as seats.

After arriving back at their basecamp, Josh dropped his pack and moved straight to the firepit. He needed to keep his mind busy and was glad for the work they had done the day before. He grabbed several pieces of wood and began placing them in the pit. Carefully Josh stacked a few of the cut limbs into a small teepee shape, which would help to feed the flames by allowing air to flow easily. He then placed some kindling on the bottom and ignited a match.

The kindling quickly began to smolder, but Josh needed to lean in and gently blow onto the flames to get the wood to truly ignite. Once the fire caught, he stacked additional wood in the pit. It was more wood than was necessary, but in the back of Josh's mind, a large fire was going to be needed to fight off the quickly encroaching darkness.

Susan and the professor were standing a short distance away. Josh could hear them debating what the next step should be. Now that they were back in the perceived safety of camp, the apprehension they had previously experienced was dissipating.

Michael wanted to go back up the next morning and set up some trail cameras. He even stated they had probably left too soon. Susan, on the other hand, was advocating for a more cautious approach. She pointed out how Jane Goodall and other primatologists would spend months just getting the primates acclimated to their presence before even considering trying to interact with them. This debate went back and forth. An agreement had not been reached when the sun went down.

Josh threw another log on the fire, then grabbed a couple of the dehydrated meals they had brought with them. While the campfire provided warmth and comfort, it was not ideal for cooking. For that, Josh set up a Coleman propane stove not much bigger than a thermos.

Placing a tin cup on top of the stove, Josh boiled some water. Once boiling, he added the water to a pack of dehydrated lasagna then sealed the contents inside. After letting it sit and reconstitute for a few minutes, he reopened the pack and dished out three even portions onto some plastic plates they had brought with them.

"Dinner's ready," Josh said and he passed the plates of warm food to Susan and Michael.

"Thanks, Josh," Susan said, taking the plate of lasagna and sitting on a log near the fire. Michael also took a seat. For the next several minutes, they ate and discussed how much the dehydrated camping foods have improved over the years.

With food in their stomachs, and a warm fire burning, the normalcy of life returned and their moods lightened. Josh even started to feel better. They found themselves telling humorous stories, laughing and joking aloud.

"So, Josh," Michael began, "after today's discoveries, what have we learned?"

Before Josh could answer, a small rock, not much bigger than a quarter, bounced off the side of the firepit and came to rest at Josh's feet. They all looked down at it.

"Did I just see that?" Susan asked more to herself than the group.

"Incredible," Michael exclaimed. They all stood up and looked into the darkness. For several moments, they peered into the shadows.

"I can't say how many stories I've heard that include elements of Sasquatch throwing rocks," Michael stated, breaking the silence.

Josh quickly moved to one of the tents. After rummaging through a pack, he returned with three flashlights. They all clicked on the lights and began scanning the woods around them.

"What does it mean? The rock throwing?" Josh asked.

"It could mean any number of things, Josh," Susan responded as she pointed her flashlight in another direction. "Some think it is playfulness or curiosity. As if they are watching and get bored, so they throw some rocks to illicit a reaction. Other accounts believe it is done as a warning. Basically, letting the people know they had gotten too close."

As they searched the woods with the lights, another small rock struck one of the logs they had been using as a seat. All three jumped a little. Grabbing two more pieces of wood Josh rapidly threw them on the fire then returned to scanning the woods with his flashlight.

Just moments later, another rock landed between Susan's feet.

"Okay, Michael! I'm um, ready for any suggestions," Susan said uneasily.

"Listen," Michael began, in an attempt to take control, "it's night, and would be too dangerous to leave. If we run, it could also provoke a predator response we don't want." He shined his flashlight on a shadow. "The only thing I think we can do is stand our ground."

They continued to search the woods with their flashlights. The beam from Josh's flashlight illuminated a tree. From behind a branch, partially obscured by the leaves, a pair of large eyes reflected the light back. The eyes did not move. Josh gasped. Susan and Michael promptly spun their flashlight on the tree.

As the eye-shine stared back at them, on the opposite side of the tree, an immense hairy arm wrapped around the trunk. About three inches in length, the hair was a dark reddish brown. The massive open hand displayed all five fingers. They looked like large sausages. Long, incredibly filthy nails, combined with the dark grayish skin gave the arm a ghoulish appearance. Unconsciously they all took a step back, putting distance between themselves and the tree.

A deep growl rose from behind them. It resonated inside their chests. The sound reminded Josh of something a tiger might make, if that tiger happened to be as large as a school bus. They all spun and shined their lights in the direction of the growl. Remembering the ghoulish arm, Josh spun his light back towards the tree. The arm was gone.

"Oh shit!" Josh exclaimed. Quickly he reached into his pocket and pulled out a Swiss Army knife. He opened the blade, one of the little, red knife's many tools. Looking down at the small two-inch blade, not much sharper than a butter knife, he realized the stupidity of even holding it and let it drop from his hand.

Their flashlights began moving frantically back and forth, searching for the beasts. The ground beneath their feet seemed to shake a little as if from an impact tremor. Then another. The trio spun their lights in the direction of the vibration.

All their lights came to rest on the same spot. A pair of gigantic feet covered in hair stood just a short distance from the fire. In unison, all three began to raise their flashlights. As they slowly elevated their lights, the beams kept going higher and higher, never seeming to reach the top of the creature.

A pair of incredibly muscular legs was initially illuminated. Enormous arms hung relaxed at its sides, its hands flexed by its knees. As the light shined upon the barreled chest, Susan observed a jagged scar that zigzagged from one side of its chest to the other. The shoulders, appearing like basketballs, were as wide as she was tall.

When the flashlights eventually came to rest on the creature's head, the glow from the fire danced in the large black eyes that stared back. Other than the wide flat nose, the face was completely covered in hair. A grayish white streak in an otherwise black mane ran from his deep brow to the back of his neck and speckled its shoulders. The creature began to rock back and forth.

With a mixture of wonderment and horror the three stared. As they did, the creature's expression changed from that of neutral ambivalence to something different. The eyes narrowed and its brow lowered. Then the creature's lips parted exposing large teeth. It began growling. For Susan, this growl seemed to come straight from the depths of hell.

She wanted to run as the panic started to overwhelm her. Time seemed to slow. While trying to control her emotions, Susan saw another rock fly through the air. It landed at the creature's feet. As the light from her flashlight fell on the rock, she realized it was black and oddly shaped like a small soda can.

While her mind tried to absorb all that was happening the oddly shaped rock exploded in a bright flash and the loudest boom she had ever heard. As if she had been struck, Susan fell backwards landing hard on her butt. While her ears continued to ring, she blinked her eyes, rapidly trying to clear the bright spots created by the flash.

Through the spots in her eyes, Susan saw a Sasquatch charging towards her. It was not as large as the one with the scar but in the light of the fire, its shaggy hair seemed unmistakable. In a desperate attempt to flee from the approaching monster, she started to scramble and backpedal on her hands and feet. Her eyes began to clear just as the creature reached out for her. Susan screamed when its steely grip grasped her by the forearm. Then the creature yelled.

"If you want to live through this you need to come with me now!"

Susan was unsure she had actually heard the creature before her say anything. That would be crazy. The ringing in her ears was lessening. Confused, she stared at the hairy monster that had seized her by the arm.

While she tried to wrap her mind around what was happening, Derek yanked her to her feet. ◉

CHAPTER 17
"CABIN"

When Derek tossed the Combined Tactical Systems (CTS) flash-bang distraction device, he closed his eyes. Upon landing at the creature's feet, the 175-decibel explosion sounded like a howitzer cannon going off in the quiet forest. Combined with the 12-million-candela flash, anything not prepared would be completely disorientated. However, before Derek even opened his eyes the monster had already disappeared into the darkness. Derek knew, once it realized it was not truly injured it would be back. He rushed to the trio.

Susan had fallen over. Derek grabbed her by the arm and yanked her to her feet. Josh and the professor were staring openmouthed at him. None of them appeared to understand what was transpiring.

"If you want to live through this you need to come with me now!" Derek yelled. "Take ahold of one another and keep your flashlights pointed outward!" he commanded as he physically moved them into a single column formation. "Follow me."

For the first five minutes, they did what they were told and followed Derek into the creek. Unlike in the spring, when the runoff from the melting snow flowed into the rivers, the creek was relatively shallow this time of year. The water was not moving fast but it was extremely cold and almost immediately soaked their feet.

As they crossed, Susan slipped on a rock and nearly fell, but Derek, grabbing her by the elbow, steadied her. Once on the other side, they continued to move quickly along the gametrail. They scanned the forest with their flashlights while they jogged, trying to keep pace with Derek.

As the shock of what had befallen them began to wear off, the professor commenced to protest.

"Wait! Who the hell are you? What's going on?" Michael demanded as he slowed his pace to a mere walk. Susan and Josh, followed suit in quiet solidarity.

Derek knew they did not have time for this. He spun and grabbed the professor by the collar and pulled him to within a few inches of his own face. The camouflage paint on his face combined with the bushy hat of his ghillie suit gave him an inhuman, almost demonic, appearance.

"Listen carefully," Derek began, a threatening tone in his voice, "I am the fucker that just kept you all from getting ripped apart. Now you have two choices. First, you can shut the fuck up, follow me, and live, or second, I can leave you here in the dark to fend for yourself! Now which will it be?"

When the professor did not respond, Derek took it as compliance. He looked at Susan and Josh who suddenly seemed eager to get moving. Derek turned and they all began jogging quickly again.

Another two minutes passed without anyone speaking. Only their heavy breathing and feet stepping on dry leaves could be heard. Then, off to their left, what sounded like a herd of elephants crashing through the woods, breaking branches, and knocking over trees, brought them all to an abrupt halt. The monstrosity was rapidly approached them. Not aware they were doing it, the trio seemed to cluster closely around Derek.

"Close your eyes and plug your ears!" Derek ordered as he removed another flash-bang from his load-bearing utility vest.

They did as instructed.

Derek pulled the pin on the flash-bang and tossed it in the direction of the rampaging creature's approach. The explosion once again had the desired effect as the beast clearly changed directions and began fleeing from the concussive noise and bright flash. A long, deep, howl, nearly as loud as the flash-bang accompanied its retreat. Without waiting, Susan and the others turned and started running, following Derek.

They scrambled up a small incline. Loose debris and vegetation made movement difficult, and they all slipped a handful of times. On several occasions, they assisted each other by grabbing small tree limbs, then pulling one another up by their hands.

Their advance slowed as a crashing noise came from a short distance ahead of them. Finally, as they reached the top, Derek began to feel some relief. He knew they were merely a few hundred yards from his vehicle. They were going to make it, he hoped.

The thought of escape quickly dissipated as they rushed out of the brush and onto the Forest Service road. His vehicle was not where he had parked it. Derek turned on his own flashlight and scanned the immediate area. The reflection of the SUV's taillights shined back at them.

They all pointed their flashlights at the vehicle. Derek's government SUV looked like a freight train had struck it. The vehicle was laying upside down, off a small embankment. It would have tumbled farther down into a small ravine but a number of trees had kept it from rolling farther.

"Well, that sucks!" Derek said, as the humor of how he was going to have to wordsmith the GSA-vehicle accident report crossed his mind.

A half howl, half scream made them all jump. It was less than fifty yards away.

"What now, Rambo?" Josh yelled as he scanned the woods in the direction of the howl with his flashlight.

Without a word, Derek turned and began jogging up the Forest Service road. Susan, Josh and Michael followed without question.

It did not take long. Less than a quarter of a mile, Derek led them to the abandoned Ranger Cabin he had driven past earlier. It was situated at the base of the canyon. The cabin was only about thirty yards off the road. The vegetation had reclaimed the area around the cabin and the forest was closing in on it. The four of them scrambled up onto the porch. Derek was about to kick open the front door when he decided to test the lock. He grabbed the doorknob and turned it. The door swung open.

The four hurried inside. Derek shut the door and reached for an interior lock, only to discover there was none. Since there was nothing inside to steal, there was no reason to have locks on the door, Derek surmised. They shined their flashlights around the cabin's interior.

It was one small room, about ten by twelve feet. A couple of wooden bunkbeds, without mattresses, were situated on one side, and a wooden table and benches filled the center of the room. The only other item in the cabin was an old cast-iron woodstove that was covered in cobwebs. The stove's telescoping chimney pipe extended through the ceiling.

Derek grabbed one side of the heavy wooden table. Without being told, Josh grabbed the other side and the two of them moved the table against the door. They did the same with one of the benches.

They had not been in the cabin more than a few seconds before a loud bang occurred on the back wall as if a large hand had struck it. This knocked years of dust loose as they all jumped.

Derek stood in the center of the room. He held his rifle in a low-ready position and he turned in a slow circle, pausing and listening intently. Over the next ten minutes they said nothing as the cabin was stuck two more times on different sides.

Feeling temporarily secure, Derek dropped his backpack and began peeling off his ghillie suit.

"I think we are okay for the moment," Derek announced.

"How do you figure that?" Josh questioned.

"Because we couldn't keep a cow out of this shack if it wanted in," Derek said. "If those creatures truly wanted us, they'd simply push down these walls. They might still do that, but for now I think we're good."

As Derek was explaining, he began using his Shemagh to wipe the camouflage paint from his face. Derek noticed Susan, her hands on her hips, staring at him intently. After a few moments, she shined the flashlight she was holding directly on his face.

"What are you, some type of crazed Bigfoot stalker?" Susan said accusingly as she realized the man standing before her was the same person she had seen at many of her lectures. "Who the hell are you and what are you doing here?" she demanded.

Derek half smiled, realizing he was going to need to come clean sooner than he had hoped.

"My name is Derek Riley. I work for the government," then pointing outside, he said, "and they are my job!"

During the next five minutes, Derek described the job of the SRT to the trio. The three stood, openmouthed, staring at him. Derek avoided discussing the Research, Disinformation, and Destruction task the PsyOps unit performed, nor did he tell them how Smith wanted them all killed. He would get to that eventually, he told himself. While Derek spoke, they all jumped, as another loud bang occurred on the outside of the cabin.

"So you know all about these beings?" Michael asked, as the first of a plethora of questions crossed his mind.

"No, not exactly," Derek began. "When a new member is brought into the SRT we are given some information, but I recently discovered we aren't being told the truth."

"What do they tell you?" Susan asked.

After a long pause Derek asked, "Have any of you heard of the spotted owl?" ◉

CHAPTER 18
"THE SPOTTED OWL."

"When we initially begin our assignment with the SRT, like any group working together, we need to be united by a common goal," Derek began. "Most of the SRT members are prior military and believe in patriotism. You know, Mom, apple pie, baseball, and the protection of our country.

"Once hired, new members are brought into a classified conference room and given a national security briefing. It is during this briefing we are informed that the government has been keenly aware of these creatures, the Sasquatch, since the early part of the twentieth century," Derek stated.

"Are you saying the government has been aware of this discovery for well over one hundred years?" Michael asked incredulously.

"Yes, that is what I am saying, but that is just the beginning," Derek said matter-of-factly as he looked from one to the other. "Throughout the better part of the twentieth century when a story arose or a photograph emerged, it wasn't a great concern to the government. There was no global internet, no cellular telephones; there were only three television news channels. If a story came out, the government could simply ignore it or chalk it up to some 'wildman' or simple misidentification.

"Then in the late 1960s the Patterson-Gimlin film emerged," Derek continued. "Still the government was not overly concerned, as the ability for mass global communication had not yet come to fruition. But to keep this film controlled, they portrayed the film as a hoax and leaked a story that it was a Hollywood special effects artist. Despite any information to the contrary, the 'man in a suit' story became the main belief. It was in the late 1980s and early 1990s two major changes forced the government to re-address the issue."

Derek moved his backpack and set it against the wall on the far side of the cabin. Walking over to one of the wooden bunkbeds, he broke off two pieces of the frame. Handing the wood to Josh, with his thumb, Derek pointed at the cast-iron stove over his shoulder.

"See if you can get a fire going," Derek said.

Josh took the wood and stepped around Derek. He began putting the wooden legs in the stove happy to have a job to perform.

Turning back to Susan and Michael, Derek continued his story.

"The first major change was the urban sprawl that began to encroach on the Sasquatch's natural habitat. The second was the spread of cable news and the rise of the internet."

Derek saw that the three, immersed in his story, were staring at him intently. Susan and Michael had taken a seat on the other wooden bench while Josh had paused in his task.

"Those of us in the SRT were told, elements of the government wanted to know what would happen if an 'endangered species,' such as a great ape was discovered in North America. So, they ran a test case," Derek explained. "In 1991, the government let it be known that the spotted owl's habitat was being endangered by the logging industry.

"This immediately triggered tremendous outrage and numerous court battles between environmentalists and the logging industry. Occasionally, when the tree-hugger crowd came to protest in some logging communities, the issue caused bitter street fights. Protesters were beaten and hospitalized by loggers. The protesters would, in turn, spike trees with metal bars so loggers would be injured if their chainsaws cut into them.

"This conflict between the environmentalists and loggers continued until 1994, when eventually, the public outcry came down in support of the environmentalists." Derek took a breath before continuing.

"The Clinton Administration put the owls on the 'endangered' list and millions of acres of timberland were set aside for an owl no one had ever heard of until just a few years earlier. This decimated the logging industry in some communities. The timber industry, by some estimates, lost over 30,000 jobs and billions of dollars in revenue."

"Well, wouldn't that be a good thing? Having a habitat designated for these animals?" Josh asked, his question meant for both the owl and the Sasquatch. He had gotten the fire going and was warming his hands near the stove.

"On the surface one would think so," Derek replied, "but this is where the national security element came into the briefing and was the point of the government's entire Spotted Owl test. The Endangered Species Act of 1973 was able to completely shut down logging in one area of the country simply for an owl. What would happen if a 'critically endangered' intelligent primate were to be discovered in North America?" Derek paused to let them consider.

"The government crunched the numbers," Derek began, answering his own question. "Strictly speaking, there are roughly 2.9 million jobs in the forestry industry; 423,000 of these jobs are in the Pacific Northwest alone. That's a combined, taxable payroll of approximately $128 billion dollars. The GDP associated with paper, wood, and furniture manufacturing totals an additional $107 billion. There is another $92 billion in other forestry-related businesses. Combined, we are talking roughly ten percent of our country's GDP.

"Then add in the numerous people who have gone missing in the national forests over the last hundred years. There have been literally thousands." Derek let that sink in for a moment.

"If it became known that the government was aware of the presence of these animals and did nothing to alert the public, there would be literally thousands of wrongful death lawsuits filed against the Forest Service and other agencies under the FTCA for every person who ever went missing in the wilderness. This would tie up the federal courts and cost taxpayers additional untold billions." The three looked shocked.

"But here is the real kicker. All that," Derek continued, dramatically waving his arm in the air, "what I just told you is nothing more than 'smoke and mirrors!'" Derek said, repeating the phrase Smith had used.

"Just two days ago, I learned the actual reason for the government involvement makes the Spotted Owl test pale in comparison, and the government will stop at nothing, including killing people, to keep it quiet." Derek watched the expressions on their faces change from intrigue to horror as the three absorbed his last statement.

Everyone remained frozen. Susan, Michael, and Josh stared at Derek, with the realization of what he just said. The fire began to crackle in the stove behind them.

"Are you planning on killing us?" Susan finally whispered. "Is that why you are here?"

Derek looked her in the eyes. "If I wanted to do that, you'd already be dead." No one spoke as they looked back and forth between one another.

"Listen," Derek began, "because of what you were about to expose, you have been deemed a threat to national security. They will be sending teams to your home and lab to locate, collect, or destroy any evidence you have and they will most likely already have planted stories to discredit you."

"They can't do that! It's illegal!" Michael protested.

"So is murder, and that doesn't seem to bother them. I was ordered to kill you. But I am not a murderer," Derek said. That statement again silenced everyone.

"What can we do?" Susan eventually asked, despair in her voice.

"I am not sure," Derek stated. "They will keep sending people until you are dead. These people have the money, resources, and power to do it. I can think of only one thing we might be able to do to stay alive."

"What's that?" Michael queried.

Derek paused, collecting his thoughts before answering. He had made his decision.

"We have to get ahead of it. We need to get to the media. Maybe even bring in a local senator or politician. I think if we all explain our jobs, who we are and what we do we can create such a media circus, they won't be able to kill us without causing more questions than they are willing to answer. We need to make it advantageous for them not to kill us."

"Will that work?" Josh asked.

"Honestly, I don't know," Derek replied. "They are going to try and discredit us. That is one thing I know for sure. They may come after us other ways too."

"How?" This time the question came from Susan.

"Well, for one thing, they will bring pressure on your employers to have you sacked. Which they will. Finding another job in your fields will be a virtual impossibility. They may send the

IRS after you for some made-up tax fraud or other bullshit. Our homes may be foreclosed on. Basically, our lives as we currently know them will end. But we will be alive."

Bang!

The side of the cabin shook from the impact and everyone, even Derek, jumped. Then, to everyone's surprise, a voice echoed from outside. For Derek the closest thing he could compare it to would be a combination of an angry chimpanzee and one of those old Japanese movies when Samurai warriors would yell threats to one another!

"BÄ RAM HO RÜ KHÄ HÜ!"

"What the fuck!" Susan exclaimed. Standing she spun and faced the door.

"SÏ MËKH DZJAÖ GLÖ PÜ" came the booming inhuman voice from the north side of the cabin.

"PÄ KÖ DÜ TÜ SEKSÏ KHÏ" seemed to come in response from the opposite side.

This back and forth "communication" continued. At times, the voices would scream at one another simultaneously, with only brief momentary pauses. The speed and intensity varied dramatically giving the dialogue an even more human yet somewhat demonic tone.

For nearly ten minutes, Derek, Susan, Michael, and Josh stood in silence, listening to the voices outside. Derek watched Susan. Her eyes were closed, and she appeared to be focusing her senses, concentrating on the sounds.

"What is it, Susan?" Michael asked. Derek looked over at him. He, too, was watching Susan intently. She kept her eyes closed. Instead of answering, she held up her hand in the universal sign of "stop." Both Derek and Michael recognized what she wanted: silence.

When it finally grew quiet outside, Susan opened her eyes. Both shock and awe were prominently displayed on her expression. She looked at the others and saw they were all watching her. She spoke, slowly.

"I can't be sure. But I swear they were talking to one another."

"What!" exclaimed Josh. "How is that possible? Aren't they just large apes?"

"Listen, I know this sounds crazy," Susan said, "but several years ago, I heard a story that a researcher captured some vocalizations in the Sierra Mountains. According to the story, these recordings underwent a yearlong analysis at the University of Wyoming. Apparently, the university discovered the sounds were not made by human vocal cords or any other known source.

"Then a former Navy linguist conducted a second study," Susan continued. "This linguist discovered there were morpheme streams within the vocalizations. I thought this story was just a bunch of bunk, so I never seriously looked into it. Now I think I should have.

"As you know one of my doctorates is in linguistics," Susan explained. "I've been trained to hear things most cannot or do not recognize. And what I am hearing out there," she said, pointing, "is language."

"Please explain, Doctor," Michael urged.

"Okay," Susan began, pausing to gather her thoughts. "In essence, a phoneme is a sound. The phonemes we are hearing in those vocalizations are phonetically similar to human speech. This means they are using their tongues, lips, and teeth to form these sounds."

Susan was attempting to explain years of academic study in a short, simple explanation.

"These sounds are forming morphemes or what is commonly referred to as syllables. These syllables become morpheme streams or words."

"I thought language was strictly a human trait?" Josh asked.

"The function of language is indistinguishable from language itself. Verbal communication of meaning through utterances is the very purpose of language. The use of language is what humanity has used to define itself and separate us from the lesser species. We cannot think of an object without also forming that word in our mind.

"There are over 6,500 languages in the world from Celtic to Mandarin," Susan continued. "There are also numerous dead or forgotten languages. If all we were dealing with was a simple primate, then I would be dubious too. But everything we've seen and everything we know is pointing to these creatures being something more."

"What are they saying, Doc?" Derek asked.

"Well, there is no way to know," Susan said, looking at him.

"Language is not simply a set of sounds unrelated to one another. It is a total comprehensive arrangement of blending behavior, context, reference system, and individual perspective. Almost every word in our language has many shades of meaning, and therefore needs to be interpreted by the situation.

"There could be drastic results if a statement was taken out of its intended context," Susan continued. "Take the word *shoot* for example. It has multiple meanings. To a solider it can mean to fire a gun, but it can also be a euphemism as in, 'Shoot, that was a great dinner,'" Susan explained.

"Until we sit down with one and they point at a rock and say 'rock' in their language we will never be able to know what they are saying. We haven't done that yet, have we, Derek?" Susan asked almost accusingly.

"No," Derek said, suddenly realizing, his interaction with Smith had changed his perspective and he was no longer sure what really had been done.

"KHU' FÄ LIP ÄBÄSJ" came the voice from outside. This was followed by another loud bang as something again struck the side of the cabin. ◉

CHAPTER 19
"BETRAYAL"

Sometime around 4:00 a.m., the activity outside the cabin ended. Susan, Michael, and Josh, exhausted, had all collapsed on the floor near the woodstove. Derek had been sitting against the wall facing the front door. His rifle lay across his lap. Eventually he, too, drifted off.

As usual, Derek's sleep was not restful. Disturbing images of war filled his dreams. Except now, monsters were added to his nightmares. Derek awoke startled and quickly grasped his rifle. Glancing over at the trio, he saw they had not moved. Michael was snoring lightly, which did not seem to bother the other two.

With his forefinger and thumb, Derek rubbed the sleep from his eyes, then glanced at his watch. It was just after 6:30 in the morning. Derek estimated he had gotten about two hours of sleep. Light from the morning sun had begun to creep through the poorly constructed boarded up window and along the edges of the cabin's doorframe.

Derek leaned his rifle against the wall and stood. After performing some mild stretching, he placed his hands on his hips and twisted his torso until he felt the vertebra in his lower lumbar area pop.

Leaving the rifle where he had set it, Derek walked over to the trio and gently shook them awake.

179

"Come on, people, time to get up. We have a long walk ahead of us," Derek said, as he stood and began reorganizing his backpack.

"Have they left?" Michael asked as he slowly got up. He used the wall for support as he pushed himself off the floor. Fetching his hat from the table, Michael adjusted it on his head.

"There hasn't been any sign from them for the last few hours. But we'll be cautious when we leave," Derek replied.

"What's the plan?" Josh asked. The others looked at Derek also wondering the same thing.

"Well, since my SUV seems to be upside down in the ditch," he said half smiling, "the way I see it, we have two choices. First, we can go to the vehicle you folks used to drive in here. That means we backtrack several miles through 'their' territory." Derek motioned with his thumb and they all understood.

"Once we get there we may find it has also been flipped over by our hairy friends. And, after last night's fiasco, I don't think they will be too keen on us strolling back through their living room."

"What's the second choice?" Susan asked quickly.

"We have about a fifteen-mile hike in the opposite direction to where we may get some cell phone reception," Derek answered.

No one had any better idea and none wanted to risk going back through where they had been the night before. Derek and Josh moved the table. Slowly they edged the cabin door open. Everyone, even Derek, had visions of a giant hairy creature charging in. Instead, sunlight came washing into the dusty interior of the old cabin.

For a few moments, they all stood there looking outside before Josh, Susan, and Michael stepped out. Derek threw his backpack over his shoulder and was about to follow the others out when he remembered his rifle resting against the far wall. As he began to walk over to retrieve it, he heard Susan give a startled exhale followed by the thudding sound of a falling body.

Fearing the worst, Derek reacted instinctively. Upon hearing the commotion, Derek dropped his pack and rushed through the door and into the daylight leaving his rifle behind. None of the others were immediately visible in the front of the cabin.

Once outside, the noise coming from the far side of the cabin was the unmistakable sounds of a scuffle. As he advanced around the corner, Derek immediately saw the "Huge Brothers," SRT members Mike Davis and Patrick Bennett. Their presence brought Derek up short. The expression on their faces and the posture they displayed scared him more than the previous evening's events.

Josh was on the ground before them, resting on one elbow. With his opposite hand, he was wiping blood from under his nose. Professor Wainwright stood just to the right of Josh. Both his hands raised in the universal "surrender" position.

Davis was leaning against the old moss-covered picnic table. A sarcastic grin on his face. Both of Davis's arms were casually crossed in front of his waist. In his right hand, he loosely held a pistol, his index finger floating dangerously close to the trigger.

Bennett and Susan stood to Derek's left, facing him. One of Bennett's muscular arms was wrapped tightly around Susan's neck. He, too, was grinning. Derek locked eyes with Susan. An unspoken communication passed between them.

"Good morning, Major," Davis said. "I hope we didn't wake you from your beauty sleep?"

"Boys," Derek began, keeping the expression on his face neutral to conceal his real concern. In the back of his mind, Derek knew these former SEALs had the tactical advantage and he needed to slow the situation down.

"Glad to see you both! We had a rough night last night. How'd you find us?" Derek took a cautious step forward.

"Oh, that was easy," Davis said. "Originally, Smith tasked us with the professor here." Davis casually pointed his pistol at Michael. "But then he said he wanted to test you."

"Which you fuckin' failed!" Bennett hissed.

"But Smith likes redundancies," Davis continued, ignoring Bennett's interruption. "So just before you left, he had us place a GPS tracker in your vehicle." Davis nodded his head in the direction of the Derek's destroyed SUV. "By the way, good luck with explaining that to the bean counters."

Davis returned his gaze to Derek. "Anyhow, we were already monitoring the professor here, but we thought it would be best to stick on you. Looks like we made the right choice."

"Guys, I don't know what Smith told you, but I am still on mission here!" Derek said as he took another casual step forward. "Smith is going to want to hear what these folks have to say."

"Leave it to some stupid fucking MARSOC guy to fuckup a simple hit on a couple of bookworms!" Bennett said as he squeezed Susan's neck a little tighter.

Though her eyes widened, Derek saw Susan was remaining calm. He could see she knew the severity of the danger they were in. By the look in her eyes, Derek realized she, too, was trying to come up with a plan.

"Now, Pat, there is no need to get personal here," Davis teased. "I am sure the major has good intentions and Smith wants to see what he's capable of so we are going to give him a chance to make things right by putting a bullet in the bookworm's head." Derek slid his right foot forward a few inches.

"How are you two associated with Smith?" Derek said, continuing to stall as he inched closer.

"We've been working with Smith for almost three years now," Davis stated matter-of-factly. "He brought us on board and tasks us with the occasional odd job." Davis smiled. "Like the bookworm here. He also has us look into potential new recruits such as yourself."

"Listen, these are good people. They could be useful. They don't need to die." Derek slowly raised his hands with his palms facing Davis. "Let's talk this out."

Derek took another casual step with his left foot. Judging the distance between himself and Davis, he was almost within arm's reach.

"What could they possibly have or say to Smith that he doesn't already know?" Davis asked incredulously.

"Well, that's between us and Smith," Derek said. He shifted his weight to his front foot.

"That was the wrong thing to say," Davis said with a sigh. Before Derek could react, Davis brought the pistol up and pointed it at Michael's head.

The gunshot echoed off the canyon walls. Michael's head snapped back from the bullet's impact. As the fedora fell to the ground, Michael's body simply buckled and collapsed.

Derek was already moving even before Davis began to turn the pistol towards him. Derek stepped to the right of Davis's arm and caught it with both hands. Then in one swift movement, he pulled Davis's arm straight bringing him off-balance.

As Davis's weight shifted to his front leg, Derek struck upwards against Davis's straightened and locked elbow. Derek heard a distinctive popping sound as Davis's elbow became dislocated. Derek grabbed the slide of the pistol and twisted it out of Davis's grip while simultaneously performing a thrusting kick against Davis's exposed and planted knee.

With a shout of both shock and pain, Davis crashed to the ground holding his shattered knee with his one good hand.

Clutching Davis's pistol with deadly intent, Derek began to spin towards Bennett. Unfortunately, the giant ex-SEAL was faster than Derek had anticipated. Before Derek was able to fully turn, Bennett had flung Susan away, rushing forward.

Bennett performed a tackle that would have made any NFL coach proud. His shoulder struck Derek in the side. Derek was taken completely off his feet as he felt the full weight of Bennett bringing him to the ground.

As the two landed, the impact caused Derek to drop Davis's pistol. Derek felt rocks and gravel scrape across the side of his face and along his right ear. Derek's breath was knocked out of him and he felt a sharp pain in his rib cage as Bennett's 240 pounds landed on top of him.

Bennett straddled Derek's chest and began to rain punches towards his head. Derek knew he was in trouble. He brought both his arms up tightly around his head to help absorb the impact of the punches. In a trained synchronized movement, Derek turn onto his side and used his right hand to push downward on Bennett's knee. With his knee blocked, Derek brought his own leg underneath and moved into what jiu-jitsu practitioners call the "half-guard."

Though this was only marginally better, Derek knew he could at least begin to attempt an escape from beneath the SEAL. Bennett did not care as he began to crash elbows down violently attempting to strike Derek's head.

As Derek began another jiu-jitsu move, Susan and Josh leaped into the fight. Initially, the shock of seeing Michael murdered immobilized them. However, as Derek and Bennett struggled on the ground, they realized their lives were also in imminent danger. This comprehension broke their paralysis.

Davis, who had regained some composure, was crawling towards the pistol that lay on the ground. Josh pounced on Davis's back. Susan, on the other hand, had picked up an old piece of firewood and charged towards where Derek and Bennett were grappling.

With all her might, she swung the block of firewood at the back of Bennett's head. Unfortunately, years of sitting in the elements had rotted the wood to its core. Upon impact, the firewood merely erupted into hundreds pieces of soft particles. The attack only mildly hurt the big SEAL. Mercifully, however, Susan's attack had distracted Bennett.

When he turned to look at her, Derek used the opportunity to scramble out from beneath Bennett. The two men began to circle one another. As Derek sidestepped, he and Susan came nearly shoulder-to-shoulder. Together, they faced off against Bennett. This caused Bennett to hesitate as he began calculating this change in his circumstances.

"I got this! Go help, Josh!" Derek urged Susan.

She looked over at Josh and Davis. Though injured, Davis was a trained professional and Josh was merely a skinny graduate student. As they were battling over the pistol, Susan saw Davis was beginning to get the upperhand. Leaving Derek, she rushed to assist her friend.

Both men's eyes briefly followed Susan before returning to one another. Time slowed as the two warriors maneuvered, purposefully planning their next assault.

"Enough of this bullshit! I'm going to kill you the old-fashioned way," Bennett said as he began reaching for his own holstered pistol.

Derek had anticipated this. In one decisive movement, Derek bounded forward.

As Bennett began to draw the weapon from his holster, Derek grabbed the big man's wrist with both his hands and attempted to hold the pistol in place. Strong as he was, Derek was no match for the strength of the SEAL. Slowly the pistol began to rise out of the holster.

Quickly, Derek ascertained he had only moments to spare before Bennett was going to be able to clear the pistol from its holster. Once out, Bennett would be able use it against him. In unison, Derek widened his stance while at the same time he stuck his index finger into the exposed trigger-guard of the pistol. Derek then pressed the trigger. The weapon discharged.

To Derek's good fortune, two things happened. First, as the weapon had not come completely out of the holster, as it fired, the holster interfered with the designed movement of the pistol's slide. This caused a malfunction in the weapon. The pistol would have to be cleared before the pistol could operate properly again. More importantly however, the bullet that did fire, struck Bennett in the foot. He screamed in pain.

Derek, still holding Bennett's wrist, brought the pistol the rest of the way out of the holster. Once exposed, he then slapped it from Bennett's hand.

The shattered bones in Bennett's foot caused him to drop to one knee. Not done fighting, the SEAL began reaching for the combat knife on his belt. Derek however, had already drawn his own knife.

In one swift attack, Derek moved behind Bennett and clutched his chin with his left hand. Derek pulled Bennett's head up and to the left as he simultaneously plunged his knife into Bennett's neck just below his right ear. Derek pushed the blade forward slicing through the SEAL's carotid artery and jugular. In a heap, Bennett collapsed motionless to the ground. Blood pooling around his head.

Exhausted and breathing hard, Derek took one staggering step away from Bennett's body. He was about to turn to help Susan and Josh deal with Davis when the gunshot rang out.

Derek spun, preparing to charge into the fray. It was not necessary. Davis had crumpled backwards to the ground. His legs folded underneath him. A knife was prominently displayed in Davis's hand. Josh was on his back, holding his hands before him in a defensive position. Susan, a small cut on her forehead, was standing just behind Josh. She was still pointing the pistol she clutched in her hands at the now dying Davis.

As the adrenaline left Derek's body, the pain began to enter. His head, especially his right ear was throbbing. At some point in the skirmish, he had tweaked his left knee, which was now starting to ache. Instinctively he held his left arm protectively over his rib cage as he limped over to Susan.

"It's over. We're alive," Derek said compassionately as he slowly reached out and placed his right hand over the top of the pistol Susan was still pointing. Initially, Susan did not seem to notice him, but as Derek's hand touched hers, the trance she was under seemed to break.

They looked at one another. Derek watched as her expression seemed to display the wave of emotions stemming from the last several hours. Shock, despair, fear, and saddness appeared in her eyes. Slowly he pulled the pistol from her hands.

Josh groaned as he brought himself to a seated position. Susan rushed to help him up. Together they walked over and knelt before Michael's body.

The avalanche of grief seemed to overwhelm them. Having been in similar situations, Derek knew they were thankful to be alive, despondent over the loss of Michael, and fearful of what was to come.

With their arms around one another, they quietly began sobbing. Derek stood behind them, giving them space and time to grieve. This was a personal moment for them. Not only did he feel as if he was not invited to participate, he felt responsible for their anguish.

Unlike Susan and Josh, his emotions were laser focused, bordering on fury. Derek looked at Davis and Bennett's lifeless bodies and quietly vowed to kill Smith. Even as this thought crossed his mind, the realization of their predicament began to take hold. Derek began to survey the scene and glanced towards the flimsy cabin they had used as a fortress the previous night.

Then he saw it. Standing behind the cabin, just inside the tree line. A prominent scar zigzagged across its barreled chest. The grayish white streak of hair adorning its otherwise black mane. The creature's dark eyes stared at Derek. Unmoving, Derek stared back. Then it turned and disappeared into the forest. Derek could have sworn it had smiled as it moved away. ◎

CHAPTER 20
"NEPHILIM"

They had been driving for nearly an hour along the Forest Service road. Following the events at the cabin, it had taken considerable effort for Derek to get Susan and Josh moving. While they grieved for the professor, Derek had removed a set of vehicle keys from Davis's pocket and located the now deceased SEAL's SUV a few hundred yards south of the cabin.

Quickly going through the vehicle, Derek took inventory of the equipment Davis and Bennett had brought with them. Aside from the two full sets of tactical gear and weapons, they had some food and water as well as a couple of government-issued smartphones. Derek knew these phones would not do them any good. Each phone had its own unique 10-digit pass code. He discarded them next to their corpses.

From their wallets, Derek removed what little cash they had on them. It was only a few hundred dollars. Derek was also concerned Smith may have placed an additional GPS tracking device on Bennett and Davis as well. While going through their equipment and the SUV, Derek thoroughly checked for any hidden devices. He found none.

Finally, Derek took the mediocre medical kit from the glove compartment. With some of the bottled water, he cleaned the blood and dirt from his face as best he could. Then did the same for Josh and Susan. He put a Band-Aid over the cut on Susan's forehead. His broken ribs made breathing painful. They would eventually need to do a better job of caring for their injuries, but this would suffice for now.

Initially, Susan and Josh wanted to bring Michael's body with them. Derek explained how they were going to have to lay low and having a dead body with them would be hard to explain. He told them they needed to get off the mountain and come up with a plan before more of Smith's men arrived.

They decided to move Michael's body inside the cabin to keep the animals from it. They left Bennett and Davis where they lay. Since it is possible to track cellular telephones, Derek had Susan and Josh throw theirs as far as they couuld into the forest. He did the same with his own issued smartphone.

From there they drove in silence for nearly the entire hour. Susan and Josh stared out the windows. Each running through the events of the last twenty-four hours in their minds. Even Derek had a hard time contemplating all that had transpired. He had not told Susan or Josh of the Sasquatch, he had seen following their fight with the Huge Brothers. He did not know what to make of it. In his mind, Derek had begun referring to this creature as "Scar" due to the large jagged scar running across its chest.

Eventually, they left the old Forest Service road and pulled onto the asphalt of Highway 20. After about twenty minutes, they came to the small town of Sedro-Woolley. While paused at a stoplight along the main street, Derek noticed a small general store. Derek pulled the SUV into the parking lot and told Josh and Susan to wait in the vehicle.

With Davis's pistol concealed on his hip, Derek casually entered the store. Initially he was a little concerned that the clerk or patrons would take notice of him in his dirty camouflage and banged up head. His concern was unfounded as this was a small country store and half the folks inside appeared to be similarly dressed.

Derek grabbed some more bottled waters and a couple of candy bars. From another aisle, he grabbed a number of bandages, ice packs, rubbing alcohol, some aspirin, and a neoprene slip-on brace for his knee. Then he picked up what he truly wanted, two disposable telephones, which he found on a stand near the main counter. Using some of the cash he had taken from Bennett and Davis, he paid for the items then returned to the SUV. He handed the candy bars and water to Susan and Josh.

While they hungrily wolfed down the candy bars, Derek popped open the bottle of aspirin and quickly swallowed four. He then removed one of the telephones from its packaging and went through the process of activating it. Derek linked the telephone via Bluetooth to the vehicle and dialed a number from memory.

"Okay, we're in this together. Don't say anything," Derek said as the phone began to ring. "Just listen and maybe we can get some answers." Susan and Josh both nodded in agreement.

The phone was picked up after a couple of rings.

"This is Pettiford," came the voice over the SUV's internal speakers.

"Marcus, no names, do you know who this is?" Derek said, hoping Marcus would not say anything that someone standing nearby may overhear.

"Yeah, I know. What's up, boss?" Marcus said. Derek winced slightly as even the term *boss* could give a clue to who he was talking too.

"Are you in a position where you can talk without being overheard?" Derek asked.

191

"Give me a minute," Marcus said and the line clicked as he placed it on hold. About two minutes passed before Marcus came back on. "Okay, I just moved into the Trophy Room. There's no one in here with me."

"Did you have a chance to look up any of that information I ask you to?" Derek asked.

"Absolutely," Marcus began. "If I didn't know what we did for a living, I would say this was starting to move into the realm of 'crazytown!' Each thing you had me look into was a little weirder than the previous one. I know you wanted me to keep it on the down-low, so I tried to do as much open-source checking as I could but still had to do a little computer snooping."

"That's great, Marcus," Derek praised, a little worried as to how much 'snooping' Marcus had actually done. "Give me the high points."

"First," Marcus began, "regarding Admiral James Forrestal. He was appointed the first Secretary of Defense in 1947 by Truman. He held that position until 1949 when he supposedly did a 'Peter Pan' out of the sixteenth floor window of the Naval Medical Center in Bethesda. They said he was being treated for depression. This is where the crazy begins to enter.

"Forrestal's brother adamantly denied James was depressed and that he and other family members had been refused access to him while he was being held at Bethesda. Additionally, the official report made no mention of what might have caused the fall from the sixteenth floor, nor did it make any mention of a bathrobe sash that had first been reported to have been tied around his neck," Marcus reported. Josh and Susan were leaning forward in an unconscious effort to hear better.

"So, hold on to your seat; we are about to enter the Twilight Zone," Marcus continued, "It is theorized that Admiral Forrestal was one of the founding members of a secret government group called Majestic-12 or MJ-12. This group is said to have been founded by President Truman to research and control information related to UFOs.

"Following the Roswell incident in 1948, it's speculated," Forrestal became despondent with what he was learning about aliens and wanted to go public with the information. So instead, they threw him into the psych ward at Bethesda and then had him 'suicided' to keep him from talking. In the mid-1980s, some supposedly secret documents were made public regarding MJ-12 and the Forrestal connection. These were quickly labeled a hoax by the government," Marcus stated.

"What is your personal opinion, Marcus?" Derek asked. He glanced at his companions. Josh and Susan were absorbing every word Marcus was saying.

"Honestly, boss," he began, "as a connoisseur of all things conspiracy. This has all the fingerprints of the same type of RDD campaign we would have run. First, it is true that in the late '40s and early '50s there were all sorts of concerns throughout the government regarding UFOs. So much so that in 1960s the government commissioned the Brookings Institute and NASA to evaluate, and I quote 'the implications of a discovery of extraterrestrial life.'

"The government doesn't have a report like that created without some cause," Marcus explained. "It only makes sense that they would create a secret organization to oversee it. Secondly, what was done with Forrestal and the later release of the documents in the 1980s is a classic 'Disinformation and Discredit' campaign.

"If you asked me to do the RDD on this," Marcus continued, "I would have probably recommended something very similar. Having Forrestal whacked, however, well, that was a little extreme." Due to the recent events, Derek knew that element of the story could also be true.

Susan and Josh had exchanged a wide-eyed look. Even after what had transpired, the rabbit hole they had just entered was not what anyone could have been prepared for.

Derek understood their shock. Government conspiracies, UFOs, secret organizations, assassination plots, it was nearly too much to comprehend. Derek thought to himself, *is this not exactly what Smith had tried to recruit me into?*

"What's next?" Derek asked.

"Okay, so you asked me to research the term *Nephilim*. This was easy. The Nephilim are mentioned not only in the Bible, but also the Torah, the Qur'an, and some other religious writings. Basically, all these religious texts all say the same thing: that the fallen angels took the daughters of men as wives and the hybrids born from their marriage were the Nephilim. Here, I wrote some quotes down." They could hear Marcus unfolding some paper before he began reading.

"The Nephilim were giants, the violent superhuman offspring produced when wicked angels mated with human women in the days of Noah." He paused. "Ah, here's another one from Genesis, 'The hybrids born from this unnatural union were no ordinary children. The Nephilim were giant bullies, tyrants who filled the earth with violence. They left behind a legacy of violence and fear.'

"This quote is from the Qur'an's Book of Watchers," Marcus continued. "'They also teach them sorcery and other illicit sciences, and the outcome is disastrous. They have giant offspring the Gibborim and Nephilim, and it is these giants who wreak all the havoc on earth that caused God to send the flood.'

"The Torah mentions the Nephilim a few times as well. In 13:32–33 it says where the 'Twelve Spies report that they have seen fearsome giants in Canaan. The land, through which we had gone, in spying it out, is a land that devours its inhabitants; and all the people whom we saw in it are men of great size. There we saw the Nephilim.'

"Boss, I am not a religious person," Marcus admitted, "but knowing what we do, this piece of information, if it's true and not just some religious BS, has me re-evaluating quite a bit." Susan thought she heard some concern in Marcus's voice.

"Okay," Derek said, breaking the silence. "What did you learn about our Mr. John Smith?"

Marcus gave a nervous laugh on the other side of the line.

"Well, this one was hard," Marcus started. "As you can imagine, just doing a data-mining search on a John Smith, is nearly impossible. Simply typing that name into any white pages web search gets you over 70,000 hits. Since we know it is an alias, I tried looking through different agencies, CIA, NSA, DHS, etcetera for a comparison, checking names, approximate age, and gender. This also was fruitless and I gave up pretty quickly."

Derek knew it would be difficult but was becoming disappointed.

"Were you able to find anything on him?" Derek asked still hopeful.

"Well, kind of," Marcus responded. "Since I was getting nowhere going the usual informational routes and we didn't even have a true name to work with, I ended up doing a Hail Mary. As you know, we have cameras everywhere around our headquarters. So, I took an image we captured of him while he was here. I then uploaded that image into our facial recognition software." Derek saw where Marcus was going.

"I figured he wants to maintain a low profile, correct? Well, even if a person wants to maintain a low profile and move covertly around government installations without drawing too much attention, they will at least need some type of government ID.

"As you know," Marcus continued, "in 2004, there was a Homeland Security Presidential Directive to enhance security and standardize government identifications. Nearly all government employees in all agencies were made to obtain a PIV Credentials. Management of this credentialing program was assigned to GSA's Managed Service Office. Well," Marcus said proudly, "I hacked into the credentialing centers and ran our image against those they have on file.

"The results just came back about two hours ago." Marcus paused. "I have a facial recognition hit with a ninety-eight percent certainty reading. Peter Baxter is the name in the GSA file. He's our guy, boss," Marcus said triumphantly.

Susan, no longer able to contain her curiosity, blurted out! "What's it say about him?" She quickly glanced at Derek, a look of apology on her face.

"Who was that?" Marcus asked, sounding a little concerned.

"Don't worry about her, buddy; she's working with me," Derek reassured Marcus and smiled at Susan. "What does the file say?"

"Well, this file is also a cover." Marcus returned to his narrative. "It says that Baxter is with the Department of the Interior, but maintains both a 'Q' Clearance as well as a Top Secret clearance with all the bells and whistles. It says he has been given blanket access to pretty much all classified programs. Which as you know is total bullshit; nobody has that kind of access. There are really no other records of Peter Baxter matching our guy, but I then ran the surname Baxter through the other agencies to see what I could come up with.

"A few have come back and they match our guy perfectly." Marcus took a breath before continuing. "There is a Paul Baxter with the CIA and a Patrick Baxter with the NSA. Then we again entered the Twilight Zone."

As Marcus paused for dramatic effect, Derek was beginning to get an uneasy feeling in his gut. Anyone who could have multiple covert files spread throughout several intelligence agencies had some serious horsepower backing him.

"So on a whim, I hacked into the national archives and ran both the name Baxter and the image through their records. Now a number of things came up, most of which I completely discounted. Honestly, I would have discounted everything but due to the secret agent crap and the Nephilim religious connection, I thought the next few pieces of information were worth mentioning."

"Go ahead," Derek encouraged.

"First, though, I don't think it's our guy simply because he would be too old, but there was a Philip Baxter with the OSS Detachment-101 during World War II. The records say Detachment-101 operated in the China-Burma-India Theater during the war. They conducted covert operations and prisoner interrogations. By all accounts, they were highly successful mainly due to their brutal tactics.

"Now, some of their success was partly credited to this Philip Baxter guy and his linguistics abilities. The reports say he spoke four languages fluently and had a working knowledge of at least five others. But, swear to God, boss, that couldn't be our guy. He'd be way too old." As Marcus said this Derek thought differently.

"The second thing I got from the archives was a letter dated in 1980. It was from the US State Department to the Archbishop Giuseppe Caprio. He was the Vatican City's president-designee of the administration of the Patrimony for the Holy City. I had to look that part up to see what that meant," Marcus explained.

"Basically, this Archbishop guy was in charge of the Vatican's finances and church property. The State Department was requesting the Vatican grant a Mr. Peter Baxter, access into their secret library xchange for some 'monetary foreign aid.'

"Finally, there was a brief mention about a Keith Baxter and his lead involvement in the MK-Ultra Program," Marcus said casually.

"What was the MK-Ultra Program?" Susan asked, having never heard of it before.

"Basically, the MK-Ultra Program was the secret government experiments the CIA ran for nearly twenty years ending in the early seventies," Marcus explained already accepting Susan's presence as part of the team.

"The CIA was conducting mind-control testing on unwitting American citizens using different drugs such as LSD and such. Again, other than the absolute sick nature of that particular experiment and that Smith is a creepy motherfucker, I really have nothing else tying him too it.

"That's about it, boss. I haven't had time to research much else," Marcus apologized.

"No, that's great, Marcus. More than I expected even," Derek praised.

"What else do you need me to do, boss?" Marcus asked. He had developed great respect and loyalty for Derek over the years they had worked together and would do nearly anything asked of him. Derek knew this but did not want to take advantage of their friendship.

"Nothing right now, Marcus," Derek said. "Just keep your head down and eyes open. I'll get in touch with you in a day or two if I need anything else." Derek provided Marcus the number for his disposable phone. "If something important comes up. Use that number."

"Copy that, boss!" Marcus said. Derek visualized Marcus saluting the telephone and smiled.

An audible "tri-tone" could be heard over the vehicle's speakers as Marcus hung up the telephone.

Derek retrieved the disposable telephone and was about to also disconnect, when a second *clicking* sound came over the vehicle's speaker system. Derek disconnected, immediately concerned. ◉

CHAPTER 21

"MARCUS"

Pleased with himself was an understatement. Usually, when the teams deployed, Marcus would remain back at headquarters providing computer assistance. Though his job was important, the regular members of the SRT frequently called Marcus and the others in the PsyOps division "POGs." One of Marcus's PsyOps coworkers, who had not previously served in the military, once asked him to explain the term POG.

"People Other than Grunt," Marcus explained. "It's what those in the infantry call soldiers who work in supply or back at base and are never exposed to any real danger."

Though he knew they were only teasing, Marcus still had feelings of guilt as if he was not doing his fair share. When he did get the opportunity to help someone like Major Riley, Marcus truly felt as if he was contributing.

Marcus had great respect for Derek, not only was he one of the top operators within the special operations community, Derek always had time for him and treated him with as much respect as he did any other member of the team.

A few years earlier when Marcus was struggling to maintain his shooting qualification scores, Derek came in on his own time and helped coach him up. On top of that, Marcus thought Smith was a creepy "motherfucker!" Marcus knew he was up to no good.

Taking the files he had compiled for Derek, Marcus stuck them in a manila envelope, which he slid into his athletic bag. Slinging the bag over his should Marcus left the computer room. He only had a couple hours left in his shift and since there was nothing currently pressing that required his computer talents, he would spend that time in the gym.

As Marcus strolled through the complex, he thought about the date he had arraigned for later that evening. He had met the girl on a dating site a few months back. Her name was Teri and the two seemed to hit it off. They had finally agreed to meet.

Marcus turned off his telephone. He had not been laid in six months and nothing was going to keep him from this date. He had high expectations.

For the next hour and a half, Marcus worked out. Running on the treadmill and lifting weights. The focus of his workout today was going to be on his arms. Marcus wanted them to look "jacked" for his date. After showering, Marcus changed into his civilian attire. He grabbed his bag and began walking through the complex's hangar to where he had parked his car.

Marcus paused as a flurry of activity drew his attention. A few more vehicles than normal were parked inside. B-Team was scheduled to be off duty, yet several members of B-Team were hustling towards the Trophy Room. Marcus stopped one as he was moving past.

"Hey, Adam. What's all the commotion about?" Marcus asked curiously.

"What, you didn't get notified?" Adam, one of B-Team's designated snipers, asked without breaking stride. "They called everyone in. Apparently something has happened with Riley."

A sickening feeling struck Marcus square in his stomach. A little over two hours had passed since his conversation with Derek. Forgetting his date, he began to follow the members of B-Team.

It was standing-room only in the Trophy Room. Marcus slid into a corner where he could see everyone while simultaneously trying to maintain a low profile. Everyone present seemed to be having quiet conversations. Mostly, everybody was attempting to guess what had occurred.

Glancing around, Marcus saw Brian Hall, Derek's assistant, had taken a seat at the conference table. Apparently, whatever had occurred was important enough that even injured they wanted Brian in attendance as well.

As Marcus looked to the front of the room, he saw Colonel Harris standing at the head of the table. Then to his horror, sitting directly behind Harris was Smith. Marcus felt a chill run up his spine.

Smith's dead eyes were staring intently at him. Two men Marcus had never seen before stood behind Smith, flanking either side of him. They wore black tactical uniforms. Their emotionless expressions reminded Marcus of mafia enforcers. With as much nonchalance as he could muster Marcus looked away from Smith.

"Okay, people, settle down." Harris raised his hands to emphasize his statement. The room immediately became still. "I'm going to cut right to it. What I am about to say does not leave this room. We do not yet have all the information, but preliminary reports indicate Major Riley has murdered Davis and Bennett."

The room immediately erupted in disbelief.

"Quiet! Quiet down!" Harris commanded while using both hands to motion everyone back down. "I know this is hard to take in and we are trying to get more information.

"Apparently, what we are being told, is Davis and Bennet came upon the Major as he was in the process of killing his girlfriend's rival," Harris explained. "When they tried to stop him he killed both of them as well."

"Sir, this is bullshit!" Brian exclaimed, coming halfway out of his seat. "Derek didn't have a girlfriend and he didn't kill either of those pricks." Several team members in the room concurred with Brian's assessment.

Before Harris could respond, Smith reached out, his long fingers wrapped around the colonel's forearm, stopping him from saying more. The room again grew silent as Smith stood and took the colonel's position at the head of the table.

"I know this is hard for you all to hear," Smith began, his gaze moving from one team member to the next, willing them to silence, "but your Major Riley has been having a clandestine relationship with a Ms. Susan Parker for nearly a year."

Marcus saw Brian adamantly shaking his head no. Smith saw this too.

"Is it not true, Mr. Hall?" Smith began. Marcus noted Smith knew exactly who Brian was. "That over the last year you personally have driven him to see her no less than a half dozen times?" Before Brian could answer, Smith continued.

"I realize this is hard for everyone and we definitely will get the major's side of the story; however, right now he is a fugitive. A fugitive who has enough information inside his head to hurt this country's national security. Until we have him contained, we have to assume the worst. Besides, innocent people typically don't run, which is exactly what he is doing."

"What are you expecting from us?" Captain Hammond, B-Team's second in command, asked. "Are you saying we have to hunt Riley down? One of our own?"

"Absolutely not!" This time, it was Colonel Harris who stepped back to the head of the table standing alongside Smith.

"Listen, Mr. Smith here is a specialist from DC. He and his men will be working with the US Marshals as well as the local authorities to bring Major Riley in peacefully and safely," Harris said assuredly.

"You all are being told this in case the Major reaches out to any of you," Colonel Harris continued. "If he does, you must alert us immediately."

"Let me add to what the colonel just said," Smith took over.

"To be clear. We all want to help your Major Riley; however, if he contacts you, the best way you can help him is to immediately come to us. If you do not, you will be charged with aiding and abetting a murder suspect and subject to the same penalties as he is. Do I make myself clear?"

A number of the members grumbled their disapproval and dismay. Several asked additional questions but mostly the same information was repeated. The main points emphasized by both Harris and Smith, were to do nothing and report any contact with Riley.

As the crowd stood and began to shuffle out of the Trophy Room, Smith whispered to Harris. Prompted, Harris blurted, "Hall! Pettiford! I need you two to stay back for a minute!"

Marcus and Brian exchanged a look of concern. Brian sat back down in his seat. Though he was bordering on the verge of panicking, Pettiford stood as casually as he could. Faking a yawn, he hoped they could not see his knees shaking. As the last member of B-Team stepped from the room, Harris began.

"Listen, neither of you are in any trouble. However, because both of you work so closely with the major, Smith here wanted to ask you a few questions. Now I told Smith you'd be cooperative; and remember, this is in everyone's best interest," Harris stated.

"Like I said, that is all bullshit," Brian said, repeating his earlier statement. "Derek did not do what this guy says he did."

Brian pointed an accusatory finger at Smith. "It's simply not possible. He wasn't having a relationship with Dr. Parker. Even if he did kill Davis and Bennett, it was probably their fault. Colonel, even you know how psycho those two shit-stains were!"

"There is more at stake here than your friendship with the major," Smith cautioned, not letting Harris answer. "Isn't your wife pregnant? Amy's her name, correct?" Marcus saw Brian turning red at the obvious threat. Even Colonel Harris looked incredulously at Smith.

"What will happen to her and your unborn baby if you happen to lose your job, or worse, end up in prison?" Smith asked coldly.

"Now wait one goddamned minute," Colonel Harris said, having a hard time containing his own anger. "These are good men here. There is no need to threaten them."

"I am merely speaking the facts, Colonel," Smith replied as he threw Harris an icy glare.

Harris turned to Marcus.

"Pettiford, could you step outside for a minute while we talk with Brian." As Marcus turned to walk out the door, Smith was about to protest when Harris added, "Don't go far. As soon as we are done with Brian, we will want to talk with you."

Marcus stepped out and immediately hurried down the hall. He knew what was going on. Derek was innocent. Davis and Bennett may have been killed, but Smith was pulling a disinformation and destruction campaign focusing on Derek.

Remembering the documents in his bag, Marcus knew he could not be caught with them. They needed to get to Derek. Quickly Marcus developed a plan. He had to hurry and headed back towards the locker room.

Approaching the locker room, Marcus glanced to his left and noticed the accounts disbursing office. An idea popped in his head and he rapidly amended his plan. Marcus cracked the door to the dispersing office open and peeked in.

No one was inside. This was typical, especially this time of day. Looking to his left and right down the hall and seeing no one, he stepped inside and moved immediately to a file cabinet behind the main desk. Thankfully, it, too, was unlocked. One thing about working in an ultra-secret facility, some people get overly comfortable with their personal security and leaving things unsecure often became commonplace.

It is not well known, but the National Security Act of 1947 authorized some government agencies, those primarily tasked with clandestine projects, to receive and maintain a "black budget." In 2018, the Trump administration asked for $81.1 billion for the following year's black budget. This was to support both military and non-military programs. A portion of this black budget was distributed to DOE's SRT program.

Marcus knew, aside from their congressionally approved budget, Hanford's SRT maintained one of these off-book black budget accounts. He was also aware that this account currently had access to nearly thirty-seven million dollars of unaccounted for black funds.

In addition to other uses, frequently SRT members would be dispatched on covert travel assignments. Often no one wanted an official record of these assignments. In order to cover expenses or procure equipment a debit card associated with this clandestine account would be used. As a result, every member of the SRT knew, the disbursing clerk maintained a stack of debit cards linked directly to this account in the top drawer of this file cabinet.

When an SRT member needed covert funding, they would be temporarily issued one of these debit cards. So long as the expenses did not exceed a single, five-thousand dollar expenditure, rarely did any receipts from this account get audited, and then only internally. The Government Accountability Office or GAO, never reviewed these black accounts.

Opening the top drawer, Marcus saw there was a bundle of cards lashed together by a simple rubberband. In actuality, there were more debit cards than he had originally thought likely. Knowing they would not be noticed as missing for an extended period, if ever, he grabbed two cards from the back of the stack.

In the file next to the cards was a printout with each card's specific pin number and activation code. He jotted down the associated numbers on a yellow sticky note he had taken off the clerk's desk.

Shutting the cabinet, Marcus placed the cards and sticky note in the manila envelope along with the other information. He then left disbursing and rushed to the locker room.

Two minutes later, Marcus was headed back to the Trophy Room. Apparently, Smith and Harris had already finished talking with Brian, as Marcus stumbled across him in the hangar. Brian was with Hammond and Hernandez, two members of B-Team who had remained behind. They appeared to be having a discreet conversation.

"Hey, Brian!" Marcus exclaimed. Brian turned and looked at Marcus. "You need to get those dirty socks out of your locker," Marcus said this loudly, not sure who else might be listening. "They're starting to stink the place up."

Initially, Brian looked confused. Marcus remained watching him until he saw understanding cross Brian's face.

"Okay, sorry, man," Brian said, raising his hand and turning towards the locker room. Glad to have relayed the message, Marcus headed for the Trophy Room.

As Marcus entered the Trophy Room, Smith looked more than irritated whereas Harris appeared worried.

"Where did you go?" Smith said accusingly. The way Smith was staring at him, Marcus was certain Smith knew what had just transpired.

"I had to take a shit!" Marcus replied with as much sarcasm as he could muster.

"Empty your bag," Smith ordered, as one of Smith's goons rounded the table. Before Marcus could protest, the man in black removed the gym bag from Marcus's shoulder and dumped the contents on the table. He quickly went through the items.

"Do you have anything else on you?" Smith asked. Marcus did not have time to answer. The goon who had dumped his bag began a thorough pat down of Marcus, reaching into every pocket. He retrieved Marcus's cell phone and wallet then set them on the table.

Nodding at Smith, the agent walked back to his post behind Smith.

"Listen, Marcus," Harris began gently, "I'm sorry about this, but Mr. Smith here believes you have been in contact with the Major. Is there any truth to that?"

"Absolutely not!" Marcus blurted out. However, he could tell not even Harris fully believed this.

"Okay, Marcus, go home. If the Major gets in contact, you need to let us know. Do you understand?" Harris directed.

"Yes, sir," Marcus said. Though he tried to remain calm, Marcus had to will himself to keep from sprinting from the room.

As Marcus was leaving Smith threw a cold glance at Agent Baldwin, one of his security men. Agent Baldwin nodded, understanding Smith's silent direction. ◉

CHAPTER 22
"MOTEL 6"

Contemplating the implications of what Marcus just told them, after Derek hung up the phone, they all sat in silence for a few minutes. Susan and Josh were still coming to terms with what Derek had exposed them to the previous evening, now these revelations were almost too much to fathom.

"This is unreal," Josh exclaimed, breaking the silence.

"What part is unreal?" Derek sarcastically asked as he smiled at both of them. "The government conspiracy, the assassination plots, demons and angels, the UFOs or the Abominable Snowman?" This caused everyone to laugh.

"Touché," Susan exclaimed. The mood in the cab had suddenly become lighter than it had been all morning. The ridiculousness of their predicament was almost humorous.

"Okay, Derek," she continued, "Josh and I are way out of our depth here. We recognize that if you hadn't shown up last night, there is a good chance something would have killed us. Human or otherwise. So thank you." Susan reached out and touched Derek's forearm. "But what do we do now?"

"We need a place to hunker down and regroup. Then I think we have to stick to the original plan. We need to get to the media," Derek replied. "Josh, do you have a credit card?"

"Yes," Josh responded cautiously, not sure where Derek was going.

"Okay, here is the first thing we are going to do." Derek put the vehicle in drive and pulled out of the Sedro-Woolley Country Store's parking lot.

"On my way out here, I saw a Motel 6 in Burlington, about ten miles from here. If those hunting us haven't already begun, they soon will be looking for Susan and I. This means they will be monitoring our credit cards. Specifically, when and where those cards are used." Susan and Josh understood, but Derek continued anyways. "However, nobody is aware of Josh here. At least not yet."

"So first thing, we are going to do is find a place to get some supplies. We have plenty of guns and tactical gear from what we got from Davis and Bennett, but we need regular clothes, toothbrushes, etcetera. Then, Josh, you are going to check us into that motel." The vehicle turned onto Burlington Boulevard.

Derek was pleased to discover a Fred Meyer's superstore adjacent to the motel. Concerned there may still be an undiscovered tracking device in their vehicle, they parked on the far side of the Fred Meyer's. After leaving the SUV in the store's parking lot, he and Susan began shopping while Josh walked over to the Motel 6.

In the store, Derek and Susan bought some clothing and jackets as well as a couple of ball caps. One said John Deere while the other sported the Seattle Seahawks logo. Finally, they grabbed some additional first aid supplies and basic toiletries.

As they were standing in line at the checkout counter, Josh strolled up to them and handed them both a key card for their room. Unlike the Sedro-Woolley Country Store, the clerk at this business looked at the three of them strangely. They all were dirty, with cuts and scrapes and smelled from not having bathed since before they had entered the forest.

Susan, noticing the clerk's disapproval, smiled politely.

"We've been dealing with a busted water pipe under our house." This seemed to satisfy the clerk's concerns and she immediately began ringing them up while talking about her own issues with her kitchen remodel.

Leaving the SUV in the parking lot of the Fred Meyer's they walked to the motel carrying the Huge Brothers' equipment bags as well as the items they just purchased. Josh intelligently had gotten them a room in the back of the motel on the bottom floor.

Once inside the room, Derek and Susan dropped their bags on the bed. Derek walked over to the window and drew the curtains closed. Susan rummaged through the bags and collected her newly acquired clothes and toiletries. After placing her watch on the dresser, she then retreated into the bathroom.

"I'll see you boys in a week," she said, smiling as she shut the door. Almost immediately, Derek and Josh heard the shower turn on.

"Okay, Josh, our next big issue is the vehicle." Josh glanced out the window, but the vehicle was nowhere visible. They had left it on the far side of the store's parking lot.

"What's wrong with it?" Josh asked.

"Well, aside from the fact I am not convinced it doesn't have a tracking device in it, we've been driving around in a big, blacked-out SUV with government plates. Eventually someone will take noticed. The only problem is I don't see any other solution." Derek scratched his cheek. He was speaking aloud, more to run the problem through his own mind than anything else.

"We don't have enough money to buy a car, even a cheap one. We could steal another vehicle, but that would just be swapping one problem for another."

"Ah, I might have a solution," Josh stated, smiling.

"Spill it!" Derek said hopefully. "At this point there are no bad ideas."

"Well…." Josh was hesitant but remained grinning. "You see, I have this cousin who, ah, doesn't exactly play within the lines, legally speaking. I bet I could swap him the SUV for a different vehicle."

Derek knew they did not want a stolen vehicle and said so.

"Though I appreciate the idea, Josh, like I said, that would just be changing the problem. We can't be driving around in a stolen vehicle!"

"But that's the beauty of it!" Josh exclaimed triumphantly. "It wouldn't be stolen."

"I need you to explain," Derek stated curiously.

"Okay, so my cousin Jeremy, well he does steal cars. However, he doesn't keep them." Josh was getting animated in his explanation.

"Immediately after he steals a car, he and his boys strip it of all its parts. I mean the seats and everything." Derek listened intently. "Then after the car is completely stripped they place the hulk of the car, basically what's left of the vehicle, and at this point it's mostly just the frame, out on the side of the road.

"So then the cops come by and see the hulk on the side of the road." Josh continued. "They check the VIN number and see it was reported stolen. The remains of the vehicle are recovered and brought to some impound lot. This next part is the beauty of the plan. You see, the insurance company eventually looks at the hulk and claims the vehicle is a total loss, as it would cost too much to replace all the parts. The hulk then goes up for auction."

As Josh continued to explain, Derek immediately understood.

"Then my cousin swoops in and buys this hulk vehicle at auction, VIN numbers and all, for literally pennies. He has all the stolen parts placed back in the vehicle and he owns it outright and legal. He then turns around and sells it for top dollar."

Derek thought about it for a few moments then said with a smile, "That is truly some Dr. Evil shit right there, Josh."

"Well to be honest, he got the idea from some Russians he had been working with several years earlier," Josh explained. "They were doing the same thing but with Porsches and Mercedes then shipping them overseas. But the plan still works."

"Will he be willing to help us?" Derek asked.

"Jeremy? Shit, yeah! He hates the cops!" Josh paused and looked at Derek. "No offense. And besides, he loves me."

They discussed the plan for a few more minutes. As it turned out Josh's cousin lived only about fifteen minutes away. Derek agreed to Josh's plan. He passed Josh the second disposable telephone and told him to get back as soon as he could.

After Josh left, Derek inventoried Davis and Bennett's equipment bags. Aside from the rifles and handguns, they had two complete sets of tactical gear, including ballistic vests, radios, and night-vision equipment. As he was finishing reorganizing and storing the equipment, Susan came out of the bathroom.

"All yours, cowboy!" she stated. Derek looked over at her. Susan was rubbing her hair with a towel, the wet ends dancing on her shoulders made the top of her T-shirt damp. They momentarily locked eyes. Derek thought he saw her blush. Quickly she turned away and retrieved her watch from the dresser.

"Where is Josh?" Susan eventually asked. Derek explained their plan to swap out vehicles.

"Is it safe for him?" she asked with concern.

"The most dangerous part will be when he is initially driving to his cousin's. I told him to follow all traffic laws enroute. If he is stopped in the government SUV there could be problems. However, I am sure it is too soon for there to be a BOLO on that vehicle," Derek explained.

"Few local cops are going to stop a vehicle sporting 'federal government' plates without a very good reason. So I think he should be good. I would have gone, but Josh didn't think his cousin would deal with me."

"My turn," Derek said as he stood. Grabbing his fresh clothes, he stepped past her into the bathroom.

The warm water of the shower reopened the cuts on his head and they began to ooze blood again. As Derek stood under the shower, he reached up to clean the wounds with soap. That was when his ribs reminded him they, too, were broken. Derek cursed loudly.

Susan knocked lightly on the door and cracked it open.

"I heard you yell. Are you okay?" she asked.

"Give me a couple minutes. I'll be right out," Derek replied.

After showering, Derek dried off as best he could. He slid the neoprene brace over his knee then secured it tight with Velcro straps. He then pulled jeans over the top of the brace. Leaving his shirt off, Derek stepped from the bathroom. His towel draped over his shoulders. Susan was staring out the window.

"I'm going to need your help with a couple of things," Derek said.

Susan turned from the window to face him. Immediately Susan noticed his muscles, which until now had always been hidden from her view. Susan began to realized she had not been on a date since she and Eric broke up. Blushing for a second time, she internally told herself to *snap out of it*. Then Susan saw the real issue.

Blood was trickling down the side of Derek's head, especially around his ear. Additionally, the left side of his rib cage had turned a dark shade of purple.

"Oh my God!" Susan exclaimed. "Does that hurt?"

"Only when I breathe," he replied, smiling.

Susan took Derek by the arm and pulled him to the small motel table, which sat near the window. She half pushed him into the seat. Then Susan opened the curtains just wide enough to let some daylight shine in.

Standing over Derek, Susan examined his injuries. She collected the bag of medical supplies they had purchased and dumped the contents on the table. Derek winced as she used some cotton balls to dab hydrogen peroxide on the cuts and scrapes around his ear.

After thoroughly cleaning the cut, she had him hold a small hand towel to the side of his head and apply pressure until the bleeding stopped. It did not take long. Once stopped Susan used a couple of butterfly bandages to close the largest of his wounds.

"You're definitely gonna need to wear that hat." Susan joked as she finished dressing his head wounds.

"Okay, let me look at those ribs," she said and watched Derek grimace as he slowly raised his arm over his head.

"You really should see a doctor…," Susan began.

"Aren't you a doctor?" Derek asked, smiling, then added, "We can't take the chance it wouldn't immediately be reported. There isn't much they could do anyways."

Derek talked Susan through what he wanted her to do. With the athletic tape, she firmly put several layers across the left side of his rib cage. Then taking an ace bandage, Susan completely wrapped his torso as tightly as Derek could stand it. This immobilized his ribs as best they could under the circumstances. Derek knew wrapping was not always the correct thing to do with broken ribs. The wrap would make it difficult to take deep breaths. However, the need to remain mobile was more important, so the wrap was necessary.

He stood and moved around a little, twisting slowly. Though the pain was still present, it was manageable.

"Well, I won't be running any marathons in the near future. But that should keep me moving. Thanks."

"So now that you're all bandaged up. What do those tattoos mean?" Susan asked, pointing at Derek's arm.

Prominently displayed on his left shoulder was an eagle standing on top of a globe and anchor, the symbol of the Marine Corps. Just below, covering his bicep was a shield in dark blue. Inside the shield were five white stars, which formed a semicircle around a skull. It was the Raiders Unit's insignia.

"Those were from my days in the Marine Corps," Derek explained without elaborating. He picked up his T-shirt and immediately groaned as he attempted to slide it over his head. Susan reached out to help him get it the last few inches over his shoulder. Again, for a long time, they looked at one another without saying a word.

"Do you think we are going to make it out of this?" she finally asked in all seriousness.

"I certainly hope so," Derek replied with a smile.

"You hope so!" she laughed. "Hey, you're supposed to be all positive and encouraging," she said, playfully punching him in the left shoulder, instantly regretting it as Derek winced in pain.

"Sorry," she said with a half smile. She picked up one of the first aid icepacks they had purchased and handed it to Derek. He held it against his ribs. Finally, she passed him a few more aspirin. He swallowed them without water.

They spent the next forty-five minutes planning their next course of action. Derek thought they should head straight to a local news channel, but that was before Susan mentioned she had previously met a state congresswoman who was an alumni of her university. Susan thought she might be willing to assist.

As they sat at the table discussing their plan, a truck suddenly pulled up just outside the window. Derek adjusted the pistol tucked in his waistband, then he and Susan moved to the door. As they walked outside, they saw Josh stepping out of the cab of a 2015 Toyota Tacoma.

"Hey, look what I found!" Josh exclaimed leaping from the cab, a colossal grin on his face.

"Your cousin loaned that to you?" Derek asked a little shocked that the plan actually worked.

"More than loaned!" Josh reached into his back pocket and pulled out two pieces of paper, handing them to Derek. Derek looked at the papers. One was a bill of sale; the other was a vehicle title with Josh's name prominently displayed in the owner's box. Derek looked up shocked. Josh was grinning from ear-to-ear.

"I told him he could keep the SUV," Josh paused, considering; "I hope that was okay? Anyways, Jeremy said after he was done with the SUV he'd probably come out ahead about $10k. So we did a straight trade."

"You did good, young man," Derek praised. The three walked into the motel room. Josh flamboyantly pushed a button on the key fob and the truck beeped as the doors locked.

"You realize you're going to have to pay the sales tax on that truck when you take it in for the registration," Susan said over her shoulder as she walked back into the hotel room.

"Wait. What?" Josh said, stopping in his tracks. ◉

CHAPTER 23
"FIRST DATE"

When he first left SRT headquarters, Marcus was extremely apprehensive bordering on paranoid. The meeting with Smith scared him. Not only was he a creepy bastard, but Marcus felt an instinctual fear he could not quite describe.

The drive home took nearly forty-five minutes. As he pulled into his driveway, the dread he previously felt had greatly subsided. Marcus had purchased his modest home, along with a couple of acres of property, about five years earlier. It was located in the county not far outside the Kennewick City limits. Though he had no immediate neighbors, a developer had recently begun building homes for a new subdivision just down the street.

Marcus had mixed feelings about the development occurring. He did not really want the addition of neighbors, but the Starbucks that would surely follow within walking distance of his home would be a benefit.

As Marcus stepped from the car, his phone chimed indicating a new text message. It was Teri. She was asking what time he would be picking her up. After Marcus responded, Teri replied with a heart and thumbs-up emoji. Marcus, smiled and rushed into his home. He needed to quickly clean and change before leaving to meet her.

Walking swiftly through the kitchen, Marcus pushed the wooden dining room chairs under the table. He then threw the dishes that had been accumulating around the sink, into the dishwasher. After entering the bedroom, he quickly made the bed. Marcus then gathered up the dirty clothes that had piled on the floor. While holding a bundle of dirty socks and T-shirts in his arms, he glanced around deciding what to do with them. He settled on throwing them into a heap in his closet and shutting the door.

Checking his watch, Marcus realized he had a few minutes left before he had to leave. Grabbing the laptop off the nightstand, Marcus typed in his security code and began scrolling through his email.

Though most of it was spam, there was one lengthy email from his mother asking how his date had gone. Marcus smiled. Always the momma's boy, he knew she would get an email from him in the morning. However, depending on how the date went, he probably would not be describing all the details to his mom.

Closing the laptop, he grabbed his keys and headed towards the front door. Marcus briefly considered bringing his Glock 9mm pistol along but decided against it. Some people are simply not comfortable around weapons. Marcus did not want to take any chances that being armed might derail the date.

After locking the front door, Marcus stepped to his car and programmed Teri's address into the vehicle's navigation system. He then backed out of the driveway.

"In a quarter of a mile, right-turn," the robotic female voice of the navigation system began directing Marcus.

Fifteen minutes later, Marcus was arriving at the small Pinecrest Apartment complex in Pasco. After pulling into the parking lot, Marcus sent Teri a quick text. She replied, stating she would be right out. Marcus stepped from his car and stretched with nervous anticipation.

Teri came walking up the sidewalk a couple of minutes later, a bashful smile on her face as she approached. Marcus, too, began smiling the moment he saw her. She was in her early twenties, about seven years younger than Marcus. Her hair, a sandy blond, had been pulled into a ponytail. Teri wore a floral sundress and held a small handbag. She nearly skipped the last couple feet up to him.

"It's nice to finally meet you," Teri said after their initial awkward hug.

"You as well," Marcus replied as he opened the car door for her.

They both wanted a relaxing evening without pomp and circumstance. As such, they settled on the Atomic Ale Brewpub and Eatery. After arriving, the date began to really take off. For the next couple of hours, while drinking beer and eating french fries, they laughed, talked, and got to know one another.

Teri was a senior at Columbia Basin College. She was obtaining her bachelor's degree in education. Teri beamed as she told Marcus how she always wanted to be an elementary school teacher.

Deliberately downplaying what he did, Marcus told her he was *just* an officer with Hanford Patrol. He stated his job mostly consisted of performing cyber security. To Teri's credit, she seemed genuinely interested in him and said she thought his job sounded exciting.

With dinner over the couple walked hand-in-hand a short distance to Howard Amon Park. There they strolled along the riverfront continuing to giggle and joke. Marcus, was trying to build up the courage to kiss her. He decided to wait a few minutes when he saw the two joggers quickly approaching. He thought their presence might ruin the moment.

As the runners passed, Teri beat him to it. She leaned in and kissed him. As they embraced, their arms wrapped around one another. After a few minutes, she pulled away.

"Why don't you show me your house?" Teri suggested chastely.

For the second time today, Marcus had to contain himself but for different reasons.

They drove in relative silence in modest anticipation. Teri would occasionally fiddle with the dials on his radio and ask polite questions about his home. The short drive seemed to last forever.

Pulling into his driveway, Marcus quickly got out. He rushed around to Teri's side of the car and opened the door for her. She kissed him again as she stepped from the car. Arm in arm they walked to the front door. Teri wrapped her arms around Marcus's waist as he fumbled with the key to the deadbolt.

The door swung open and together they stumbled in laughing.

As Marcus turned on the light, disbelief filled his mind. Smith was sitting casually in his living room. With his legs crossed, wearing that impeccable suit, Smith held what appeared to be a brandy in his right hand.

"Oh. Hello," Teri said, half startled to see the stranger before her. She turned and looked at Marcus for an explanation.

Two large agents, Smith's men, who Marcus had not previously seen, grabbed on to his arms and lifted him off his feet. Marcus's disbelief became a fear that washed over him like a tsunami.

Before she could react, a third agent stepped from around the corner. He grabbed Teri. Wrapping one hand around her waist he threw a large palm over her mouth just as she began to scream.

Marcus and Teri struggled ineffectually against their abductors. Within moments, the agents had them tied with zip ties to the wooden chairs of the dining room table. A gag was thrown in Teri's mouth just as Smith began to stand and walk over to them.

Confident they could not escape, the three agents stepped back, just as Smith strode up next to the couple.

"Hey, what's going on? Why are you doing this?" Marcus began begging as he pulled on his restraints.

Smith ignored him. He turned towards Teri and began to caress the top of her head in a grandfatherly but disturbing way. She began to whimper through the gag. Marcus saw terror in Teri's eyes. Tears began running down her face as she stared at Marcus for help.

"Just let her go!" Marcus begged Smith. "She doesn't know anything! We only just met this evening!"

Smith did not respond. Instead, he held up one long index finger, signaling Marcus to remain quiet. As he did, Marcus watched as a fifth man stepped from his bedroom. This man was skinny and his dark hair looked as if it had been greased back. Marcus saw he was wearing latex gloves and carrying his laptop.

"It took me a while, but I was finally able to hack into it," the greasy haired man said as he placed the laptop on the table in front of Smith.

"Thank you, Mr. Russo. Your work here is done. Please go wait outside," Smith commanded.

Reaching into his pocket Smith pulled out his own set of latex surgical gloves. As Russo closed the front door, Smith pulled the gloves on and turned towards Marcus's laptop. He began examining the files on the home screen.

A few minutes later, apparently satisfied with what he saw, Smith pushed the laptop away and pulled a third chair out from the table. He sat just a few feet from Marcus. Close enough Marcus could smell his breath as he exhaled.

"You should have been honest with us earlier today, Mr. Pettiford," Smith began. "We could have avoided all this unpleasantness."

"I was being honest," Marcus replied hesitantly. Smith only smiled and looked at his agents.

Two of them stepped around the table. One held a cut piece of garden hose about one foot in length. The other held a bottle of vodka and a funnel taken from Marcus's kitchen.

Grabbing Marcus under the chin, the agent with the garden hose tried to put it in his mouth. Marcus clenched his jaw shut and began twisting his head away from the agent. The agent with the hose looked at Smith for guidance.

"Cooperate and open your mouth, Mr. Pettiford," Smith said with a tone of exasperation. "Otherwise, your date will be punished." As he said this, the third agent grabbed Teri by the ponytail and pulled her head back. She screamed through her gag as he placed the edge of a knife to her neck.

Reluctantly, Marcus opened his mouth.

Almost immediately, as the garden hose was jammed in his mouth, Marcus felt it forced part way down his throat. The funnel was placed on the opposite end of the hose. The second agent promptly began pouring most of the contents of the vodka bottle down the funnel. It took less than a minute to empty nearly the entire bottle.

Marcus coughed uncontrollably as the hose was removed.

"Okay," Smith said, apparently pleased with how the events were transpiring. "It is question-and-answer time."

"I don't know where Derek is," Marcus said his head down, feeling ill.

"I didn't ask if you did," Smith replied with a raised eyebrow. "I am not concerned about that."

"Then what is it you want?" Marcus stated. He could feel the warmth of the vodka in his stomach.

"After you spoke with Major Riley on the telephone, who else did you discuss your findings with? Who else knows what you discovered?" Smith's tone had turned hard, though he did not raise his voice.

Marcus looked at Teri. Mascara covered her cheeks as the tears continued to flow. At this moment, Marcus thought she was the most beautiful person he would ever see. Regret, for all the things that would never be, filled his heart.

Even if he told Smith the whole truth, they were dead. Marcus knew neither he nor Teri would ever see the morning. That is when Marcus decided he would not give Brian up. The image of Brian and his pregnant wife in this same position sealed his resolve.

"No one," Marcus said as his head hung low defeated. "No one else knows. Derek told me not to involve anyone." He could feel the vodka begin to take effect.

Smith studied him for several moments before speaking.

"Very good, Mr. Pettiford. I do regret having to put you through this little drama."

Turning back to the laptop, Smith opened a Word Document on the computer. He began typing. Marcus could not see what he was writing. After a few minutes, Marcus watched as Smith accessed his email account.

Once done, Smith looked at the agent standing behind Teri. He stepped forward and cut the zip ties that bound Teri to the chair. He then removed her gag. She looked up at him as a glimmer of hope crept across her face. Keeping a firm grip on her shoulder, the agent had her stand then pushed the chair back up under the table.

"Don't move," the agent commanded as he stepped to the right positioning himself between her and the front door. Teri remained frozen like a deer caught in the headlights of a vehicle. She did not know what to do. The alcohol had Marcus's head spinning.

"Marcus?" Teri said pleadingly.

It happened quickly. The agent standing behind Marcus pulled a pistol. Teri's eyes widened just as the gunshot rang out. The bullet struck her in the chest just above the heart. She spun around falling against the wall before sliding to the ground.

"You fucking bastard!" Marcus howled. He knew they were going to be killed. That did not make seeing Teri shot any easier.

"Surely you know how this goes, Mr. Pettiford," Smith said nonchalantly. "Your death will play out this way. You were drinking heavily, as your blood alcohol level will show. When you brought your date home, she refused your advances and in a drunken rage, you shot her. Then, with remorse, you killed yourself. Of course the note you left on your computer and the email you will be sending your mother explains all this."

"Go fuck yourself, Smith," Marcus whispered as tears ran down his face.

Smith nodded to the agent.

Crying, Marcus watched Teri take her last breath. He barely noticed the muzzle of the pistol pressed against his temple nor did he hear the gun discharge. There was a bright flash then nothing. Marcus slumped over in the chair dead. His hands still bound. The agent that shot him dropped the Glock 9mm, Marcus's pistol, on the floor next to him. The agent then pulled off his own gloves.

"Take his restraints off," Smith directed. "Then send the email and leave the laptop open to the note." Smith began walking to the front door. "Clean this place up so there is no trace we were here." Then as an afterthought. "Oh and Mr. Baldwin, be sure to lock up when you're done."

"Yes, sir," replied Agent Baldwin. ◉

CHAPTER 24
"FIVE-0"

They did not have a computer or even a smartphone that they could link to a search engine. They initially tried going old school and using the telephone book in the motel room. Unfortunately, this directory only contained local county listings so finding a reporter to talk with was not going to happen via the phonebook.

They then looked at the government listings for the state congressional offices. These only listed the generic capital switchboard number. Not wanting to leave any type of messages on the public information line and wait around for a response, they tried dialing 4-1-1, the number for information. They asked the operator for the home numbers for both the congresswoman and a well-known reporter. The operator told them both those numbers were unlisted.

As it was late in the afternoon, they decided that first thing the following morning they would go to the local library and use the computer there to research both the reporter and congressional person.

"If the numbers are unlisted, how will the computer research help?" Josh asked.

"Okay, so the congresswoman's district is in Spokane County, and we can assume that since the news station is located in Seattle, the reporter lives in either King County or a neighboring county." As Derek was explaining how to track people down using public resources, Susan and Josh listened intently.

"After, we get on the library's computer and access the county assessor's web page for those counties where we believe they reside and conduct a property search. Typically, we can type in either an address or name; in this case, we would use their names. If they own a home, they will be listed. Since they are both professionals, it is a good assumption they own a home.

"Once we have their physical address," Derek continued, "we have two avenues. First we can either perform a reverse directory on the physical address, typically, this will give us a phone number to call; however, I think it would be best if we simply showed up on the reporter's doorstep. After we convince the reporter of our story, we get the reporter to contact the congresswoman."

"Okay, the library it is," Susan said after brief consideration. They used the last of their cash to have a couple of pizzas delivered.

"Tomorrow, I will go to a local bank and clean out my checking account. That should get us about $10,000," Derek said as he finished off a slice of pepperoni.

"Won't that get flagged?" Josh asked.

"Yes, but unless they have frozen my account, which they may not have yet, we will be long gone before anyone gets notified or is able to respond to the bank. We will just need to make sure we park far enough away that they won't be able to pull any surveillance tapes and get a picture of the vehicle we are driving." The plan seemed as sold as they could make it.

"Okay, now let's talk about these." Derek stood and lifted one of the equipment bags. Susan saw a slight look of pain cross his face as he set the bag on one of the room's two beds. He pulled a rifle and handgun out.

"Do either of you know how to use a gun? I mean loading, unloading, dealing with malfunctions, etcetera."

"My dad taught me how to shoot a long time ago. But do you think that is really even necessary?" Susan replied. Josh shook his head no.

"Well, yes," Derek responded. "We have already seen they will be sending people after us. They intend on killing us. Period, full stop. If I am not there to protect you, it will be up to you to survive. Understand you won't be able to negotiate with these people."

Movies always make handling a firearm look simple. As if anyone could merely pick up a gun and be able to use it competently in an actual gunfight. Reality is far different. Even holding a semiautomatic handgun incorrectly could induce a malfunction.

For the next few hours, Derek taught them the ins and outs of basic weapons manipulation. Showing them how to load and unload, how to use the weapon's sights, and fix malfunctions. He had them get into different shooting positions. He then ran them through several drills until they both had a good conceptual understanding.

Susan and Josh, to their credit, realized what they learned could truly mean the difference between life and death.

When they finally went to sleep, all three crashed hard. The events of the last few days draining them completely. Though they both objected, Derek slept on the floor, a pistol within arm's reach. He borrowed a blanket and pillow from each of the beds.

The floor was far more comfortable than many of the places he had slept in the past. Derek's dreams were again disturbing: trapped by monsters, Derek struggled to free himself, only to see the monster morph into a grinning John Smith.

They woke early. As neither the bank nor library would be open until 9:00 a.m., they cleaned up. While Josh brushed his teeth,

Susan decided to turn the television on. When she saw her own image, staring back at her on the local news, Susan gasped.

"Turn it up," Derek said quickly. With one hand over her mouth, Susan pressed the volume button on the remote.

"Again, our top story this morning," the news anchor began. "The Skagit County Sheriff's Office, US Forest Service, and FBI are at the scene of a triple homicide that occurred in the Snoqualmie National Forest, just north of the town of Concrete." The television showed the image of a police command-post. It appeared to be bustling with activity.

"According to police," the anchor forged ahead, "yesterday at about 8:00 a.m., two forest rangers were brutally killed when they came across the body of Professor Michael Wainwright. Professor Wainwright had allegedly been murdered by these two persons of interest." Images of Susan and Derek flashed onto the television screen.

"Susan Parker, a professor with the Washington State University," the news anchor continued, "and her boyfriend Derek Riley. Sources close to the investigation are telling us Riley is a disgraced former US Marine, who was apparently forced to resign from the Marine Corps for allegedly committing war crimes in Afghanistan."

The news anchor shook her head.

"Though the apparent reason for the murder is not yet known, sources tell us that the two professors had conflicting theories regarding, and I quote, 'Bigfoot'..."

Derek noticed the television anchor roll her eyes. Even having to use the term, Bigfoot offended her.

"...and that Riley murdered Professor Wainwright at the behest of Riley's girlfriend, Susan Parker." The news anchor shuffled some papers dramatically, though Derek knew she was just reading off a teleprompter.

"It is believed the two are mentally unbalanced and should be considered armed and extremely dangerous. An intense manhunt is underway—" Derek took the remote from Susan and hit the Mute button.

For several moments, the three sat and stared at the television. Then Derek spoke.

"They anticipated what we might do. Even if we go to the media now, we have been labeled crazy murderers. Whoever we go to, no matter how sympathetic they may be, all we can do is try to convince them of the truth. Without any proof, that will be nearly impossible to accomplish."

Derek closed his eyes, trying to come up with an alternate plan. Susan, concerned, reached out and placed her hand on Derek's forearm. He opened his eyes and was about to speak when his disposable telephone rang. They all looked at the phone. Derek had only given that number to Marcus. He grabbed the telephone and pressed the hands-free Answer button.

"Do you know who this is?" came a voice over the telephone's tiny speakers.

"Yes," Derek answered, recognizing Brian Hall's voice on the other end of the line. Susan and Josh sat up, listening intently.

"No time to talk. You might have less than five minutes before Five-O crashes your party. I'll call you back in twenty." The line went *click* as Brian hung up.

Derek knew the term Five-O was a street slang term for police. Grabbing their bags Derek rushed Josh and Susan towards the door.

"We have to get out of here," Derek said, tossing the equipment bags in the back of the truck's bed. Taking the keys from Josh, he said, "Get in." Susan and Josh, understanding the urgency of the situation, did as they were told.

Derek backed the truck away from the motel and onto Burlington Boulevard. He immediately turned into a Haggen's grocery store, which stood directly across from the Motel 6. He positioned the truck to have clear observation of the motel while remaining inconspicuous in the parking lot.

"What are you doing?" Susan asked. "We need to get out of here!"

"Not yet," Derek said. He grabbed a set of binoculars he had taken from one of the gear bags and began scanning the scene. Brian was wrong. The police did not arrive for nearly ten minutes.

First, two Burlington Police sedans, blocked both the north and southbound traffic along the boulevard. Then two Ford Explorers from the sheriff's office pulled into the entrance and blocked the access to the motel. A police K9 unit arrived and staged just a half block away. Finally, the SWAT Team arrived in a bullet resistant vehicle called a "Bearcat."

Men in green tactical uniforms leaped from the truck. Several carrying ballistic shields and pointing rifles, approached the motel room Derek and the others had just occupied a few minutes earlier.

Derek watched as one of the SWAT Team members hit the door with a battering ram. As the door broke off its hinges, another officer tossed in a flash-bang grenade similar to the one Derek had used just two nights ago. After it went off, the team entered the room.

A few minutes passed, then the SWAT Team emerged from the motel room with their rifles casually hanging from their chests. Derek watched as one of the officers, probably their team leader, removed his ballistic helmet as he spoke into his handheld radio.

It did not take long. Two blacked-out SUVs pulled past the roadblocks and stopped next the SWAT command vehicle. Derek watched as several men wearing black tactical uniforms stepped from the vehicle. Then one of them opened the rear door of the second vehicle.

Derek recognized him immediately as his long skinny frame slid out of the car. Smith looked up and down the street, then walked over to the SWAT Team leader.

As Smith turned to face the team leader, Derek saw he was sporting a windbreaker with the letters "FBI" stenciled across the back.

"That's him," Derek said as he passed the binoculars to Susan.

"Who?" she asked as she leaned forward scanning the group of cops across the street with the binoculars.

"Do you see that guy wearing the FBI jacket?" he asked Susan as she was adjusting the binocular's focus.

"You mean the tall, old, skinny guy?" she asked after a few seconds.

"That's the one. His name is Smith," Derek paused then added "or Baxter. And he's not in the FBI. He's the one Marcus told us about yesterday. That's the son-of-a-bitch that has orchestrated this whole thing."

"And tried to have us all killed," Susan added.

Susan passed the binoculars to Josh who had been sitting in the back seat. As he leaned between Susan and Derek trying to get a better view the disposable phone rang. Derek answered.

"I am about thirty minutes away," Brian said. "We need a safe place to meet."

"I might know a place," Josh said without pulling the binoculars from his eyes, volunteering yet again. ◉

CHAPTER 25

"BRIAN"

After doing a quick check to see if there were any surveillance cameras in the immediate area, Derek pulled the truck into the back parking lot of the Burlington Lutheran Church. Grabbing the John Deere ball cap, he put it on, pulling it low on his head. Checking himself in the mirror, he stepped out of the cab.

"I'll be back in twenty minutes. If something goes wrong or I'm not back in thirty, head to your cousin's," Derek said, looking Josh in the eyes. Josh nodded his agreement to their prearranged rally point.

Keeping his head down and his hands in his jacket pockets, Derek began walking. To the average onlooker, Derek was just out for a stroll. In actuality, every step Derek took was tactically planned. Glancing ahead, he evaluated each vehicle, building and bush, in order to establish what would work as appropriate cover or concealment available to him if needed.

Using either his peripheral vision or by directly viewing reflections in the many glass windows of the stores and cars he passed, Derek assessed all potential dangers. Vigilantly, Derek evaluated every approaching person or vehicle.

Nothing moved without his notice.

Two blocks later, Derek arrived at a Bank of America. His bank. After reaching the front of the building, Derek paused at the double glass doors of the bank's entrance. He peered inside to confirm all was well.

The last thing they needed was for him to stumble unwittingly into a robbery in progress. Satisfied, Derek entered, keeping his head down. He casually stood in line and waited for the bank teller to call him forward.

"Next," the teller stated, looking at Derek. "How can I help you today?" she asked in a well-rehearsed manner as Derek stepped up to the teller's window. A large counter separated the customers from the bank employees.

"I'd like to make a withdrawal," Derek said, removing a debit card from his wallet. Keeping his head low, he punched the pin-number into the card reader that sat on the counter.

"And how much would you like to take out?" the teller asked.

"Nine thousand, five hundred, in fifties and hundreds, please," Derek requested. Though he had a little more in his account, by keeping the amount under ten thousand he kept the bank from mandatorily reporting the withdrawal. This might allow them a little more time before Smith was made aware.

"Okay, I don't have that much in my drawer; I will have to get the manager to collect that amount from the vault," the bank teller said while typing onto her computer's keypad.

Derek closely watched as she and another bank employee, he assumed was the manager, met at the vault. Derek scrutinized their every movement. A few minutes later, the teller returned to the window. She painstakingly counted out the $9,500 in front of him. Derek thanked the teller and collected his money.

As Derek was about to exit the bank, he paused at the main door. Removing his ball cap, Derek turned and faced the many surveillance cameras inside. Smiling, Derek raised his right hand and extended his middle finger towards the cameras.

After slowly mouthing the words "Fuck you, Smith," Derek put the ball cap back on his head and stepped outside. Though silly, Derek hoped this minor act of defiance would aggravate the crap out of Smith when he eventually reviewed the bank's digital footage.

Though just as cautious, Derek's return walk was uneventful. After arriving back where they had parked, Derek climbed into the truck.

"Okay, Josh, which way?" Derek asked as they pulled out of the church parking lot. As Josh began giving directions, Derek texted the information to the telephone number Brian had used to call him.

One of the primary ways to get to the reservation is to cross the Swinomish Channel over the Rainbow Bridge. This two-lane, deck-arch bridge had been built in 1957. Faded orange paint covered the entire bridge giving it a generally run-down appearance. Arriving on the far side, Derek, Susan, and Josh drove their truck onto the Swinomish Reservation.

Thousands of years before white settlers arrived, the coastal fishing tribe of the Swinomish people traditionally inhabited the Skagit Valley and Puget Sound islands.

The Treaty of Point Elliott established Swinomish Reservation in 1855. This treaty reserved the part of Fidalgo Island, known at the time as Shais-quihl, for the tribe. With just under one thousand members, surrounded by twenty-seven miles of shoreline, most of the Swinomish tribe still lived on the reservation.

After crossing the rainbow bridge, Derek glanced immediately, to the west. There the tribal cemetery greeted all those entering the heart of the reservation. Many of the houses spread along the main road consisted of similarly built, single-story ramblers in different states of repair.

Though some residences appeared maintained, many homes and yards were in poor condition and run-down. As they drove through the reservation, Josh began speaking.

"Russell Means, a Native American Activist and cofounder of the American Indian Movement, testified before the US Senate in the late 1980s. At the time he said, 'If you want to see an example of failed socialism, go to an Indian reservation.'"

Derek looked over at Josh who was staring out the window as they drove past the homes.

"For decades, Native American tribes have been dependent on the US government. The Bureau of Indian Affairs was created nearly two hundred years ago to help 'make our lives better.'" Josh made air quotes with his hands as he said this.

"The BIA has a large budget and serves all the federally recognized tribes," Josh continued. "It has been cited as the least effective and most mismanaged agency in the US government," Josh began explaining, with a mixture of both pride for his heritage and despair for the state of affairs.

"But isn't the BIA needed?" Susan asked, trying to understand.

"It's not a money issue, it's a government issue," Josh explained.

"There are somewhere between six to eight million Native Americans and roughly 574 tribes in the United States. The BIA has an annual budget of over two billion dollars. You could literally give each tribe three to four million dollars a year and do away with the BIA completely. This would save the taxpayers billions of dollars, and we'd be no worse off than we are right now!

"As it currently stands, depending on the reservation, unemployment rates can vary between thirty-five to eighty-five percent. Compared to just under four percent for the rest of the country. Nearly 30 percent of Native Americans live below the poverty level. Many live in conditions similar to those found in third world countries. Some reservations don't even have running water," he continued, shaking his head.

"It wasn't until the government stuck us on reservations and stripped us of our freedoms that we began living in these conditions. So, to fix the first problems they created, the government developed social programs they thought were in our best interest. It was then that our issues began to compound. Like I said, it is not a money issue; there is no pride in letting a government take care of you," Josh explained.

"It is an impoverished, dependent lifestyle. Addicted to the federal wallet and programs that we didn't need to begin with. Now, whether we're talking substance abuse, suicide rates, educational dropout rates, despite the billions spent on these social programs, in nearly every statistic, Native Americans are worse off than any other minority in our country.

"After two hundred years," Josh said, shaking his head, "you'd think the government's BIA could figure it out. I actually laugh when I see a portion of this country's population wants to adopt similar socialist programs for themselves and be put on their own metaphorical reservations, so to speak.

"Increasing government spending doesn't solve anything," Josh said. "We have begun to recognize a need to find our own independence and entrepreneurship. It wasn't until our tribe began seeking our own way, rejecting the government and embracing capitalism, that things began to turn around for us."

Derek saw Josh sit a little straighter.

"We now have a tremendous medical and dental center, childcare facilities. We are creating businesses and jobs. Everything about our lives is slowly improving despite the government, not because of it! We have a long way to go before we change the mindset that took generations to develop."

They pulled down Moorage Way, passing the Village Store and gas station. At the end, they came to a small marina filled with fishing boats. Numerous trucks occupied the parking spaces along the shoreline. Crab pots and fishing nets sat along the side of the road. They saw a handful of people performing various tasks both around the marina and on the boats.

After parking between some very similar vehicles, they waited. Josh continued to talk about growing up on the reservation and the pride he and his family felt when he was accepted into Washington State University.

After about twenty minutes, Derek noticed an older model, light blue, Chrysler Sebring driving past the village store. It came to a stop near the front of their truck.

"This is him," Derek said as they all stepped from the vehicle.

Brian emerged from the Chrysler and walked up to Derek. The two men hugged one another as warriors in combat do after surviving an engagement. Derek then made introductions.

"Next time you come to one of my lectures you should stay for the whole thing," Susan said as she also gave Brian a hug.

Initially Brian was a little shocked that Susan both recognized him and hugged him but as the shock wore off, he returned the hug, smiling.

"Sorry, Doc, spy shit," Brian said as a lame excuse.

"Sorry to get you involved in this, Brian," Derek interrupted.

For the next several minutes, Derek explained everything that had occurred since he departed SRT headquarters just a couple days earlier. Occasionally, Susan or Josh added their perspective. Brian told them of the meeting B-Team had with Colonel Harris and Smith.

"We knew you didn't do what that scumbag Smith said you did," Brian stated. "There are a few of us ready to come help however you need us to!"

"How'd you find us anyway?" Derek asked.

"Marcus," Brian answered and looked down.

Derek perceptively noticed Brian's response.

"What about, Marcus?" Derek said, concern obvious in his voice.

"So you haven't heard?" Brian realized and took a deep breath before continuing. "Yesterday after the meeting where they said you killed the Huge Brothers, they had Marcus and I remain behind. I left first but Marcus had left an envelope in my locker for you,." Brian paused.

"A short time later, maybe a couple hours," Brian continued, "we got word Marcus had gotten drunk and killed some girl he was on a date with, then shot himself." Brian paused briefly seeing the look of shock on Derek's face.

"They're calling it a murder-suicide, complete with a note and everything. Personally I believe Smith had him whacked," Brian exclaimed. "I mean you've know Marcus longer than I have. Have you ever known him to get drunk? Or be suicidal for that matter?"

Derek's jaw clenched. Slowly he turned away from them and faced the truck. The others watched as he placed both fists against the vehicle. Derek's head bent low as his body shook and he tried to gain control of the overwhelming sense of sadness and guilt that wanted to crush him.

Susan, who had only heard Marcus on the phone, put her hand on Derek's back and gently rubbed. Her eyes, too, began to water.

Brian and Josh remained quiet for a couple minutes. Quietly Brian walked to his vehicle and retrieved the manila envelope Marcus had left in his locker. He waited until Derek raised his head and turned back around before saying anything.

"Marcus left me your phone number," he said, handing the envelope to Derek. "After we heard what happened to Marcus, we figured everyone might be a target. I had a couple of the guys come over to stay with Amy while I tried to find you," Brian continued to explain.

"I borrowed my mother-in-law's vehicle. I figured Smith couldn't have foreseen me using it, so there's no way they could be tracking it. She was not too happy about that by the way," Brian said, smiling trying to lighten the mood. "Then I bought a disposable telephone."

"Anyways," Brian continued, "the POC has been monitoring what's been going on. They saw Smith and his goons were working with the Skagit County Sheriff's office on obtaining a warrant. Apparently, since you were hiding in a public place they want to look above board. When I found out I began driving."

Derek wiped a tear from his eye then took the envelope Brian had given him and opened it. He began to read its contents.

"I hope you don't mind," Brian interrupted Derek as he read, "but a couple of the guys and me," he hesitated briefly, "well when we heard about Marcus, we all read the file."

"I wish you hadn't done that," Derek said concerned. "It only puts you, Amy, and the others in more danger."

Derek paused as Josh had begun walking away from their little group. They all watched as he waved at an older man who had stepped off a small fishing boat and was walking up the pier.

Josh greeted him at the entrance to the marina. As the two men began to talk, Derek noticed, though the newcomer appeared to be about thirty years older and a hundred pounds heavier than Josh, he had a familial appearance. Derek turned back towards Brian.

"Marcus also grabbed you these," Brian said, handing him the two debit cards and the yellow sticky note.

"Here is another thing most of the SRT doesn't know: Jeff, the guy who works in dispersing." Derek looked up from the debit cards and nodded. "Well, he and I served together. We're tight. I haven't spoken to him, but he will help if I ask." As Brian spoke, Derek remained quiet, considering his options.

"Boss, Hammond and Hernandez, and I are also on-board for anything you need us for. We know this is all bullshit," Brian offered.

Derek took a deep breath.

"I need you all to stand down. Especially you," Derek commanded. Brian was about to protest when Derek continued.

"You've already done more than I could ask. Look at what happened to Marcus. You need to think about Amy and the baby! I mean it. Stand down," Derek said firmly.

"Okay," Brian replied as a child who had just been chastised.

As Josh returned, Derek and Brian said their goodbyes. This time Brian initiated the embrace with Susan. As he hugged her, out of Derek's view, he slipped a piece of paper in her jacket pocket.

"That's my phone number," he whispered in Susan's ear. "Keep me in the loop."

As she pulled away from the embrace, she smiled and gave Brian a slight nod. Derek was eyeing them both suspiciously. He knew some conspiratorial bond had just occurred, but he did not want to push it. As Brian drove off in the Chrysler, Derek turned to Josh.

"Who was that?" he asked only a little concerned. Their safety required they continue to maintain a low profile.

"That was my uncle James. I told him what was going on and asked for his advice," Josh said matter-of-factly.

Seeing that Derek was about to get upset Josh put up both his hands before he could say anything.

"Whoa your horses there!" Josh began smiling.

"Trust me. Nobody here likes government. My uncle believes we need to go talk with my grandfather. He went to get him," Josh explained.

Derek thought about admonishing Josh. He was still concerned about the ever-increasing number of people who were becoming involved in their dangerously fatal game. However, he also realized Josh had come through many times in the last couple of days.

"Well hell, why not? Let's go see your grandfather. Lead the way," Derek said as they climbed back into the truck. ◉

CHAPTER 26

"STORY OF THE GIANTS"

Just a short distance from the Marina, they arrived at the Swinomish Tribal Center. As they entered the structure, Derek thought it reminded him of a Viking longhouse. The two-story main hall was both long and wide. Tall wooden pillars rose to a ceiling held in place by thick oak beams. The sunken wooden floor and interior balcony provided the appearance of a senate chamber. Traditional Native American art, including many woodcarvings, mostly of animals and fish, lined the walls.

The interior lights were off. However, the skylight, which ran the entire length of the ceiling, bathed the chamber with the midday sun. No other people were present. The three walked the length of the structure. Under normal circumstances, they would have paused to admire a carving or painting. Now however, Derek barely took notice.

When they eventually arrived on the far side of the building, they all took a seat on the some wooden benches. The benches, which appeared to have been set out for some previous event, were placed on the wooden floor near the chamber steps.

The entire chamber demanded reverence. Quietly they spoke about the history of the structure. From weddings and celebrations to funerals, Josh told them of the different community events that had been held within this building.

Soon, the door on the far side opened. They all turned in their seats. As the two men entered, the doors shut automatically behind them. Derek immediately recognized the uncle Josh had spoken with at the marina. He was leading a frail-looking elderly man Derek assumed he was Josh's grandfather.

Slowly the old man shuffled through the chamber towards them. Derek guessed this man was no more than 125 pounds, though the thick Seattle Seahawks jacket he wore hid his true size. He was a couple inches shorter than Susan was and his gray hair had been cut tight in the style of a military flattop.

As they closed, Josh stood. Susan and Derek followed his lead. Josh rounded the bench, walked over to his grandfather and gave him a hug. A huge smile crossed the old man's face.

"Grandfather, these are my friends, Susan and Derek," Josh said as he took a step back. The smile faded from the old man's face. Derek thought the wrinkles on his face looked like a road map to history. He estimated Josh's grandfather was pushing a hundred years old, but judging by the sharp gaze in his eyes, Derek knew he was not only fully aware, but also cunning.

Josh introduced his uncle James and then said, "This is my grandfather, Jacob."

"Pleased to meet you," Derek said and extended his hand. Jacob looked at it, then stepped around the benches without shaking Derek's hand.

Both Jacob and James sat on the steps across from the benches. Derek, Susan, and Josh also sat. For a long time Jacob stared at Derek. Understanding he was being assessed, Derek never broke Jacob's gaze. Everyone knew Jacob was the one who was to speak first.

In a monotone voice, Jacob slowly began speaking. "So you are the government man I have seen on the TV?" Derek nodded.

"And, so you are also the man who has placed my grandson in danger?" Again, Derek nodded.

"It does not require many words to speak the truth," Jacob said. "So before I help you, I have one question." Derek remained quiet, waiting for the question.

"Will you guarantee my grandson's safety?" Jacob asked intently watching Derek's eyes.

"No," Derek said without hesitation. He continued to maintain eye contact. Susan and Josh both looked at Derek as if he had just lost his friggin' mind.

"We are heading into danger," Derek continued. "I can't guarantee any of our lives. I do promise to give all I can, including my own life to protect theirs."

The chamber remained quiet for what seemed like an eternity to Josh and Susan. This time it was Jacob who nodded.

"Ours is a sad history," Jacob said. "Truth and the government never seem to connect. Politicians often make promises but rarely do they keep them." Jacob paused briefly before continuing. "After the government made its promise to us, your President Ulysses S. Grant, attempted to unilaterally change the western boundary of our reservation. This unlawful attempt to take a portion of our land and other violations of the treaty remain a painful part of our history. We have little faith or trust in agents of the government," Jacob continued. "If you had made a promise you could not possibly keep, I would have walked out." Jacob paused, considering.

"Then there is my grandson. He is loyal and dedicated to you." Jacob was looking at Susan as he said this.

"He believes your fight is a righteous one. He trusts you both. He surely will follow you regardless of whether I help. If I do not help you, I am also not helping my grandson." Jacob paused looking down.

To Derek, it seemed as if he was considering a path forward. After a moment, he looked up directly at Derek. A decision had been reached.

"Dzoonokwa. Ba'wis. Skookum. Every tribe has a name for the ones you seek. For us they are as much a part of our history as any other. Some believe they have the ability to move between both the physical and spiritual realms."

"I am going to tell you the 'Story of the Giants,'" Jacob said, "told to me by my grandfather, who was told by his grandfather and so on, back to the beginning." Jacob looked at all three before his gaze drifted past them, remembering.

Then Jacob began.

"There is a long ridge in the central part of the South Dakota. It looks out of place. There was a time when it was not there. Many people drive by it every day. To most, it is only a long hill. A few of us, though, still remember the story, of how Eia was defeated.

"They say it was a summer of storms, when Red Calve's people were camped south of what is now known as the Missouri River.

"Cloud and Plum were married in the moon of ripening berries.

"Two evenings later, a storm blew in. Big black clouds rolled across the sky and the thunder shouted, their angry eyes flashing with the light of a hundred suns. But the storm was not the worst thing that happened, something dark and ugly came out of the night, ripping into the village."

"Cloud and Plum huddled in their lodge.

"From the darkness, they heard cries of terror, women and children screaming. Something ripped into their lodge. A mountainous black figure. It was Eia, the Giant, with the strength of a thousand men, the blackest of hearts and a bottomless hunger. A hand, larger than a grown man, snatched Plum away from

Cloud and tossed her into a mouth like a large hole in the ground and she was gone.

"Eia tore apart the village to satisfy his hunger. No one could stop him.

"He grabbed girls and young women and tossed them into his wide slobbering mouth, then he was gone into the blackness of the stormy night.

"By dawn the storm weakened. Red Calve gathered the counsel of old men to consider what to do.

"There was no use to do anything, some said; Eia is too big and powerful.

"Move the village and hope he doesn't return, others advised.

"Cloud didn't intend to make the move; he was angry and announced he would gather his weapons and strike out after Eia. Seven others joined him. Eight young men headed east armed with lances, knives, and bows and arrows.

"Eia's trail was easy to follow. His footprints were so deep, rainwater collected in them. They found him asleep on a hillside. He was an ugly beast, naked and unwashed. Twigs and branches caught in his long and tangled hair.

Derek glanced at Susan. She was mesmerized by the story. Leaning forward she was absorbing every word.

"Cloud and the others had never seen Eia," Jacob continued. "They knew him as an imaginary creature in the stories told by the old ones. Now there he was, bigger than any living thing. Inside his stomach were Plum and the other girls.

"Black Fox asked the question in all their minds, 'how will we defeat such a thing?'

"'We will think of something,' Cloud said.

"Eia arose and walked eastward, flattening everything in his path. They followed until the giant stopped at dusk to sleep in a gully. The young men made camp and Cloud suddenly thought of an idea to kill him.

"'We will trap him,' he announced. 'He has a weakness: he is always hungry. We will use it to trap him. I will offer myself. I will get him to chase me, and I will lead him to the trap, a hole in the ground that we will dig.'

"Through the night they talked. Six would dig a hole while Cloud and one other would decoy Eia to the trap. The place for the trap was a dried creek where the sand was soft and easy to dig. They made stone axes. The digging started and Cloud and Yellow Hawk left to find the Giant.

"They would keep him decoyed. When the signal fire was lit they would know the trap was ready. Then they would lead him to it.

"They found him easily, for Eia never bathed and could be located at great distances when the wind was right.

"The others dug and dug. Dirt piled up on each side of the trench as they dug deeper and deeper. Days and nights passed. The diggers worked without rest. Out on the prairie Eia set out with long strides. Cloud and Yellow Hawk ran to keep pace.

"All went well until Eia spotted them. With a yell of surprise and anger, he stumbled after them. The ground shook. Eia's feet were like boulders crashing to the earth. Yet they were able to stay away from him.

"It was a dangerous game and Cloud and Yellow Hawk grew tired because they could not rest.

"Back to the west, the trench was growing deeper and deeper. The others worked their fingers bloody but the thought of their women inside the ugly giant's stomach was enough to make them work harder.

"The trench was as deep as five men standing on top of one another. It was finished. It was time to signal Cloud and Yellow Hawk.

"The diggers gathered driftwood and dried brush to cover the trench. Then another pile of wood was set on fire.

"Cloud and Yellow Hawk saw the fire in the distance. The others had finished the trap. Now Cloud would have to lead the giant. He prayed and made offerings, then went after the angry and dangerous Eia.

"It was easy to get him to follow, but to stay alive Cloud had to keep out of the giant's long reach. The chase continued through the day and Cloud was tiring. He led Eia across the prairie and towards the trench.

"The others saw Eia approaching and hid. If Eia fell into the trench they had to collapse the mounds of earth into the hole. Closer Eia came, looming larger and larger. They saw a man running before him. It was Cloud, stumbling badly. Soaked in sweat he ran only on sheer willpower. He fell many times but fought mightily to stand and push on.

"On a grassy slope Cloud lost his footing and slid. Eia's hand came down like a falling tree. Cloud rolled and barely avoided being flattened. But he had no more strength, he was too exhausted to be afraid. He had given everything he had and could do no more.

"Closing his eyes he waited for Eia to crush the life out of him. But somewhere, deep inside, he found a pebble of strength, one last spark of hope to save Plum and the other women.

"With a bellow of rage he rolled away from Eia's outstretched fingers and leaped to his feet.

"The ground shook under Eia as Cloud ran for the trench. Behind him Eia's mouth was curled into a snarl, his yellow teeth bare and his long black hair swirling like black smoke.

"Cloud reached the trench and was halfway across when he heard a shout of triumph and Eia's cry of surprise and a loud cracking. Eia had followed Cloud and broke through the trench covering. He was far too heavy and he went down into the trench.

"Eia fell to the bottom, caught firmly in the hole. Dust bellowed upward as he struggled, filling the air with his deafening yells of rage.

"The others collapsed the dirt down into the trench. Eia's yells turned to whimpers. His arm reached up, one hand clawed at the edge of the hole. But he could not free himself. Eia struggled with all his might, coughing as dirt covered his head. His struggles weakened and he coughed no more.

"Silence fell over the land.

"All the young men stood gaping at the dead giant. Somehow they had defeated it. Cloud jumped into the trench and sliced open Eia's stomach. Foul air and a green yellow slime leaked out. He reached in and pulled out the body of a girl, more dead than alive.

"With a yell the other young men jumped into the pit as Cloud enlarged the opening and found more bodies. All the young women and girls were barely alive. The young men pulled them out of the giant's stomach and took them to the nearby stream. In its cool waters they were gently revived and cleaned.

"The young men filled in the hole to cover Eia's body and the dirt piled higher and higher until it became a long ridge. In time, grass and cactus grew on it.

"Cloud and Plum grew old together. They raised two children along the way and heard the laughter of several grandchildren.

"On stormy summer nights Plum would gather her grandchildren and tell them the story of a terrible, ugly giant. The little ones would ask Grandma Plum if giants were real and she would only smile.

Jacob leaned back on the steps as he finished his tale. There he sat, content to remain quiet while the others considered his story. Derek felt as if this silence, too, was a test.

Breaking the silence, Derek finally said.

"Cloud and the other men were the true giants, not Eia. It was a story about never giving up."

Slowly, Jacob began to nod as he smiled at Derek for the first time. ◉

CHAPTER 27

"JOURNEY"

"We have learned the only way to win against the government is to survive and persevere," Jacob said. "For you to win this battle with the government you too must survive." Jacob paused looking directly at Derek. "And persevere."

Derek watched in silence as Jacob seemed to study him. He realized Jacob was not so much looking at him but instead over his shoulder. Several moments passed before Jacob spoke again.

"You have a strong spiritual presence standing beside you, government man. He has been sheperding you for many years. He told me he will continue to guide you and keep you safe."

With that, James helped Jacob stand, indicating their meeting had come to its conclusion. The trio stood as well.

Though the time they had spent with Jacob had been interesting, Derek was becoming concerned it was time wasted. Nothing more than developing a better understanding of Native American folklore. They had no answers or direction and were no better off than they had been an hour earlier.

Derek was about to ask Jacob for guidance when, as if on cue, he saw Jacob and James exchange a look. James nodded. Reaching into his pocket, James retrieved a folded piece of paper, which he extended to Derek.

"The truth you seek," Jacob advised. "as well as the answer to your problem can be found there. Though the answer may not be what you expect."

With that, Jacob said his goodbyes, giving Josh another hug. Before turning away, Jacob paused and looked at Derek. Then surprising everyone, he offered his hand to Derek.

"Good luck, government man," Jacob said as the two men shook. Derek, Susan, and Josh watched quietly as Jacob, escorted by James, walked slowly out of the chamber. Their departure left the three with an empty, vacant feeling.

Josh and Susan gathered around Derek.

"What is it?" Susan asked as Derek unfolded the paper. Other than two seemingly random sets of numbers, the paper was blank.

48.712128, -121.916586.

It only took Derek a moment of scrutinizing the paper before understanding what the numbers were. With that realization, Derek smiled, instantly knowing what Jacob had given them.

"These are map coordinates," Derek said. Holding the paper in front of him, Derek looked at Josh and Susan.

"Your grandfather is a crafty old fox, Josh," Derek said with admiration. "Listen. If I am correct, these coordinates will lead us to our hairy friends." Susan looked at Derek with concern as Josh took a physical step back as if he had been pushed.

"How can that possibly be helpful?" Susan finally asked.

"Okay, follow my logic," Derek began as he began walking in a small circle, collecting his thoughts.

"Smith has discredited us. He has planted stories in the media that we are a couple of 'nut cases' who have committed multiple murders over a disagreement regarding Bigfoot." They all recognized how crazy that sounded.

"If we simply show up to the media and start spouting off about what we know, no one will believe us. Just more ramblings of the crazy folks." Susan and Josh nodded their heads in agreement.

"However," Derek continued, "if we have actual proof of the existence of Sasquatch, then it will lend credibility to our claims. It will be difficult for anyone in the media to ignore our stories."

Susan and Josh, beginning to understand the plan began to nod their heads in agreement.

"Alternatively, if we choose, we can use that proof as leverage against Smith. Threaten to go public with the proof if he doesn't back off coming after us." Derek was starting to gather steam and he felt a second wind catching in his sails.

"So we go to these coordinates. Gather what proof we can. Then we take our chances," Derek stated hopefully.

"Do you think it will work?" Susan asked.

"Frankly, I don't see us having any other choice," he said. They discussed the option for a couple more minutes but none of them had any better idea.

Instead of blindly charging forward, the three of them sat back down on the benches and began developing their scheme. For nearly an hour, they discussed the plan and wrote out what supplies they would need. Finally, with the decision made, they all agreed on the path forward. Leaving the Tribal Center, they walked to where they had left the Toyota Tacoma. There was no more time to delay.

It took about forty-five minutes to drive from the reservation to the Bellingham REI, an outdoor gear and apparel store popular in the Pacific Northwest. Taking exit 252, they arrived at the REI less than five minutes from Interstate 5.

Derek parked near a Starbucks. The three crossed the parking lot and entered the outdoor store. Though considerably smaller than some, this REI had more than enough equipment for their needs.

Racks of name-brand outdoor clothing such North Face and Patagonia filled the store. Hiking boots, sandals, and specialty shoes were overflowing along one entire wall. Dozens of mountain bikes hung from the ceiling, dangling over varieties of rain gear, while many other bikes lined numerous racks.

Copious amounts of first aid and survival equipment was readily available. As winter was approaching, skiing equipment boasted the biggest sales. Fishing gear and multicolored climbing ropes saturated other areas of the store. Tents of various sizes, water purification bottles, small and large Coleman propane cookers and more dehydrated meals than anyone could eat filled the aisles.

Susan and Josh grabbed two big shopping carts, and then systematically began acquiring the items on their lists. The three shopped for nearly an hour acquiring new tents, sleeping bags, backpacks, and other camping equipment. They purchased new coats, boots, and clothing. Additionally, they bought trail cameras and recording equipment. Derek was not concerned about the cost: he was going to use one of the debit cards Marcus had obtained for him.

The purchase went smoothly. After wheeling the carts of gear through the parking lot, they took another twenty minutes unpackaging everything and organizing their new backpacks. Pleased with their preparation, they stowed the packs in the bed of the truck and drove off.

It took about an hour before they arrived at the Forest Service road and another hour before they came to a stop. Derek had been using the GPS he had purchased and programmed the coordinates into.

"Okay. This is as far as we can drive," Derek said as they stepped from the truck. "We have about a fifteen-mile hike before we reach the map coordinates Jacob gave us. We only have a couple hours of daylight left, so here is the plan," Derek explained as he began pulling the packs out of the bed of the truck and handing them to Susan and Josh.

"We will hike until dusk. That will get us about five miles in. Wherever that ends up is where we set up camp for the night. Tomorrow, we take our time and move slowly to the map coordinates." Derek pulled out a Green Trails map and laid it across the hood of the truck. Susan and Josh looked on.

"Here we are." Derek pointed to a spot on the map. "And this is where we are going." Taking a pen from his pocket Derek marked an X on their final destination.

"Okay now this is the interesting thing." Derek paused and they both looked at him. "Though we are taking a different route in, this spot is less than ten miles from that cabin we sheltered in a few nights back. Because of that fact alone, I believe these coordinates are going to be accurate."

Susan and Josh agreed but apprehension began to creep into their demeanor as they thought of their last encounter. As they tightened their packs, Susan saw Derek wince in pain as he slung his own pack.

"Are you okay?" she asked.

"Yup. Just the ribs reminding me they aren't happy," Derek responded.

With their packs on, Derek reached into the back seat of the truck and retrieved the two rifles. He slung one and handed the other to Josh. Derek then handed Susan one of the pistols. She stuck the pistol in her waistband. Making some last minute adjustments with their packs, the three turned and walked into the woods.

The hike was not as bad as Derek had been anticipating. Just a slight incline in elevation and mild vegetation slowed their progress. Lost in their own thoughts, none of them spoke much during their hike.

Derek frequently referred to the handheld GPS he carried. Their direction had been true and rarely did he need to make a course correction.

As the sun began to settle behind the mountains, Derek called a halt to their progress. Moving quickly, they set up their three, single-person tents. Each was just large enough for one person to crawl into with their sleeping bag.

Though they kept them sheltered from the elements these tents provided little protection from any potential threat they may face. More for reassurance than security, they placed each of the tent's opening towards one another. This allowed them to look out of one tent and into the others. None of the tents were more than a couple feet apart.

With their camp put together, Josh broke out the Coleman stove and immediately went to work on their dinner. He seemed to relish the idea of being the camp-cook.

"What do you think we will find out there tomorrow, Susan?" Derek asked the thought that had been on his mind since Jacob handed him the coordinates.

"I have no idea," she replied. "But I am both terrified and excited to find out."

As they ate, Derek broke out the map and discussed how he wanted to approach the target tomorrow. It would take them most of the morning to move in and he wanted to circle wide around it to the north.

The map showed an elevated position about a half mile away from the coordinates that should provide a clear view of the entire area, he explained. Once there, they could then adjust as needed. The others agreed, knowing this was Derek's expertise.

All were apprehensive about going to sleep. They knew sleep would just bring tomorrow closer. Instead, Susan and Josh told funny stories about their childhood. Derek in turn gave accounts of some of the insane adventures he and his Marine buddies had embarked on. However, as the night grew ever colder each crawled into their individual tents. They had to squirm around so as their head was positioned near the opening.

Still they were hesitant to close their eyes. Derek lay on his back looking up at the stars through the opening of the tent. Josh and Susan were mirroring him.

"If you had to choose a different occupation, what would you have done with your life?" Josh asked Susan.

"I would have been a 'Hot-Shot' or smoke Jumper!" Susan said confidently after a long pause. "You know, one of those firefighters that fights seasonal fires! That would combine all of the things I enjoy: the outdoors, protecting the environment. I think that would have been a satisfying job."

Derek and Josh both agreed they could picture Susan as a smoke jumper.

"What about you, Derek?" Josh asked. "What would you do differently if you could?"

"I'd be a florist," Derek said without hesitation. Susan and Josh both turned in their tents to looked at him before breaking into laughter.

"What?" Derek asked with a false sense of incredulousness. "I can arrange a mean bouquet." This caused Susan and Josh to laugh harder.

"I have to use the little girl's room," Susan said, crawling out of her tent and turning on her flashlight. They sat quietly and listened to her walk a short distance away from the camp.

"You know she likes you, right?" Josh said to Derek in a low tone so Susan could not overhear. Derek rolled over and looked at him.

"Even with all the bad stuff that has happened, I can't remember the last time she's seemed happy like this," Josh reflected.

"Well, the feeling's mutual, Josh," Derek said, taking a deep breath.

Josh was about to say more when they heard Susan make a strange noise. Almost as if the wind had been knocked out of her. Both rolled onto their elbows and looked at one another. Josh's eyes had gone wide.

"Susan!" Derek said loudly, already crawling out of his tent and grabbing his rifle.

"Susan!" Josh repeated, having also gotten up.

They began shining their flashlights in the direction where they had seen Susan wander. That is when Derek noticed Susan's light laying on the ground just thirty feet from their tents. As he went to retrieve it, the beam from his own flashlight landed on an unmistakably large print in the dirt next to it.

"Susan!" Josh yelled, holding both hands to his mouth. He was close to panicking. Josh was turning to run into the woods when Derek grabbed him by the back of his collar nearly yanking him off his feet.

"Wait!" Derek commanded. "We can't just charge blindly into the night."

"We can't leave her out there!" Josh demanded as the tears began forming in his eyes.

"We aren't," Derek said, grabbing Josh by both his shoulders. "We know where they're taking her!"

Derek reached in his tent and retrieved the GPS. Holding it in front of Josh.

"We have no choice but to trust the coordinates!" Derek held Josh tightly until he shook his head, yes.

"Throw what you can in your pack and grab your rifle. We are leaving here in two minutes," Derek commanded.

"GO!" Derek yelled as he and Josh began moving with a sense of urgency neither had felt before. ◉

CHAPTER 28
"TRIBE"

All pretext of moving quietly had been thrown out the window the moment Susan had been abducted. Derek and Josh charged through the woods as fast as they could travel in the dark. They were led only by the glow of their flashlights, the beams bouncing along the ground ahead of them.

Derek did not have to encourage Josh. Both knew what was at stake. Neither wanted to think about what they might discover, if and when they caught up to Susan and her abductors. The uneven terrain and vegetation continuously grabbed at their ankles causing them to stumble and fall several times.

Tree branches scratched and poked at their faces as they crashed blindly through the brush. Derek reflected back on the story Jacob had told them. He wondered if this was how Cloud felt trying to get Plum back from Eia.

As dawn arrived, Derek slowed their pace. They had traveled to within just a half mile of the coordinates Jacob had provided. Josh wanted to keep charging ahead, but Derek, not unaccustomed to high-risk situations, stopped him.

"Listen," Derek said compassionately, "it has been several hours since Susan was grabbed. Whatever was going to happen has already happened. We will not be able to change this fact by blindly rushing in."

Josh was breathing hard, both adrenaline and exhaustion coursing through his body as every muscle screamed at him.

"We need to be smart now." Derek looked Josh in the eyes. He was a coiled spring, ready to launch. "It could make many things worse if we don't slow down and start thinking clearly."

"Okay," Josh finally agreed. "What do we do next?"

Derek had already reverted to his days as a scout sniper. Decades of training and experience took over.

"Move where I move. Step where I step. Slow your breathing and focus." With that, Derek moved around Josh and began stalking forward.

As he started advancing, Derek began closely observing the ground in front of him, picking the best spots to plant his feet. Avoiding small branches or leaves that would snap or make noise. Instead, his feet found the moss and soft dirt, which masked each step.

Every few paces he would pause and observe the environment allowing his senses to takeover, slowing his breathing, and becoming acclimated to the natural sounds of the forest. Josh, to his credit, mimicked everything Derek did. For all intents and purposes, they had become virtually silent in their actions.

A quarter mile from the coordinates, Derek restricted his movement to traveling between one concealed position to another. During one pause, Josh reached out and touched Derek's arm.

Slowly he turned and looked at Josh who was tapping his ear. Derek had noticed it too. The forest had gone quiet. The birds had stopped chirping, crickets, and frogs were no longer making noise. Even the breeze in the trees seemed to have gone quiet. Derek nodded in understanding.

Two hundred yards from the clearing, Derek and Josh began crawling. Through breaks in the foliage, Derek could see movement in the clearing ahead, but he could not ascertain what was moving. Slowly they crept forward. Derek had chosen an area with a large tree surrounded by several large ferns as his final position. He moved deliberately towards this location.

Crawling on their forearms and knees, Derek and Josh moved up shoulder to shoulder. Hidden behind a bushy fern, they peered into the clearing together. Both quietly gasped at what they beheld.

The clearing itself was picturesque. The sun shone brightly down, warming everything. Small particles of pollen glittered in the sunlight. Grass and wildflowers covered the field.

On the far side just inside the tree line, almost directly across from Josh and Derek was a large mound. This embankment seemed to recede into the hillside. It appeared as if there were some type of cave opening near the base of the mound.

The beauty of the meadow was not what astounded them. Instead, Susan sat almost directly in the center of the clearing. She did not appear hurt or even overly concerned. As Derek watched her, he saw fascination on her face.

Susan moved slowly and deliberately. Though she never stood, occasionally she would turn to observe the different activities occurring all around her. Throughout the meadow, several Sasquatches seemed to be relaxing in the morning sunlight.

The first two Derek and Josh noticed were sitting together off to one side. Both had reddish brown hair similar to that of an orangutan. One sat with its arm draped over its knee. In the creature's other hand, it held a small tree limb while it slowly chewed on one end.

The other looked nearly identical. Derek wondered if they were siblings. It sat behind the first. With both hands, this creature picked through the first one's hair. This grooming behavior was comparable to what Derek had seen other great apes do in documentaries.

An obvious female strolled through the meadow. Its appearance and stride reminded Derek of the Sasquatch from the Patterson-Gimlin film with one big exception. This one had honey-blonde hair. She stood approximately seven feet tall and topped out at probably 500 pounds. In her arms, she carried a bushel of branches and leaves.

A loud, high-pitched scream came from the area of the mound. Two apparent juveniles came charging out of the trees. Both were much thinner than the others were. Neither stood more than five and a half feet tall.

They ran through the field on all fours. They reminded Derek and Josh of a couple of young chimpanzees playfully chasing one another. As the two rushed past Susan, one reached out and brushed her hair with its fingers. Susan turned to watch as the blonde female grunted in apparent displeasure at the juveniles.

The female stopped a few feet from Susan and dropped the bushel of branches and leaves at her feet. Derek thought he heard Susan speak, but he could not make out what was said. He watched as Susan gathered up some of the branches and began to weave them together. The female squatted next to her and seemed to do the same.

For nearly twenty minutes, Derek and Josh watched in awe of what was occurring before them. Neither really knowing what the right thing to do was. Finally, Derek spoke.

"I'm walking in there." Josh did not say a word. He just stared at Derek as he unslung his rifle and set it on the ground next to Josh.

"I don't know what's going to happen. However, no matter what occurs to me. Do not react." Derek paused. "You will need to try and get her out if I fail.

"Remember what I taught you," Derek said as he looked at the rifle Josh held. "If you have to shoot, aim center-mass. Keep pressing the trigger until the target falls. Then find a new target. Don't forget, those are armor piercing bullets you have in that magazine."

With that, Derek slowly stood. Taking a deep breath, he stepped around the tree.

Understanding basic animal behavior, Derek recognized direct eye contact could be considered a threatening posture. Keeping his gaze cast low Derek tried to observe everything with his peripheral vision. He kept his arms visible in front of him with his palms facing outward.

Susan seemed to be the first to notice him. She sat erect as Derek saw the first look of fear cross her face.

The blonde female stepped in front of Susan, while the two involved in grooming stopped and stood, facing Derek. That is when a howl echoed through the clearing. Derek stopped in his tracks as a previously unseen, male Sasquatch came crashing out of the tree line across from him.

It was much larger than any of the other Sasquatches present. Nearly eight feet tall with thick muscles covered by jet-black hair.

This monstrosity brought both fists down, slamming them on the ground. Derek felt as if the whole clearing shook from their impact. Black then charged towards him. It propelled its body forward on its knuckles. With a roar and bared teeth, Derek thought this black one had begun urinating as it barreled violently towards him.

"Oh shit," Derek whispered to himself and he froze as the black creature quickly closed the distance.

Shutting his eyes Derek imagined the tackle Bennett had done to him a few days earlier. He was certain that was going to feel like a love tap compared to what he was about to endure. Derek inhaled deeply and waited.

Several moments passed. When the life-crushing impact did not happen, Derek slowly opened one eye, then the other. He saw Susan first. She remained where she had been. Her eyes were wide as she held both hands in front of her mouth.

The female and two siblings that had been grooming one another were not making any noise. Instead, they seemed to be gently swaying back and forth as if they were standing on the deck of a ship at sea.

Black, the one that charged him, had come to a complete stop just fifteen feet from Derek. Though it was displaying its teeth and breathing heavily, it was no longer looking at him. It was however, looking just past Derek's right shoulder. Even before he looked, Derek sensed his presence.

As slowly as he could, Derek began to turn. It stood just feet behind him. Derek gradually raised his eyes. Scar was even larger than the black one that had charged. As it inhaled, its barrel chest prominently displayed the zigzagged scar, which Derek instantly recognized. Its silver gray hair, the creature's second most prominent feature.

As adept as he is in the forest, Derek was amazed at how quietly this giant had been to be able to step within feet of him without his knowledge. Though he knew better, Derek looked Scar in the face.

As Derek locked eyes with it, Scar grunted and brought its arm forward. The impact, though not harder than a parent might reach out and grab a child, knocked Derek to the ground. He grimaced in pain as his ribs reminded him he should be relaxing at home and not interacting with giants. Scar stepped around Derek.

"DZJAÖ SÏ GLÖ MËKH PÜ" Derek felt the strength of Scar's voice as it vibrated within his chest.

The black one that had charged, grunted at Derek in what seemed to be either frustration or anger. Then, Black, as Derek began referring to him, turned and walked towards the mound throwing a hateful glance in Derek's direction.

Scar looked down at Derek. For several moments, the two stared at one another, before it, too, walked towards the mound.

Slowly Derek picked himself off the ground and Susan came rushing over to him. She flung her arms around his neck and hugged him tightly to her.

"Oh my God! This is incredible!" she exclaimed not releasing the hold she had on him.

"Are you okay?" Derek asked, taking her face in his hands.

"What? Yes, yes of course!" she said.

"They are like an entire community. And my God they are so intelligent." Susan was almost ranting. She pulled away but took ahold of his hand as she began leading him towards the center of the meadow.

"After I was brought here last night, it was like they all sat around and had a council meeting and decided to adopt me or something. Well, actually I think the black one wanted to eat me, but the female and Scar seem to be the Alphas."

Derek looked at the female. She stood not too far away, observing them closely. Her face, though not pretty, was surprisingly human with almost a motherly look. Hair covered most of her face, but where it did not, Derek saw many wrinkles showing her true age.

Her mouth was two to three times larger than a normal human's. The space between the bottom of her nose and top of her lip looked to be nearly four inches. As Derek looked into her large brown eyes, he saw both intelligence and kindness.

Susan dropped to her knees and pulled Derek down into a sitting position. "I've counted twelve distinct beings so far," Susan began explaining. "They have shown both great ape and human behaviors and they definitely have a language.

273

"I'm not sure," Susan continued, "but I believe there is an underground chamber that can be accessed over by that mound." She pointed towards the cave Derek had noticed earlier.

"Susan, we have to go," Derek stated, taking her by the shoulders. She looked at him as if he had just slapped her.

"We have to get our gear and record as much of this as we can!" he said, reminding her of their plan.

"No!" Susan said. "We can't. If we let people see what we've discovered it will destroy them. We have to keep this place secret. We have to protect them!" She was pleading.

For more than a minute Derek looked at her. He had only been in the meadow a few minutes but was also beginning to feel as if they had been given a special blessing.

Remembering the words of Josh's grandfather, *the answers may not be what you expect.* Derek could not explain it, but he agreed with Susan and began nodding his head. These creatures needed to be protected, not exploited.

"Well, Smith be damned, I guess we're gonna be fugitives," he said, smiling.

"Thank you!" Susan exclaimed and again threw her arms around him hugging him tightly.

Derek saw her react first. The blonde-haired female was no longer looking at Derek and Susan as her head had turned towards the tree line. She suddenly barred her teeth. Then Derek heard the noise as well. He knew what it was before he saw it.

During his time in the Marine Corps Special Operations Command, Derek had been involved in a number of clandestine direct action missions. These required him and his team to covertly enter and leave enemy territory. To accomplish this, they occasionally used HU-60 Ghost Hawk helicopters. These are the military's premier covert stealth helicopter.

Aside from the shape and design of the radar dampening airframe, much of the noise created by helicopters comes from the rotor blades; the Ghost Hawk corrected that issue with state-of-the-art noise reduction technology in the blades and a tail rotor placed within a shroud. Now the helicopter is virtually silent until it is almost on top of its target.

As the helicopter cleared the tops of the trees, it began to turn broadside to Derek and Susan. The female Sasquatch looked at Derek. He saw fear in her eyes. ◉

CHAPTER 29
"WARRIOR'S BOND"

As the helicopter came broadside, the side door slid open exposing the gunner within. Suspended by a stabilizing arm, the M134 mini-gun opened fire. Its six rotary barrels spun like a Gatling gun spitting out nearly six-thousand rounds per minute like a dragon's breath.

The female Sasquatch screamed in pain as she was struck. The multiple impacts of the 7.62 caliber bullets spun her around and she fell. Her large brown eyes filled with horror as she lay on the ground.

Susan began to move towards the female when Derek grabbed her. He pulled Susan to the ground covering her body with his own as rounds from the mini-gun impacted around them throwing clumps of dirt in the air.

The two siblings with the reddish brown hair began running towards the tree line. The helicopter's gunner turned the mini-gun on them. Derek watched, as one was struck squarely in the back. The multiple impacts propelled it forward. The Sasquatch landed hard, facedown, just feet from the trees. It remained motionless.

Derek grabbed Susan by the arm and yanked her to her feet. They began sprinting towards the opposite tree line. The gunner sent a burst of fire at their feet, stopping them in their tracks. Derek looked up at the helicopter. The gunner had the mini-gun locked on them. There was no place for either of them to run. Slowly Derek raised his hands, surrendering.

Susan was looking over at the wounded female who appeared to be struggling to breathe. Derek knew Susan wanted to rush to her aid, but he grabbed on to her arm keeping her from provoking another response from the helicopter.

With the gunner fixed on Derek and Susan, the helicopter began to land. As it touched down, four men, including the gunner stepped from within. The pilots remained inside as the rotor blades continued to spin. They were not planning to stay on the ground very long.

Three of the men wore full black tactical uniforms and held rifles at the ready. The fourth man was Smith. A triumphant grin crossed his face. They casually strolled towards Susan and Derek. As tears rolled down her face, Derek held tightly to Susan's forearm.

"Major Riley," Smith gleefully began as he clasped his hands together in front of himself. He walked close enough to touch Derek. The three, armed agents spread out, keeping their rifles pointed at Derek's chest.

"I must say this has been a very interesting run," Smith said, rubbing his hands together. "Rarely am I surprised by a series of events, but you, Major, have managed to surprise me."

"Well, why don't you have these guys lower their weapons and I'll be happy to surprise you again!" Derek said, not masking his contempt.

Smith laughed. "Oh, I think they will stay just as they are."

"How did you find us?" Susan spat.

Smith raised his eyebrows in mock shock.

"Well, you showed us dear. If it wasn't for your cooperation we would have never gotten this far nor would we have found this place," Smith proclaimed.

A look of confusion crossed Susan's face.

"I don't understand. I would never help you! You sick bastard!" Derek felt Susan's body wanting to lunge forward and attack as her muscles flexed under his hand. He tightened his grip on her.

Smith was again laughing as he reached out and grabbed Susan by her wrist. This is when Derek lost his composure and let go of Susan's arm. He took an aggressive step towards Smith.

One of the agents, anticipating Derek's reaction, swung his rifle. The rifle's stock struck Derek hard across the shoulders and base of his neck. Derek fell onto his hands and knees in pain. Smith looked at him then turned back to Susan.

"It was your watch, dear," Smith said as he removed her watch. "Before I sent this to you I had a tracking device installed in it."

Smith began examining the watch then tossed it on the ground where he immediately stomped on it. It cracked under the weight of Smith's boot.

Derek looked up at Smith and began calculating. He was not going to die on his knees. Not to this man.

"We nearly had you at the hotel," Smith continued to explain. "Then we tracked you to the reservation, however, I elected not to send armed agents onto an Indian Reservation to collect you. The last thing we need would be for some Indians garnering sympathy for some sensational news coverage like what happened at 'Wounded Knee' in 1973."

Smith was relishing his victory. He wanted Derek to know how much he had been in control of the situation.

"So we tracked you here to the forest. When I realized where you were going," Smith said, looking around the field while theatrically waving his hand, "I decided to let you lead us here. This way we could kill two birds with one stone, so to speak."

"You don't have to do this!" Susan pled. "They aren't harming anyone. They just want to live their lives."

"My dear," Smith said coldly, "they are abominations and need to be eradicated."

Smith turned towards Derek who met his gaze.

"Unfortunately," Smith sighed, "so do the two of you."

Smith glanced at one of the agents and gave a half nod. The man stepped forward and raised his rifle, aiming it directly at Derek's head. Derek was about to make his final charge when the shots rang out.

Three rounds impacted the agent square in the chest. The armor-piercing bullets easily penetrating through his body armor. The agent fell to the ground dead. This sudden change in events caused everyone, except Derek, to hesitate.

Derek leaped to his feet and tackled the man closest to him as Josh stepped from the tree line aiming his rifle. He began firing rapidly at Smith and the third agent as they began sprinting towards the waiting helicopter.

Susan ran towards the wounded female as Derek wrestled with Smith's agent. The agent was younger and faster than Derek. Each movement caused Derek shooting pains from his broken ribs and other injuries. As such, it did not take the agent long before he was able to break free of Derek's grip.

The agent's rifle had come off during the struggle. As they scampered to their feet, it remained on the ground between them. Slowly they began to circle one another. That is when Derek saw him.

Without a sound, Black had charged out from the tree line. A look of pure hate and fury on its face. The large black Sasquatch moved faster than when Derek first saw him. He froze in utter fascination. The other man saw Derek's gaze had changed. Instinctually he turned to see what Derek was looking at. He did not even have enough time to scream.

Black was on him. One massive hand reached out and grabbed the agent by his load-bearing vest. The black Sasquatch lifted him high in the air over his head. Then in one violent motion, he brought the man down headfirst striking the ground. Derek likened the noise to the sound a water balloon might make after being dropped onto concrete.

Smith had reached the helicopter and had climbed in. However, Josh had winged the agent running with him. This man had fallen behind clutching his leg and limping badly.

The sounded was the combination of air raid siren and a lions roar. Derek looked in that direction. Scar had also charged out of the trees. The gray speckled hair on its broad shoulders was standing straight up. It was making a beeline directly towards the wounded agent and helicopter. Scar almost appeared to be gliding across the meadow.

The agent Josh had wounded had also heard the howl. He turned and at the last moment brought his hands up defensively. It made no difference. As Scar reached him, his massive hand engulfed the agent's head. Without breaking stride, in one swift motion Scar detached the agent's head from his torso. He then flung the head across the field like a softball as he continued his charge towards the helicopter.

The Ghost Hawk had quickly lifted off the ground. It was nearly thirty feet in the air and rising when Scar leaped. Derek thought he was going to make it. Scar missed striking the helicopter by only an arm's reach. The valley echoed from Scar's scream of anger as he landed. The helicopter banked sharply away.

As it flew past, Derek saw Smith staring down at him. He felt the venom coming from Smith's glare. Derek raised his arm and gave Smith a middle-fingered salute.

Black was standing over Susan and the female utterly ignoring Derek. Though painful, the injury to the blonde female did not appear life threatening. Derek did not think she would be using her arm anytime soon.

While Derek watched, Susan and Black help the female to her feet. Josh had stepped from the trees and was slowly walking towards them. He had slung his rifle and had entered the field just as Derek had earlier. Scar was pacing him stride for stride, flanking him. Scar watched Josh closely. Josh, having just seen Scar pop a man's head off, was eye balling him back just as closely.

"Did we win?" Josh finally asked as he stepped up to the group. Derek looked around and shook his head.

"No, Josh. I'd call this one a draw." Derek stopped talking.

The unmistakable squelch of a radio transmission had begun. Derek quickly ascertained the noise was coming from the headset the dead man at his feet was wearing. Derek reached down and removed the radio. After wiping blood from the transceiver, he held it to his ear.

"Reaper-Six. Reaper-Six. This is Cleaner, Over." Derek recognized Smith's voice.

"Cleaner this is Reaper-Six. We have you five-by-five." Derek understood the terminology and realized Smith was talking to a pilot. They were using their call signs and the one designated Reaper-Six was acknowledging they had a good radio signal with Smith.

"Reaper-Six, you are cleared hot on your primary target," Smith directed.

"Confirmed, we are cleared hot on primary target located at 48.712130, -121.916590."

Derek recognized the coordinates as nearly the same as the ones given to them by Jacob. The redundancy in the communications was standard to ensure mistakes are not made.

"We are three minutes at fifteen even. Doors open. One Mark-77...."

Derek dropped the headset; he had heard enough. The meadow they were standing in had been targeted for a bombing run. Obviously, Smith had the plane on standby.

The pilot, Reaper-Six, had said they were at 15,000 feet and were going to drop a MK-77. The MK-77 is the direct successor to the MK-47, better known as napalm. This was the primary incendiary weapon currently in use by the United States military.

"We have to go! Now!" Derek commanded. He looked at Scar. He did not know how to communicate the urgency. Using his arms and pointing Derek yelled, "They're coming back!" Scar stared at him. Using both hands Derek tried to push Scar. The giant did not budge. "They are going to blow everything up!" Derek pleaded. Scar looked at Derek then towards the horizon. Derek nodded.

Grabbing Susan and Josh by the arms. "Run. As fast as you can!" he yelled. "Don't look back." They took off at a dead run. Derek followed behind them.

"Faster!" he urged.

As they reached the tree line, Derek paused and glanced towards the meadow. Scar and the others were gone. In the distance, he saw the unmistakable bat-shaped wing of the B2 stealth bomber. It had flown over the mountain and was coming directly at them. He turned and followed Susan and Josh into the forest. ◉

CHAPTER 30
"ROAD TRIP"

The Tacoma's radio was tuned to a news channel. The female broadcaster was just changing stories.

"In local news, the fire that has been raging in the northern Cascades has currently burned over 200,000 acres. Local fire officials stated the blaze is only 10 percent contained. According to officials, the remote location and difficulty in getting firefighting apparatus into the area are the largest obstacles."

"With us now is chief meteorologist, Richard Kirkland. Richard, thank you for being here."

"My pleasure, Carol," the male voice came across the radio.

"Richard, could you please explain to our listeners what you were telling me earlier?" the news broadcaster asked.

"Absolutely. Though this fire has taken hold late in the season, it is not terribly unheard of. Several factors have helped produce the conditions that we find ourselves in," the meteorologist stated.

"Like what?" prompted the news broadcaster.

"Well, the Global Climate change had helped spur a drier-than-normal summer. This coupled with some recent lighting strikes in the area, sparked the fire we see today.

"What many people don't realize is that the temperatures generated in a forest fire can sometimes reach upwards of 1500 degrees. That's as hot as a crematorium. This literally means the fire could destroy everything in its path. It will take decades for the area to fully recover."

"Thank you, Richard," the female broadcaster stated. "In other news the CDC...."

Derek reached over and with a click, turned the radio off.

"Do you think they escaped?" Susan asked, concern filling her voice.

"We did," Derek responded.

It had been nearly a week since their run from the bomber. Derek realized what a diabolical plan Smith had devised. The B2 bomber would not have been picked up on any civilian radar and the MK-77 incendiary bomb would destroy any evidence of the Sasquatch or their skirmish with Smith and his men. In essence, all history would ever show was there was once a forest fire in a remote area of the Cascades.

After escaping the forest, Derek, Susan and Josh met again with Jacob. Though divulging what they learned about Scar and the troop of Sasquatch had been taken off the table, even if they wanted to, there was no proof. Still, they needed to clear their names. To do this, evidence would be required. Jacob had told them to meet with a cousin of his in Nevada. According to Jacob, his cousin was a wealth of knowledge on Sasquatch and other cryptids. This is where they were currently headed.

They did not know if Smith was still looking for them. The fire caused by the incendiary bomb had spread quickly. With any luck, Smith may believe they had perished in the fire. Unfortunately, Derek did not believe Smith would make that assumption. Regardless, they were still considered fugitives. As such they had to maintain a low profile and avoid law enforcement contacts.

Derek had begun growing a beard. Susan had cut her hair short and had dyed it blonde. No one knew Josh; he had become their ace in the hole.

Brian Hall was insistent on helping as much as he could. He had been able to recruit a couple more members of the SRT to covertly assist them. This included a good friend of Marcus from the PsyOps unit. Brian had been able to obtain a couple of the false identification documents. The SRT teams sometime used these false identifications when working on covert assignments. With the assistance of Marcus's friend and by hacking into the DMV and other databases, they were able to develop a solid cover.

They had been traveling nonstop since leaving Washington, each sharing a turn driving and only stopping to fill the gas tank and use the restroom. To avoid unnecessary police interaction they made sure the cruise control was always set for the posted speed limit.

The last several hours had passed in silence. As 2:00 a.m. rolled around, Josh had fallen asleep in the back seat while Derek was snoozing in the front. Susan had taken over driving around 10:00 p.m. They had been traveling on State Route 95 since passing through Reno almost two hours earlier.

Route 95 was a very long, remote, straight stretch. There are virtually no streetlights, towns, or even buildings lighting their way. Theirs was the only vehicle on the road, with the Toyota's headlights the only illumination.

Derek sat up.

Immediately he was awake and alert. Derek did not know what had disturbed his sleep, but he knew it had not been one of his recent nightmares. He looked over at Susan; the soft glow of the dashboard illuminated her beautiful face. Feeling his stare, she looked at him. Neither spoke.

They drove in silence for a couple minutes. That is when Derek first noticed it. The glowing "orb" appeared to their east, nearly on the very edge of the horizon. As Derek watched the orb, Susan continued to drive. She remained looking straight ahead and did not appear to notice.

To Derek's amazement, within the span of a mere few seconds, this orb crossed the entire distance from the horizon and traveled to a spot just fifty yards directly in front of their vehicle. It had in essence, cut them off.

In complete and utter fascination, Derek and Susan watched as the orb immediately began pacing their truck. The glowing object maintained both its speed and separation.

Derek estimated the orb was about the width and height of a large vehicle. It glowed as bright as the high beams of any approaching car. This brightness however, did not require Derek to shield his eyes.

It maintained its momentum and distance with them, hovering roughly ten feet off the ground. As Derek watched, he could not see into or beyond the light. Neither could he make out any shapes other than the orb being a large, circular light.

For nearly twenty seconds this inexplicable light maintained both its speed and distance. Then without warning, it shot up into the western sky at nearly a forty-five-degree angle. It traveled away so fast to Derek's perception, its departure looked somewhere between being a blur of light to almost instantly disappearing.

Derek and Susan continued traveling in silence for what seemed like a several minutes.

"Did you see that?" Derek finally asked.

"Yes," Susan replied after a long pause.

"Do you want to talk about it?" Derek queried.

"Nope," she said.

With that, Derek turned and rested his head against the window. The high-strangeness they had been dealing with over the last few weeks had dulled their ability to be shocked and Derek drifted back off to sleep. They were still a few hours from Las Vegas. ◎

CHAPTER 31

"THE FUGITIVES"

Caesars Palace opened in 1966 and was Vegas's first themed resort. Some of the biggest names in entertainment including, Elton John, Celine Dion, and even Diana Ross have performed at the Casino. With over 4,000 rooms, Caesars Palace covers eighty-five acres in the heart of the Vegas Strip. Though sixty years have passed since it was originally built, Caesars is still one of the premier resorts and casinos in Vegas.

Of the six different towers, their room was located on the third floor of the Octavius Tower. Derek, out of habit, had always insisted they only take rooms located either on the second or third floors. When Susan asked why, he explained that rooms typically located on the first floor are easy targets for criminal activity within the United States and terrorism overseas.

Further, Derek informed both Susan and Josh that many countries outside the United States, do not have firefighting apparatus capable of reaching the higher stories. However, by selecting a room on the second or third floor, they would be able to escape relatively easily through any hotel room's window without too much risk of injury. This was important for other reasons as well.

Over six months had passed since the confrontation and fire in the forest. They were still on the run from Smith and his sadistic agents. Initially, Derek was hesitant to make Las Vegas their "hide-out" and in essence, their de facto base of operations. No place on earth has more surveillance cameras than Las Vegas. Derek knew agents working for Smith could use facial recognition software to identify them. However, after considering the downside, Derek recognized several factors worked in their favor.

First, each hotel and casino administer their surveillance systems independently. These systems are off-grid, not accessible through the internet and manned twenty-four hours a day, seven days per week. As such, they cannot simply be hacked. If Smith wanted his people to steal the images for review, they would need to physically break into each casino, and bypass the security measures and people in place, without being caught. This would mean each casino would be its own separate difficult operation and any mistake could expose Smith's covert activities.

Second, Smith could not overtly seek random warrants for the surveillance footage without probable cause for a specific location. There are over one hundred casinos in Las Vegas, each with two thousand or more cameras. Even a corrupt judge would have a difficult time justifying signing off on such a warrant. Additionally, absent a specific legal reason, the images from these cameras typically would only be maintained by the casinos for, at most, thirty to sixty days.

Finally, there are millions of visitors to Las Vegas every year. Derek knew it would take a whole team of personnel time to review the images and they may still never be identified. This was especially true since the arrival of an international pandemic. This virus provided the easiest way to remain completely anonymous. Specifically, for several months, everyone was required to wear a mask over their face. Even though the infection numbers have since dropped, and restrictions have eased, it was not uncommon for many people to still be seen wearing masks. Derek and Susan frequently used this to their advantage. By merely wearing hats, masks and walking with their heads down, it would be simple to avoid unwanted detection so long as they did not become complacent.

Not wanting to become overly familiar with members of any hotel staff, every few weeks, Derek, Susan, and Josh would move to a different hotel and casino. Derek realized they could do this indefinitely, never staying at the same hotel twice in a single year. However, some hotels were definitely more luxurious than others. This was their first stay at Caesars.

When they first went on the run, Derek and Susan initially considered quietly disappearing. Josh could even return to his life before Smith. This option would have been the easy route. With the help from sources close to Derek, he and Susan had acquired a number of false identifications. These identifications could easily pass even the most thorough inspection by law enforcement. More importantly, the two off-the-books credit cards provided to Derek were linked to millions in a "black budget." Few people knew about these and it was highly unlikely they would ever be audited. Over the last few months, Derek had used these to set up a number of legitimate credit cards linked to their many false identities.

Instead of disappearing, however, Susan and Derek wanted to clear their names and bring Smith and his killers down. For that, they needed evidence. This had been the start of their quest for the truth. Something else happened during the last several months as well. Without expecting to, Derek and Susan had fallen in love.

Derek sat up. Another nightmare had awoken him. As the sweat dripped from his forehead, he looked over at the woman lying next to him. Susan, concern in her eyes, was watching him closely.

"You had another bad dream?" Susan asked as she sat up in the bed, the sheet dropping to her waist.

Susan reached out and touched his tattoo. Prominently displayed on his left shoulder was an eagle standing on top of a globe and anchor, the symbol of the Marine Corps. Over the last few months Susan had grown accustomed to Derek's many nightmares. Though he did not speak often about his experiences in the Marine Corps and never openly discussed his dreams, she knew he had seen more disturbing events than most people would in their entire lifetime. As he had grown older, these experiences where manifesting in what most would describe as post-traumatic stress disorder.

Derek smiled as he looked at her. When they initially went into hiding, Susan had dyed her hair blonde. Recently, she had let it return to her natural color. Now, after a night of sleep, Susan's brown hair was in a general state of pillow disarray.

"Just a dream," Derek said out of habit. Then after a short pause, "except there was something different: Scar was there!"

Susan looked at Derek a little shocked.

"Tell me about it?" Susan queried.

"Well, there really isn't much to tell," Derek explained. "I was in the desert with some of my Marines and Scar appeared." Derek paused briefly before saying, "He said 'Help us!'" Without humor, he laughed at this last statement.

Susan considered for a long moment before speaking.

"We've learned that these creatures are highly intelligent and seem to even have a language. You and I have seen the work some researchers have put forth. For the most part, this is considered a viable theory. Even our own experiences at the cabin suggest they have this ability—"

"Yes, but English…?" Derek interrupted. "I highly doubt that."

"Not so fast," Susan shot back. "I don't believe they can speak English either. But let's not discount the possibility of communication entirely."

Derek slid out of the bed and pulled on a pair of jeans.

"Go ahead, Doc. You have me interested," Derek said as he took a seat in the plush chair found in most of the Caesars Palace hotel rooms.

"So, psychic connections, though not understood by any stretch, have been both identified and documented. Take the CIA's 'Remote Viewing' project we stumbled across last month. Even domestic dogs have been shown to have some type of psychic connection with their masters. How many stories have you heard of pets going to the window or door before the owner even arrives home? Or those stories, and there are many, of a pet being left behind when a family moves across the country only to find their way to the owner's new home?

"Additionally," Susan continued, "there have been reports, of Sasquatches, 'mind-speaking.' Honestly, when I first heard of this phenomenon, I completely discounted it; however, I don't believe going forward we should ignore any possibility."

"I highly doubt I have a psychic connection with Scar," Derek said, nodding.

"Well, probably not," Susan replied, as she, too, slid out of the bed. "But we shouldn't disregard it either. We are probably the only humans Scar even remotely trusts."

Susan walked over to where Derek sat. She bent forward and kissed him.

"I'm going to jump in the shower," she announced.

"Do you want some company?!" Derek smiled as he began to stand.

"Down, Clyde!" Susan laughed as she pushed him back into the seat. Since they were both fugitives and a couple, Susan had occasionally referred to Derek and herself as Bonnie and Clyde. "Order me some breakfast."

As the door to the bathroom closed, Derek stood and peered out the window. Their room overlooked the several pools of the casino. These pools had been decorated to look like old Roman architecture with pillars and marble lions. The largest, a circular pool in the center sported a golden statue of Julius Caesar standing in the middle.

Though early in the morning, and following the hotel's social distancing guidelines, a few people had already gathered in the lounge chairs arranged near the different pools. While looking at them through the window, Derek picked up the telephone and pressed the nine button.

"Room Service. How may we help you?" the voice on the other end of the line said. Derek ordered two deluxe omelets with bacon and hash browns, as well as two cups of coffee and orange juice.

While Susan showered, Derek dropped to the floor and knocked out a quick two hundred push-ups. He then rolled over and did an equivalent number of crunches. Derek was in the middle of stretching when he heard the shower turn off. A few moments later, Susan turned on the radio they had placed in the bathroom. A country western song was playing. Derek heard Susan begin singing along. Smiling, he continued to stretch.

Several minutes later, there was a knock on the door.

"Room Service," the voice on the other side said.

Always cautious, Derek tucked a pistol in the back of his trousers before peering through the peephole. Satisfied it was safe, he opened the door. Leaving the door open, the young hotel staff member pushed the serving cart into the room. As the waiter placed the two meals on the small round table near the window, Susan came out of the bathroom wearing jeans and a T-shirt. Smiling at the waiter, she took a seat at the table. Derek signed the check and thanked the young man.

As the waiter left the room, Derek began to shut the door. A hand came up and stopped it from closing. Josh casually pushed the door back open.

"Good morning, my peeps!" Josh said.

Before Derek could invite him in, Josh walked into their room with a swagger in his step. When Derek and Susan initially went on the run and they suggested Josh return to his normal life. He had staunchly refused. He was caught up in the events and fully committed to seeing it through to the end.

Josh entered their room every day at about the same time. He had a copy of their room key and they had his. Derek had explained the redundant keys were for security if there was ever a need. However, instead of knocking, Josh, oblivious to personal boundaries, frequently used the key anytime he wanted to talk with them. On more than one occasion he nearly caught Derek and Susan in a compromising position.

After crossing the room, Josh took a seat opposite Susan. As Derek watched, Josh picked up a fork and began cutting into his omelet. This, too, had become a common theme for Josh. Derek smiled.

"What's on the agenda for today?" Josh asked. "Hand-to-hand training or are we going to the range?"

Derek shut the door to the room. Over the last several months, he had been training Josh and Susan almost daily on different aspects of combat. Occasionally, Derek would even have them drop in at a local Jiu-Jitsu school so they could practice what he had taught them.

Josh, in fact both of them, had become quite the adept students. Since that first confrontation with Davis and Bennett at the cabin, Susan and Josh had come to realize how important combat skills may become necessary. Josh had even cut his hair in a style similar to Derek's. Susan once quietly told Derek, it was out of admiration, as Josh's own father had never spent much time with him.

"Oh, you have to try the bacon!" Susan said, pointing with her fork. Josh picked up two pieces and stuffed them in his mouth.

Derek, still smiling, walked across the room and retrieved the coffee from the table. It was all he really needed. They had become an odd sort of family, he thought.

"No, Josh, we aren't training today. Remember we have a meeting in a couple hours," Derek reminded them both. "It took us a couple weeks to set this meet up. I don't expect any issues, but we shouldn't take any chances. We should try to get there an hour or so early just to check the place out."

Neither were listening to Derek but instead giggling about something silly Josh had said. ◉

CHAPTER 32
"THE MEETING"

After being framed for murder, Derek and Susan had two goals. The first was to clear their names. The second was to bring down Smith and those who worked for him. They decided the best way to do this was to discover proof of the government's conspiracy and cover-up then turn the information over to the media. That was easier said than done.

Initially, the focus was narrow, as they were only looking to determine what the government was hiding regarding Sasquatch. They had traveled to Nevada to meet with Jacob's cousin. He in turn introduced him to another source who then provided the name of yet another person to meet with. Over the next several months, this is how their investigation expanded.

Many of the people they met were only able to provide anecdotal evidence to their theories. Unfortunately, few wanted to come forward officially and none so far had been able to provide anything resembling proof in a court of law, let alone something that would clear their names. Like pulling on a string, one meeting led to another. They hoped their luck was about to change.

About one month ago, Derek and Susan met with a former physicist who had previously worked at Los Alamos National Laboratory. He told them that a few years earlier he had been recruited to work on a project at the S-4 Site located near Area 51. His specific task involved reverse engineering the propulsion system of an "alien space craft." Again, this scientist was only able to provide witness testimony to what he had personally seen.

To Derek and Susan's dismay, again, he did not want to say anything official. Even if he had, Derek knew his testimony alone could be easily discredited. During their last meeting, the physicist provided them with the contact information for a quasi-friend who apparently had actual proof.

Derek, Susan, and Josh had become proficient at performing countersurveillance. Derek taught them the importance of awareness and blending in. They practiced frequently and became increasingly more adept after each meeting. Today was no different. Sticking to the plan, Josh called an Uber, leaving about thirty minutes before Susan and Derek.

As Smith and his agents were unaware of Josh, he was going to arrive early and casually perform a reconnaissance of the area, specifically looking for government vehicles or people loitering without purpose. Anything, or anyone, out of the ordinary would warrant further scrutiny and they would not hesitate to pull the plug on the meeting if necessary.

As Derek and Susan pulled out of the Caesars Palace parking lot headed towards the meeting, Josh telephoned them.

"It looks good," Josh said. "I had the Uber driver drop me off a block away and I walked in. I didn't see anything that stood out."

"Where are you now?" Derek asked as he turned their Toyota Tacoma north onto Las Vegas Boulevard.

"I took a seat at the back of the restaurant facing the door like you taught me," Josh replied.

"Okay, call us back if anything changes," Derek directed and hung up.

It took about fifteen minutes to drive to the Denny's Restaurant where Derek set up the meeting. As this was to be the first interview with this informant, Derek had told him that, both he and Susan would be wearing Seattle Seahawks baseball caps. This would make it relatively easy for the contact to identify them.

They turned onto East Charleston Boulevard, driving west for about ten minutes. Pulling into a residential neighborhood, Derek circled back onto Bishop Drive, where he pulled over about a block north of the Denny's. Derek grabbed a pair of binoculars. The restaurant shared a common parking area with several other businesses including a Walmart. While Susan checked to make sure no one nearby was watching, Derek scanned the area with the binoculars. He did not see any concerning activity.

Pulling away from the curb Derek drove into the parking lot. Casually he cruised up and down each row of cars. Everything seemed normal. People pushing carts of groceries, mothers corralling their children and a mixture of civilian vehicles was the common theme. Satisfied they were not in any immediate danger, Derek parked closer to the Walmart than the Denny's. Then he and Susan stepped from the truck.

Due to the pandemic, wearing a face covering had become second nature. It provided Derek some level of comfort knowing they would not be easily identifiable. Still, as they crossed the parking lot both Derek and Susan scanned the area.

"Paranoia will keep us alive," Derek would often say when planning these meetings. Both half-expected to see men, clad in black tactical uniforms, rushing towards them. None appeared.

Derek chose this particular restaurant precisely because it was in a residential neighborhood. Unlike the Vegas strip, other than inside Walmart, there were no cameras in the parking lot or restaurant. Additionally, the residents of any area, always have a different look than tourists or outsiders. Anyone nonlocal would become easier to pick out of the crowd.

As they entered the lobby of the Denny's, a sign was posted indicating they needed to wait for the hostess to seat them. Scanning the restaurant, Derek saw Josh sitting in the back not far from the restrooms. Josh was facing the front door. Aside from momentary eye contact, Josh ignored them entirely. He had set up a laptop and looked like any college student writing a paper. There were a few other folks in the dining area, but as the lunch crowd had not yet arrived, the restaurant was mostly empty except for the staff.

A young girl in her late teens, walked up to them. She was wearing an apron and a nametag identifying her as "Kelly."

"Just the two of you?" she asked with a pleasant smile as she grabbed two menus from the hostess podium.

"We are expecting a third," Derek replied. Kelly turned and grabbed a third menu.

"Can we have that booth right there?" Derek pointed to a large booth situated between Josh and the front door.

"Absolutely!" Kelly replied as she walked them to the booth.

Susan slid in first as Derek sat next to her. The red vinyl of the booth's seat squeaked as they sat. They both were facing the front door. A large picture window provided them an unobstructed view of the parking lot. Derek knew Josh had their backs covered.

"Can I get you anything while you wait?" Kelly asked as she handed them the menus.

"Just coffee for now," Susan replied with a smile. Kelly hustled away.

"I'm going to take a quick look around," Derek said as he stood.

"Hurry back!" Susan grinned as she began to rearrange the salt, pepper, tabasco sauce, and various packages of jelly that had not been uniformly placed on the table.

Derek first walked to the restrooms. He would have Susan check the ladies' room momentarily. The men's room was small with only a couple of stalls and two sinks. There was no one inside and only a small window that no adult could fit through. This was both good news and bad. No one could approach them from that direction, but they also could not escape that way either.

As he returned to the table, Derek glanced in the durchreiche, the serving hole that separates the dining area from the kitchen. Two men in white chef's jackets were working near the grill beside a pantry and freezer; there was an emergency door at the back of the kitchen. It was propped open. This seemed normal but did give Derek some concern. The final emergency exit was located on the far side of the dining area.

Kelly dropped off their coffee, two glasses of water and walked on. Derek sat and explained to Susan their primary and secondary escape plans if it became necessary.

They sat quietly for about thirty minutes. Occasionally, Kelly would return and top off their coffee or ask if they needed anything while they waited. A few other people had entered the restaurant. A young couple and one family with an obnoxious two-year-old. Kelly sat the family at the far side of the restaurant so the child's tantrums would not bother the other patrons too much. Derek decided he would tip her well for that.

A man shuffled into the restaurant. His shoulder-length gray hair still had streaks of brown. It was receding and looked as if it had not been washed in more than a couple of days. His goatee was untrimmed and stubble lined both sides of his face. Though he looked considerably old, by the wrinkles around his eyes, Derek estimated he was actually just a couple years older than himself.

Under the tattered cardigan sweater, his dirty white tank top had a mustard stain that remained prominent above his beer belly.

Besides a worn leather satchel, blue sweatpants and wool socks inside Birkenstock sandals completed his attire.

Derek was ready to dismiss the newcomer as a homeless man until he made eye contact with him. Ignoring Kelly, the man turned and walked directly towards Derek and Susan.

"This is our contact?" Susan whispered under her breath as the man slid into the booth opposite them.

Kelly sat a glass of water on the table then poured the gray-haired man a cup of coffee.

"Can I get you anything to eat?" Kelly asked doing a stellar job hiding her general disgust with the newcomer's appearance.

"We're fine," both Derek and Susan said in unison.

The gray-haired man set the leather satchel on the red vinyl seat next to him then clapped his hands together.

"I will have the chili-cheese burger with extra onions. I will also have a large Diet Coke. And my friends here have graciously stated they will be picking up the check," he said, indicating with both hands towards Derek and Susan.

Having written the order down, Kelly stuffed her note pad and pen in her apron, collected up the menus and headed towards the kitchen.

"I believe introductions are in order," he said, smiling through his shaggy goatee. "I do like the Seahawk's though they never seem to actually start playing until late in the third quarter!"

"I'm Derek and this is my colleague, Susan," Derek said, leaning across the table and extending his hand.

The sleeve of his tattered cardigan dipped into his coffee as he took Derek's hand.

"You can call me John," he said. "John Winoski." ◉

CHAPTER 33
"DISCLOSURE"

For the next twenty minutes, John explained his initial time in the military and how he was hired onto the Protective Forces at the NTS. Susan sat enthralled as he told the story of the "Gillman" he discovered in a warehouse. It was not until he began talking about his first meeting with Smith that Derek became truly interested.

"Well," John continued, "Smith didn't exactly threaten my life. He said I had two choices. The first being I could work security at the Groom Lake facility. What most people would call Area 51. For my second choice, he said my life, as I currently knew it, would become quite uncomfortable." John made air quotes with both hands as he said that last part. "The death threat was implied."

"So, they just brought you into the secrecy fold?" Derek asked suspiciously.

"Not exactly," John said while he shoveled in a bite of the chili-cheese burger Kelly had brought him.

"For the first couple of years, they kept a pretty tight leash on me. They had me providing security for the low-level facilities at Groom Lake. So, I kept my nose clean. Eventually, it was as if they forgot to be concerned about me. As it is to this day, almost everyone working out there is flown in daily via JANET Airlines."

"I'm sorry, did you say JANET Airlines?" Susan asked. "I have never heard of them."

"Of course," John said, grinning; a little piece of chili had stuck to his front tooth. "JANET Airlines is the covert airline the CIA uses. Other than a red strip running down the fuselage the aircraft, typically a Boeing 737, is unmarked. We always joked JANET was an acronym that stood for Joint Army, Navy, and Extraterrestrial. Anyways, they fly out of McCarran." He paused and wiped his chin on the sleeve of his cardigan before explaining.

"That's McCarran International out of Las Vegas. Some employees would stay in the barracks for a few days. Others would simply perform shiftwork flying in and out. The air traffic controllers working at McCarran did not really pay attention to the unmarked JANET planes comings and goings as they had been a common theme for nearly forty years. The security on the site performed random searches of the employees from time to time as we left to ensure we didn't bring any materials out."

"If they searched you, how were you able to sneak evidence out?" Susan asked.

"Easily. It was my buddies working security who were performing the searches. Just like police officers don't write each other speeding tickets, there was a level of professional curtesy afforded between the officers I worked with," John explained.

"Anyways," he continued, "like I was saying, after a couple of years of me keeping my nose clean, I think Smith forgot about me. Manpower issues had my supervisors assigning me to higher and higher-level security details and eventually I was assigned to the S4 Facility.

"Once there, I had access to just about everything. Then my wife left me about ten years ago. When I retired in 2018, like everyone who leaves or retires, I was told if I ever talk about my work at

Groom Lake and specifically S4, I would be charged with treason at a minimum. So, I've been just banging around here ever since."

"Why did you choose to come forward now?" Derek asked.

"That's easy. Six months ago, I was diagnosed with pancreatic cancer," John stated matter-of-factly.

"I'm so sorry," Susan exclaimed, reaching across the table and touching John's forearm.

"Don't be, dear," John said as he patted her hand. "My doctor says if I undergo extensive chemo, I might extend my life by a year or so. Well, fuck that! I'm going to go out of this world on my terms. What in the hell can that shit-fuck Smith possibly do to me? Kill me, I'm already dead. Kill my ex-wife and in-laws? Well, I certainly hope so!" John said with a half-laugh.

"Not trying to be insensitive here, John," Susan began, "but how could a lowly security guard obtain the highly classified information you state you have?"

"No offense taken, but amazingly, most scientists think like you. Actually, it was relatively easy," John replied. "Just because a person doesn't have formal degree, doesn't mean a person isn't intelligent or educated. Most people see security personnel as little more than furniture. Over time, they forget we are even present. I began collecting information as early as 1989," John explained.

"At first I was simply listening. We had one big cafeteria on the main site, though S4 was a different animal. There, we mainly just had breakrooms. Anyways, I would often plan and take my lunch breaks sitting at tables near different scientists. While I pretended to read the paper or work on a crossword puzzle, the scientists would often talk openly about what they were working on or discuss issues they were having with different aspects of their projects. As they did, I would write key words and phrases into the boxes of the crosswords. Then later, after I got home, I'd transcribe the conversations up as best as I could remember it.

"As personnel had to fly out of the site nightly," John continued, "the protocol was to ensure all classified information was properly secured before they departed. Typically, the scientist viewed security as an inconvenience they had to tolerate. Many considered locking up classified material as ridiculous as they were in a secure facility that required a chartered flight to even get there. When they left their offices, more often than people realized, the scientists would simply leave their material and offices unlocked. Out of curiosity, I once asked one why. She told me it was a waste of their time as they would just have to get the information back out of the safe the very next day.

"So, the S4 facility has five levels. One ground level and four below ground." John was smiling as he described the site. "The first two levels were designated for the back-engineering programs of the different crafts and materials they had control of. Levels three and four where designated for the EBE's cooperative and uncooperative testing programs and living quarters."

"Excuse me, but what is an EBE?" Derek asked.

"I'm sorry, everything is acronyms," John said fanning his hands out as if to encompass the world around them. "EBE stands for Extraterrestrial Biological Entities. Finally, the lowest level was where they did their dark testing and human experiments."

"What do you mean human experiments?" Susan sounded horrified as she asked the question.

"I will come back to that," John answered. "Anyways, like I was saying, security at the main Groom Lake facility was not too tight. Hand geometry and access codes were the standard. But the S4 Facility, that was where security was top notch, at least on initial appearance. Each floor required retinal scanning and other increasingly more difficult security measures the deeper into the facility you went."

"I thought retinal scanners were a Hollywood concoction," Susan stated.

"Actually, the first retinal scanners came about around 1975, but that is another story," John continued. "So, access to each floor was incrementally more difficult unless you were part of the security forces, which I was. Once a person entered each individual level, security frankly broke down and was a joke. During the nighttime rounds, I would frequently find unsecured doors. Before I secured them, I would snoop around.

"Back in the late 1980s and early 1990s," John continued, "very little was kept on secured computer terminals. If I found something interesting, I would either walk it down to the Xerox machine or simply take notes. Rarely did I report the unsecured door. If I did, the scientist would have gotten a security infraction and it would have made them more cautious in the future. As security measures changed or became enhanced, I figured out ways around them.

"Even when computers first became common in the 1990s, security enhancements typically were little more than a password. Again, most of the same scientists simply wrote their passwords on a yellow sticky note and left it under their key-board or in their desk drawer." Derek found himself nodding in agreement with everything John was saying. He had seen this basic disregard for security firsthand.

"So, what do you have for us?" Derek asked.

"Well before we get into that, I think a little history lesson would be appropriate." John smiled as he dipped a few french-fires into some ketchup.

"Absolutely, why not?" Derek said. Having removed his mask earlier, he took a sip of his coffee and leaned back in the booth.

"The United States formal UFO cover-up essentially began with President Harry Truman," John recounted. "He had been the vice president for barely eighty-two days when he had to take over the Office of the President following the death of Roosevelt. Remember he was thrust into a running World War. He first became aware of the Manhattan project and had to make the decision to drop the atomic bombs. He inherited a world in chaos. Then, with all that going on, imagine what was going through his mind when the head of the OSS, a guy named Bill Donovan, knocked on the door to the Oval Office and told him what military intelligence knew about alien contacts."

Derek thought about what John was saying. Truman had to have been under tremendous pressure following the end of World War II. Then jumping right into the cold war with Russia, a country that had also just obtained atomic weapons. Concealing information must have been almost second nature.

"Truman became so concerned about what he heard"—John's history lesson continued—"by Executive Order, he formed a secret group within the government to monitor, collect, and control all information related to UFOs. This secret group was codenamed Majestic Twelve or MJ-12. Truman then appointed Admiral Forrestal to be in charge."

Susan and Derek exchanged a glance upon hearing Forrestal's name. They had first heard of Forrestal when Derek asked his friend Marcus Pettiford to look into Smith. What Marcus told Derek was that it appeared as if Forrestal had been murdered when he made it clear he wanted to come forward with what he knew. Subsequently, it was shortly after that conversation, Marcus himself was killed by Smith's men.

"The code name MJ-12 has changed a number of times over the years. I don't know what they are currently calling themselves." John took a drink of his Diet Coke before he continued.

"The first UFO recoveries came in the late 1930s. There were a few more in the early 1940s. Most people never knew about those. Then came Roswell, which the public found out about. They recovered two live aliens from the Roswell crash. One died shortly thereafter, but the other one lived until about 1956.

"From that, the government found out there are eighteen different alien species currently monitoring earth. Some of them are good, some are hostile, but most are simply indifferent to us," John said flatly. As he spoke, Susan realized she was staring openmouthed.

"Wait!" Susan interrupted. "From everything I have ever heard, I thought aliens were supposed to be enlightened and were here, visiting Earth, to help us!?" Even as she spoke, the words, Susan instantly regretted them. She realized she had been asked very similar questions during her own lectures regarding Sasquatch.

"You would be wrong," John replied. "Look, before I came to meet you, I looked you up. You're an anthropologist. In nature, when does the prey animal ever dominate the predator?" Before Susan could respond, John answered his own question.

"They don't. Rabbits will never rule over the lions. Even in our own cultures, where have the weak ever dominated the strongest or most aggressive? It simply doesn't happen. In fact," John continued, "many consider the Tibetan Buddhist monks to be some of the most enlightened people on our planet. For the purpose of this analogy, let's call them the sheep. Their society, for all practical purposes, hasn't advanced an inch in a thousand years.

"Sure, some now have smartphones available, which they didn't create, but in the truest form, their culture, or society has not changed. The only reason the Chinese Communist Party, let's call them the wolf, hasn't wiped them off the face of the planet is because the United States and other strong nations stand up for them. Like a sheep dog.

"So, if this is the cycle throughout nature and human history," John summarized, "that the strongest or most violent are in charge, why then would an alien culture be different? Why would we assume the most dominant advanced alien species be the rabbit and not the wolf?

"Then ask yourself this," John continued, "if aliens were simply here to 'help us,'" he again made air quotes, "what is it they are waiting for? Are they waiting until the global climate change has destroyed the planet? Or are they waiting until we actually shoot nukes at each other? Point being, they aren't here to help us and they really don't care about climate change. That's just wishful thinking bordering on fantasy."

"I can't argue with any of that. But if they are not here to help us, why are they here?" Derek asked.

"What MJ-12 has discovered during the last seventy years is the human race has been the experiment or product of an alien presence whom we don't believe we've met. Nor do we know who they are. What we are sure of, is the 'greys' are biological cybernetic organisms. Basically, they're nothing more than glorified biological robots or drones, that occasionally operate with a collective brain. The greys are here at the behest of their employers. These beings look like giant bipedal praying mantis. They are monitoring us through abductions. However, that is just the tip of the iceberg, other alien species are abducting us too."

"Are the greys or their 'employers' good or evil?" Derek asked with an emphasis on employers.

"That would depend on which side of the abduction you are on," John replied. "Let's go back to the enlightenment theory. Even scientists from societies who consider themselves enlightened take animals out of their natural habitat, abduct them so to speak, then perform experiments on them. From the scientist's point of view, they are doing so for basically three reasons."

Holding up his hand, John began ticking off numbers with his fingers. "One, to increase their understanding of nature. Two, improve the life of the species they are abducting or, finally, to enhance their own society. For the scientists, and governments funding them, these reasons may seem lofty and noble, but from the animal's point of view, would be considered hostile." John paused and took a bite.

"Now look at the human race; although we are all human, every culture within humanity is different. Here in the United States, we eat cows," John said, pointing at his plate with a fork. "But Hindus consider the cow to be sacred. When performing experiments on animals, the way animals are treated during medical experiments is vastly different in the United States than in Russia for instance.

"So, let's go back to the alien abductions. I know for sure one group is performing these abductions with both the blessing and cooperation of our government. There could also potentially, be other groups within the same species. These groups may view and treat humanity differently. In other words, just because members of one 'group' within a species is good doesn't mean another 'group' of the same species is as well." John took another bite from his chili-cheese burger.

"What are the experiments about?" Susan asked.

"The EBE's the government is working with have never actually told us, and MJ-12 has never been able to find out," John said. "Even if we were told, we could not be assured it was the complete truth. They are both liars and deceivers."

John's term, *deceivers* reminded Derek of how his Sunday School teacher once described, Satan and his minions.

"We do know," John continued, "that we have been externally corrected multiple times and they frequently refer to us as 'containers.'"

"Containers? What does that mean?" Derek asked.

"There was some speculation that the souls our bodies contain are the reason for the experiments. Though most of the scientists working at S4, don't believe in God, they theorize the experiments have to do with reproduction and DNA. But as far I have been able to determine, there has been nothing proven.

"Personally, I think there are several experiments occurring. Once, while on the fifth level, before the door closed, I saw Smith and some others in a room with some greys. There was a woman there. She was strapped to a medical table and was obviously terrified. A short time later, I saw her as they wheeled her from the room. She appeared comatose. Almost like a zombie. I never did discover what they did during these experiments."

"Are you saying the people they are abducting are being taken to Area 51?" Susan said incredulously.

"Well, S4 actually," John replied. "For all practical purposes Area 51, Groom Lake, has been shut down. There has simply been too much media attention over the last fifteen years. S4 is still in operation. Most everything else has been moved to other bases around the world. From White Sands in Utah to Antarctica, there's the underground facility in Dulce, New Mexico, even the Pine Gap facility located smack dab in the middle of the Australian outback."

"I understand what you are telling us, but from everything I understand the earth is on the far edge of the galaxy. It would take too long to travel such a great distance. We are talking thousands of years or more. It would not be worth the effort," Derek said.

"Yes, that would be true if you are thinking about our current technology," John replied. "Even a hundred years from now, we won't have the ability to travel such great distances without cryogenically freezing ourselves. But that is assuming two things. The first being that the aliens are merely a few hundred years more advanced than we are. What if they are a million years more advanced, or a billion?

"The second is one dimensional; what if some of these beings can travel through multiple dimensions? Some of the research conducted at S4 had to do with advanced propulsion technologies that are capable of gravitational time dilation. Drawing energy from the vacuum and utilizing wormholes. Point being, our understanding of time, propulsion, and travel, for all intents and purposes has barely begun.

"Since about 1938 we have lost over two hundred aircraft to UFO hostilities and thousands of soldiers. Most of these were called training accidents. Since that time, several hundred thousand civilians have also disappeared without a trace.

"Then there is the slightly more horrible phenomenon known as human mutilations which have occurred," John said as he sipped on his Diet Coke.

"Excuse me? Human mutilations?" Susan exclaimed sounding a little shocked.

"These are similar to cattle mutilations," John described. "Humans are taken, then their bodies are returned usually about forty-five minutes to an hour later with their rectums cored out. They've had their genitals and eyes removed from their sockets and their bodies completely drained of blood." Chili sauce dripped onto John's goatee as he took another big bite of his chili-cheese burger.

"In all cases," John continued, speaking while chewing, "it appeared as if the mutilation procedures occurred while the subjects were still alive and conscious. One of the scientists at S4 speculated that the humans had to be alive for the samples to be of any real value."

"Okay, no offense, John, but this is getting a little bit far-fetched," Derek said, preparing to end the interview.

John put his fork down and reached into the leather satchel with both hands. Derek and Susan watched as he flipped through several stacks of papers. After a few moments, he produced an eight-by-ten, color photograph and dropped it on the table in front of them.

"Here we have a picture of a twenty-two-year-old male who went missing from his own backyard. The police looked for him for two days. Then his body suddenly returned to that same backyard." Susan inhaled audibly as she and Derek looked at the photo.

It was as John described; the young man was completely naked. His eyes, genitals and ears appeared to have been surgically removed. No blood was visible. Derek flipped the photograph over as Kelly approached them. None of them spoke as she topped off their coffees.

"Abductions occur throughout the United States almost on a daily basis," John began when Kelly walked away. "When the government first learned of this, they protested to the grey they had at DOE's Y2 Facility in Los Alamos."

"How did they overcome the language barrier?" Susan asked as one of her doctorates was in linguistics.

"I am not exactly sure," John admitted. "I did hear some talk of telepathy and the use of pictographs. There were also some rumors about certain members of our government learning their language, but unfortunately, I have no real information on that.

"Regardless, meetings occurred and after some back and forth, the government or rather MJ-12 agreed to limited abductions in exchange for some of their advanced technology. MJ-12 was periodically provided a list of abductees. To almost no one's surprise the number of abductions was a substantially greater than agreed to and the technology we received was considerably less."

"But the United States is being provided alien technology?" Derek asked.

"Yes, we then back engineer it," John answered. "Think about this. For at least 5,000 years, maybe longer, humans traveled by horse and cart. We were still using horses and carts during the first world war barely a hundred years ago. Then in the span of roughly sixty years, we went from horse and cart to landing a spaceship on the moon. That didn't happen simply because we suddenly became smart on our own. We had some guidance."

"What kind of guidance?" Derek asked.

"Okay, so do either of you know anything about, Muroc Army Airfield and Test Center? It's now called Edwards Air Force Base, if that helps," John asked.

"Isn't that where Chuck Yeager broke the sound barrier?" Susan replied. Derek looked at her, impressed. Most people would not have been able to answer the question.

"It's one of my favorite movies," Susan said with a shrug after catching Derek's gaze.

"Yes," John confirmed. "Anyway, it was shut down for three days in 1954, from February 19 through February 21. At the same time, President Eisenhower left Washington without alerting the media, which caused quite a stir. He had to because Eisenhower was meeting with another alien species at Muroc.

"This EBE suggested they could help get rid of the greys for us. Unfortunately, Eisenhower turned them down because they refused to provide our government with any advanced technology as the greys had been doing.

"For Eisenhower, it became apparent the perceived notion of God, at least as he had come to understand it, was incorrect. During this meeting, we also discovered that some aliens had been using their technology to influence different religions. This bothered Eisenhower so much he had 'In-God We Trust' put on all of our currency and in the Pledge of Allegiance to reaffirm the public's faith in God. Of course, different reasoning was given to Congress for these additions.

"Since then, the greys have been trickling the technology to us such as magnetic weaponry. Did you know we have conducted nearly one hundred tests of magnetic weapons? Of course, this has caused the deaths of thousands of birds and put many citizens in the hospital with neurological issues. But when you consider the 'greater good....'" John again mockingly made air quotes.

"Much of the EBE technology is now run through DARPA," John said, then remembering his earlier statement about acronyms added, "The Defense Advanced Research Projects Agency. Some overtly. Some covertly—"

"Okay, this is a great story," Derek said, interrupting, "but do you have anything to corroborate what you are saying?"

"It is hard to keep secrets," John said with a sly smile. "And rumors immediately came out that Eisenhower met with aliens at Muroc. In fact, at about the same time, a radio talk show host named Frank Edwards, who had millions of listeners, reported and discussed this openly on his show. But that is not everything." John motioned towards the eight-by-ten picture and again began digging in his leather satchel. He produced another eight-by-ten photograph. This one was a black and white.

"The government loves its pictures. Knowing this was going to be a historical meeting, a photographer assigned to Army Intelligence took a number of photographs," John said as he dropped the photo in front of them.

Derek picked it up as he and Susan studied it intently. Eisenhower was prominently centered in the photograph. Several men in suits and a few uniformed officers Derek did not recognize were standing behind him. At first glance, Eisenhower appeared to be greeting just another human but upon closer inspection the differences were obvious.

This being was quite tall, well over six and a half feet but slender with almost delicate features. Its eyes were large, at least two or three times the size of a normal person's. Though he could not tell by the black and white photograph, his straight shoulder length hair appeared blond. Derek thought this entity looked like one of the elves from those books about the "Hobbits."

For several moments, Derek and Susan just stared at the photo. Then John broke the silence.

"We call them the Nordics, but we think they actually come from the Pleiades star cluster. From what we understand, they have been here since the beginning. After this first meeting, Eisenhower enacted a policy of absolute secrecy on UFOs and EBEs."

John dug through his bag one more time and produced a copy of a Department of Defense Document. It was classified "Top Secret." Derek quickly scanned the document a few words leaped out at him.

DOD Document
Dated 1 March 1954
Mandate 0463
"Under no circumstances are the general public or public press to learn about the existence of these entities. The official government policy is that such creatures do not exist."

"In the late 1950s, NASA was formed to collect and obtain all information about the aliens," John explained. "The government sold NASA to the public by claiming it was strictly for space exploration and all information would be public knowledge. This was far from the truth. What the public did get was highly sanitized.

"Those involved in the cover-up regularly eliminated anyone who was part of the operation and made even the slightest inclination on disclosure," John said flatly.

Derek and Susan looked at one another. They knew from firsthand experience that this type of direct action could occur. Smith had sent a couple of assassins to kill them both. When that failed, he had them framed for murder.

"The project and associated cover-up began to get bigger and bigger," John continued his story. "The defense budget had to be inflated to meet the demand. That was not enough. So, the government got into the drug business, and that was still not enough.

"It is so out of control now many involved want immunity or simply out; however, there is so much deception and double and triple blinds in place it is unlikely it will ever be completely dismantled especially when you consider the amount of money and power that is associated with disclosure," John stated flatly.

"How is that even a consideration? What about the good they could do?" Susan asked.

"So sure, a person might think, what about the limitless energy potential, or medical advancements such as a cure for cancer. Those ideas would be true if the government's motivation was based on the betterment of mankind." John paused. "But what if the government's motivation is about control?

"So, it appears, one of the primary propulsions utilized by the crafts that have been studied involve anti-gravity technology. If this information was released and became mainstream, it would provide a cheap and effective alternate energy source. Basically, it would make obsolete the need for oil, coal, nuclear, and any other energy sources," John explained.

"This means the annual loss of trillions of dollars, huge industries and a complete shift of the global economy. You can make the same statements about the medical and pharmaceutical industries and the trillions of dollars they make annually. Then consider, which politicians do these industries donate to?

"Recently the government began to disseminate insignificant pieces of information such as the blurry 2004 'Tic-Tac' video. But for the most part they are still not disclosing what they truly know. Even if the government decided to provide additional information to the public, it would be so watered down all they will really say or release would be something like, 'yes we are aware there are craft, but we don't know much about them.' At absolute best the government may say, 'yes we did collect a flying saucer and there was a body.' I doubt any of the other information would ever come out," John concluded.

As an afterthought, John added, "And all that is assuming the government themselves are not being manipulated by the EBEs."

"Okay, you have our attention," Derek replied while Susan nodded her agreement. "Unfortunately, there isn't anything here that could stand up to the disinformation campaign that would surely happen. Do you have anything more useful?"

John smiled broadly.

"I only brought a few things with me, but I have access to thirty years' worth of material. I'm talking documents describing classified programs, research and back-engineering projects. I have the names of some of the abductees who were taken and held at my facility. I have photographs of spacecrafts, alien bodies, and aliens meeting with government officials such as Eisenhower. Not just computer images but the old 35mm and 8mm negatives and films."

"These negatives and films are the originals that couldn't be easily faked. They were in archives at the S4 Site. Once they had been transferred into digital images, no one ever really reviewed the originals. Turnover was such that most may have forgotten they were even there. I also have a directory of every person who worked at S4 from about 1990 until I retired in 2018."

Derek knew they had hit the motherlode, then John dropped the bomb shell.

"I also have Smith's personnel file." ◉

CHAPTER 34
"SURVEILLANCE"

Jimmy Russo's transfer had come through three months ago. His new area of operation was southern Nevada, which included the S4 site. Smith had primarily tasked Jimmy with monitoring recent retirees from S4. Unfortunately, there were now so many retirees and others it would have taken a hundred agents to consistently monitor everyone. Instead, Jimmy had to prioritize and put them on a rotational list.

During Jimmy's first month in Nevada, he mainly monitored the women. That was until Smith chastised him for taking images having little to do with national security. Not wanting to disappoint Smith further, Jimmy began taking his job seriously. He focused on everyone equally, usually never spending more than a day or two on any specific individual. He was mostly monitoring them for abnormalities in their daily routine.

Today, as he had two new recruits in training, Jimmy picked what he considered a low-level threat. Some old dinosaur who once upon a time worked security at the site. If one of the recruits made a mistake, it would not matter much. This was the fourth time Jimmy had conducted surveillance on Winoski. The man never did anything exciting.

They began following Winoski when he had left his home. Jimmy thought it odd that he made a few completely random turns but according to everything Jimmy knew about this person, he was by nature, odd. Their target pulled into a Walmart parking lot and circled the building twice before parking. Jimmy and the recruits watched as Winoski shuffled to the Denny's restaurant next door.

Though he could requisition an official vehicle from the Homeland Security motor pool, Jimmy was always trying to perfect his craft. To do this, he avoided anything that screamed "government." Unfortunately, all the GSA vehicles stood out. A few months earlier, shortly after arriving in Nevada, Jimmy presented Smith with a sound argument and was subsequently rewarded with some discretionary funds to purchase and set up a couple of surveillance-specific vehicles.

Today they were using two. One of the recruits sat in a silver Honda Accord. They used this vehicle to follow and give chase if necessary. It remained parked out of view a short distance away. Jimmy referred to the agent in the chase vehicle as Tweedle-Dee.

Jimmy and the other recruit, who he called Tweedle-Dumber, sat in an older-model Honda Odyssey minivan. The minivan was the primary surveillance rig. Jimmy had even attached a couple of bumper stickers to each vehicle. One read, "baby on board" while the second said "Proud Parents of Hyde Park Middle School Honor Student." Both vehicles were completely nondescript and downright boring.

Either would have seemed normal in any suburban setting. Initially, Jimmy was not happy about having to use excessively dark tinting on the windows. It was necessary to keep the cameras and other equipment inside hidden from the casual observer. However, as this was the Nevada desert and sunny almost year-round, it was not uncommon for many vehicles to have some level of tinting.

What Jimmy did not know was that the recruits had flipped a coin to see who would be stuck in the minivan with him. Neither cared for Jimmy and considered him somewhat of a weasel. While the recruit who won the coin toss sat in the chase vehicle, remaining hidden a few blocks away, Jimmy and the other had continued to follow Winoski.

They had parked a short distance away. As Jimmy watched from the back of the minivan, Winoski entered the Denny's restaurant. He passed the digital camera, equipped with a massive Canon EF 800mm lens, to the recruit. Unconcerned anything was going to happen; Jimmy retrieved an empty water bottle and began to pee into it.

"Ah, sir," the recruit said just as Jimmy began to urinate, "it looks like Winoski is meeting up with some people inside."

Jimmy's research and prior experience with Winoski had him pegged as a loner, one step from being a homeless hermit. Meeting people for lunch was out of character. Jimmy hurriedly fastened up his trousers. He did not care that he had dribbled a little urine onto the floor of the minivan or down the front of his khaki pants as he did so.

With damp fingers, Jimmy took the camera from the recruit. He immediately zoomed in and adjusted the manual focus. As the trio finished shaking hands Jimmy began snapping pictures. Jimmy had access to long-range listening devices. These could pick up sounds by bouncing micro lasers off objects such as glass. Not believing this surveillance would amount to much, he had not brought them along.

For a moment, he considered sending the recruit into the restaurant. There, he could sit near the trio and hopefully pick up on their conversation. Unfortunately, this kid looked like a poster boy for "G-man Magazine." Jimmy figured he would be made as an agent fifteen seconds after he walked in. Since the primary key to covert surveillance is to remain covert, Jimmy decided digital images would have to suffice.

They watched as Winoski passed some papers across the table.

"What is he passing to them?" the recruit asked while looking through the extra set of binoculars.

Even the massive telephoto lens was not able to pick up what the papers had been. Jimmy took more pictures. The couple must have removed their masks shortly after arriving inside the restaurant. Jimmy zoomed in on their faces and took more images. There was something familiar about them, he thought. Especially the female.

For nearly forty-five minutes, Jimmy and the recruit monitored the trio in the restaurant. As Winoski appeared to finish his meal, he stood. Jimmy took more digital images with his camera as Winoski again shook the couple's hands.

"Sir, do we continue to follow him?" the recruit asked as Winoski began to walk out of the restaurant.

"Of course not, you idiot!" Jimmy spat. "We know who he is. We need to identify who these two are and where they are going."

A few minutes after Winoski left, the couple walked out the front of the Denny's, Jimmy watched as they pulled their face masks up. This now looked more like an attempt to conceal themselves rather than as protection from a virus. He expected them to walk to a vehicle parked near the front of the Denny's. Instead, the couple was walking towards them.

As he continued to observe, Jimmy noticed that the man seemed relaxed, though purposeful in his movement. The female however, only gave the appearance of being casual. Jimmy zoomed in. Although her face was covered with a mask, her eyes were not. Jimmy saw she was scanning the parking lot while trying not to appear as if that was her intent. He moved the camera to the man's face. Though not as obvious, he was doing the same thing.

"Holy shit!" Jimmy said. "They're doing countersurveillance." To Jimmy's horror, he realized they were going to walk right past their surveillance van.

"Close your eyes. Don't move. Don't even breath," Jimmy told the recruit.

Having spied on people nearly his entire life, Jimmy believed people can sometimes sense when others are watching them. He even tested this by staring at people from across a room until that person looked up from whatever they were doing and made eye contact with him.

As the couple closed the distance, Jimmy looked down focusing his gaze on his own feet. Less than twenty feet away, they walked past the van. Jimmy did not think they noticed.

"Watch them," Jimmy said when they were far enough away. "We need to know what vehicle they get into." Jimmy picked up the handheld radio, calling the recruit in the chase vehicle.

"Merlin to Baby-Bird," Jimmy said, using the radio call signs he had decided on. "Wake up and standby for a rolling surveillance."

"It looks like they are getting into a silver-gray Toyota Tacoma," the recruit sitting next to Jimmy said. "They are pulling out onto East Charleston Boulevard." Jimmy passed the information on to the chase vehicle. Jimmy slid into the front seat of the minivan and started it up.

A few moments later, both surveillance vehicles were following the Tacoma. To avoid being obvious, they took turns as the either lead or trailing vehicle. Neither got closer than three car lengths from the Tacoma they were targeting. Due to the high volume of traffic coupled with the nondescript vehicles they were using, Jimmy knew it would be very difficult for them to be discovered on a rolling surveillance.

"They're pulling into the parking lot of Caesars Palace" came Tweedle-Dee's voice over the radio.

"Wait three minutes, and then follow them in. Find out where they parked, then let us know," Jimmy directed.

"What should we do now?" asked Tweedle-Dumber.

"Do you have your Homeland Security credentials on you?" Jimmy inquired.

"Yes," he replied as he pulled his credentials from his pocket.

"Okay, good," Jimmy stated. Then hesitantly said, "I need to call Smith." ◉

CHAPTER 35
"THE VATICAN"

Reading any travel brochure, a person might get the impression Rome always smelled of coffee, spices, and a mixture of floral scents. As many things often are, the truth can be terribly disappointing. Like any big city, a person could frequently come across walls or curbs that reeked of urine or puke. Other common odors included rotting food from alleys or exhaust fumes from buses and taxis. However, on nights like this, following a heavy rain, the ancient sewage and drainage lines, not designed to accommodate the addition of millions of tourists, have the streets of Rome stinking like an overfilled port-a-john.

Though a Cadillac logo on the grill was prominently displayed, the vehicle was actually designed and built by General Motors. It only looked like a sedan. It was actually a heavily armored vehicle built on a truck chassis. It was similar to the one used by the President of the United States. That vehicle was codenamed "The Beast" by the Secret Service.

Foot-thick doors and bulletproof glass were only some of the security features. The vehicle had been designed to withstand a hit from a rocket propelled grenade or roadside bomb. It even had built in tear-gas launchers and an emergency medical station equipped with the protectee's blood type.

As the limo turned onto Viale Viticano, the road bordering the Vatican, the driver had to expertly navigate the narrow streets. Unlike in the United States, large vehicles are not as common in Europe. This is not because the Europeans prefer compact vehicles or because they are more Earth-friendly than Americans. Instead, large vehicles are not common simply because they are not practical for navigating through the many ancient cities with cobblestone streets that had originally been designed for slow moving horse-drawn carriages.

Smith sat in the back reviewing the dossier he had been provided. He had worked within the shadow government since he was nineteen. That was near the end of World War II when he was recruited into the Office of Strategic Services or OSS. It was, however, his intelligence and willingness to do whatever was necessary to complete the mission without remorse, which brought him to the attention to the newly formed Majestic-12. His fluency in multiple languages was also advantageous. It did not take long before he was their go-to man when a problem needed to "disappear." Once again, a tasking had been assigned.

There are two well-known entrances into Vatican City. One is through the Vatican Museum, accessible from Viale Vaticano along the northern side of the city. The second main entrance is St. Peter's Basilica, on the southeastern side of the city. This entrance is accessible from Via Della Conciliazione. There is even a third formerly "secret entrance" known as the Passetto Del Sant'Angelo. This connects the Vatican to Castel Sant' Angelo. During the siege of Rome in 1527, this secret entrance allowed the Pope to escape from the German and Spanish mercenaries.

On top of Castel Sant'Angelo is a statue of the Archangel Michael. According to religious accounts, during the dark ages, following the fall of Rome, a plague descended upon the city. Bodies of the dead filled the streets. Pope Gregory led a prayer for the end of the plague. As he watched, the Pope observed the Archangel Michael appeared on top of Castel Sant'Angelo. Radiating brightly, the Archangel brandished his sword, ending the plague.

Then there is a fourth, almost unknown entrance. Hidden in the wall along the western side of the city, the door, barely large enough for a man to step through, is virtually invisible. It can only be opened from within the Vatican. Known as the Exploratorem Ostium, it was used to shuttle the Church's spies in and out of the city 500 years earlier.

As the limo pulled up to this concealed door, Smith set the dossier on the seat next to him. Few people knew his true identity. This anonymity provided its own level of security. Still, for his personal security, Smith always traveled with a two-agent protective detail. After the vehicle came to a complete stop, Jack Baldwin, one of Smith's specialized agents stepped from the vehicle. Slowly he scanned up and down the street searching for potential threats. Satisfied it was safe, Agent Baldwin opened the limo's door for Smith.

When Smith slid from the vehicle, the hidden door to the Vatican opened. A Wachtmeister, or sergeant of the Swiss Guard stepped through to greet them. The Vatican has been protected by the Swiss Guard since the fifteenth century. Most people see the Swiss Guard standing near entrances or performing ceremonial duties. Tourists frequently can be seen photographing the Swiss Guard as they wear the traditional blue-and-orange-striped uniforms with puffy trousers, holding halberds and occasionally wearing shiny armor. Underestimating them was common. It would be wrong to do so.

To become a member of the Guard, recruits must be single males, Catholic, and of Swiss citizenship. Though the general requirement is that they must have completed basic training with the Swiss Armed Forces, most members of the Swiss Guard formerly served in the Swiss Special Forces. Following the assassination attempt on Pope John Paul II in 1981, enhanced training in weapons and tactics became standard.

The Wachtmeister of the guard gave Smith a quick salute as he approached.

"I apologize for utilizing the Exploratorem Ostium, signore. His Eminence, Cardinal Contarini requested it," the Wachtmeister stated with complete sincerity.

"It is perfectly fine. Being discrete is my preference as well," Smith replied with a smile.

As Agent Baldwin, assigned to protect Smith, began following, the Wachtmeister held up his hand. "I am sorry, signore only Mr. Smith."

Smith looked at Baldwin and gave a slight nod. The agent stepped back to the limo. Standing near the passenger door, Agent Baldwin faced the secret entrance to the Vatican and crossed his hands in front of his waistline. Regardless of how long he was gone, Smith knew Baldwin would be standing in that same position when he returned. Entering the Vatican grounds, Smith followed the Wachtmeister.

The Secretariat of State, is the cardinal who oversees the Vatican's relations with other countries and serves as the top ranking official in the Holy See's bureaucracy. This cardinal's position is the oldest and most important dicastery of the Roman Curia, second only to the Pope. Over the last few decades, the office of the Secretariat accumulated increasing authority over finances and job hires, taking on roles analogous to prime minister and chief of staff in the papal court, as well as that of top diplomat. Rumors of corruption were whispered throughout the halls of the Sistine Chapel.

Pope Benedict XVI, was ill prepared to deal with the internal politics of the Church. The stress became too much and in 2013, he became the first Pope in nearly six hundred years to retire from the position.

Following Pope Benedict's retirement, Jorge Mario Bergoglio became Pope Francis when he was elected the 266th Pope of the Roman Catholic Church. Pope Francis did not have the problem with leadership Pope Benedict had. His first order of business was to disrupt the bureaucracy of the Church. He started at the top; ending the power of the Secretary of State by "retiring" Cardinal Tarcisio Bertone. He then dismantled the overreaching power of the office, reshaping the department to one solely involved in diplomacy.

Pope Francis then appointed Cardinal Gasparo Contarini to the position. Unlike Contarini's two predecessors, who preferred to be chauffeured around in limousines along with their many aides, Cardinal Contarini frequently walked alone. His approach to the position was much more evangelical.

Smith's concern was not that the new cardinal could not be as easily corrupted as his predecessors. Smith even respected the honesty of the man. Instead, Smith's interest was for the cardinal's background and the direction Cardinal Contarini had been influencing the Pope to take the Church.

Cardinal Contarini was a man of science. He had obtained his Bachelor of Science in 1979 and his master's in Operations Research a year later at Massachusetts Institute of Technology, known to all as MIT. The cardinal then went on to obtain his PhD in planetary science from the University of Arizona's Lunar and Planetary Laboratory.

After his postdoctoral research and teaching at the Harvard College Observatory, he was ordained. Contarini was then assigned as an astronomer to one of the oldest astronomical research institutions in the world, the Vatican Observatory. Ten years later, the Pope asked him to serve as a member of the Council of Cardinal Advisers.

Cardinal Contarini's push towards radical changes within the church needed to be curtailed.

As they walked between the immaculately trimmed hedges of Lourdes Gardens, a bishop approached them. He was wearing the traditional black robes and red fascia. The bishop's head was down, apparently deep in thought. As they grew closer, the bishop raised his eyes and briefly smiled preparing to greet Smith and the Wachtmeister. That was until he caught Smith's gaze. Instinctually, the bishop dropped his sight back to the ground. Shuddering involuntarily as they passed, the bishop crossed himself and said a silent prayer.

The Apostolic Palace, also known as Papal Palace, is home for both the administrative offices and many who reside in the Vatican.

Smith followed the Wachtmeister into the Palace. Together they began climbing several flights of stairs. Reaching the top, they walked down a long hall, their footfalls echoing off the stone and marble construction. They passed several large meeting areas including the ornately decorated Clementine Hall. At the end, the Wachtmeister brought Smith to a sturdy wooden door. Knocking hard, the guard stepped to one side.

Slowly, the door opened revealing Cardinal Contarini standing on the other side. Though he greeted Smith with a smile, there was no warmth behind it.

"Come in, Johnathan," Contarini said believing he was using Smith's given name.

"Thank you, Flynn. Please wait here. This should not take very long," Contarini said, looking at the Wachtmeister. Smith was not surprised the cardinal knew the Wachtmeister's first name. He was that type of person.

"I appreciate you seeing me on such short notice," Smith said, walking into the room.

Contarini's smile faded as he closed the door. He regarded Smith for several moments before speaking. Contarini was a foot shorter than Smith and quite thin. Though he was in his late sixties, Contarini's face was youthful, almost boyish. He radiated energy.

"I cannot say that I am pleased to see you, Johnathan. However—" Contarini briefly paused before continuing. "—when a distinguished member of the little conspiracy between your country and my Church calls, it is the least I can do." As Contarini spoke, he did little to hide his displeasure. He turned and entered the small room.

They were not meeting in Contarini's official office but instead his private study. The room was not very large, though quite comfortable, almost homey. Covering one entire side of the room was a floor-to-ceiling bookshelf that was lined with numerous first edition books and other writings. Many of these first editions had little to do with religion or theology.

On the opposite wall was a fifteenth-century painting of the Madonna. Below the painting, nearly twice the size of a beach ball, sat a large sixteenth century, Italian mahogany globe. The globe was enriched with gold foil finishes and nautical maps from that era. Centered in the office was Contarini's wooden desk. It was positioned to provide the cardinal with a view of St. Peter's Basilica.

"Your Eminence," Smith began, "we are not yet ready for the Church to reveal the truth. I realize you were not present when our arrangement was made and I appreciate you may not agree with it. You must, however, understand that at the time we all determined this was in the best interest of all our people."

"Maybe there once was a time when such considerations needed to occur," Contarini said, sitting at his desk. "But that time has passed. People are far more knowledgeable and accepting in this modern age."

"Are you not concerned about how people will react?" Smith asked. "All the research we have conducted indicates the truth could have drastic consequences. What of the scandal?"

"Of course, we recognize some people will be upset, however the Church has withstood other scandals. We will survive this. Fortunately, extraterrestrial intelligence exists whether people wish to believe in it or not," Contarini replied.

"The best thing the Church can do," Contarini continued, "is to get ahead of it and ease our faithful into this acceptance. Doing so will ensure the shock is not as traumatic. It will be better for all to know, than to discover not only of the existence but that their Church has been lying to them about it."

"So, can you at least tell me how the Church plans on exposing the truth without damaging its influence?" Smith asked. "Surely, the Pope is not planning on coming forward with everything all at once, I hope?"

"The existence of other life does not preclude the existence of God," Contarini replied. "Belief or faith of one does not have to be at the exclusion of the other. The first sentence of the Bible is 'God created the Heavens and the Earth.' Well, what are the heavens if not other planets and peoples?

"The Church already started down this road a few years ago when we acknowledged the possibility of existence. Though I personally would like to move a little more quickly, I believe his Holiness will want to proceed with a little more caution. Over time, maybe a year or so, we will slowly disseminate information to the population. The first order of business is to get the people comfortable with the idea that existence is possible," Contarini said, explaining the plan.

"Is the Pope settled on this course of action? Is there nothing I can say or do to persuade you otherwise?" Smith asked, already knowing the answer to both questions.

"Fear of the unknown is often worse than the actual unknown. My mind is set, but the Pope will require a little more convincing. I have a meeting with him in the morning to discuss possible paths forward," Contarini replied.

"Very well," Smith sighed. He knew the actual unknown was worth fearing. "If that is the path you have chosen, I will not attempt to change your mind further." Looking at the globe Smith asked. "Can I make us a drink to celebrate this new chapter in our cooperative histories?"

"Why not?" Contarini replied with a smile. He began to feel considerably more relaxed. He had been expecting a difficult fight with Smith to include threats coming from Washington.

Smith walked to the wooden globe. It was in actuality a hidden liquor cabinet. Hinged at the meridian level, Smith began to open it. Raising the top revealed not only a bottle of Louis XIII Cognac in a crystal decanter but a few elegant Tulip glasses widely agreed to be the king of cognac glasses.

"That is a very interesting painting you have on the wall, your Eminence," Smith said nodding his head at the fifteenth-century painting of the Madonna. While talking, Smith removed the decanter and began to pour two glasses.

Contarini stood and walked to the painting. Turning his back to Smith he began admiring the art hanging on his own wall.

"That is the Madonna with Saint Giovannino," Contarini said in appreciation of the painting. "It was illustrated by Domenico Ghirlandaio during the Renaissance."

Smith's hand moved slowly over one of the tulip glasses. Even had Contarini been watching closely, he might not have seen the clear, odorless, and tasteless liquid Smith expertly added to the cognac. Satisfied, Smith extended the glass to Contarini.

"The painting was hung at the Palazzo Vecchio in Florence," Contarini said, taking the glass from Smith. "When I showed an interest, they were generous enough to allow me temporary custody of it."

"To the Madonna," Smith said, raising his glass.

"And the future," Contarini added.

Smith saluted with his glass. While taking a sip, Smith carefully watched Contarini drink from the tulip glass he had given him. Smith began a silent count in his head.

"Did you notice anything strange about the painting of the Madonna, Johnathan?" Contarini said, taking another taste of the cognac.

"No," Smith said, smiling slyly. "What did I miss?"

"Do you see the shepherd and his dog standing behind the Madonna?" Contarini asked. "Look closely at them."

Smith began scrutinizing the painting more meticulously. Then he saw it. Standing in the painting's background was what appeared to be a shepherd and his dog. Neither were looking at the Madonna. Instead, they were both peering up into the sky. Above them was a disc-shaped object looking much like a UFO.

"Interesting," Smith admitted.

Contarini smiled and returned to his desk. After another sip, he set his glass on the desk.

"Were you aware much of history's most famous artworks are littered with aliens and UFOs?" It was more a statement than a question.

"Leonardo da Vinci, famous for his hidden images, painted the face of an alien in his Saint John the Baptist," Contarini pulled on his collar with his index finger as he spoke. Smith began watching him closely.

"The Baptism of Christ, painted by Aert De Gelder, also depicts a disc-shaped object shining beams of light on John the Baptist and Jesus. Even throughout the written word of God, to include the non-published scrolls, stories of extraterrestrials are intermixed with our own. Such as the book of Ezekiel which describes creatures visiting Earth in a wheel-shaped craft." As Contarini spoke Smith observed beads of sweat begin to form on his bald forehead.

"There was a thirteenth century book, *Otia Imperialia*," Contarini continued, "which includes accounts of a being descending from a flying craft over Bristol, England. Even the log from Christopher Columbus's first voyage onboard the Santa Maria contains a report of strange lights rising up from the ocean, then circling his ships." Smith was nodding in understanding of what Contarini was saying.

"In 1604, to end a dispute in the Anglican Church, King James the First, ordered the creation of a standardized bible? The King James version remains the most famous and common Bible in history. However, there are only sixty-six books within the King James Bible, while the Catholic Bible has seventy-three books, and the Ethiopian Orthodox Bible has eighty-one books. So, the question then becomes, why were so many books edited out over time?" Contarini quizzed Smith.

"I do not know the answer to that," Smith admitted.

"It was because, not only do these texts infer the possibility of extraterrestrial life, they also show a very different side of God. For example, the priests at the time considered the Book of Enoch too controversial to handle so it was concealed and hidden from the population," Contarini explained.

"Throughout many ancient cultures, China, Greece, Egypt, India, even Sumeria, there have been detailed accounts of extraterrestrials. None has the detail as The Book of Enoch. It is because of this controversial detail that the text was removed from the Bible.

"For instance, in the Book of Daniel there is a group of angelic entities known as watchers." Contarini's breathing began to sound more labored. "These watchers are briefly mentioned, saying they have been ordained by God to direct the affairs of man. They look over our world and help control our destinies.

"Nowhere else can you find a description of the watchers, except in Enoch. While only briefly mentioned in Daniel, these beings are the primary focus of the book of Enoch. Enoch teaches that not all encounters were of a divine nature. In Enoch, two hundred of these watchers ended up descending to earth. They were known as the shiny ones." Contarini shook his left arm.

"When the Dead Sea Scrolls were discovered, Biblical scholars ascertained these were of significant religious importance. Within these scrolls were copies of the Bible that were more than a thousand years older than any previously known copy. This included chapters from the Book of Enoch not previously identified, as well as the Book of Giants, which supposedly had been written even before Genesis. Unfortunately, these, too, failed to meet canonical criteria.

"Religion never wanted to say that human beings were the center of the universe. This is a misunderstanding of the old cosmology. Acknowledging that extraterrestrials have coexisted with our histories would certainly inspire theologians to develop new ways of thinking about topics like original sin, the immortality of the soul, and the meaning of Christ's redemptive act." As Contarini spoke, his eyes began to show internal concern.

"I am suddenly not feeling too well," Contarini said and began to stand looking to Smith for assistance.

Placing his glass of cognac on the edge of the desk, with a catlike grace, Smith moved towards Contarini. Initially, he thought Smith was coming to his aid. Then Smith grabbed him. With a strength belying his age and slight frame, Smith forced Contarini back into his seat.

As one hand held Contarini's shoulder, pressing him into the seat, his other hand pushed up on Contarini's chin, closing his mouth. Using his two long middle fingers of the same hand, Smith pinched Contarini's nostrils closed, essentially shutting off his ability to both yell for help and more importantly, breathe. Contarini's eyes widened in panic as he struggled against Smith's grasp. Smith leaned in mere inches from the cardinal's face.

"Forgive me father for I have sinned," Smith said, smiling. "It has been decades since my last confession and I have committed every sin. Including, most recent, murder. The reason you are not feeling well is because you are having a heart attack." Smith leaned closer.

"Point two six grams," Smith whispered into Contarini's ear. "That's what your soul weighs." Contarini continued to fight in vain against Smith's viselike grip. Slowly the struggle lessened until it ended all together.

Releasing his grip, Smith propped Contarini back in his chair in a more natural position. He then picked up his own glass of cognac. Smith raised his tulip glass towards the dead cardinal then in one gulp finished the cognac.

Developed by the clandestine services of the CIA, the poison Smith had used causes its victims to quickly succumb to a massive cardiac arrest. One of the benefits was it could not be detected even during laboratory testing. Smith, however was always cautious. Taking the glass of cognac he had given Contarini, Smith poured it out the window. He then wiped down both glasses and returned everything to where they had originally been.

Satisfied the death scene looked "natural" Smith stepped to the large wooden door. He opened it just wide enough for him to slip through. Smith's tall frame blocked the vision of the Wachtmeister standing outside. Smith closed the door behind him.

"His holiness said he needed time to pray and reflect. He asked not to be disturbed but requested you escort me back to my car," Smith said as casually as a person asking for the time of day.

"Of course, signore," the Wachtmeister said.

Ten minutes later, Smith was in the back seat of the Cadillac satisfied that even if his presence threw suspicion on the cardinal's death, nothing could be proven. While his security detail was driving him back to the airport where his private plane waited, his phone vibrated.

"Mr. Russo, don't tell me you are calling to complain about one of my agents again." Smith answered after reviewing the caller ID.

"No, sir," Jimmy Russo replied with obvious concern in his voice. "We were conducting surveillance on retiree John Winoski, when it appeared he had a clandestine meeting." Smith vaguely remembered the name.

"Did you document it?" Smith asked.

"Yes, sir. I am sending you an image now."

Smith's phone chimed indicating the arrival of the message. Opening the image, Smith used his fingers to enlarge the picture. Derek Riley and Susan Parker stared back at him. Smith's eyes momentarily widened. He grew quiet.

Two minutes passed in silence as Smith considered both the ramifications and his options. Having had no sign of them for several months, Smith had hoped Riley and Parker had perished that day in the forest. Unfortunately, he always suspected they had survived. The ever socially awkward Jimmy finally broke the silence.

"Ah, sir. Are you still there?"

"Be quiet: I'm thinking!" Smith snapped.

Another couple of minutes passed before Smith finally spoke.

"Do you know where they are at this moment?" Smith queried.

"Yes, sir," Jimmy replied, happy to have an answer. "They parked at Caesars palace. I have had their vehicle tagged and we are identifying what room they are staying in as we speak."

"Okay, listen carefully," Smith began. "I'm going to email you an encrypted file. I want you to save it to your hard drive."

"Okay?" Jimmy replied, a little confused.

"Now this is what I want you to do." For the next couple of minutes, Smith gave Jimmy precise instructions. He made Jimmy repeat the instructions back to him. Satisfied, Smith hung up the telephone. He smiled.

If Jimmy were to be successful, this little problem would be solved. If he failed, the backup plan would be initiated. Either way, Smith did not think Jimmy, or the agent trainees would be alive much longer. That however, was not important. They could be replaced. ◉

CHAPTER 36

"HOMELAND SECURITY"

Before departing, Derek passed John Winoski a disposable telephone. This was so they could call one another anonymously without concern of government agents listening in. Derek had programed his number into it. They all agreed to meet back at their hotel room in Caesars Palace in two days. John Winoski said he would bring copies of everything he had. He said there was enough material that it could easily fill two suitcases. Meeting at the hotel would be good cover, as he would look like any other guest checking in.

Once in the room they would be able to sit down in relative safety as John went through and explained each piece of evidence. From there, they would be able to catalog and prioritize it. At John's insistence, he recommended he provide a video testimony to what he knew and saw. Derek knew it was important to get this on the record, due to John's terminal cancer.

When Susan and Derek finally left, Josh waited an additional ten minutes before following them out.

After returning to Caesars Palace, Derek and Susan decided they wanted to get some exercise. The excitement they felt about the direction John would be able to take them had their adrenaline pumping. After changing, they planned to utilize the hotel's fitness center.

Josh however wanted to get in a little target practice. He told Derek and Susan he was going to the Clark County Shooting Complex. He said he would meet back up with them when he returned. Derek said he thought it would be a good idea for them to all go to dinner that evening.

This would be both a quasi-celebration of this recent turn of events as well as to conduct a debrief of the day's activities. Susan often teased Derek about his inability to step away from his role as a Major with the SRT.

After grabbing his range bag, Josh took the keys for the Toyota from Derek and quickly departed. He knew if he waited too long, the afternoon crowd would fill the shooting range. As their adrenaline began to diminish, Derek and Susan, began to drag their feet about working out.

About forty-five minutes after returning to the hotel, they finally made it to the fitness center. Like most hotel fitness centers, this one was fairly small with only a couple of treadmills, some dumbbells and a universal machine.

They were the only two in the center. Using the limited equipment available, Derek quickly developed a series of exercises patterned after some common CrossFit training he had previously done. They would sprint a quarter mile on the treadmill, followed by a number of pull-ups and body weight exercises, then repeat the process. They did not slow down for nearly forty-five minutes. Susan, to her credit, kept pace with Derek nearly stride for stride in every exercise.

Once done with their workout, Derek and Susan decided to walk around the casino's property for a cool down. They had worn their swimsuits under their T-shirts and shorts. Stopping at one of the many pools, they stripped down. Both climbed into the warm water and swam a couple of causal laps. Even this time of year, Vegas can be hot.

"Do you believe John was telling us the truth? That he actually has everything he says he does?" Susan asked as she rested her elbows on the side of the pool. Slowly she began fluttering her legs in the water behind her.

"I mean, the more I think about it, the crazier the whole thing sounds." Susan rested her chin on her forearms, which she had crossed casually on the pool's edge.

"If we told someone our story, they would probably think the same thing about us," Derek replied as he pulled himself out of the water turning to sit on the side of the pool next to Susan, his feet still dangling in the water.

"I believe he believes what he said. But here is what I do know. John is currently our best and only shot at getting out from under Smith's grasp. We, of course, won't know for sure until we've had some time to review what he has. However, if it is even half as credible as what he says, we will have a good chance to blow the lid off this bitch," Derek said encouragingly.

"You know I love you?" Susan said quietly.

"I love you more," Derek replied, placing his hand to her cheek.

They spent a couple minutes discussing where they would go to dinner that night. Susan was insistent on having a margarita, so they decided on the El Dorado Cantina Mexican restaurant on the Vegas Strip. Derek stood and helped Susan climb out of the pool. Slipping their T-shirts and shorts on, they held hands while walking back to their hotel room. As they stepped onto the elevator that would take them to their floor, Susan rested her head on the side of Derek's shoulder.

A few minutes later, they arrived at their room. The door's lock beeped as Derek used his key card on it. A small LED light turned green as it unlocked. Susan stepped into the room. She pulled her

T-shirt off, which was soaked through from her swimsuit and headed towards the bathroom.

"I'm going to take a shower," she said, tossing the sopping T-shirt on the floor. Looking over her shoulder at Derek, she said. "You could join me if you'd like!"

"You don't have to ask me twice!" Derek said, hurriedly pulling off his own T-shirt while simultaneously hopping on one foot towards the bathroom as he removed his shoes. Entering the large bathroom, Derek closed the door.

Derek and Susan lost track of time while they showered together. Stepping out of the shower, Derek grabbed two of the hotel's large, plush towels. He handed one of the towels to Susan as he began to dry himself off.

"I think we were in there too long," Susan said while using the towel Derek had handed her on herself. "I've become a prune."

"I like prunes," Derek said, stepping forward to kiss her.

"Didn't you get enough of that already?" Susan giggled. "We need to start getting ready." Stepping back, she wrapped the bath towel around herself and grabbed a hand towel. Susan began vigorously rubbing her hair dry. "Josh could show up any minute."

"Okay fine," Derek said, sticking his lower lip out in mock disappointment as he wrapped the towel around his waist. He stepped towards the bathroom door and began to open it.

"Don't pout," Susan laughed and lightly whipped the hand towel at his arm.

Derek, too, began laughing, but froze as he entered the main room. Susan, curious why Derek suddenly stopped moving, turned and walked up to him. That is when she saw them.

Two men flanked Derek and Susan. They were standing on opposite sides of the room. One stood between Derek and the main door. The other had positioned himself on the opposite side closer to the balcony's sliding glass door. Though they looked young, maybe in their midtwenties, their physiques and dress gave all the appearance of government agents.

What gave Derek pause was the suppressors attached to the weapons. Both held SIG Sauer P226 9mm handguns, which were currently pointed directly at Derek. Legitimate government agents who intend to "arrest" a suspect typically do not attach suppressors to their weapons.

Sitting between the two agents, at the table Susan and Josh had eaten their breakfast at earlier that morning, was a thin little man with greasy hair. What appeared to be a computer bag hung around his chest. He was smiling broadly as if someone had just told him a joke.

"Ah, shit," Susan muttered.

Derek recognized her tone as being more frustrated than fearful. Derek raised his hands. Susan raised one hand. The other hand she used to ensure the towel wrapped around her body did not fall to the floor.

"I was beginning to wonder how long you two would be in there," Jimmy Russo said still smiling. "I was about to send my boys in to get you."

Derek started to take a casual step forward.

"Not so fast, slick!" Jimmy said as both the younger agents raised their weapons a little higher, focusing more intently on the couple.

Derek recognized, with their weapons out and the way they had positioned themselves on opposite sides of the room, there was little chance he would be able to disarm one before the other began firing. He would need to buy time.

"Have a seat on the bed. You too, sweet-tits!" Jimmy said, staring at Susan with hunger in his eyes. Susan stared back as both she and Derek slowly moved to the side of the bed.

"So, boys, I am pretty sure we didn't order any room service. May I ask who you are?" Derek said, taking a seat on the edge of the bed.

The agent standing near the balcony was closest to him. Still clutching her towel, Susan had taken a seat on the bed nearer the agent by the main door. Jimmy sat between them though he never completely took his leering eyes off Susan.

"We are with Homeland Security," Jimmy said proudly, "and you two are wanted fugitives." Derek adjusted his sitting position so his body weight was evenly distributed to his feet. Out of the corner of his eye, he saw Susan was mirroring his posture.

"And who might you be?" Derek asked, continuing to stall for time. He needed the agents holding the guns to drop their guard before he could even make an attempt at disarming them.

"I am Supervisory Special Agent in Charge Russo and these men work for me," Jimmy said as if that was the first time he had ever made such a statement. Derek observed the agent closest to him roll his eyes.

"And what are you planning on doing with us, Supervisory Special Agent in Charge Russo?" Derek asked with more than a touch of sarcasm. The agent nearest him smiled. Jimmy also saw this and Derek watched as a flash of anger crossed Jimmy's eyes.

"So here is what is going to happen," Jimmy began. "My men are going to handcuff you. Then we are going to have a video conference with my boss."

"Can I be allowed to get dressed before your men handcuff me?" Susan asked incredulously.

"Oh, I don't think that will be entirely necessary, sweet-tits," Jimmy said, smiling again. He kept his thoughts about what he was going to do to her to himself. "We are after all, professionals here."

"I sincerely doubt that," Susan muttered under her breath.

"Who is your boss?" Derek asked as the man closest to the door took a step towards Susan. As he did so, he began to lower his weapon.

The beep of the door's lock sounded incredibly loud as a key card was inserted into it. The agent who had been approaching Susan, pivoted towards the door. Jimmy and the agent nearest the balcony also momentarily diverted their attention to the main door. Derek was about to make his move when Susan beat him to it.

"Josh!" Susan yelled, as the alarm in her voice alerted Josh to the danger he was walking in on. She and Derek both knew he was the only person with a key card who would have entered the room without knocking first. She leaped from the edge of the bed.

The agent, sensing Susan's movement, began to turn back towards her. He was too slow as she was already on him. Susan thrust her leg out in a front kick that would have made any martial arts practitioner appreciative. The kick landed squarely on the man's sternum, knocking the wind out of him. He bounced backwards against the wall near the main door.

Knowing they were committed, Derek had to trust Susan and Josh could handle the agent by the door. He came off the bed a fraction of a second after Susan. The agent closest to him began to brandish his pistol in Derek's direction. Derek threw a low leg kick that landed between the agent's ankle and shin.

The kick swept the agent's feet out from under him and he began to fall forward. Derek simultaneously grabbed him by the back of the neck. Aided by gravity, Derek used the agent's falling momentum, to forcefully guide his head into the corner of the hotel room's wooden dresser. The agent's head snapped backwards as it made a cracking sound upon impact. He was unconscious before he hit the floor.

Derek spun towards the main door ready to jump in and assist Susan and Josh. It was unnecessary. After retrieving the suppressed SIG Sauer handgun from the unconscious agent, Derek resumed his seat on the bed.

Josh had been able to disarm the agent Susan had kicked in the chest. The agent was lying face down on the floor still struggling to catch his breath as Josh covered him with his pistol.

Susan, on the other hand, was having a field day with Jimmy. After kicking the first agent, Jimmy had attempted to run. Susan struck him in the face with the palm of her hand, nearly breaking his nose.

As blood began to run down Jimmy's face, he bent forward placing both hands over his nose. Still clutching her towel, Susan stepped back and threw another kick, similar to what a punter would do. The kick landed squarely on Jimmy's groin and he made a squealing noise. The sound of the impact caused both Derek and Josh to wince in sympathetic pain.

Jimmy fell to the floor; a little vomit came from his mouth as he curled into the fetal position.

"Clear," Derek said casually, to also get Susan and Josh refocused.

"Clear!" responded Josh as he continued to cover the agent with the pistol.

"Real clear," Susan said, still clutching her towel to body. Then as an afterthought, "You fucking little troglodyte!" Susan said as she kicked Jimmy in the ribs. He remained on the floor curled up and crying.

"Okay, we might have to get out of here quickly. Susan, you should get dressed," Derek said, "while Josh and I deal with these guys."

Susan angrily grabbed some clothes then stepped into the bathroom closing the door. As Josh secured the agents with their own handcuffs, Derek continued to watch Jimmy lay on the floor. Once they were secured, Derek and Josh lifted the two agents onto the bed placing them facedown. Derek ensured the unconscious agent was still breathing. Susan stepped from the bathroom fully dressed.

Derek lifted Jimmy, who was still clutching his testicles with both hands, into a nearby seat. He removed Jimmy's computer satchel from around his shoulder and handed it to Susan.

"Okay, Supervisory Special Agent in Charge Russo. Let's start this conversation over," Derek said, patting him on the head with the muzzle of the suppressed pistol. "Who sent you?"

"Fuck you, man!" Jimmy spat in an attempt to gain back some of his bravado. Derek was about to say something intimidating, but Susan beat him to it.

"He asked you a question, twerp!" Susan yelled as she took an aggressive step towards Jimmy.

Susan brought her hand back as if she was going to strike him again. Jimmy flinched instinctively, already fearful of the beating he knew she would put on him. Susan looked at Derek and winked. Derek tried not to smile.

"Josh," Derek said casually, "open the balcony door."

Jimmy's eyes darted between Derek, Susan, and Josh, who had begun pushing the sliding glass door open. "What are you going to do, man?" Jimmy asked with trepidation.

"It is quite simple," Derek said casually, "I'm going to ask you one more time. Then, if you don't answer, I'm going to throw you off the balcony."

"Bullshit." Though he said it, Jimmy's voice cracked, betraying his confidence.

"Are you sure, Supervisory Special Agent in Charge Russo? I mean, since we are already wanted for multiple homicides. Quite frankly, what is one more?" Where there had once been hunger, Derek saw dread enter Jimmy's eyes.

"Who sent you?" Derek asked again. He waited exactly five seconds, then grabbed Jimmy by his neck and the back of the trousers. Lifting him from the seat Derek, halfcarried him towards the balcony.

"Wait! Wait! Wait!" Jimmy yelled. Derek dropped him on the floor. He instinctively curled back into the fetal position. "It was Smith! Smith sent us!" Derek saw Josh and Susan exchange a look of concern.

Susan moved to the table and sat. Pulling the laptop out of Jimmy's satchel, she powered it up. Josh, clutching the pistol a little tighter, walked to the main door. After looking through the peephole, he secured the inner locks.

"And what were your orders?" Derek asked.

"We are supposed to put you on camera and let Smith watch as we shot you both in the head." Jimmy was in tears as he began hyperventilating.

"What is the password to the laptop?" Susan demanded. When Jimmy hesitated, Susan began to stand up. That was all the encouraging he needed.

"Flesh Missile double-oh-seven," Jimmy replied, curling even tighter defensively into a ball.

"Seriously," Susan said incredulously while shaking her head. She sat back down. "What a little shit-weasel."

"Shouldn't we be bailing out of here?" Josh asked anxiously.

"I think we are good for about an hour," Derek answered. "If he was supposed to put us on camera so Smith could watch that means Smith isn't nearby. He would want to be here if he could," Derek explained his reasoning.

"Also, they had no way to know for sure when we would be back in the room, so there wouldn't be a specific check in time. I think we have about an hour before Smith sends anyone else or begins to make inquiries." Josh nodded in agreement.

Derek got dressed as Susan began going through the laptop. Once dressed, he told Josh to pack up as quickly as he could. Derek spent the next ten minutes questioning Russo about what he knew and how he had come across their meeting. Russo explained in detail.

Completed with his questioning, Derek gathered some 5-50 cord and flexible zip ties they had previously stored in their tactical gear. He thoroughly bound all three. Derek ensured Jimmy's nose had stopped bleeding and that he could both inhale and exhale through it. After stuffing some hand towels in each of their mouths, he duct-taped the towels in place making sure to leave enough space for them to breathe. Derek reviewed his handywork and was satisfied the three would not be going anywhere without help. Josh was back in the room with his bags in tow.

Susan pointed to a few files on the computer. Some files were basic pornography obviously for Jimmy's personal use. One file appeared older and of poor quality. It was of some teenaged girls in a locker room. Others however, were unmistakable surveillance photographs. Each file had a name and date time stamp indicating whom the surveillance was on and when it had occurred. These seemed to confirm Russo was telling the truth.

"Open that one," Derek indicated the one time stamped for today. Susan clicked on the file. Images of John Winoski and their meeting at the Denny's appeared. Susan scrolled through the images.

"Well, at least we know exactly how Smith found us," Susan said.

"What is that one?" Derek asked, pointing to a file only identified by a twelve-digit number. Susan tried to open the file a couple of different ways. With each attempt, it would only come up scrambled.

"It won't open," Susan said with frustration. "I think it's encrypted."

"Okay. Shut it down," Derek ordered. "We need to pack up and get out of here just in case I am wrong about how much time we have."

"But what about the file?" Susan asked.

Derek dropped his head to the floor considering. After a few moments, Susan saw his shoulders slump. Without raising his eyes from the floor, Derek replied, "I think I know someone that can help us with that." ◉

CHAPTER 37
"TURNING BACK THE CLOCK"

As they stepped from their hotel room, Derek hung the Do Not Disturb sign on the door handle. House cleaning had already come for the day, so there was not much concern of their showing up again. If nothing else, the sign may at least give them a couple hours' head start before anyone entered the room.

Arriving on the first floor of Caesars Palace, Derek took his disposable telephone and called John Winoski. When John answered, Derek told him they had been compromised and what had happened.

Initially, John was angry, blaming Derek and Susan. He went on a rant about how he had been gathering information for nearly thirty years without an issue. John was ready to break all communications with them. Then Derek explained how Russo had been assigned to conduct surveillance on all former S4 employees. It had only been a bad coincidence that he was following John on this particular day. Nevertheless, they were now both compromised.

Derek told John he and Susan were going into hiding for a few days. He recommended John do the same. John agreed, saying he had a place off-grid he could go to that no one knew of. Discovering Russo had only stumbled upon their meeting, they both concurred that the disposable phones they were using were most likely still good, but they would keep them turned off just in case. John agreed to call Derek in one week's time. They would then move forward with their previously agreed upon plan. With that, they hung up.

Knowing Smith would eventually be able to gain access to the information from the hotel, Derek, used his knife to destroy the false identification and credit card he had used to book the rooms. Having an abundance of false identifications was helpful.

Previously, when Susan and Derek dealt with Smith, his agents had placed tracking devices on their vehicles. Concerned the Toyota they had been driving was now compromised, all three agreed to leave it in the hotel parking lot. Even if a tracking device had not been installed, they could not risk having Smith leak the vehicle's information to local law enforcement.

Instead, they took an Uber to a nearby dealership. Once there, Derek, using another one of his many false identifications, purchased another Toyota Tacoma. It took less than an hour to close the sale.

The used car dealer noted the speed for which the purchase was made had been a personal record. Derek paid for the vehicle in cash explaining to the salesperson how he had just hit a "jackpot" at one of the casinos. Amongst themselves the three of them frequently mused at how everyone should have access to millions in a black budget no one cared about.

After loading their bags into the bed of the truck, they climbed in. A block from dealership, Derek pulled to the side of the road. Pulling a telephone from his pocket, Derek stared at it briefly. As he took a couple of deep breaths, Susan and Josh watched him curiously. He almost looked nervous, Susan thought.

Using his pass code to open the phone, Derek dialed a phone number he seemed to have committed to memory. Susan heard a voice on the other end answering. The voice was male but she could not understand what was being said.

"This is Riley," Derek spoke hesitantly. There was a pause on both ends of the phone before Derek spoke again. "I am sorry to call you like this. You can say no if you want, but we need your help."

Again, Susan could hear the voice on the other end but was unsure if it was excitement or anger coming through the telephone.

"Thank you," Derek eventually replied. "We will be there in about nine hours. Probably sometime around midnight. There are three of us," Derek said. With that, he powered down the telephone and set it in the vehicles center console.

"Who was that?" Susan asked her curiosity peeked.

"An old friend," Derek answered. His desire not to talk was more than obvious. Susan decided to let it be for the moment. He put the car in gear and pulled away from the curb.

Stopping only for food and gas, they drove straight through. Taking Interstate 15, they traveled to Bakersfield, California. From there they cut across to Interstate 5 and headed northbound.

Derek was quiet for most the trip, though he did laugh with them when Josh made the occasional joke or recounted how Susan had kicked Russo in the groin while trying to keep her towel from falling off. Susan was having an ever-more difficult time determining Derek's mood. She eventually settled on sad.

Stopping at the Buttonwillow Rest Stop, Susan and Josh stepped inside to use the restrooms. Their bags were loose in the truck's bed. Besides their clothing, they contained their multiple false identifications, but also numerous weapons and equipment. Not wanting an opportunist thief to steal their bags, Derek remained with the vehicle.

Once done, they strode out of the restroom. At the same moment two immaculately clean, black and white, California

Highway Patrol vehicles pulled into the rest area. Susan and Josh watched in dismay as the police cruisers approached their parked truck.

Slowly, they came to a stop, parking on either side of their new Tacoma. Nonchalantly, as if he had no care in the world, Derek stood there, leaning his back against the truck's fender. His arms were casually folded across his chest.

"What do we do?" Josh asked Susan under his breath.

Though they had been framed, they were still fugitives wanted for multiple homicides. Even if it meant Smith would end up capturing them, Susan knew they would never hurt a law enforcement officer for any reason. Taking a deep breath, she interlaced Josh's arm with her own and together they began to walk forward to meet their fate.

As they grew closer, Susan and Josh watched as the two Highway Patrol Officers, decked out in their tan, highly recognizable uniforms, stepped from their vehicles. One adjusted the duty belt around his waist while the other put on a set of mirrored Oakley sunglasses.

Susan was amazed when Derek turned and greeted the officers. He then deliberately engaged them in a conversation. As Susan and Josh arrived at the truck, one of the officers stepped away and retrieved a Thomas Guide map book from his car. Upon returning, both officers began providing Derek some directions.

As they finished, Derek thanked them. Because the pandemic had made handshaking a taboo, he gave them both a fist-bump while telling them to "stay safe." The officers smiled at Susan and Josh as they walked past heading towards the restrooms.

"What was that about? Why did you go out of your way to interact with them?" Susan asked as they climbed back into the Tacoma.

"It was about absolutely nothing," Derek replied. "But I have learned one of the best ways to stay hidden, is to appear obvious and not look like you are trying to stay incognito."

As they drove away from the rest stop, Derek then recounted how he had once breached a military base during a heightened security drill. He was able to do this merely by wearing a hardhat and holding a clipboard. Acting as if he had no care in the world, Derek was able to stroll right through the front gate.

Approaching their destination, Derek and Susan discovered Josh had never been to San Francisco or seen the Golden Gate Bridge. Derek himself had not been to the Golden City in nearly twenty years. Since it was not going to add too much time to their trip, Derek decided to drive through Oakland and cut across the San Francisco-Oakland Bay Bridge.

Night began to fall as they approached San Francisco. Derek knew that traveling along North Point and Jefferson Street would give them a quick view of both Alcatraz and the Golden Gate. It was not an ideal way to do any sightseeing but would have to do under the circumstances.

Once upon a time, San Francisco had been one of the country's greatest cities. Not anymore. Failure to enforce basic standards of public behavior had made the city nearly unlivable. For nearly thirty years, the city council had conducted a failed social experiment all in the name of compassion for the homeless. The result had become quite the opposite, making nearly everything worse.

Like something out of a third world country, misery and squalor were the actual view they had from their vehicle. Homeless camps seemed to have overtaken the streets. Derek would not have been surprised if they had witnessed an assault or robbery during their short excursion.

Drug usage had obviously skyrocketed as they observed people shooting-up as casually as a smoker may have lit a cigarette three decades earlier. People wrapped in blankets were laying in the street next to what appeared to be human feces, garbage and hypodermic needles. This behavior could be seen everywhere along their drive.

Initially he had been excited to be visiting San Francisco, even if only briefly for the first time. Unfortunately, looking out the passenger window, Josh became increasingly more disturbed. They traveled through one depressed area after another.

Cutting their sightseeing trip short, Derek turned south and headed towards Silicon Valley. Besides San Francisco, the valley is comprised of the southern bay regions including Palo Alto, Sunnyvale, and Santa Clara.

Due to the tech industry boom that occurred in the 1980s and 1990s, the valley is now home to some of the country's most expensive neighborhoods. Despite this and both the local and state government's skyrocketing expenditures to deal with the homeless problem, the valley's homeless issue was no better than that of San Francisco.

They all grew quiet as they drove through. Each contemplating how any government could allow this type of decline. Finally, Derek spoke up.

"The government has tried to solve the problem with money and good intensions. That has obviously failed. I guess they've never heard of the Broken Windows Theory."

"Broken Windows Theory, what's that?" Josh asked.

Derek smiled. He knew if he did not answer, Josh would spend a few hours thoroughly researching the topic until he knew it well.

As Derek drove, he turned the vehicle towards the Woodside Hills not far from the Pulgas Ridge Preserve. The contrast was astounding. The city lights of Palo Alto and view of San Francisco Bay were more than noticeable the higher their vehicle climbed.

They passed one gated, luxury home after another, each seemed to have their own private swimming pool. A person reviewing recent real-estate listings would quickly discover, one such home recently sold for nearly twenty-two million dollars.

"Shouldn't we be concerned about Smith having your friends under surveillance?" Susan asked as she realized they were growing closer to their destination.

"No," Derek replied. "I am sure we are good. Though Smith does have considerable resources, I don't believe even he could muster enough people to cover everyone I know especially for any extended period."

Near the top, on Mountain Home Road, Derek pulled their truck over into a large, gated driveway. A seven-foot stone and mortar wall seemed to encircle the property. The wall obstructed any attempt at observation. As Derek pulled up to a wireless security intercom, a motion-activated flood lamp bathed their vehicle in light. Derek rolled the driver's window down and pushed the transmit button on the intercom.

Susan recognized the red blinking light of a security camera affixed to the wall. It was facing the entrance, recording them. Glancing up and down the wall she noticed several other cameras equally spaced. These security cameras were pointed in a number of different directions. They were entering a fortress, she thought.

"Yes?" came the deep voice from the other side.

"It's Riley," Derek said. Seconds later a buzzing sound could be heard. Slowly the cast-iron gate began to open. Putting the truck into gear, Derek took a deep breath and drove through.

Moments later, they pulled onto a horseshoe driveway stopping in front of a large multistory mansion. Walkway lights illuminated the path to the front door. Ahead of them, parked near the unattached four-car garage, sat a red convertible Tesla Roadster. One of the garage doors was open. Inside, Derek could see the unmistakable front end of a black Hummer H1 Slantback.

After coming to a stop and shutting the vehicle off, Derek, Susan, and Josh stepped from the pickup. Derek leaned backwards, placing his hands on his hips to help stretch his lower back. Both of the large front doors to the mansion swung open.

Susan watched as the figure stepped out. He was a black man who stood just a little over six feet tall. His dark polo shirt was pulled tightly over his body-builder physique. As he approached, Susan estimated, from his short graying hair and the wrinkles around his eyes, he was in his early fifties. She almost did not notice the limp. Almost.

Never taking his eyes from Derek, the man walked directly to him, stopping a mere foot away. Susan could not read the expression on the man's face. Slowly, Derek extended his hand.

"Thanks for helping us," Derek said almost submissively. The man looked down at Derek's outstretched hand for several moments. Then, with a big grin, he grasped it and pulled Derek into a colossal bear hug. Derek returned the embrace. They hugged one another for several long moments.

"I'm so sorry," Susan heard Derek half whisper. She saw his body slouch in the man's grip.

"It wasn't your fault, brother," the man exclaimed with tears forming in his own eyes. "It was never your fault." Not understanding why, Susan knew there was a significance in the reunion. She found herself caught up in the moment as her own tears began running down her cheek.

After a few moments, they separated. Susan noticed Derek briefly turn away. With his left hand, Derek wiped something from his eyes. She knew he was too embarrassed for her to see him cry.

Then clearing his throat, Derek turned to the group.

"These are my friends," Derek said with a half smile as he gestured with his hand. "Dr. Susan Parker and Josh Williams."

The man stepped forward and grabbed the two of them. Without a thought, he pulled both into an unexpected hug. After the initial surprise, Susan wrapped her arms around the man's thick torso. Instantly she knew this was a person she could trust completely.

"I am very pleased to meet you both," the man said as he released them from his embrace. "I am Michael King. You can call me Mike."

Helping them grab their bags, Mike quickly ushered them into his home.

"My wife and her girlfriends are away on a wine-tasting trip through southern France," Mike explained his empty home. His deep voice seemed to echo, reverberating off the living room's vaulted ceiling.

"I went once a few years ago. Longest month in my life," Mike continued. "Even worse than that month I spent at Landstuhl Medical Center in Germany. Bunch of pompous frogs." Mike laughed loudly as he insulted the French.

"Anyways, Sheri got so pissed she told me I couldn't come on any more trips. Best thing to happen to me in years!" He chuckled again.

It was nearly 1:00 a.m. when Mike finished the tour of his home. He brought them to the guest rooms.

"I made up three rooms. Didn't want to assume anything," Mike said.

"Oh, they only need one room," Josh offered helpfully as Susan blushed.

"Anyways," Mike said, smiling, "I know you've had a rough trip so I will let you get some sleep. Bathroom is down the hall and there are extra towels on the counter. I will have breakfast ready in the morning." Looking at Derek, he said, "I can't tell you how good it is to see you again." With that, Mike turned and walked away.

Josh dragged his bag into his room and shut his door. Derek and Susan did the same. After their long drive, they used the bathroom to clean up before eventually crawling into bed. Susan curled up in Derek's arms.

"You served with him of course," Susan spoke.

"Tomorrow." Derek kissed her on the forehead. "We will talk about it tomorrow." With that, exhaustion overtook both of them and they quickly fell fast asleep.

Three hours later, Derek sat up. The Kuwaiti road and Scar had again entered his dream. The Sasquatch's face, yelling at him for help still fresh in his memory. Derek looked over at Susan. She was laying on her side with her back towards him. Inhaling deeply, Derek lay back down on his pillow. Quietly, he hoped sleep would return.

Derek was unaware Susan had been awake. Listening to his nightmare. Her eyes open and troubled.

CHAPTER 38

"FORGOTTEN FRIENDS"

Morning came quickly. While Susan showered, and though still tired, Derek went through his morning routine of push-ups, crunches, and stretching. When she returned, it was his turn to jump into the shower. Fifteen minutes later, they were walking towards the kitchen.

As they approached, Mike's immense voice, in a cappella, could be heard echoing in perfect pitch off the walls. "The Marine's Hymn," it was a song Derek had rarely heard since his days in the Corps and never with the passion Mike sung. Derek and Susan both paused at the door and watched him. Mike's back was to them. While cooking, Mike was both singing and swaying in unequaled rhythm at the stove.

"From the Halls of Montezuma
To the shores of Tripoli
We fight our country's battles
In the air, on land, and sea.
First to fight for right and freedom
And to keep our honor clean: We are proud to claim
The title of United States Marines.
Our flag's unfurled to every breeze

From dawn to setting sun: We have fought in every clime and place,
Where we could take a gun.
In the snow of far-off Northern lands
And in the sunny tropic scenes; You will find us always on the job: The
United States Marines."

Sensing their presence, Mike turned. Continuing to sing, he smiled and, using a stainless-steel spatula, motioned for them to take a seat at one of the counter's tall stools. They complied eagerly. Without breaking a note, Mike dished up two plates of eggs and sausage. As Josh stepped into the kitchen, Mike ushered him to another stool and set down a third plate.

"Here's health to you and to our Corps
Which we are proud to serve:
In many a strife we've fought for life
And never lost our nerve.
If the Army and the Navy
Ever look on Heaven's scenes,
They will find the streets are guarded
By United States Marines."

As Mike concluded the hymn, he dropped a stack of pancakes on the counter next to them. Susan grinned and applauded as he finished singing. "You're a fantastic singer," she proclaimed.

"Thank you, very much, young lady." Mike bowed. "That's my Southern Baptist upbringing coming out. Momma had us attending church every Sunday where we sang praises to the Lord."

"I know we can eat a lot, Mike, but I think that's a little bit much even for us," Derek said pointing at the mountain of food Mike had made.

"Oh, I didn't make that just for you three," Mike said, smiling at the inside joke only he knew. "Didn't I tell you? We are having company this morning. And these boys can eat."

Almost on cue, the doorbell rang.

"Come in!" Mike's voice boomed.

Derek eyeballed Mike with the suspicion of a person about to receive an unexpected gift. He did.

Although both were thirty years older, Derek immediately recognized Ernesto Rios and Shawn Jackson as they strolled into the kitchen. Rios's had grown his hair into a long ponytail and he sported a goatee, both of which had streaks of gray. Jackson however, had shaved his head. Though he still looked fit for a man in his fifties, he had developed a little bit of a gut.

Derek stepped from the table and walked to greet the two newcomers. They hugged one another like a long-lost family finally reunited. Rios and Jackson were grinning from ear to ear. Though not as severe as the previous evening, Susan saw moisture appear in Derek's eyes once again.

Derek made introductions around the room. Rios and Jackson hugged both Susan and Josh.

"You all served together, I assume?" Susan asked.

"Are you kidding? We were the team back in the day!" Jackson exclaimed as he threw some pancakes on a plate. "And this man saved all our lives! More than once," Rios chimed in, using both hands to point at Derek.

"That's not what happened," Derek said with a note of remorse coming to his voice.

"That is exactly what the fuck happened!" Mike said, putting his own fork down. Susan heard a touch of annoyance entering his voice for the first time since she'd met him the night before.

"Twenty-Two!" Mike proclaimed. Everyone was silent for several moments.

"Twenty-Two? What's that?" Josh asked as he looked back and forth between Derek and Mike.

"That is the number of veterans who commit suicide everyday, Josh," Rios explained solemnly.

"Most people think this is because of what they had to do," Jackson continued. "For some that is true, but for many, it is the overwhelming guilt they feel having returned home when many of their friends did not."

"For our boy Derek here," Mike took over, "that is especially true. He has seen and done more than most. Been in combat and shot at numerous times, had bombs go off next to him, and has lost men. Yet he's never even been scratched. It is like someone has been looking out for him." Derek shifted uncomfortably in his seat.

"This is long overdue. You saved all our lives!" Mike announced.

Turning towards Susan and Josh, Mike began telling them of the events on the Kuwaiti road. Occasionally, Rios and Jackson would interrupt. Adding details from what had been their perspective at the time. Back at the counter, Rios stood beside Derek with his arm draped across his shoulder. Derek wanted to run but felt that Rios would hold him in place if he tried to get up. Derek almost felt as if this were some type of intervention.

When Mike concluded the story, Susan and Josh were staring at Derek with different admiration.

"Holy crap!" Josh said. "I never knew that happened. You guys must have all gotten medals or something?"

"Hardly," Jackson spat.

"It's fine," Derek countered, then looked over at Josh. "Josh, we never did anything so we could earn medals. People who act in order to obtain prestige or medals are reckless and stupid. What we did, we did for each other."

"Hell, it was Wetmore's fault anyways," Rios explained as he released his grip on Derek's shoulder walking around the counter to pour himself a cup of coffee. As he did, Rios threw a sausage link in his mouth.

"What do you mean?" Susan asked.

"You see," Mike began, "most people don't really understand the importance of the Gulf War. Yes, the Iraqis invaded Kuwait. Yes, the Saudis, Kuwaitis, and a number of other nations asked the United States for assistance and yes, the US economy was reliant on the oil fields of the Middle East. That was all true and important to the politicians for selling the war to the public.

"But the military had a different agenda." Mike continued to illustrate. "This was the first actual war the United States had been in since Vietnam. The military had taken a fifteen-year public relations beat-down following Vietnam. Jimmy Carter screwed up the Iranian Hostage Rescue; the Marine Barracks in Beirut was blown up. About the only thing the military did partly right was the invasion of the tiny little country of Panama. However, even that was filled with mistakes. Poor planning caused a number of needless deaths and it still took ten days to get Noriega to surrender.

"So, the military's morale was low, and the public didn't believe what we were capable of. Then this war came along. The Pentagon knew they needed to win in a big way to get back the military's luster. Think about it, when did the 'thank a veteran' movement begin?

"The military encouraged the news media to become embedded with many of our troops. That had never been done before. They held frequent press conferences with General Schwarzkopf, which made the war look like a sanitized video game. Shit, even Dan Rather and the *60 Minutes* news broadcast did a piece specifically on our unit. Anyhow, they could not afford any serious bad press. When friendly fire occurred, the leadership went to great lengths to keep it quiet," Mike concluded.

"Shit, they even made a movie about how the military covered crap like that up," Jackson said. "What was it called?" Jackson was looking at the floor snapping his fingers trying to remember the name of the movie.

"*Courage Under Fire*," Rios replied. "With Denzel Washington and Meg Ryan."

"Oh yeah," Jackson said, looking up. "Not to mention, if anyone got a medal, someone else would also have to take the blame."

"Again, Wetmore," Rios replied. "Did you know his uncle worked at the Pentagon?"

Looking at Derek, Mike continued, "Medals be damned. You saved our lives. I am here because you pulled me into that ditch. We are having breakfast because of your quick thinking. I have a lovely wife, three children, and four grandchildren all of whom I adore. My business, everything I am is all owed to you."

"Actually, one of us did get a medal." Jackson half laughed as he used his fork to cut into his stack of pancakes.

"Who?" asked Josh excitedly.

"I got the Purple Heart," Mike said, lifting his pant leg and exposing his titanium prosthetic.

"Well, you almost didn't get that," Rios exclaimed angrily.

"Why not?" asked Susan incredulously.

"Again, Wetmore!" Rios replied with disgust.

"You see, the criteria for awards would change from time to time. Initially, when I was in Germany, after my second surgery my father had flown in and he asked," Mike explained.

"They told him that because the injury was not a result of enemy action, I did not rate a Purple Heart. When Riley here heard that Wetmore hadn't put me up for a Purple Heart, he wrote a letter to my congressman. Two weeks later. It was pinned on my chest by my dad." Mike's already large chest expanded with pride.

"So, do you all work together now?" Susan asked.

"Well, while I was recovering, I began taking a number of computer courses. You know, programing, engineering, shit like that," Mike explained. "One thing led to another, now I am the owner of a fairly successful company that has a couple of divisions. One develops motherboards and CPUs for many of the companies in the Valley while another works on coding and such.

"I hired Rios here as my head of security," Mike said, pointing at Rios. Rios gave a half salute with a butter knife, while he chewed.

"So, how rich are you?" Josh asked, oblivious to etiquette faux pas.

"Are you kidding?" Jackson said, answering for Mike. "When he and Bill Gates go to lunch, Bill makes Mike pick up the check!"

"Well, that's a bit of an exaggeration!" Mike laughed.

"And do you work for him too?" Susan asked, looking at Jackson.

"Oh, no way, man!" Jackson answered. "That computer shit is too complicated for me. I am just a lowly chauffeur."

"By chauffeur," Mike said, laughing, "Jackson here means he is the owner and operator of his own exclusive helicopter shuttle service."

"You see," Jackson said, using a pompous British accent, "the rich and famous, like our Mr. King here, cannot be bothered by frivolous little things such as traffic. So, they hire me. I land my helicopter on their front lawn and take them wherever they need to go. For which they pay me a bunch of money."

"I am proud of you, boys." Derek finally spoke. "I should have looked you up sooner and for that I apologize."

They continued to laugh and talk over breakfast. Eventually, they all adjourned to the main patio.

"Are either of you married?" Susan asked Rios and Jackson, while sipping on her second coffee.

"Divorced," Rios said.

"And you?" Susan asked, looking at Jackson.

"Divorced," Jackson laughed. "But to be fair, that was kind of my fault. You see, my ex kinda caught me making-out with a socialite in the back of my helicopter."

"Kinda your fault? Is that what you call it?" Rios roared with laughter. Turning to Susan. "This shithead was fully butt-ass-naked, high in the saddle, with the rich daughter of the cofounder of an enormous social-media site.

"His wife showed up and caught him. She then tried to brain him with a crowbar that she'd taken out of the trunk of her BMW." They all were laughing as Rios continued his animated story.

"So, now picture the socialite running down the runway of the airport, half-naked as our boy here is wrestling in the buff with his wife. That is when the cops show up and shot him in his ass with a Taser!"

"That story can't be true?" Susan asked as she wiped tears of laughter from her eyes.

"Every word," Jackson acknowledged with a grin and a slight nod of his head. Rios and Jackson told increasingly more embarrassing stories about one another for the next ten minutes.

"So, does any of the old squad also live around here?" Derek asked, genuinely interested when the conversation began to slow.

"Well, you know, Doc Comfort got his medical degree. He's now the head of surgery at UCSF. We play golf together a couple times a month. I believe Skiers opened a dive bar in Sacramento."

After another hour of war stories and laughing, Mike turned to Derek.

"We all know those stories about you in the news are bullshit." Rios and Jackson were nodding their heads in agreement. "So, what is it you need help with?"

"Okay," Derek said, taking a deep breath. "I'm going to have to brief you guys on a few things and I need you to try and remain openminded."

This time it was Derek who told the story with Susan and Josh occasionally interjecting. For nearly twenty minutes, he explained about the SRT and their covert mission to hunt Sasquatch. The old Marines just stared wide-eyed as he told them of how he had met Susan and Josh.

Derek described the assassination attempts Smith orchestrated and how Professor Wainwright and Marcus had been killed. Finally, he described what they had learned about Area 51. At the conclusion, they all sat quietly for a few minutes. It was Rios who finally broke the silence.

"I knew it! I knew all that shit was real!" Rios was up and pacing frantically. "God damn government assassinations and cover-ups! ETs giving anal probes to civilians! Bigfeets snatching hikers! I knew it!"

While the former members of the 1st Battalion 8th Marines asked clarifying questions of Josh and Susan, Derek stepped inside. A few minutes later, he returned with Jimmy Russo's laptop. After powering it up, he handed it to Mike.

"This is the computer we took off that douche-canoe Susan beat the crap out of," Derek said with a smile remembering the groin kick. "He was the guy who was going to assassinate us in the Vegas hotel. Anyhow, most of the files are surveillance photographs. However, there is an encrypted file on the computer. We need to access it."

Mike pulled a set of reading glasses out of his shirt pocket. Placing them on the bridge of his nose, he looked at the file for a few minutes.

"This shouldn't take too long," Mike said after studying the file. Standing, he took the laptop and disappeared into the house. Jackson began entertaining them all with stories of the rich and famous whom he'd had the pleasure of flying around the state. Many of the stories painted them in a less than glamorous light.

About fifteen minutes later, Mike stepped from the house carrying the laptop.

"I had to call one of my tech guys to help me out with the finer aspects, but I got it open for you." He handed it Susan.

Taking the computer, Susan began scrolling through the file. While she did, Mike, Jackson, and Rios began showing Josh some old-school Marine Corps hand-to-hand combat moves on the lawn.

"I'm pretty good at all things related to combat!" Josh exclaimed to the combat hardened veterans. This caused all the Marines to burst into laughter.

"Typical millennial," Rios teased. "Think they invented the wheel but aren't capable of changing a tire." The group proceeded to take Josh to "school."

"Oh shit!" Susan said after a few minutes. Looking up, she caught Derek's eye. As he walked over, she turned the computer screen towards him.

Reading through the file, Derek became more and more horrified. Apparently, Smith and his goons had been able to capture a troop of Sasquatch. Not just any troop but Scar and six others. This was the same group of Sasquatch Susan and Derek had come across in a secluded meadow several months earlier. The file was complete with photographs. Like any creature trapped in a cage, maybe even more so due to their humanlike faces, the Sasquatch in the photographs appeared abused and defeated.

As Derek read, he saw that the captured Sasquatch were scheduled to be transported from their current location at the Army's Yakima Training Center to a site in Utah. There they would be studied, dissected, and disposed of. The file provided the transport date and route of travel to the Utah facility. Looking up from the file he and Susan locked eyes.

"That's why you were seeing him in your dreams! We have to do something," she implored. "We cannot leave them in Smith's control."

"We won't. I promise," Derek replied as he reached out and grasped her shoulder. They became acutely aware the others had stopped talking. Looking up, Derek and Susan saw Mike and the others had gathered around them.

"You two look like a couple about to make some really stupid life choices," Mike finally said, breaking the silence.

"So, I guess you can count us in," said Rios as Jackson nodded in agreement. Everyone looked at Mike.

"Well, shit, my wife's out of town. I have nothing better to do." He smiled. ◉

CHAPTER 39
"THE PLAN"

Six days. According to the file, that is how much time they had until the convoy transporting the "packages" reached their destination. That is how the file referred to the troop of Sasquatch. As such, Derek and the others assumed the lingo and began calling them packages as well. The timeline gave them three days to plan and prepare, one day to travel, and one day at the location to walk the ground and alter the plan as necessary. On day six, they would execute their plan.

They moved into Mike's entertainment center. It was slightly larger than a normal living room. Mike's 105-inch NanoCell television nearly covered one entire wall. Several plush leather recliners were positioned in a semicircle around the television. A large coffee table was in the center. They all took seats.

"I wanted a bigger TV," Mike bragged as he connected the laptop to the television, "but my wife wouldn't let me knock out the back wall."

Mike began operating the computer projecting different images including an aerial map onto the television screen. They spent the next several hours developing their plan. As lunch came and went, Mike had a couple of pizzas delivered.

They all knew Derek had the most experience. As such, the others let him do most of the planning. They would ask questions and interject ideas whenever necessary. At certain critical points in the planning, Derek would have Mike and the others attempt to pick holes in the plan and discuss what they would do to counteract. If a solid counter to their plan was developed, they would alter it; however, they all knew no plan would ever be perfect. During the planning, as essential equipment was identified, they made notes where the equipment could be obtained.

Susan and Josh were for the most part quiet. They were amazed at how these men, who had not seen one another in decades, began working together seamlessly. She found it especially interesting that they did their planning backwards, starting at how they would escape and working their way to the initial assault. She asked why they did reverse planning. Derek explained that if a "need" was established to be necessary at the end of the operation, but had not been prepared for at the beginning, it could effectively alter the plan. This might potentially force the planning process to begin again.

They reviewed the travel itinerary for the convoy on the laptop. The convoy was to consist of three vehicles and twelve agents. Derek began referring to the agents as "Tangos." He explained to Susan and Josh, that *Tango* was an old-school, easily understandable term used over a radio to identify a terrorist.

The convoy's lead and chase vehicles consisted of heavy-duty Sportsmobile 4x4 vans. The lead vehicle would be occupied by four agents and was to travel about one to five miles ahead of the other two vehicles. According to the file, it was tasked with identifying potential issues and diverting the other vehicles as necessary. The chase vehicle was occupied by four additional agents and the convoy's commander for a total of five occupants. Finally, there was the transport vehicle. This was a custom-built Freightliner Cascadia semitruck with sleeper cab. Three agents occupied this vehicle. The "packages" would be in the reinforced trailer being hauled.

The itinerary had the convoy leaving the Yakima Training Facility and traveling south on Interstate 84. It would cut through both Oregon and Idaho. Once in Utah, they would skirt past Salt Lake City and Provo. From there they would travel on State Route 6 until it connected to Interstate 70, eventually arriving at the Green River Testing Complex, also known as White Sands.

Derek and the others agreed that the best place for them to ambush the convoy was on Route 6 as the semi was traveling uphill. This was a secluded mountain pass. Woods and hills would surround them and civilian traffic would be limited. The truck's speed would be greatly reduced by the steep incline.

Further, if they initiated the ambush on an S-curve they could keep the three elements separated and occupied. However, this would make it harder for them to support one another. They picked a point near "Soldier Summit." Not only was this site ideal for the ambush but also afforded them multiple escape routes. Susan thought the name of the ambush location sounded fitting.

"Okay," Derek began, recapping their mostly finalized plan, "we will only be using drop-phones. Our personal phones will be left at Mike's to avoid any possible tower triangulation. Josh will be the spotter. He will position himself in a location where he can identify the vehicles, then follow them along the highway. They shouldn't be hard to spot, each is a custom-made vehicle sporting a government license plate. Once he identifies them, Josh will keep us posted on their location and ETA.

"At fifteen minutes out," Derek continued, "because we do not want to involve any local law enforcement, Susan will make an anonymous telephone call to the Wasatch County Sheriff's office. She will tell them she saw an off-duty officer shot on the far end of the county. This should divert all legitimate police officers as far away from us as possible. This will be broadcast as Phase Line Alpha over our radios.

"I will initiate the assault on the target vehicle by detonating a shaped charge. Susan will provide overwatch." Derek indicated a place on the map.

It was determined that since Susan and Derek were both known to the Sasquatch it would be safer if they were the ones present when Scar and the others were released from the back of the trailer.

"We cannot know what state of mind they may be in," Susan said.

"We will call this Phase Line Bravo. The lead vehicle should have already, passed our location. Once the assault begins, depending on how far ahead they are, it should take them between two to five minutes to get turned around and in a position where they can respond. Rios and Jackson will engage and occupy them before they round the corner of the road and have a visual on the trailer. The chase vehicle will be the tricky one. Mike, that is on you and Josh. Keep them pinned down as long as you can.

"When I am able," Derek resumed, "I will breach the trailer. This will be Phase Line Charlie. Once the 'packages' are released, I will call out 'bingo' over the radio. At that point, everyone needs to break contact and initiate our escape and evasion plan. Any questions?"

"What are our rules of engagement?" Rios asked, though he had already made his mind up.

"Though unlikely," Derek began in earnest, "if a local law enforcement officer does stumble in and becomes involved, do not engage with them. Break contact if necessary. However, everyone needs to understand, these agents working for Smith are some evil SOBs. They have already tried to assassinate Susan, Josh, and I on more than one occasion. They will not hesitate to kill any of you.

You should give them the same courtesy. These guys represent everything that is wrong with our government."

They were all quiet for several moments. Derek eventually broke the silence.

"Guys, I know this is some heavy shit I am asking of all of you. If you are not able to help, if you want to back out, now is the time. It is completely understandable. There will be no hard feelings," Derek said, giving everyone an out.

Rios was the first to speak up.

"I can't speak for the others, but this is the most fun I've had in years. It's like having an All-Access Pass at Disneyland." Rios began rubbing his hands together in anticipation. "You couldn't keep me away from this trip even if you wanted to."

"I'm with him," Jackson stated. "I don't think I could listen to one more celebrity complain about how difficult their life is. This is actually the first time in a long time I've felt like I'm involved in something important."

"Well, the way I see it," Mike said, smiling, "we've been on borrowed time for the last thirty years." Derek looked at Susan and Josh. Both were nodding their approval.

"Okay then." Derek smiled. "Let's go shopping." ◉

CHAPTER 40

"SHOPPING SPREE"

Initially, Derek was most concerned about weapons. Then he remembered he was talking with some Marines. He, Josh, and Susan would be utilizing M4 rifles and the handguns they had previously acquired several months earlier. Derek also had his suppressed, bolt action .308 Rifle. However, it was Mike who put the icing on the cake.

Walking them to his basement, Mike opened a huge walk-in gun safe. Inside Mike had an array of weapons on display, including a couple of Heckler & Koch MP5s and an FN-249 SAW belt-fed machine gun.

"What can I say?" Mike said with a shrug and a smile. "This may be California, but... hey, I'm rich!"

Not only had Mike acquired an arsenal of weapons, he had also replaced all the firing pins, barrels and extractors with after-market parts. As such, if a fired shell casing was obtained by law enforcement, it could not be directly traced back to him. Mike was also an avid reloader. Often, he would spend hours in the basement using specialized equipment to reload his ammunition. He had thousands of cartridges in various calibers. Rios and Jackson would be borrowing a couple of Mike's firearms.

With the weapons issue solved, Derek, Mike, and Jackson went to Enterprise Car Rentals. Rios however, remained at the mansion with Susan and Josh. There they went over how each weapon operated. Then they cleaned and lubricated each one thoroughly. With that done, they jammed magazine after magazine full of ammunition.

At the car rental, using one of his fake identifications, Derek rented three Toyota Tundra 4x4 trucks. The team then drove the rented trucks to East Bay Motorsports where Derek purchased three Polaris Ranger XP-1000s utility terrain vehicles, as well as all needed accessories including the trailers necessary to haul them. Mike occasionally offered to purchase something, but Derek had to keep reminding him those purchases could be traced.

After loading the Polarises onto the trailers, they headed back to Mike's home. On the way, Derek stopped and purchased six handheld radios and over a dozen disposable cellular telephones. Then one final stop at a hardware store, where he made a variety of purchases.

Derek's time in the Middle East, especially as a member of the Marines Corps Special Operations Command, exposed him to many of the techniques used by terrorists and insurgents. The Marine Corps had also put him through the Special Operations Forces Explosive Ordinance Disposal Level One Course. Like reverse planning, at the Level One Course, he was taught, before a person can learn how to dismantle an IED they must first learn how they are built.

For their ambush and rescue operations, they determined a number of explosives would be needed to assist them. So, with the supplies he had purchased, Derek got to work on creating them.

First, he used a number of easily obtained household chemicals, such as acetone, peroxide-based bleach and hydrogen peroxide. With the formulations taught to him, Derek developed a Tri-acetone Tri-peroxide explosive, most commonly called TATP. This was not only the most frequently used explosive in IED attacks in Iraq, but by terrorists worldwide.

Next, Derek took some large piping and a metal plate he had acquired and combined them to create a couple of platter charges. This particular shaped charge works off the pressure created by the explosives packed around it. Upon detonation, the metal plate is shaped into a cone, squeezed by the intense pressure until it shoots out of the front of the pipe.

Contrary to popular belief, this cone or carrot-shaped projectile is not molten, but despite being solid, it behaves like a liquid upon impact due to the intense pressure it is under. The plan they had come up with was to use this shaped platter charge to precisely take out the front end of the semitruck.

With the primary explosives completed, Derek took some smaller piping he had bought, as well as the smokeless gun powder Mike used for his reloading. He combined these into a number of pipe bombs. To increase the amount of shrapnel each created, Derek hot-glued about one hundred ball bearings along the outside of each pipe bomb. Derek estimated they would have a kill radius of ten to fifteen meters with a wounding radius of possibly double that.

Their ambush plan called for zero collateral damage. Because they would be using all of these explosives on a roadway traveled by civilians, Derek attached one of the disposable cellular telephones to each of the explosives. Each would have to be command-detonated by calling the cell phone attached to it, which would then act as the detonator. The numbers were programmed into the phones. If a civilian were observed too near any explosive, the team knew they would not be able to detonate them. Derek and

Susan would be responsible for the platter charge while pipe bombs one through three would be under the control of Rios and Jackson, leaving bombs four through six in the control of Mike and Josh.

While Derek worked on the explosives, Mike and Rios left. They told the others they had an errand to run. After returning, Derek asked what it was they had to do. Mike only smiled and told them, "It's a surprise."

The next day they drove two hours to a large private ranch owned by a friend of Mike's. There they had access to thousands of acres where their activities would not be observed.

The first order of business was for them to all practice driving the Polarises. Susan especially enjoyed the way the little Ranger could tackle just about any off-road obstacle. She almost needed to be dragged off the little utility vehicle.

Once done training on the Polarises, each zeroed their weapons. Then Derek ran them through a few malfunction- and close-quarters-marksmanship drills to shake out any cobwebs they may have collected. He was pleasantly surprised none seemed to have lost a step in the years since they had been operational.

With the marksmanship done, Derek wanted to test the explosives. With the extra explosives he created, Derek had each group detonate one of the pipe bombs by using the cellular phones to initiate the detonation. Before each test, he set up some cardboard at various distances to help confirm the explosive radius.

From behind cover, nearly a hundred yards away, they detonated the pipe bombs. Each worked perfectly and the ball-bearing penetrations of the cardboard confirmed the accuracy of Derek's kill-radius estimate. Confident in the pipe bombs, Derek tested the extra platter charge.

The property owner had left an old rusted-out pickup truck abandoned in a field. Derek aimed the shape charge at the front quarter panel and engine compartment. The charge worked as designed and effectively atomized the front of the pickup including the rusty engine. Derek would need to be very precise to avoid harming the Sasquatch secured in the trailer the semi would be hauling.

With all the testing completed, Derek had the group rehearse the ambush multiple times. During each of these rehearsals, Derek threw different twists at each of them. With each scenario he increased the difficultly level to see how they would react.

During one of the breaks, while Derek began to set up a new drill, Susan approached Mike.

"We appreciate all you have done," she began, "but do you mind if I ask you a question?"

"You want to know why myself and the others are risking everything we have built," Mike said, anticipating Susan's question.

"Well, yes," Susan replied.

"That's easy," Mike began. "First, regardless of the time we've spent away from one another, we are brothers. What we went through will forever ties us together. You don't leave a brother to fend for himself when you have the ability to help. Second, the cause you and Derek are fighting for is righteous and we believe in it."

Mike sighed before continuing. "Then there is the final part I don't expect you to appreciate."

"Please tell me?" Susan asked honestly.

"Understand, we are all getting older," Mike began, a little embarrassed. He gestured at Rios and Jackson before continuing. "And well, I guess we just want to have one last hurrah at making a difference in this world before the end comes for us. You see every old man has at least one good fight left in him. This might be ours."

Susan nodded her understanding and gave Mike a hug.

"Okay, people. Let's set it up again," Derek instructed as he finished setting up the next drill. Susan touched Mike's arms and they smiled at one another as they stepped to their starting points.

As dusk began to fall, Derek, satisfied everything was as ready as they were going to be, directed the team to pack up and head back to Mike's. The next day they would be traveling to their ambush location.

Derek was often nervous before executing a mission. Especially those he had planned and was in charge of. The responsibility to Susan, his brothers and indeed to any team he had ever commanded weighed heavily on his mind. Because this mission was not sanctioned by "King and Country" and the team he was leading was comprised of people he loved, that feeling was amplified. Were they doing the right thing?

That night, Scar visited Derek in his dreams again. ◉

CHAPTER 41
"HOSTAGE RESCUE"

They spent most of the fourth day traveling. Whenever they stopped for food or gas Derek quizzed them on their respective elements of the plan. He wanted to leave nothing to chance.

On day five, they arrived at the ambush site. They parked their trucks on a number of different remote access roads identified during the mission planning. There they unloaded the Polarises and drove into the target area.

When the rescue was complete and it was time to escape, each team would hightail it out of the area on their Polaris. They would travel in different directions to make pursuit more difficult. Few vehicles would be able to follow them several miles cross-country. When they arrived at their trucks, the Polarises would be stashed in the brush and left behind. They would then drive the trucks to a predetermined rally point. Even if the Polarises were eventually discovered, they would only be traced back to one of Derek's false identifications.

As Derek walked each through their area of responsibility, he helped them develop optimal fields of fire and identified the best locations for the pipe bombs to be located. They also enhanced their positions by camouflaging them with brush and using stones to build small protective walls to help keep them safe from small-arms fire. When completed, Derek stood in different areas of the road to ensure the positions were completely concealed from any approaching point of view.

While reviewing his position, Derek began using a speed limit road sign for targeting. He watched as the occasional semitruck drove through. They were traveling the same path the target vehicle would the following day. He began estimating each truck's speed and using the road sign as an indicator of when to detonate the platter charge. Derek became confident in his ability to do so with great accuracy.

Once everyone was comfortable with their positions, Derek again had them walk through the plan. Though there was little traffic, they rehearsed without weapons to avoid any unwanted attention by potential passersby. Derek ended the day's rehearsals with each of them driving a Polaris along their escape path. They were as ready as they were going to be.

The next day, they arrived at their positions early. Except for Josh, the others parked their trucks several miles away on different access roads and drove their Polarises to the ambush point. Each donned their tactical gear and checked weapons, putting fresh batteries into their optics. Derek helped Susan and Josh with their equipment.

Josh saw Derek and the other Marines each rip three strips of duct tape off a roll. They placed each of the strips, all several inches long, on their thighs.

"What's with the duct tape?" Josh asked with complete curiosity.

"You never know," Rios replied.

"Any number of things, Josh," answered Jackson. "If, in the middle of a firefight, your shoelace breaks, answer: duct tape. If you lost the pin to a grenade but need to secure the spoon: duct tape. If you capture a tango and need to keep him quiet: duct tape."

"What he is saying, Josh," Derek further clarified, "is we may never need to use it, but if we need to secure something quickly, we have the ability to do so." With that, both Josh and Susan placed three strips of tape on their own thighs.

With the equipment and radio checks completed, they placed the explosives in their predetermined positions. They were now prepped. Before Josh departed in his truck to spot the convoy, Derek brought them all together.

Hugging each one he said, "Be safe. Do not take any unnecessary chances."

As Josh was about to step into his rig, Mike spoke up.

"Ah, guys, one last thing." Mike fished a small box out of his pocket and opened it. "This was the surprise I told you about," Mike explained the items to the group. Derek smiled.

Shortly after Mike finished passing out his surprise, Josh left. The rest moved to their predetermined positions and hunkered down to wait. For the first fifteen minutes, Susan clutched her rifle and continuously attempted to remain covert peering over and around cover as if the enemy could appear any moment. That was until she looked over at Derek.

Sitting on the ground, Derek was leaning against a small tree with his ankles crossed in front of him. He appeared completely relaxed with his rifle laying across his lap and his hands folded over his stomach. Derek had pulled his ball cap down over his eyes. Susan almost thought he was sleeping.

"What are you doing?" she whispered.

With one hand, Derek raised the ball cap slightly and smiled at her. "Trust me. After nearly forty years of this shit, you learn to rest when you can. Take a break and try to relax."

Susan tried to assume the same nonchalant relaxed posture, but she could not bring herself to loosen up. This was, after all, her first ambush.

Nearly three hours passed before Derek's cellular phone finally began to vibrate. It was Josh. Derek sat straight and repositioned his ball cap.

"I have eyes on the vehicles," Josh said. Derek could hear the adrenaline in Josh's voice. It had just become real for him. In his mind, Derek could see where Josh was. He had him take up an observation position along an overpass about 60 miles to their north. This allowed Josh both optimal field of view and the ability to jump in behind the convoy as it drove by. Derek estimated this would give them just under an hour before the convoy arrived.

"Thanks, Josh," Derek replied. "Stay back at least a half mile, but keep your eyes on them." Picking up his radio, Derek transmitted.

"Josh has eyes on the targets. They're about one hour out. Everyone perform one final equipment check."

Time began to slow down. Derek could feel all his senses begin to become sharper. He was used to this feeling. He looked at Susan. Both her hands were shaking. Seeing him watching her, she looked up and smiled.

"I don't know how you were able to do this all those years? My hands are shaking so badly." Susan raised her right hand to show Derek.

"It's just adrenaline. The shaking will stop shortly," he said assuredly. "You will do fine. Remember to breathe and trust your instincts." He reached out and squeezed her shoulder reassuringly.

Every ten minutes Josh called with an update and a mile marker. When they were approximately fifteen minutes out, Derek had Susan telephone the sheriff's office dispatch.

"9-1-1, what are you reporting?" the dispatcher calmly asked.

"Listen," Susan said, the stress in her voice not an act. "I don't want to get involved, but I just saw an off-duty officer shot!"

This time it was the dispatcher's turn to sound stressed. "Where did this occur, ma'am?" the dispatcher asked. Susan provided an approximate predetermined location then, abruptly hung up the telephone.

"Phase Line Alpha," Derek transmitted over the radio.

"Copy that," replied Mike, his deep voice booming over the radio.

"Roger. Phase Line Alpha." Rios, Derek's former radio operator, sounded calm and professional as he spoke over the radio.

Ten minutes later the lead vehicle came into view. The engine of the heavy-duty Sportsmobile van could be heard before it was even seen. Subtlety was not what the agents driving the van were going for.

The van almost appeared to be something out the Road Warrior movies. Painted completely flat black, a large push bar encompassed the front end. The bar was similar to the type police vehicles used for conducting Pursuit Immobilization Techniques. The enlarged multipurpose tires and upgraded suspension were obvious, but it was the three additional antennas arrayed on the roof of the vehicle that truly screamed government. Derek knew these were for their enhanced communications and mobile data terminals.

The vehicle seemed to slow as it entered Derek's predetermined ambush point. Though he did not know why, the hair on the back of his neck began to stand up.

Derek transmitted. "Lead vehicle in sight. Stay down." Two clicks could be heard over Derek's radio as Rios and Mike provided their nonverbal acknowledgment.

Five minutes later, the convoy's semitruck appeared. Derek could hear the driver down shift as it began the steep incline. "Thirty-seconds," Derek transmitted.

At the speed limit sign, Derek estimated the semi was moving at no more than forty miles per hours. "Phase Line Bravo! Phase

Line Bravo!" Derek announced over the radio. He then set off the platter charge.

The platter charge had been timed perfectly. The shaped explosive sent the metal carrot flying through the air. It collided with the front portion of the semitruck nearly cutting the engine compartment in half. The truck came to an almost immediate stop. It partially jackknifed, as the truck itself seemed to lean at an odd angle. Smoke rose from both the engine compartment and cab area. Derek grabbed his rifle and rushed forward.

Within seconds of the platter charge detonation, Derek heard Mike open up with his belt-fed machine gun. He knew this meant Mike had begun engaging the chase vehicle. Soon the level of gunfire increased as the agents began returning fire on Mike's position.

As Derek approached the semi, he held his rifle at the ready. He saw that the driver appeared unconscious or even dead in the driver's seat. He moved around the front of the smoldering engine compartment. Three explosions occurred almost in unison from where Mike had placed his pipe bombs. Derek wanted to rush to his friend's aid but remained committed to his current course of action. He had to trust the plan and his people.

As he rounded the opposite side of the semi, Derek saw that the passenger door had been opened. He had two potential danger areas to contend with, the inside of the cab and the wood line behind him. Pointing his rifle at the cab Derek began to peer inside. That is when he heard a branch snap behind him.

Instinctively, Derek dropped to the ground and spun just as a rifle fired behind him. The bullet made a thwacking sound as it struck the semi where Derek's head had been a second earlier. Pointing his own weapon Derek shot as the agent was readjusting his aim. The bullet found its mark in the center of the agent's face.

That's two down, Derek thought. Where is the third?

This question was quickly answered. Before he could stand, Derek heard an exchange of gunfire occurring from the back of the trailer towards the hillside where Susan was positioned on overwatch. Derek looked under the truck. A pair of men's combat boots stood at the rear corner of the trailer. Derek could see the empty shell casings falling to the ground after each shot.

Aiming his rifle from the prone position, Derek's first bullet hit the agent in the foot, his second struck the man in his knee cap. This caused the agent to fall to the ground in full view. Now seeing the agent's exposed head, Derek fired a third round. The agent lay motionless.

As Derek stood, explosions and gunfire began to occur in Rios and Jackson's area of operation. There was no time to waste.

Derek rushed to the back of the truck. The doors were secured with a large lock. Derek had anticipated this. As he began to pull a set of medium-sized bolt cutters from the back of his utility vest Susan arrived at his side holding her rifle. Derek positioned the hardened-steel cutting edges along the lock. Using both arms, he grabbed the tubular handles near the ends to amplify his leverage. The lock snapped easily.

With the lock cut, Derek began to swing open the doors to the trailer. "Phase Line Charlie! Phase Line Charlie!" Derek transmitted. Susan grabbed his shoulder smiling. They were going to make it.

With the doors full open, Derek and Susan peered inside. Except for the security camera affixed to the far wall, the trailer was empty. The red light below the camera indicated it was on and recording them.

It took Derek less than a second to process this new piece of information. His realization turned to dread as he grabbed Susan by the elbow, pulling her away from the truck. Together they began sprinting towards their Polaris.

"Dry Hole! Dry Hole!" Derek yelled into his radio. "Everyone break contact! Break contact! It's a trap!"

As Derek and Susan ran, gunfire was still occurring where Mike and Josh were engaging the command vehicle. The area Rios and Jackson were operating in however had gone eerily quiet.

That is when everything, the planning, rehearsals, and execution began to come undone. ◉

CHAPTER 42

"MURPHY'S LAW"

First quoted by German Field Marshal Helmuth von Moltke in the late 1800s, "No plan survives first contact with the enemy." When you add Murphy's Law to the equation, specifically, "If something can go wrong, it will." It is easy to understand why military planners frequently develop redundancies into their planning. Derek had not anticipated the convoy was actually a trap nor the use of helicopters by Smith's agents. This was about to bite them in the ass.

They had nearly gotten to their Polaris when the first of two HU-60 Ghost Hawk helicopters flew over the ridgeline making a beeline directly at Susan and Derek. These were the premiere stealth helicopters in the government's arsenal. They were equipped with state-of-the-art noise reduction technology. Smith had previously used one of these helicopters against them. It appeared he was doing so again.

Throwing his rifle into the bed, Derek leaped on the Polaris and started it up. Susan jumped in next to him. The ground erupted in front of them. Derek looked out the window. The side door of the helicopter was open. A gunner, sitting in the side of the helicopter, aimed a M134 mini-gun at them. The mini-gun's six rotatory barrels were capable of firing nearly 6,000 rounds per minutes. The gunner could have easily destroyed the Polaris and killed them. Instead, he had fired a warning burst, which caused the ground to erupt in front of them. Looking out the passenger window they saw that the other helicopter had also come broadside.

"They want us to give up," Derek said, looking at Susan. "Way I see it, if we give up now, they will capture us and maybe the others too. Or...."

"Or we can buy them some time," Susan said, ending his sentence. Derek nodded.

Susan leaned across the cab of the Ranger. As her hand rested on his cheek, she kissed him on the lips.

"What is the SRT motto you once told me?" Susan asked as she pulled away from the embrace.

"To the ends of the earth. Faithful even after death," Derek replied, understanding.

"Fuck it!" Susan replied, smiling. "Let's give the boys some time to escape."

Without another word, Derek threw the Polaris Ranger into gear. The UTV leaped forward. Within moments, the Ranger was at maximum speed.

"It worked! They're both following us!" Susan yelled as she cranked her head around to peer out the Polaris's windows.

Derek drove the Polaris into a gully. As one helicopter moved to intercept, he turned sharply and headed in another direction up the mountain. Derek deliberately drove away from where the others had concealed their pickup trucks. He only hoped they had been able to break contact. He had to have faith.

As they continued to evade the pursuing helicopters, five minutes passed, then ten. Not only could they no longer see the ambush site, they could no longer even see the road. Occasionally, they lost sight of the helicopters as they traveled under the tree line. This was the most difficult terrain to travel, though, as the heavy brush seemed to hinder the Polaris the most. However, this provided Derek an idea. Pulling into an especially dense area of forest, Derek stopped the Polaris and shut the engine down.

"What are you doing?" Susan asked.

"Okay." Derek took a deep breath and looked Susan in the eyes. "This is where I buy you some time."

"Absolutely not!" Susan protested. "Where you go, I go!"

"Listen." Derek grabbed her by her shoulders. "I can move quickly and hopefully occupy them long enough for you to get away. I want you to hide over there"—he pointed at some thick brush—"until I am out of sight. Then wait ten minutes. Once it is safe, begin working your way back to our truck."

"No!" Susan continued to object. The sounds of the helicopters circling above the forest's canopy could be heard only a few hundred feet above them.

"Someone needs to find out what happened to the others. Someone needs to get to Winoski. We both can't get away." After several moments of consideration, Susan reluctantly nodded her agreement.

They stepped out from the Polaris. As Derek grabbed his rifle from the back of the vehicle Susan wrapped her arms around him, hugging him tightly.

"I love you!" she said.

"I love you more!" Derek replied with a smile. With that, Derek turned and sprinted up the hill.

About two hundred yards from where he had left the Polaris, Derek came to a clearing. Deliberately exposing himself, Derek stepped into the open and leveled his rifle at the nearest helicopter. He began firing. Within seconds, those on the helicopter became aware of his location. The helicopter he was firing on began banking away as the second helicopter turned broadside, leveling the mini-gun in his direction. Before they could fire, Derek ran back into the wood line.

After running another few hundred yards, Derek stepped out and repeated his actions. This time however, he only saw one helicopter. After firing, Derek turned preparing to move back into the wood line. That is when he saw the second helicopter.

About five hundred yards up the mountain; the helicopter was hovering fifty feet off the ground. Derek watched as a dozen heavily armed agents began to fast-rope out the sides. Using only gloved hands and ankles wrapped around the two-inch-thick rope, each man quickly descended to the ground like a firefighter sliding down a pole when an alarm sounds.

Looking back at the first helicopter, Derek saw it, too, had agents fast-roping onto the mountain below him. He was boxed in.

It is now a ground battle, Derek considered. He performed a quick situational assessment.

Checking his rifle, he discovered it contained a half-loaded magazine. He had two additional magazines remaining in his tactical vest. He also had three full magazines left for his handgun. Derek had a canteen of water strapped to his hip but no food.

The sun had moved behind the mountain and it would be dark in an hour. He had no night vision or thermal capabilities, which the agents surely would have and employ. When the sun went down, the temperature would definitely drop. Derek's light clothing poorly equipped him for a nighttime and mountainous, forest operation. Smiling he recognized his rookie planning mistake. He chalked it up to being rusty. Derek made a mental note that the next time he would need to consider this possibility.

"Well, I guess the odds are even," Derek said aloud partly to encourage himself.

Purposefully, Derek began moving from one position of cover to the next. Often, he would crawl pausing frequently to listen for sounds of the approaching agents. Nearly fifteen minutes passed before he saw the first of them. They, too, were moving very cautiously. Peering out from under some brush, Derek saw they had formed a skirmish line.

Moving slowly, they were communicating with hand and arm signals. He assumed they may have also been using radios and whispering into throat mics when necessary. Derek knew the group below him was maneuvering towards him the same way. He needed to disrupt their plan and create a hole in the skirmish line he could escape through.

Aiming his rifle, Derek picked two agents moving in close proximity to one another. He squeezed the trigger. The first shot struck the nearest agent squarely in the head. Derek transitioned his aim to the second agent and fired before the first agent had fallen to the ground. After the second agent collapsed, the grass, dirt and pine needles around Derek's position erupted with impacting bullets. Several agents had zeroed in on his position and had begun firing.

Derek rolled away and rebounded into a standing position. He sprinted to a thick tree nearly four feet in diameter. As Derek leaped behind it, bark splintered from the tree's trunk as bullets from multiple shooters struck it.

Taking a kneeling position, Derek leaned to his right, only exposing enough of himself to aim. Spying an agent running in his general direction, Derek fired several rounds. The agent fell behind some brush.

Transitioning his rifle into a left-handed shooting position Derek leaned to the left side of the tree. In a mirror image of what he had done around the right side, Derek aimed the rifle. Again, he fired several rounds. Another agent dropped. The bolt of the rifle locked to the rear as the magazine ran empty. Derek ejected the empty magazine then loaded another. With a quick glance, Derek sprinted away from the tree towards his next position.

More gunfire struck the ground near his feet as he ran. This time he jumped behind a large moss-covered bolder. From a prone position, Derek fired his weapon dry again. While reloading his final, already half-empty magazine, a bullet ricocheted off the rock near his head. This shot had come from below him. Rolling onto his back Derek located the agent who fired at him. He dropped this agent with several well-placed shots. Unfortunately, his rifle was now empty.

Removing the rifle's sling from around his neck Derek dropped the empty rifle on the ground and drew his pistol. Quickly assessing the area, Derek located another large tree about forty yards away. He took several deep breaths to increase the oxygen in his lungs, then without waiting a moment longer, he leaped to his feet.

In an all-out sprint, Derek ran towards the tree. It was not that he was oblivious to the bullets whistling past his head, but rather he chose to ignore them. Miraculously he made it to the tree.

As he circled behind the tree, Derek's body collided with one of Smith's agents who had already positioned himself on the other side. The collision knocked the pistol from Derek's hand. Both Derek and the agent looked at one another with the same expression of shock on their face. Then the agent began to raise his own rifle towards Derek.

Automatically, Derek closed the distance and wrapped his left arm around the agent's rifle immobilizing it. The agent tried in vain to pull his weapon loose from Derek's grip. Drawing his knife, Derek thrust it out in rapid succession six times. The knife found its mark just under the agent's armpit. Penetrating the agent's body, the blade collapsed his lung and sliced through the axillary artery. The agent collapsed.

While turning to retrieve his pistol, another agent rounded the tree. Before the agent could bring his rifle to bear, Derek grabbed the barrel and shoved it offline, away from him as the rifle discharged. That is when this agent did something unexpected. He released his grip on the rifle and rushed towards Derek, tackling him to the ground. They began exchanging blows as each fought for a better position. As they continued to wrestle on the ground, two more agents appeared. Both pointed their weapons at Derek's head.

"Don't move, motherfucker!" the agent nearest Derek yelled as he placed the barrel of his rifle on Derek's right ear.

Derek froze. Then slowly he raised his hands and came to a kneeling position. As the man Derek had been wrestling with began to stand, Derek felt a boot kick him hard in the center of his back. The wind was knocked out of him as he face-planted into the dirt and moss.

Rough hands grabbed Derek's arms and pulled them behind his back. He felt handcuffs tightly securing his wrists. With his hands secure, the agents stood Derek up and stripped every piece of gear off him. Having been thoroughly searched, a dark cloth hood was placed over his head, blinding him.

For what seemed like ten minutes, Derek was marched through the forest. Though he occasionally stumbled, hands clutching both of his secured arms kept him from falling. Derek knew they were approaching a clearing as he could hear the sounds of a helicopter idling on the ground. As they drew near, the wind created by the helicopter's rotor wash nearly pulled the hood off Derek's head, before an agent's hand secured it in place.

Derek felt himself being hoisted up and thrown onto the floor of the waiting helicopter. He could feel people crowding in around him. The sound of the helicopter's side door sliding shut was unmistakable. Derek was dragged into a seated position. That is when he heard Smith's distinctive voice.

"Hold it. Remove his hood." Smith's command seemed louder than the sound of the helicopter's blades spooling up.

The hood was ripped from Derek's head. He blinked hard several times so his eyes could adjust. There was Smith, sitting on the far side of the helicopter's cabin. Making matters worse and nearly destroying Derek's morale was seeing Susan sitting on the bench, next to Smith. She too had been captured. Her hands were bound behind her back and a gag had been wrapped tightly around her head. Her eyes filled with tears as she saw Derek sitting on the floor of the cabin, dirt, and sweat covering his face.

Derek watched as Smith grinned at him. Then Smith brought one of his long boney hands up and began stroking the hair on the back of Susan's head as if she were his pet.

It was too much. As Derek began to rise off the floor. The butt-stroke from an agent's rifle sent his world into darkness. ◉

CHAPTER 43
"A CONVERSATION WITH SMITH"

Slowly Derek began to wake up. He did not know how long he had been unconscious. He was unsure whether it was day or night. Initially, his mind was befuddled, though slowly it was beginning to clear up. Derek was unsure if his grogginess was due to the blow to the head or if they had also given him a tranquilizer while he was out. The only thing he was sure of was that they were no longer on the helicopter.

Instead, Derek discovered he had been strapped down to some type of metal gurney. Both his wrists and ankles were secured by thick leather straps. He could feel the strap's large buckles. Due to the cold metal of the gurney against Derek's skin, he correctly surmised he had been stripped down to his boxer shorts. His captors had not cared enough to use so much as a sheet to cover him.

Derek was unable to see anything. The black hood, which was thrown over his head when he had been captured, was now replaced by some type of eye mask. The mask was similar to what a person trying to sleep might wear.

The gurney was in motion. One of the wheels made an audible squeak as it rolled. There were at least two men pushing the gurney. Derek was able to ascertain this by listening to the sounds of their breathing and other noises they made. Derek got the impression they had turned a corner. The way their footfalls resounded Derek assumed they were inside a structure. After a few minutes, the gurney came to a full stop. Derek heard one of the two men walk a short distance away. Then there was an audible click.

"Where are we taking him?" one of the male voices inquired.

"5208. I was told they have something different in mind for this one," the other answered.

Moments later, Derek heard the quiet sounds of pulleys, cables, and motors followed by the clamor of metal gliding open. The men pushed Derek and the gurney a few feet. Seconds later the sound of sliding alloy again reached Derek's ears. This noise was quickly replaced by a hum and vibration.

Deducing he was on an elevator, Derek tried to determine if he was going up or down. He could not. He approximated they had traveled several floors due to the amount of time they were on the elevator. By the number, 5208, Derek assumed they had arrived on the fifth floor.

Leaving the elevator, Derek was wheeled down a hallway, finally ending in a room. There, the men removed his blindfold. Derek's eyes were assaulted by the bright lights dominating the room. For a few moments, Derek had to squint and blink before his eyes eventually became accustomed to the light.

"Wakey. Wakey," one of the men said to Derek and patted him on the cheek none too gently. They wore light-green surgical scrubs. These gave the appearance the men were medical orderlies. It was their tight haircuts and athletic appearance that had Derek convinced they were or at least had been military of some type. Now most likely, they were agents working for Smith.

"Thank you for your service," one of the orderlies sarcastically said with a crooked grin, after observing Derek's Marine Corps tattoos. He gave a mock salute. With that, as the two walked from the room, they left Derek strapped to the gurney. Derek could hear them laughing as they locked the door behind them.

Craning his head around, Derek attempted to see what type of room he had been left in. Initially, it appeared to be an examination room. The walls were made of concrete blocks painted a light gray. The door that the orderlies departed through, was made of metal, painted slightly darker than the walls.

Affixed to the door, just above the handle was an OMNI lock. For access through this door the lock required both a PIV badge and PIN code be used. Large medical examination lights attached to moveable arms hovered above Derek. A counter and cabinets sat along one side of the room. Beyond, was a second open doorway. This appeared to allow access into some form of operating room. In the corner, near the main door, sat a standard issue government chair.

Derek tested the restraints. They were tight. He began wondering about whether dislocating or breaking his own thumb would allow enough space for his hand to slip loose. He began to give this thought serious consideration.

With his left thumb, Derek reached as far as he could across his palm. He could just about touch the base of his pinky finger. He wrapped all his fingers around his thumb and began to squeeze.

This is going to hurt, Derek thought as he bit his lip. He was preparing to break his own thumb when the door to the examination room opened.

Smith strolled in. As the door began to close Derek observed two armed guards standing in the hallway just outside. Smith paused at the foot of the gurney. He looked down at Derek and smirked.

Turning, Smith grabbed the top of the government-issued chair. Like fingernails on a chalkboard, the chair made a screeching sound, as he pulled it closer to the table. Smith sat. Even seated Smith's tall frame allowed him to continue looking down on Derek, as he lay helpless.

"Mr. Riley, I am so pleased you are awake," Smith began. "I was afraid I would be called away before we'd had a chance to finally talk."

"Where are you holding Susan?" Derek demanded. As much as he could, Derek kept his emotions out of his voice.

"In good time," Smith countered. He looked at Derek for several moments before speaking. "You know, I've been at this game a long time and honestly, I cannot recall the last time I came across any one person who caused me so much trouble."

"Yeah well, I've been told I have serious issues with authority," Derek retorted. Smith nodded.

"Fifteen of my men were killed by you and your friends up on that mountain. Several more were wounded. I have to admit, it was honestly kind of amazing," Smith said with a small amount of adoration in his voice.

"I guess that means you're starting to run out of henchmen!" Derek needled. Smith grinned back.

"Oh no, there is never a lack of people willing to join up. You were the oddity in that respect," Smith answered.

"Of course, by now you've figured out, I deliberately set the trap when I sent that encrypted file to Mr. Russo. I couldn't make it too easy or you would have guessed the purpose. I also knew what bait to use that neither you nor Dr. Parker could resist. Obviously, your sense of right and wrong would have you try to rescue those Nephilim. We even anticipated a few places where you might try to spring the escape. What I did not foresee was you bringing a couple of friends along as well. They didn't make it, by the way. Most were killed on the mountain, whereas one died from his wounds as we were transporting him." Smith sighed heavily as if disheartened by his own statement.

Derek clenched his jaw. He was not going to give Smith any more reactions. He knew Smith was a sadist and wanted to inflict psychological as well as physical damage in his triumph.

"Why, Smith, or should I say Baxter? I mean why aren't you dead?" Derek asked honestly.

Six months earlier, Derek's friend Marcus Pettiford had been with the SRT's PsyOps unit. Besides the psychological operations they performed, the PsyOps team also conducted research and intelligence. Before he was murdered by Smith's men, Marcus discovered Smith's true name was Philip Baxter and that Baxter had joined the OSS near the end of World War II.

"Simply amazing," Smith said with a raised eyebrow. "You know, there are maybe five people left on the planet that know my given name. I sometimes forget it myself." Glancing at his watch, Smith nodded his head as he looked up. "We have a little time, so I guess it wouldn't hurt to tell you a story." Derek twisted his hand in the restraint.

"Our little grey friends have been coming to this planet for thousands of years." Seeing that this admission had not shocked Derek, Smith added, "Yes, everything Mr. Winoski told you was true. We will catch up with him shortly. Of that I am sure. Anyways, these greys didn't seed our planet; mind you, we are not sure who did, but they have been using it for their own purposes. They've been performing DNA, gene manipulation and other experiments the entire time.

"Making hybrid creatures and such; though, to be forthright, they have never satisfactorily told us why. It is from these experiments that many of the legends and fables come from. There are images of hybrids in carvings, pictographs, and hieroglyphics.

Throughout Mesopotamia to South America, similar hybrids can be found but to date no one has connected the dots.

Smith continued. "Many of these hybrids, like the mythical griffin, would eventually be destroyed. Then there are others, such as the Nephilim. Let's call that one of their mistakes. Initially they were attempting to hybridize and advance a species for, in essence slave labor, but like some experiments, they lost control. Like a virus that escapes from a research laboratory, it multiplied and mutated. We now have to keep a lid on them because if any were truly captured and DNA collected, it would reveal the truth."

"And what truth is that?" Derek asked.

"That the Nephilim are a true hybrid creation," Smith acknowledged. "Many thousands of years ago they mixed human DNA with another species not native to this planet. Human women originally bore many of these offspring. Unfortunately, unlike other experiments, they were too intelligent and escaped their creators. Of course, the greys were unconcerned.

"Now many of the different religions learned centuries ago about the existence of aliens. However, few learned what their purpose was. Allowing their existence to be known meant, of course, the loss of their power over the masses. Some senior members of different governments and secret groups, such as the Freemasons, also learned the truth but kept it to themselves for the same reason.

"For hundreds of years," Smith continued, "the aliens seemed to be fine staying in the shadows. They still do for the most part. However, then came World War II. That is when something in the grey's plan changed." Smith paused for dramatic effect.

"The greys, that is how they are commonly referred to. We, of course, have a different name for them, but it would mean nothing to you. Anyways, they began working with a government," Smith continued. "Not ours unfortunately. They actually began working with the Nazis. They even worked alongside that German Schutzstaffel officer Josef Mengele and other Nazi scientists."

Knowing the abhorrent experiments Mengele performed as part of the Nazi SS, just the thought of the greys assisting him, Derek found completely appalling. *Now they are working with people in our own government*, Derek thought.

"Were you aware," Smith said without acknowledging the look that had come across Derek's face, "the Nazis believed they were the descendants of an ancient Aryan, some documents even say alien race? Himmler even set up the Ahnenerbe, the Institute for Ancestral Research, that combed Europe for evidence of this. The SS heavily researched the occult and all things supernatural. They even had a 'witch division' responsible for seeking and exploiting evidence of witches and wizardry. They were actually quite ahead of their time in my opinion." Reverence filled Smith's voice as he spoke.

"If they had all this extraterrestrial help, why didn't the Nazis win the war?" Derek asked. Although repulsed, he was actually interested in what Smith was saying.

"Well, it was not because they did not have the resources or ability. Germany's loss simply came down to bad luck, though some might argue divine intervention. In reality, some of our scientists seemingly became inspired, while at the same time the leadership of the Third Reich was greatly flawed. You know how that story ended. I imagine, if Hitler and Heinrich Himmler were not in charge, there would probably have been a vastly different outcome and we'd all be speaking German right now.

"Following the end of the war," Smith forged ahead, "instead of trying these Nazis for war crimes in Nuremberg, we conducted 'Operation Paperclip.' Secretly our government brought more than

1,600 Nazi scientists into the United States. Many of whom had committed war crimes that our government chose to overlook. The Russian's did similar with scientists they captured.

"These Nazis began working with us. Scientists such as Wernher von Braun, who was placed in charge of our space program. During the war, von Braun had been influential in the Nazi Party and was in charge of building advanced rockets to launch missiles into the civilian areas of London." Smith paused and scratched his chin before continuing.

"When we began collaborating with the Nazi scientists, two things happened. First, we realized the extent of involvement the Nazis had with the greys especially near the end of the war. Secondly, the greys approached our government and offered a proposition similar to the one they had given the Nazis. We have been colluding with them in earnest since the mid-1950s. That is where my job began," Smith said arrogantly.

"And what exactly is that, besides being a colossal, murdering, prick-of-misery?" Derek asked, hoping to irritate Smith.

"I am the fixer," Smith continued, without concern for Derek's insult. "After World War II, our government could not let the populous know we were working with the same Nazis they'd fought against just years earlier. For the same reason, we could not let them know about the greys and our collective agreement.

"Over the years, we had to keep the truth concealed while at the same time, controlling the population and narrative. No secret lasts forever. However, we needed to have it kept long enough for us to be able to obtain complete control when the information is finally released.

"To do this, we again looked at history. Take the Nazis for example. Not all Germans were evil, and we wanted to understand how nearly seventy percent of Germany supported the Nazi Party in their extermination of the Jews and other so-called atrocities. We conducted the Milgram's Experiment in the 1960s and again several variations of the experiment since then. These experiments on 'destructive obedience' have always panned out with about the same percentages even as recently as our 2015 test.

"What the Milgram Experiment taught us," Smith explained, "is sixty to seventy percent of any population will always willingly obey those perceived to be in power. They will blindly follow direction even if they disagree with the morality of it. Some will do so willingly because they do not want to be placed in the position of having to make difficult decisions. Others, because they are afraid they will get in trouble, and then the final group because they believe the people in charge must know better. With the knowledge we obtained from Milgram, we realized we can control two thirds of any population if we simply control the narrative."

"There is always the other third," Derek replied defiantly. "A third of us won't simply bend over for you and take it."

"Yes, this is true," Smith acknowledged, nodding his head. "We cannot have a third of the population standing up in defiance, so they must be contained. Once again, we've learned from history how to do this. Eighteen months before the Declaration of Independence, British troops headed to Lexington and Concord. They were not looking for rebels advocating resistance. They were under specific orders to seize and destroy arms and munitions believed hidden in the town. Had they been successful, they revolution would have never occurred." Smith appeared to enjoy his grasp on history.

"Then, take the Bolshevik Revolution. Prior to 1917, every Russian owned a firearm. This allowed the Bolshevik's to overthrow the then government. Following the execution of the Tsar, Joseph Stalin knew what the peasants could do if they remained armed. As such, he initiated a large-scale confiscation of civilian firearms, thus guaranteeing his power." Smith glanced at his watch before continuing.

"We understood that confiscating firearms would be considerably more difficult in the US, so we looked at how the Nazis controlled their defiant third. First, the Nazis instituted a gun registration, under the auspices of 'safety.' Once the Nazis knew where the guns were, they followed up with gun confiscation. Those still not falling in line were placed into re-education camps. A similar model was used in China and elsewhere.

"It is taking longer, but we will eventually reach that goal here as well. Once we have, we can move forward with the rest of the program," Smith proclaimed.

"Confiscating firearms can't by itself control a country!" Derek countered.

"True, but it is definitely a good start." Smith grinned. "It is for that reason there are multiple aspects of the program we are implementing. We have been distracting the populace by getting them focused on basic needs and creating conflict within subgroups. In doing so, most won't recognize the loss of certain freedoms when they occur. To accomplish this, we recognized the narrative must be controlled. Anything that may disrupt or alter that narrative falls to me to silence.

"The second part is quieting the final third. For that, we have funded and now control some well-placed politicians and some business executives. A few of whom are even aware of the complete program, though most are not. Many of these politicians help because they are simply eager, if for nothing else, to increase their own power base." Smith half laughed with a contempt Derek shared.

"Controlling the narrative began years ago. There was the traditional way the Nazis did it. We copied this and began heavily controlling the narrative in the early 1970s with Operation Mockingbird." When Smith noticed Derek looking at him confused, he explained further.

"Operation Mockingbird was the brainchild of Director William Colby. He served in the OSS with me. Colby recruited nearly four hundred journalists into the CIA. Some of the journalists were already established, while others were coming right out of college.

"These journalists signed onto the CIA payroll for a variety of reasons. Some wanted to be James Bond, others simply for the money. The reason did not matter but their collective voice gave Colby great control over what information the public was provided and how it was disseminated. Every director since has maintained this program and we frequently use it to manipulate the free press to our advantage.

"Take assault weapons, for example. There are maybe four hundred people a year who die from them. In comparison, nearly 500 percent more are killed with knives and several thousand more killed as a result of DUIs. But because we have controlled the narrative, the country is now on the verge of both a registration and ban under the auspices of safety. These are two of the critical pieces the Nazis and others recognized as necessary for gaining control over the defiant third.

"Another objective of the program," Smith casually explained, "is doing away with any form of paper currency or coins. We began this years ago, but the electronic age has finally made this practical. We are selling this idea to the masses as 'convenience.' However, once everything has converted to digital, we will not only be able to track everyone's movements but more importantly, we will be able to shut down specific individuals, locations, or entire states with the flip of the switch.

"People will not be able to buy food or even put gas in their vehicles unless we approve of it. Once those two elements are firmly in place, control over the populace has for all intents and purposes been achieved," Smith stated pleasantly.

"The Nazis to a lesser degree, attempted something similar when they first made Jewish citizens wear stars on their chests. Eventually, they tattooed numbers on their arms. In essence, we will be able to do the same thing using a person's bank account or social security number for identification, and ultimately, control. We are almost there."

"I think I may have heard this story before, Smith," Derek said. "My Sunday school teacher called it the mark of the beast!" Smith again nodded at the comparison but did not say more.

"So, who do you work for, Smith?" Derek asked, flexing his hand. Smith thought about the question for several moments before answering.

"Since you won't be around much longer," Smith began, "there is no harm in telling you. Technically, I am employed by the Central Intelligence Agency. Though there was once even a time when I was all about the flag and patriotism. However, as I grew older, my loyalty shifted. It became about the greater good of the program." Smith looked at Derek for several heartbeats before continuing.

"Though it may appear that our government is running the program, which, in a way, certain elements within the government do, its true direction comes from just a few wealthy individuals and a handful of politicians. Now, knowing the truth and what is eventually in store for us, I decided to serve my own interests, just like those I answer to.

"There are some benefits." Smith grinned. "I'm going to let you in on a little secret. You asked, why I'm not dead. Well, to put it simply, that is because the greys have prolonged my life. There are a handful of government officials and a few of those wealthy elites I told you about, who are aware of this benefit and have had their lives prolonged as well.

"We are not immortal," Smith explained, "however our aging process has been slowed dramatically. The greys have curtailed our genetic decay almost completely. My only regret is the greys did not introduce me to this portion of the program until I was in my sixties. Nevertheless, I am sure you would acknowledge there are many people who would willingly murder tens of thousands for that little incentive alone."

The door to the room opened. One of the agents who had previously wheeled Derek in entered. He was pushing a portable IV stand. A saline IV bag was already hanging from the top of the stand.

Both Smith and Derek watched as the agent stopped near the opposite end of the gurney. The agent pulled some tubing from the pocket of his scrubs. It was still contained in its protective plastic. Tearing open the plastic bag, he removed the tubing. Taking the spike located near the drip chamber of the tube, he removed the protective cover from the top. With the plastic cover removed, he penetrated the IV with the spike.

"Unfortunately, Mr. Riley," Smith said, glancing at his watch again. "I see our time together has come to an end. I do regret having to put you down, as you have been a most competent adversary. But I simply can no longer risk having you running around." Standing, Smith nodded at the orderly and began to depart.

"Wait!" yelled Derek. "Two last questions." Smith stopped and turned back towards Derek.

"The Sasquatch that were supposed to be in that truck. What happened to them?"

"Ah yes." Smith nodded his head. "Like I said, I knew bait was needed to lure you and Ms. Parker. They were the perfect choice.

We still have them and are in the process of conducting a number of experiments on them, but the actual convoy won't occur for another several weeks. What is your second question?"

"Where is Susan?" Derek asked all pretext gone as genuine emotion entered his voice.

"Well, that is kind of 'good news bad news' story for you there," Smith said. "The good news is Ms. Parker is still alive and probably will be for quite some time. The bad news is our hosts, the greys; are especially interested in her rare Rh-Negative blood type. They want to use her in their hybrid breeding program."

"What!" Derek blurted almost in disbelief.

"Oh, yes," Smith stated nonchalantly. "The greys have been creating alien-human hybrids for a while now. They haven't told us why, but they use human females to act as incubators. Ms. Parker will be part of that experiment for the foreseeable future. Though I don't imagine she will be fond of the experience."

"I'm going to kill you, Smith!" Derek spat.

"No, Mr. Riley, you will not. Farewell, it has been stimulating." With that, Smith turned and walked out the door.

Derek began to struggle against his restraints.

"Just relax, buddy," the agent said. "Smith wanted this to be quick." Ignoring Derek's movements, the agent tied a light-blue, rubber tourniquet around Derek's bicep. He then took a small alcohol pad and sterilized the area near the bend in Derek's elbow.

"Are you kidding me?" Derek said in disbelief. "You're going make sure I don't get an infection before you kill me!"

The agent looked amused as he palpated the target vein by tapping lightly on it with a couple of fingers. He then expertly inserted the needle and advanced the catheter. With that, he released the tourniquet and attached the IV. Taking a small vial from his pocket, he began filling a syringe.

"Once I inject this into your IV, you will simply go to sleep. Your heart will stop, as will your breathing, but you won't feel a thing." The agent grabbed the access port of the IV bag and began injecting the fluid.

It is now or never, Derek thought. He grabbed his thumb and squeezed as hard as he could. It snapped at the trapezium bone near his wrist. Derek did not even feel the pain as his eyes began to flutter. The chemical worked quickly. There was no time left as his mind began getting cloudy.

Derek tried pulling his hand out of the restraint, but his arm would not follow his commands. As Derek's eyes began to roll back into his head, the last thing he saw was the orderly lurch and stumble somewhat as he turned away from the gurney.

Derek's breathing stopped. ◉

CHAPTER 44
"IN THE WHITE"

Derek did not know if he was dreaming or awake. Every ache or pain he had or ever had was gone. All his concerns, regrets, and worries had vanished. The only thing Derek knew for sure was he felt absolute peace and relaxation.

Opening his eyes, Derek believed he was lying flat on his back, but he was not certain even that was correct. As he stared up, or at least what he thought was up, he saw nothing but white. No ceiling. No blue sky. No clouds. Just endless white.

Moving to a seated position, he looked around. In every direction the white was omnipresent. Derek looked at the ground he was now sitting on. Except, there was no ground, just white. He even noticed the pants and shirt he now wore seemed to be a soft cotton-type fabric, but they, too, were white. Derek stood.

Slowly he began turning. The view never changed, just nondescript universal white in all directions. It had no depth. Derek placed both hands near his mouth. Forming a cone to amplify his voice, Derek yelled.

"Hello!"

"Hello, Derek." Immediately came the voice from directly behind him. Derek spun. Where there was nothing only moments before now stood a person. Though, Derek could tell he was not human.

The being was tall, but not exceptionally so. He was dressed similar to Derek but had the thin build of a runner. Though his features were sharp and feminine, he had a masculine quality, which presented an unparalleled strength. His skin was smooth and unblemished, almost waxlike. Aside from his straight, shoulder length, nearly golden hair, he had no eyebrows, or other visible hair.

It was however, his piercing blue eyes that caught Derek's attention. They were twice the size of a normal persons. Stranger still was that each eye had a dual iris and pupil. He smiled kindly at Derek.

"Is this a dream, or am I dead?" Derek asked with all sincerity.

"It is both," he replied. "It is also neither."

"Well, that's just fantastic," Derek said with a touch of sarcasm paired with a half smile. "I might be dead but at least I get to have a conversation with Confucius."

"I have always enjoyed your sense of humor," he said, still smiling. "You are not dead, but you will be able to move on if you chose to do so. However, our Father is not yet done with you. You are not dreaming. Though we are, in a manner of speaking, having this conversation within your subconscious."

"And, where am I?" Derek queried.

"Your physical body is strapped to a gurney at what you know to be the S4 Site. There it has been injected with a poison. But what 'you are' is here with me," he said.

"And where is here?" Derek asked.

"This is where your kind travel to before they move on or return," he responded.

"Okay, I'll bite. Who are you?" Derek inquired as he looked more intently at the newcomer.

"I have many names. Most of which you would not be able to pronounce. In your language I am most fond of Gabriel," he replied.

"Gabriel. You mean like the archangel?" Derek asked.

"We have actually grown rather fond of that description," Gabriel replied with a smile. "Some of my siblings even enjoy enhancing that slight misconception. Although we have been with you since the beginning and many of us are the inspiration to those stories, we are not angels in the traditional biblical sense. Though, that is for all practical purposes, exactly what we are."

"So, I am basically talking with an angel. Is that what you are telling me? I have to say in all honesty, Gabriel—you look a little more like an Elf," Derek said, raising an eyebrow.

"We can manifest any form we choose," Gabriel countered. "For example, most of humanity would probably think I should appear more like this."

Quicker than Derek could blink, Gabriel's appearance changed. He was now fully adorned in shining armor that seemed to have been polished to a mirror finish. White flowing robes rustled in a nonexistent breeze. Large wings, nearly twice the size of a man and covered in white feathers, spread openly behind him. A soft glow of light radiating from an unknown source illuminated his entirety.

"Okay," Derek acknowledged with more than a touch of wonderment. "I admit that is pretty damn impressive."

"Thank you," Gabriel said and bowed slightly. Instantly he returned to his original appearance.

"So, the whole God and Devil thing is real?" Derek inquired.

"We have been presenting ourselves to humanity since your beginning. Sometimes we manifest ourselves in a physical form or at times, we project ourselves into a person's dreams or subconscious. We try to teach, inspire, influence, and protect." Gabriel sat on a chair that was not there and crossed his legs.

"As far as you referring to our Father as God. That is probably the most accurate description. He is the creator of everything," Gabriel explained. "Look around you."

"I don't understand," Derek said.

"What do you see?" Gabriel encouraged.

Derek looked in every direction. "Nothing. I see absolutely nothing."

"Exactly. Nothing. No trees. No sky. No bird. No wind. No textures or smells. Just nothing." As Gabriel spoke, he gestured to the vastness of the white with his arms. "If I wasn't here with you, there would be no one to even talk to.

"Now imagine you were here, alone." Gabriel paused. "Though you have no reference even for the passage of time, your days turn into years. Years becomes centuries. Then millennia. How would you feel after a million millennia?"

Derek considered the question before responding.

"With absolute isolation and loneliness. Frankly, I would have gone insane," Derek answered. He felt as if Gabriel was trying to guide him to some truth.

"Now," Gabriel continued, "after a million millennia, longer even, you discovered you had the ability to create anything, including life. What would that look like? How would you react?"

"I don't know," Derek began. "I would probably boil over. I guess internally, I'd probably explode. There would be joy for sure."

Gabriel smiled. "Interesting term. Because that is, what our Father did. Many of your scientists called it the Big-Bang. When our Father discovered he had the ability to create, he did just that. Not just here but everywhere throughout the universe in the time it takes to blink. Each creation, slightly different. Every world. Every organism.

"My kind were among his first and finest." Gabriel gestured to himself. "He gave almost everything to us, including eternal life. We were his favorite, his first among many. That was until he created you. Humanity is the youngest of his creations. However, you remain his proudest accomplishment. He gave humanity what no other of his children have. A piece of himself."

"A soul," Derek declared perceptively.

"Yes," Gabriel acknowledged. "He gave you a piece of himself. A soul, a God Particle, whatever you wish to call it. This was what he was striving for in all his previous creations."

"But you have eternal life," Derek said. "You apparently have super powers. We humans are actually quite fragile. Why would he give this gift only to us?"

Gabriel smiled. "It is not the shell. It is the experiences. You were created to live, experience, die, and return."

"Wash, rinse, repeat." Derek quipped.

Gabriel laughed. "In a manner of speaking, yes. Humanity is unique in many ways. When that piece of him, your soul, enters a new body, it has one purpose, to learn and grow. The person lives their life, and the soul learns from the experiences of that life."

"If that were true, why are there evil men and terrible deeds?" Derek questioned.

"Good, evil, love, hate, pain, pleasure. These are all part of humanity's design to teach the soul. You can learn just as much from experiencing evil as you can from experiencing love. The lesson may be completely different, but that does not mean it is not equally important. What matters is the experiences the soul receives. The consequence to the shell is not important," Gabriel explained.

"Tell that to the shell," Derek retorted. "And what about the death of an infant? What experiences has that child had that could possibly enrich a soul?" he challenged.

"Newly formed souls do not need many lessons. Dying is a singular lesson," Gabriel continued. "The point being, it is not the physical body or this existence that must learn but the God Particle within. The soul must learn. In some circumstances, as with a new or young soul, the first thing they must learn is death. They can then be reborn for a second lesson. However, in all these circumstances, it is not only the dying whose soul has learned but also those left behind and what their God Particle learns from that specific lesson. The reasons are many, but rarely are we privy to them."

"So, what happens in the end? Do we win a gold watch?" Derek said in an attempt to reduce the considerable implications of Gabriel's words.

"When the soul has experienced enough, has matured enough, it joins our Father on his plane. Bringing an end to his loneliness," Gabriel explained, ignoring Derek's flippancy.

"Well, I guess that's something to look forward to," Derek replied.

"But here is the issue." A note of caution entered Gabriel's tone. "Some of my race were both angered and hurt by our Father's decision to give you a piece of himself. They believe this gift should have gone to them. They have chosen to slow your transcendence through corruption. If a soul fails to learn, that soul's cycle must be repeated. If it repeats too many times it turns dark.

"Many of my siblings have lost their way. Where we inspire, they corrupt."

"You're talking about Fallen Angels? You mean the Devil?" Derek queried.

"Again, that would probably be the most common interpretation, devils or demons," Gabriel confirmed. "Worse is, it is no longer just them. Many of our Father's other children, visitors to your planet, have learned of the God Particles, the souls you carry. They are searching for answers too. Some are even working with the fallen ones and are actively attempting to find ways to remove your souls."

"Why? How?" Derek blurted with incredulity.

"Whereas some of the visitors, if we did not intervene, would simply destroy the entire creation of humanity, others are simply jealous. They want to take the God Particles within humanity and implant them within their own creation. They have been attempting to intermix or make hybrids between themselves and your kind. With this they hope to learn how to steal the God Particles."

"Why would God allow them to create hybrids or even move forward with their attempts?" Derek asked concerned.

"Our Father creates," Gabriel replied. "His avenues of creation take many forms. He does not interfere because even evil creations provide experiences the God Particle can use to learn. Except under especially rare circumstances, unless there is an extinction level attempt to destroy humanity, my kind are generally forbidden from directly intervening. We can however, influence individuals. It is once a person has died and their soul is ready to move on that we typically reveal ourselves and guide them further."

"So, what does all this have to do with me?" Derek asked, genuinely puzzled.

"Like I said, you have a choice to make," Gabriel began. "First, your soul has learned all it needed to from your current existence. You can choose to move on and begin a new life."

"What is my second choice?" Derek requested.

"The veil between the worlds is falling. There is a war coming," Gabriel stated. "It will not just be amongst men, but will involve many of our Father's children. Though your time has ended, Susan still has a great part to play in this war. For this to happen, though, she needs to escape from where she is currently being held. I can allow you to return to help make that happen. Unfortunately, if you decline, I will need to influence one of the guards to assist her. Though this may take longer and may not be as successful."

Derek's soul was tired and though the thought of the peace from moving on was appealing, he could not leave Susan. There was not even a second's hesitation about it.

"How will I find her?" Derek asked, his decision to return made.

"Leave that to me," Gabriel replied. "Just one more thing, Derek. Remember, being a harmless person does not necessarily make a person good. However, a very dangerous person who has the capacity to harm under voluntary control is, by default, a good human being. Knowing when is the key.

"There will be times," Gabriel continued, "because of one man's evil—tens of thousands of people will suffer. However, if that man is killed, tens of thousands will live. Here then, truly the blade that deals death to one becomes the sword that saves many. A warrior guided by the spirit serves humanity."

"Like I said, Confucius." Derek grinned.

With that, Gabriel reached out and touched Derek's forehead. ◉

CHAPTER 45
"THE BREAKOUT"

As the agent turned away from the gurney, his foot became entangled in the IV stand and tubing. Losing his balance, he stumbled forward as his leg pulled on the tubing. The IV stand began to tip over. Reacting instinctively, the agent quickly reached out and caught the stand before it completely clattered to the floor. This sequence of events pulled the IV's needle out of Derek's arm.

Still holding the IV stand, the agent initially looked confused as his attention bounced between his foot that was ensnared in the tubing and then at Derek's arm. It seemed to take him a moment before he apparently realized what had happened.

Gasping one huge breath, Derek was fully awake. By the look on the agent's face Derek could tell he was not entirely sure how this could be. The agent glanced at the syringe he still held. Possibly pondering whether he had used the correct vial to fill the syringe or if not enough of the poison had entered Derek's blood stream before the IV was pulled out when he stumbled.

The agent's hesitation was all the time Derek needed. With his already broken and dislocated thumb, Derek was able to gain enough space to allow his hand to pull free of the restraint. Suddenly understanding the seriousness of the situation, the agent was spurred into action. He rushed forward in an attempt to gain control of Derek's free arm.

As he approached the gurney, even though his thumb was broken, Derek was able to grab the agent by the top of his surgical scrubs. Pulling him forward by the collar, Derek brought the agent's head down to within inches of his own. Before the agent could break loose, Derek leaned his torso forward as far as the restraints would allow. He then bit down hard on the agent's ear.

The agent screamed in pain as teeth cut through flesh and cartilage. As the agent twisted his head away from Derek's bite, a piece of the agent's ear tore away.

Blood dripped onto Derek's chin. Still clutching his collar Derek again pulled the agent forward as he struck upward with his forehead. Derek's head-butt struck the agent in the jaw hard enough to knock him to the ground. Derek spit a chunk of the agent's flesh from his mouth.

Dazed from the head-butt, the agent began to stagger to his feet. Derek reached over and quickly unfastened the restraint to his right arm. Seeing that Derek was close to escaping, the agent realized the danger he was in. He turned and began to scamper for the door. Reaching out, Derek grasped a hold of the agent with both hands.

Caught in Derek's grip, the agent tried to break free. That is when everything, the agent, Derek and the gurney toppled and crashed to the floor in a jumble of arms, surgical tubing and blood.

Desperately, the agent tried to free himself from Derek's clutches. Though the two struggled, Derek's feet were still secured to the overturned gurney. After punching the agent in the nose, Derek's right hand came down on the pocket of the agent's surgical scrubs. His fingers wrapped around an ink pen. Pulling the pen from the pocket Derek wielded it like an ice pick and thrust it into the agent's neck. Over and over again, Derek stabbed with the pen. It punctured flesh and cut through the carotid artery. Eventually they both stopped moving.

For nearly a minute, as the agent's blood slowly pooled around their entwined bodies, Derek lay on the floor catching his breath. Finally, with a groan, he sat up and unfastened his legs from the restraints. Using one hand to brace against the counter, Derek stood for the first time since being thrown in the back of the helicopter.

"I guess I don't have that under voluntary control," Derek mused as he thought about one of the last things Gabriel said.

Though he was already dead, Derek performed a pat down of the agent's corpse. Other than his PIV badge and a small vial of poison that had been intended for Derek, the agent had nothing he could use. A thick streak of blood dragged behind the corpse as Derek pulled the agent's lifeless body into the adjoining room. There he removed the agent's trousers and boots. Though a little large, Derek decided both would work as he slid them on. Derek elected not to take the agent's shirt as it was soaked in blood.

Quickly, he ransacked both rooms. All he could find that would be of any use was a bag of twenty-nine-gauge syringes, medical tape and some surgical masks. Derek's left hand and thumb had begun to throb terribly. As best he could, using the medical tape, Derek wrapped his hand in a field-expedient cast. Once done, his hand looked like he had been preparing for a boxing match.

With his thumb, reasonably stabilized, Derek filled two of the syringes with the poison he had recovered off the dead agent. He then replaced the orange safety caps to the ends of the syringes. Derek set the gurney upright before turning towards the main door. He listened briefly but did not hear any movement on the other side.

Placing the agent's PIV badge in the OMNI Lock, a light began flashing near the keypad. Derek needed the access code. Unfortunately, the only person who knew it was lying dead in the other room.

The door and frame were made of metal; Derek knew he would not be able to break through without drawing considerable attention. Even the hinges required a specialized tool for removal. His only option was to sit and wait. Though waiting also presented its own issues: for instance, how long would he wait and how many people would show up. Derek knew he could take one, maybe even two, but if three or more came through the door, his chance of being victorious was low.

Grabbing the chair Smith had used, Derek pulled it to the hinge side of the door. He then turned the room's lights off and sat. Sooner or later, someone would open the door. When that happened, Derek would be hidden from view. Grasping one of the syringes of poison in his right hand, Derek leaned his head against the wall and closed his eyes.

Twenty minutes passed. Derek was physically exhausted. His body ached and his thumb was throbbing in the makeshift cast of medical tape. Despair began to enter Derek's mind. He did not know if Smith told the truth about whether his friends were alive or dead. He was unsure where to go, or even where to begin looking for Susan. To top it off, he remained locked in a room near the corpse of the man he had just killed.

He said a silent prayer.

"Okay, God," Derek began in earnest, "if Gabriel wasn't a dream. If he wasn't a hallucination brought on by a poison running through my blood stream, I need a sign. I need your help."

Almost immediately, Derek thought he heard movement in the hallway. He stood, gripping the syringe a little tighter.

The door's OMNI lock made a clicking noise, as it was unlocked. The door began to open. Light from the hallway cascaded into the examination room. Derek crouched just on the other side of the door.

"Rudy!" the man called out as he began to step into the room. "Where have you been? I've been waiting down in the morgue with the incinerator running for the last fifteen minutes."

As this new agent came fully in the room, the door began to swing shut. The agent was not much taller than Derek and he did not appear very old. At best, he was twenty-five. As he turned to flip the room's light switch on, Derek pounced.

Kicking the agent in the back of the knee, Derek simultaneously pulled him in the same direction. This brought the agent completely off-balance. Caught utterly by surprise, the agent offered no resistance as Derek wrapped his left arm around the man's neck. Still clutching the syringe, with his right hand, Derek tried to grab the door before it shut. Unfortunately, the hydraulic arm prevented him from stopping the door from closing.

Turning his attention to the agent, Derek used his teeth to pull the orange safety cap off the syringe. He then jammed the needle deeply into the agent's neck. Derek did not push the plunger down which would have injected the poison.

"Do you feel that needle in your neck?" Derek whispered in the agent's ear.

"Yeessss, sir," the agent replied. He was noticeably scared. Not only from what he had stumbled into but also now seeing the large smear of blood trailing into the adjoining room.

"Listen carefully," Derek continued. "This needle is full of the same poison that your friend Rudy was going to inject me with. Nod if you understand."

The agent nodded slowly.

"Okay, if you answer my questions, I'll let you live. If you don't, I am going to push this plunger and fill your body full of this shit. Do you understand?" Venom had crept into Derek's voice as he spoke.

"How do I know you won't kill me anyways?" the agent asked.

Derek considered this question for a moment, then replied.

"You don't. However, I will most assuredly kill you if you don't. Therefore, the only way you have any chance of getting out of this in one piece is to answer my questions. Do you understand?"

"Yes, sir," the agent replied without hesitation.

"Smart boy," Derek praised. "Okay, first question. What's your name?"

"Billy!" the agent answered in a wavering voice.

"And what day and time is it, Billy?" Derek queried

"It's Wednesday. A little after 11:00 p.m.," Billy answered, sounding somewhat confused. Derek quickly did the math. About thirty-one hours had passed since he and Susan had been captured on Soldier's Summit.

"Good. Okay, Billy, what is the pin number for your PIV badge?"

"0003911!" Billy stated without a moment's hesitation. Derek believed him and repeated the seven-digit code. He would test the number shortly.

"Next question. The woman they brought in here with me, where are they keeping her?"

"I don't know!" Billy almost seemed panicked by his inability to provide the information in his response. "I am sure she is on this level, but they didn't tell me. I just work down in the morgue."

Again, the stress in this kid's voice convinced Derek he was being truthful.

"Final question," Derek continued. "What type of security is in the hallway?"

"There are cameras covering every hallway and roving patrols of armed officers," Billy answered. "My PIV badge gives access to everything including the elevators."

"Thank you very much, Billy. You made the right decision," Derek pulled the syringe from Billy's neck and began to squeeze his left arm. He quickly added his right arm to the pressure of the carotid neck restraint. Commonly used in mixed martial arts, the technique is called a rear-naked choke. This choke blocks the blood flowing through the arteries to the brain. Though generally harmless, it does temporarily render the person unconscious.

Billy began to struggle against the neck restraining. Within a few seconds, he passed out. Derek eased Billy to the floor.

Derek removed Billy's shirt and put it on. He then placed one of the surgical masks over his own face. Taking Billy's PIV badge, which was attached to a lanyard, Derek tested the OMNI lock. It worked. Holding the door partially ajar, Derek turned the light off. Even if Billy woke, he would not be able to leave the room without his PIV badge.

"Okay, Gabriel, which way?" Derek said and stepped into the hallway. ◉

CHAPTER 46
"REUNION"

Stepping from the examination room, for no particular reason, Derek chose to turn left. As the door closed behind him, he proceeded down the hallway. Immediately, Derek noticed the security camera at the end of the corridor. It was pointed directly at him.

The green orderly scrubs he had taken from his captors and a surgical mask to cover his face helped conceal his identity, Derek walked nonchalantly, as if he had been through this hallway a thousand times. Billy's PIV badge, hung around his neck. To any observer watching on a security monitor, Derek gave the appearance of belonging.

The structure was a maze of hallways and rooms jetting off in multiple directions. Derek moved slowly. He did not want to test every door. That would surely be seen as odd by the person monitoring the cameras. Not knowing where to go, Derek moved with a hope and faith that his conversation with Gabriel was more than just a drug-induced figment of his imagination.

Still, Derek also trusted his own powers of deduction to help guide him. Slowing near each door, he would briefly close his eyes and listen for any sounds occurring on the other side. So far, he heard nothing and progressed in the direction he hoped was correct.

As Derek was about to round yet another corner, a door opened ahead of him, about halfway down the corridor.

"I'll be right back. I suddenly have to take a leak," said an agent as he stepped from the room. The door automatically closed behind him.

Peering around the corner, Derek saw the agent was dressed in black battle fatigues and wore a ballistic load-bearing vest. Besides his holstered handgun, he had a suppressed Heckler and Koch 9mm MP5, machine gun slung across his back.

Without so much as a glance towards Derek, the agent turned and began walking in the opposite direction. Staying a short distance back, Derek followed. Turning another corner, Derek watched as he entered a restroom. Derek counted to fifteen, then after removing the second syringe of poison from his pocket, followed the agent inside.

Standing in front of the toilet the agent had already begun to urinate. As Derek approached, the agent threw a casual glanced over his shoulder at him.

"Man, I had to piss like a racehorse," he exclaimed half laughing at his own joke.

Without a second's thought, Derek jabbed the syringe into the agent's neck and depressed the plunger. While one hand still clutched his penis, the agent grasped at his neck as he turned to stare wide eye at Derek. He staggered briefly before collapsing to the floor.

Quickly, Derek turned and locked the bathroom door. Stepping to the sink, Derek washed the blood off his face and hands, then took a moment to rinse the gore from his mouth. Moving to the body, he proceeded to strip the dead agent. Replacing his surgical scrubs with the agent's uniform, Derek strapped the ballistic armor across his torso. He slung the suppressed MP5 machine gun across his chest and secured the agent's holster on his hip.

Drawing the dead man's pistol, he pulled the slide open about a quarter inch and confirmed there was a round in the chamber. After replacing the pistol in the holster, Derek confirmed the MP5 also had a live round in the chamber.

Derek checked the rest of the gear. He had four additional magazines for the MP5 and a Motorola radio. Derek pressed the scan button on the radio so he could monitor all the channels. If any alert came over the Motorola, Derek should hear it.

Satisfied, he was as prepared as possible, Derek dragged the agent's corpse into one of the restroom stalls and set him on a toilet. He then shut the stall door.

Keeping his surgical mask on and Billy's PIV badge hung around his neck; Derek stepped from the bathroom and proceeded back down the hallway towards the room where the agent had first emerged. Derek paused at the door and listened. There was activity inside.

Using Billy's PIV badge and code, Derek opened the door and stepped through. Though it was larger, the room was similar to the one he had escaped from. Susan lay on a gurney in the center of the room. Bright operating room lights completely illuminated her. Derek saw she, too, had been strapped down and was struggling against her restraints.

Unlike what they had done to him, Susan had a sheet draped across her body. An IV had already been attached to her left arm. Two men stood next to the gurney. As she looked back and forth between them, a combination of both alarm and dismay filled her eyes. Her hair was matted by sweat as if she had been struggling against her captures since she had been taken.

They stood on either side. Both wore surgical scrubs and white lab-coats similar to what a doctor might wear. They seemed much older than the agents who had been assigned to deal with Derek.

One was short, and terribly overweight. He sported an atrocious comb-over. It did little to hide his bald spot. Round spectacles were positioned on the bridge of his nose. The other man was both taller and older with shiny gray hair. His nose hooked downward like a beak. Derek thought this made him look more like a ferret. The ferret held a syringe in his right hand. Everyone stopped and looked awkwardly at Derek as he stepped inside.

Without turning his back, Derek simultaneously closed the door and raised the MP5, pointing it at the ferret holding the syringe. Locking eyes with Susan, Derek saw hope replace the fear. She smiled as her head dropped in relief back down onto the gurney as if she could finally relax.

"What the hell took you so long?" she exclaimed in exasperation.

"Sorry about that," Derek countered. "I was a little tied up."

"Who are you?" the man with the syringe protested. "What is the meaning of this?" The suppressed MP5 made a sputtering noise as Derek shot him in both kneecaps.

Dropping the syringe, he fell to the floor clutching his knees. The ferret began to scream in pain. Derek readjusted his aim and pointed the weapon at the short fat man. He immediately raised his hands. A wet stain suddenly appeared near the crotch of the surgical scrubs the fat man wore. It continued to spread down his leg.

"Release her," Derek commanded. The fat man moved quicker than Derek would have believed possible and swiftly removed the restraints from Susan's wrists and ankles.

As Susan leaped from the table, the sheet that had been covering her fell to the floor. She, too, had been stripped down to her undergarments. Susan ran to Derek throwing her arms around his neck. Derek almost stumbled from the impact of Susan's body slamming against his own.

Pulling away, Susan elatedly pushed Derek in the chest with both hands, "Where have you been?" she demanded, stress and emotion evident in her voice.

"Well, believe it or not, I died," Derek replied with a sheepish grin.

Susan looked at him in astonishment.

Still clutching his knees, the man with the ferret face, began to curse.

"You motherfucker! You'll never get out of here alive! What we have planned for your girlfriend will be even worse now!" the ferret spat.

Derek stepped towards him. Knowing what Smith had told him about their plans for Susan, he became enraged. Bringing his boot up, Derek brutally kicked him in the head knocking him unconscious. Turning to the fat man, Derek stared at him. Savagery filled Derek's eyes as he levelled the muzzle of the MP5 at the fat man.

"I'm sorry! This wasn't our fault," he pleaded. "We were just following orders!"

Instantly, Susan spun and punched the fat man in the nose with her closed fist. As the spectacles flew off his head, he staggered backwards a couple of steps. His hands reached up protectively to his face as he began to bleed from both nostrils.

"You didn't protest even a little bit when Smith told you what to do!" Susan yelled. "In fact, you gave him some suggestions!"

"Smith was here?" Derek asked knowing the answer even before Susan replied.

"Yes, and do you know what they were going to do to me?" Susan turned red in the face. "These two assholes were going to drug me up then impregnate me with some alien cross-breed baby!"

"Well, that isn't going to happen now," Derek replied, then looking at the fat man, he asked, "Where are her clothes?"

"They removed them before she was brought down here," he said hurriedly. "But there is a locker room with an abundance of clothes just down the hall."

"What is the room number?" Derek commanded. The fat man frantically gave the number to Derek. Forcing the fat man to the floor, Derek passed Susan the pistol. Similar to what he had done, Derek beamed with pride when Susan immediately performed a press-check to confirm the weapon's condition. She then peered up at him with determination in her eyes. Derek explained his hasty plan.

"You move, you die," Derek said, turning to the fat man. He then stepped from the room leaving Susan with the pistol to cover the fat man.

Quickly Derek located the locker room and used Billy's PIV badge to gain access. He plundered the room as rapidly as he could. Finding a T-shirt, jeans, and a pair of boots that should fit Susan reasonably well, Derek returned to her.

Susan slipped the clothes on. They were a little loose but would work. Pulling the boots on, Susan tied the laces as tightly as she could. Taking his body armor off Derek slipped it over Susan's head. Using the armor's Velcro, he strapped it as securely around her chest and back as he could. She then slipped the fat man's white lab coat over the top. With a rubber-band she had taken from one of the counter's drawers, Susan tied her hair into a hasty ponytail.

"Okay, you will get on the gurney and cover yourself with the sheet," Derek explained. Susan jumped on the gurney and threw the sheet over herself holding the pistol tightly to her chest. Derek told her of the cameras and roving patrols. He then grabbed the PIV badges from the fat man and his unconscious friend.

"You're coming with us," Derek said to the fat man.

"Me? Why?" the fat man asked. Demonstrating his absolute desire of not wanting to tag along, he took an unconscious step away from Derek.

"Listen, fat boy," Derek said, grabbing him by the collar. "I know when we get to the elevator we will need the retinal scan of a person and their PIV Badge. Either you can come with us or I'm going to gouge your eye out with a spoon and do it without you. Your choice." The man's jowls shook as he nodded his agreement.

"Keep your eyes closed," Derek said to Susan as the fat man pushed the gurney from the room. Derek followed two steps behind, just as a guard would.

The trio rounded several corners on their way to the elevator. It appeared as if they were the only ones left on this lower level. Derek hoped the structure would be mostly empty due to the time of night. Additionally, anticipating how security typically operates, Derek believed many of the guards would have found a secluded office or dark corner where they could nap.

Slowly, they proceeded until finally arriving at the elevator. An OMNI reader sat above the elevator's Call button along with a retinal scanner. Derek nudged the fat man. Quickly he placed his PIV badge in the OMNI reader and entered his code. He then leaned forward and presented his eye to the scanner. The elevator's push button illuminated green. It only had one directional arrow. Up. This confirmed to Derek they were underground.

The vibration of the approaching elevator was what Derek had felt when they had first wheeled him in. The metal door slid open and the fat man pushed Susan and the gurney inside. Derek followed. As the door began to close, Derek thought he heard what sounded like the melody of a large cricket. He placed his hand on the elevator door stopping it from closing. He then leaned out the elevator, glancing down the hall.

It stood in the middle of the corridor, just out of view of the others. Derek's first thought was not shock or disbelief but instead about how it could have gotten so close to them. A little over three feet tall, its head was oval shaped with an enlarged cranium. The mouth was nothing more than a small slit with almost nonexistent lips. The head appeared to be out of proportion with the rest of its humanoid, light-grey, hairless body.

With what almost looked like a potbelly and concaved chest, the creature's arms and legs were thin. Each hand sported three long fingers and a fourth oddly shaped thumb. Expressionless, large, black, almond-shaped eyes stared intently back at Derek.

Derek became frozen as he locked eyes with the grey. Initially, he could not move. His hand remained immobilized as it hovered near the elevator's buttons. Like a slideshow on rapid-fire, images of a "World on Fire" began to fill his mind. As hard as he commanded his body into action, Derek's paralysis was complete.

"What is it?" Susan asked from within the elevator as she began to sit up and slid off the gurney.

The grey blinked. This seemed to snap Derek from his trance. Quickly he stepped back deep into the elevator and pressed the button for what he assumed was the top floor. Derek kept the MP5 trained on the elevator's doors until they slowly slid closed.

"Nothing. Just my imagination," Derek responded, as he tried to comprehend what had just momentarily paralyzed him. He glanced over at the fat man who quickly averted his eyes from Derek's questioning gaze. ◉

CHAPTER 47
"DÉJÀ VU"

Derek always enjoyed movies where the good guy had to escape from their evil imprisonment. Steve McQueen in *The Great Escape,* and *Stalag-17* with William Holden were among his favorites. Both were set during World War II and portrayed Americans slipping away from Nazi concentration camps. These movies always seemed to characterize the hero as honorable and the escape as some grand adventure.

When Derek was with the Raider Battalion attached to the Marine Corps Special Operations Command, or MARSOC, they had sent him through Survival, Evasion, Resistance, and Escape training, known throughout the military as SERE School. This course taught him the basics of survival and how to properly resist when captured.

The reality he was now experiencing was anything but grand. Derek knew he would cruelly murder everyone in the building if it meant Susan would be freed.

The elevator seemed to take forever. The indicator showed they had arrived on the first level. It took five long seconds before the elevator's doors slowly slid open. Derek was hesitant to look beyond the doors. Subconsciously, he was uneasy about the possibility of seeing another alien or worse. Shaking off his jitters,

Derek leaned out the elevator's door and quickly scanned their surroundings.

The elevator opened into a large hangar. It reminded Derek of the SRT headquarters hidden underneath Gable Mountain. Several large aircraft could have easily fit inside this structure. Derek estimated the hangar's ceiling was nearly 150 feet above the floor. Foot-thick metal beams crisscrossed overhead. Large floodlights evenly positioned along each beam bathed the entire area in light. The floor was made of a nonskid coating similar to the type found on the flight deck of a naval aircraft carrier.

Several doors were observable around the exterior of the hangar. The door Derek was most interested in sat on the far side, a little more than a hundred yards from where they were. This door had a sign that read Emergency Exit positioned over the top of it. A number of government vehicles, mostly trucks and SUVs were parked along one wall. However, what drew Derek's attention almost immediately was what he saw on the opposite side of the hangar.

They could only be described as a couple of traditional UFOs. Both were saucer-shaped and about 30–40 feet in diameter. Almost the color of tinfoil, these spacecraft were a shiny silver. They would have appeared to be floating, if not for the three large, viselike clamps that gripped the UFOs. These clamps secured the UFOs to the hangar's floor. Portable floodlights illuminated the underside of the crafts and two orange self-propelled scissor lifts were positioned near both of them.

As Derek scrutinized the UFOs, two men in white lab coats, the same type of coat Susan now wore, emerged as they walked around from the opposite side of one craft. One held a piece of equipment Derek did not recognize, while the other pushed a laptop that sat on top of a portable stand. Derek did not immediately see any other personnel.

"Oh my God!" Susan exclaimed as she peered around Derek's shoulder. "It's all true!"

Holding the elevator door open Derek nudged her back inside. Turning towards the fat man, Derek grabbed and spun him around. Before he could say a word, he wrapped his arms around his chubby neck and applied another carotid neck restraint.

The man struggled momentarily, but quickly passed out. Derek lowered him to the floor. He looked at Susan. Knowing what he would have done to her if Derek had not arrived, she showed little sympathy.

"Okay, here is what we are going to do," Derek stated. "We are going to walk like we own the place towards the far exit. No matter what happens, keep walking. If things go sideways, run. Once we are outside, we are going to steal the first car we come across. Are you ready?"

Susan leaned forward and kissed him. Derek wrapped his arms around her and placed his forehead against hers.

"I love you," she said.

"I love you more," Derek replied, grinning. Then together they stepped from the elevator and began walking with a purpose. Derek winced at the sounds of their echoing footfalls, wishing they could have been quieter on the hangar's floor.

They had crossed barely twenty yards before the two men standing near the UFOs noticed them. Derek and Susan continued to walk. With his peripheral vision, Derek saw one of the men raise what appeared to be a walkie-talkie to his mouth. Grabbing Susan subtly by her elbow Derek picked up their pace.

"Ah, this is Adam in Hangar Two," came the voice over the Motorola radio Derek had confiscated. "I have a man and woman walking through the hangar, and ah, I haven't seen either of them before. Are they authorized?"

"Stand-by we're checking" came the response that Derek assumed was a member of the security team obviously monitoring their movement. As they continued to walk, Derek observed multiple security cameras. They all seemed to be focusing on them.

"Stop them!" Smith's clearly distinctive voice shouted over the radio.

Derek and Susan were only halfway across the hangar, when what sounded like a submarine's Klaxon dive alarm, began. Its audible tone blaring throughout the complex. Red flashing lights also began flashing in the four corners of the hangar's ceiling.

"Run!" Derek commanded as he and Susan both began sprinting for the exit. Glancing over his shoulder, Derek observed one of the side doors directly across from them open.

Two men dressed in black tactical fatigues and carrying rifles came rushing out. Derek spun and dropped to a kneeling position. Without taking the time to aim, he fired the MP5 instinctively in their direction. Though neither was hit by Derek's gunfire, both men jumped back through the door.

The two men in lab coats, who had been standing near the UFOs, quickly ran around behind them. Derek watched as they immediately crouched down behind the scissor lifts.

Susan was nearly to the door when Derek stood and began running towards her. As she reached the emergency exit, Derek heard several more doors open. He did not bother to even turn and look this time.

Susan struck the crash-bar opening the emergency exit and stepped through. She held the door open for Derek. As he arrived at the exit, he heard the crack of a rifle sound behind him. Before stepping through, he glanced back.

A dozen men, clad in black tactical gear, were charging towards them. A couple of the guards had taken up shooting positions and had begun firing in their direction. However, what shocked Derek the most was seeing that Smith was with them. He, too, was coming after them. Derek considered taking a shot at Smith, but the volume of fire coming at him was intensifying. Bullets began striking the wall around him forcing him to duck out the door.

Nearly midnight, the sky was dark when they stepped outside. As the S4 hangar was supposed to be secret, there were no exterior lights to illuminate and guide them. Thankfully, the moon was three-quarters full and the sky was clear. This provided enough ambient light to guide their way.

Derek hoped there would be a car or truck outside he could steal, but there was none. Remembering some of what John Winoski had told them about the S4 Site, Derek surmised they were about halfway up the Papoose Mountain. They had to get lost in the valley below.

They ran across an open area of about four hundred feet of paved concrete. To make it more difficult to see via satellite, the concrete had been painted a desert sand color. Near the far side, they approached a well-established road. This road ran from their location and continued down the mountain. Derek and Susan could easily see the road under the moonlight.

"Keep going. I'll catch up," Derek said as Susan began sprinting down the road. Derek dropped into a prone position and with his MP5 machine gun and aimed at the emergency exit.

Almost immediately, the door opened and three agents rushed out. Back lit by the light pouring through the open door, their silhouettes were easy to identify. Derek flipped the MP5's selector lever onto full-auto and let loose a high volume of fire, emptying the entire magazine. All three agents dropped from the impacts as multiple 9mm bullets struck their bodies. They were no longer moving.

When his weapon went empty, Derek stood and began running after Susan. While running, he inserted a fresh magazine into the MP5 and slapped the charging handle forward. He figured the other agents inside would be a little more hesitant to rush after him knowing their friends had been killed doing just that.

Upon hearing the gunfire, Susan had stopped and turned. She waited as Derek ran up to her.

"Keep going!" Derek yelled as they both began running down the road's decline. Engaging the agents at the door had bought them a little time and distance. Derek and Susan were now almost two hundred yards ahead of their pursuers. Unfortunately, Derek could no longer see the emergency exit or parking area.

Several agents burst through the door and ran across the open space. Along the far edge of the parking area, the agents took up firing positions overlooking the roadway. Seeing Derek and Susan running below them, they began shooting down towards the fleeing couple.

Bullets began to impact the earth around Derek and Susan's feet. As fast as they could run, they quickly approached a T-intersection in the roadway. Other than a shallow shoulder there was little cover and only some small sagebrush providing them minimal concealment. Grabbing Susan, Derek pulled her into this shallow ditch as more shots whistled past over their heads.

"Stay down," he commanded as Derek covered her body with his own. Breathing hard, Derek began to consider what their next move should be. He began looking in all directions.

Susan heard the noise first. The sound of movement was coming from below them. Susan turned and pointed her pistol towards the pending threat. Derek, seeing Susan's reaction also spun around and prepared to fire. What they saw brought a glimmer of hope to both their faces. Smith had lied.

"Hold your fire!" Michael King called out as he crawled out from behind some sagebrush. Josh and Rios were accompanying him. They low-crawled to the side of the ditch flanking both Susan and Derek. For a moment, Derek stared in disbelief, and then he remembered.

A few days earlier, while Derek was preparing the explosive devices for the ambush, Mike King and Ernesto Rios had gone to the Research and Development section of Mike's company. There they acquired an ingestible GPS tracking device from one of their laboratories.

Mike told them these GPS devices were in the early production stage and were eventually planned on being sold and used by business executives and military personnel who found themselves in a hostile country. If they thought they were about to be kidnapped or captured, the person issued the GPS device was to swallow it. For any rescue team deployed, the tracker would provide critical tactical information as to where the hostage had been taken. That is exactly what Mike had used them for.

Prior to initiating the ambush, just in case they were separated, Mike had passed the ingestible GPS devices out to everyone on the team. He told them the GPS would provide about forty-eight hours of monitoring. With all that had transpired, Derek had nearly forgotten.

After the ambush had fallen apart, Mike and the others had been able to escape to their predetermined rally point as Susan and Derek led their pursuers away from the ambush in the opposite direction. Unsure what had happened, they waited for Susan and Derek. When they eventually did not show up, Mike used the GPS devices to track where Derek and Susan had been taken.

Together with Josh and Rios, they spent a day developing a hasty rescue plan. Having identified where the GPS signal was coming from, they were preparing to assault the structure in what would have surely been a suicidal attempt to free them. They were primed to commence their incursion when Derek and Susan had burst through the emergency exit.

"Did you miss us?" Mike joked as he slapped Derek on the shoulder. Rios and Josh had begun firing up the hill as Mike also opened up with his M249 belt-fed machine gun. Derek, still amazed at his friends, let lose another burst from the MP5.

As Derek reloaded a fresh magazine into his MP5, he looked up and down the ditch. His friends were putting their lives on the line to save Susan and him. He had been here before. What had been his reoccurring nightmare for the last thirty years, he was now living through once more. Everyone he cared about was laying on the ground around him. They were firing up a hill at a superior force—only protected by a small depression.

Derek could not allow this to happen again, he thought. He began considering his limited options. That was when the characteristic sound of rotor blades of an approaching helicopter reached his ears.

At first, Derek thought Smith had brought in another helicopter to attack them from the sky. Then he saw Mike's face. He was looking at Derek with a huge shit-eating grin.

"Our taxi is here!" Mike exclaimed.

The twin engine S-76 Sikorsky helicopter was flying low and fast through the valley. Its dark blue painted exterior made it nearly impossible to see in the night's sky. Before takeoff, Jackson had disabled the transponder and had turned off the aircraft's running lights. Jackson had been circling about twenty miles to the south when Mike had radioed they had located Derek and Susan.

The cavalry was about to arrive. ◉

CHAPTER 48
"IF YOU WANT SOMETHING DONE RIGHT"

Having just gotten off the telephone with Washington, DC, Smith walked into the primary control center of the S4 Site. Immediately, he observed the agent tasked with monitoring the security cameras was leaning back in his chair. With his feet up and perched on the desk, boots crossed at the ankles the agent had his back to the door. The agent was paying more attention to a magazine he had brought with him than to the security screens.

"You keep reading that magazine, instead of doing your job; I'll have you assigned to a listening post in Adak, Alaska before the end of the day," Smith stated matter-of-factly.

"Sorry, sir," the agent responded. Quickly he put the magazine down and sat straight in his chair.

Walking over to the break station, Smith poured himself a cup of coffee. He began contemplating the events of the last few days. Other than the loss of a few men, it had been a successful operation. He had just provided his after-action report to his superiors. Those bean counters were not as satisfied, but that was to be expected.

Smith decided once he confirmed Susan Parker had been established within the program, he would begin preparations to leave. Smith began to sip on his coffee considering his next action. Then the first alert came across the base station speaker.

"Ah, this is Adam in Hangar Two. I have a man and woman walking through the hangar, and ah, I haven't seen either of them before. Are they authorized?" the voice announced over the radio.

The coffee cup in Smith's hand froze inches from his mouth. For nearly five seconds Smith did not move. He was not sure he heard the radio transmission correctly. Instead, he just stared at the wall holding his coffee. It was completely inconceivable to him that Riley and Parker could be escaping, again.

"Stand-by we're checking," said the agent, sitting at the control console and now intently monitoring the security cameras.

This response spurred Smith into motion and he stepped over to where this agent was now adjusting the angle and zoom of a couple of the security cameras. As one camera zoomed in, Smith clearly saw Riley and Parker walking through the hangar. Dropping his coffee on the floor, Smith snatched the base station's microphone away from the agent.

"Stop them!" Smith yelled into the microphone.

The agent could hear the anger in his boss's throat. Not wanting this lapse in security to fall on him, the agent reached across the console and pressed a button that was labeled security alarm. Smith shot an icy glare at the agent before he turned and headed for the door just as the Klaxon began to blare. As Smith departed, the agent began wondering what Adak would be like.

As Smith briskly walked down the corridor advancing on Hangar Two, he heard several armed men running up behind him. The quick reaction force, or QRF, was centrally housed on the first level near the control center. During any security incident, this location afforded the QRF the ability to secure the lower floors or respond to any problem on the first level with equal haste. Smith stepped to one side of the corridor providing them some room as they ran past.

Smith was not far behind as the first two reached the primary door into the hangar and ran through. Several other agents were trailing only a short distance back. As Smith grew closer, the sound of weapons fire could be heard. The two agents who had initially run into the hangar came rushing back into the hall. This froze the others in their place as they tried to determine what to do next.

"What are you waiting for? Go after them!" Smith demanded as he realized most of these men had worked in this facility nearly their entire careers and had never expected there to be any real-world response.

"But, sir! He's got a gun!" one of the agents said, thinking he needed to explain the issue. Smith almost slapped him.

"And what do you have? A fucking water pistol!" Smith grabbed the agent and threw him through the door. He then began pushing the other agents through as well.

As Smith stepped into the hangar, he saw Riley on the far side. Riley had made it to the emergency exit. For a brief moment, they locked eyes. Smith wished he had a hundred men like Riley working for him. Instead, he was surrounded by imbeciles.

The agents ran across the hangar as Smith walked behind them. Two members of the QRF sniper team arrived alongside him and began to flank Smith. One was holding a semi-automatic OBR in 6.5 Creedmoor. An infrared Mark II thermal scope was affixed to the top rail.

Again, three agents burst through the emergency exit. Instantly, more automatic gunfire could be heard on the other side. This time, when the agents did not come back, Smith assumed Riley had shot them.

More members of the QRF arrived at the exit along with Smith and the two snipers. The agents were torn. They could either be shot at by Riley on the other side of the door or face Smith's wrath on this side. Ultimately, they decided being shot at was the better bargain. Together they advanced outside. Smith stepped through the door and watched as several members of the QRF ran across the parking area.

Positioning themselves on the far side, they began firing down the hill. Smith and the two snipers carefully advanced to where they could improve their tactical advantage. They took up positions along the corner of the parking area away from the main group of agents.

Smith had been looking down the hill to where Derek and Susan had jumped into the ditch. He was about to order his men to assault, when the unexpected happened. Where Derek and Susan had concealed themselves, multiple muzzle flashes and automatic fire from several different weapons began shooting upward towards them. This unanticipated increase in gunfire made everyone, including Smith duck. He had underestimated Derek's friends; they had come to rescue him.

Smith began considering his options, which included calling the NTS Protective Force for assistance. Then he heard the approaching helicopter. He watched as the helicopter swooped in and commenced firing down on his now cowering men. It then began to hover near Derek's position.

In utter disbelief, Smith scrutinized the scene playing out before him. One by one, his quarry began escaping into the waiting helicopter. Smith stood up. Both infuriated and frustrated, he grabbed the OBR rifle from the sniper kneeling next to him.

Peering through the thermal scope Smith began hunting. Finding his target, he aimed and fired. The recoil of the large-caliber weapon forced Smith to reacquire his prey in the optic. Then a moment later, he fired a second shot. Watching through the scope Smith smiled triumphantly. The bullets had found their mark.

Handing the rifle back to the sniper, Smith turned and casually walked back inside the hangar. ◉

CHAPTER 49

"GABRIEL"

Derek almost leaped for joy when the helicopter turned broadside and he saw Jeremy Skiers sitting in the open door. Mike had known they would be needing help if they had any hope in a successful rescue attempt. Since Skiers both lived nearby and was crazy enough to tag along, Mike had given him a call. Skiers did not even ask why.

With a grin on his face, Skiers began firing from the door of the helicopter onto the hillside below. The sudden appearance of the helicopter and Skiers blasting away, alone almost completely suppressed any return fire from Smith's men. As the aircraft began to descend, Derek got the others up and moving. With Skiers help, Susan was the first to climb in followed by Josh and Mike.

Rios then climbed in. He turned and offered his hand to Derek. Grabbing onto Rios's hand, he was pulled halfway into the cab of the helicopter, Derek saw Josh and Susan hugging one another. They were going to make it, Derek thought. That is when the first bullet struck him squarely in the back.

The impact from the large 6.5 Creedmoor round spun Derek around and he lost his grip of Rios's hand. It felt like he had been struck across the back with a baseball bat. The impact knocked the wind out of him.

Trying to catch his breath, Derek reached for Rios but he had a hard time raising his arm. Glancing up the hill Derek saw a muzzle flash. The second round struck him in the chest with a thud. Derek was lifted off the ground and slammed into the side of the helicopter.

Derek was unable to move. He felt himself slowly slipping to the ground. That is when both his shoulders were grabbed by Mike and Rios. Their adrenaline was kicking in and together they yanked Derek into the helicopter with little effort.

Glancing over at Skiers, Derek saw he was continuing to fire upon the hillside, though he was no longer smiling. As the helicopter began to lift and bank away, Derek saw Jackson in the pilot seat glancing back at him. Jackson was talking rapidly on the radio though Derek did not know to whom.

Susan had come off her seat and was cradling Derek's head in her lap as he lay on the floor of the helicopter. She was crying and talking to him, but he could not hear what she was saying.

Derek began coughing blood as Mike placed his hands on Derek's chest. Mike began putting pressure on the gunshot wound in an attempt to slow the bleeding. Rios had grabbed a medical bag and had removed a pressure dressing. He was ripping it open with his teeth.

Derek glanced at Josh, who was staring in disbelief, tears in his eyes. Derek reached up and put a hand to Susan's cheek. She grabbed his hand with one of her own. Both were oblivious to the blood on his fingers. That is when Derek noticed him.

Gabriel was sitting casually behind Josh. He was smiling kindly at Derek. When they made eye contact, Gabriel nodded his understanding. Derek smiled at Gabriel.

As Susan cradled Derek's head, she saw him staring past Josh. As he smiled, she looked to see what Derek was smiling at. She gasped.

All faded to black. ◉

EPILOGUE

In the early 1800s, an influx of German immigrants arrived in Montgomery County, Maryland. Once there, they set up shop and eventually founded Germantown. Located just thirty miles north of Washington, DC, for the better part of a century the area was well known for its German population and culture.

Following the end of World War II, the headquarters for the newly established Atomic Energy Commission, was moved from Washington, DC to Germantown. Though official reasons for this move were provided, the true intent of the government was to disguise and imbed a few hundred Nazi scientists into a population who already spoke German. Most Americans never even took notice. Still today, the Department of Energy calls Germantown headquarters for its Office of Biological Research.

For nearly forty years, Smith had also called Germantown home. Though his work required extensive travel, typically around the first week of every month, Smith was able to return home for a few days or more.

The time he spent at home afforded him the opportunity to liaison with the different agencies headquartered in the District. More importantly, it provided Smith the ability to meet with his superiors, politicians, and others directly involved in the program.

Typically, when Smith returned home, he spends his first evening dining alone at the exclusive Le Bilboquet restaurant. Located just ten minutes from his residence, the little French restaurant has a well-earned reputation for being one of the snobbiest in the entire District of Columbia metropolitan area. Because the restaurant cannot accommodate more than thirty people, reservations must be made days in advance and always requires a deposit.

It had been a little more than two weeks since Derek Riley and Susan Parker had attempted their escape from the S4 Site. Having done as much as he could to sanitize the situation there, Smith had returned to DC to personally deal with the fallout. Those in charge would want answers. Knowing he was coming home, several days earlier, Smith once again made reservations at Le Bilboquet.

Two valets stood near the entrance of Le Bilboquet. Upon seeing Smith's limousine approaching, the nearest valet quickly straightened his bright red vest and adjusted the nametag that sat over his right front pocket. As the limousine came to a complete stop, he hurried to open the passenger door. Baldwin, one of the two agents assigned to Smith's protection detail, stepped from the car and abruptly stopped the valet.

"We have this," Agent Baldwin told the valet as he scanned the parking area for potential threats. Satisfied it was safe; he opened the door for Smith.

"Would you like us to accompany you inside, sir?" Agent Baldwin asked, though he already knew Smith's answer.

"No, Mr. Baldwin, I will be dining alone tonight," Smith replied as he slid from the vehicle. One of the valets held open the main door to Le Bilboquet as Smith drew near.

"Good evening, sir," the valet said with a slight bow. Smith casually walked through the main door without so much of a nod of acknowledgment towards the valet.

Just a few feet inside the door, Smith was greeted by the maître d' who had been standing behind an elegant, hand-carved podium.

"Good evening, sir. Do you have a reservation?" the maître d' asked. He was holding a pen in his hand prepared to scratch Smith's name off the register.

"Of course. It is under Johnathan Smith," Smith replied slightly irritated. He had been coming to this restaurant for more than two decades. Though this maître d' seemed new, management should have made him aware that he should be considered a VIP.

"Ah, yes here you are," the maître d' stated, finding Smith's name in the register. He crossed Smith's name off.

"Right this way, Mr. Smith." Tucking a menu beneath his arm, the maître d' began escorting Smith through the restaurant. Relatively small, nearly the entire dining area could be seen from any table in the restaurant. Still, the maître d' guided Smith to the most secluded area. From there Smith was afforded a view of the entire restaurant.

"Can I get you anything to drink while you wait, Mr. Smith?" the maître d' asked as he handed Smith his menu.

"Bring me a bottle of Château d'Yquem," Smith answered. The maître d' smiled and left with his order.

Smith looked around the restaurant. It was small but fashionable. Every table was covered with a fresh, white tablecloth. Each place setting had eight pieces of silverware, all properly positioned around five pieces of fine china. A monogramed napkin lay in the middle of each place setting. Set in the center of every table was an Amber Euro Venetian candle. The restaurant's lights were bright enough to easily see, yet dim enough to set a romantic mood. In the background, almost undetectable, soft classical music played over unseen speakers.

Though the restaurant was rather expensive, Smith was still surprised so few customers were currently patronizing it. Smith assumed that due to the recent pandemic, many people were still not comfortable dining out. As he looked around, Smith observed a younger couple sitting near the main door. Both were well dressed but looked as if they would be more comfortable eating fries out of a basket at Applebee's.

To his right, near an older, well-dressed gentleman, a busboy was busy clearing off one table. The older man was clean-shaven. He wore a white fedora and four-pocket, tweed vest. He sat alone sipping on a brandy. Reading glasses were perched on the end of his nose. However, the customer who drew Smith's attention the most was the woman sitting alone at the bar engaging the bartender in conversation.

She wore a red silk, form-fitting dress. The dress was slit nearly halfway up her thigh. Her straight shoulder-length hair was nearly as red as the dress. The facemask she wore for the pandemic matched the rest of her outfit.

She was definitely a high-end call girl, Smith thought. Of course, this was not the first high-class prostitute he had seen sitting at the bar of this restaurant. Usually, though, they were accompanied by some politician or wealthy businessman.

Since she was alone, Smith assumed her "date" had been delayed. If he did not arrive shortly, Smith would have his bodyguard, Baldwin "requisition" her for the remainder of the evening. Of course, he would have to pay her considerably more for the abuse he was going to put her through. He was not worried about any complaints she might file. The prostitutes in DC were well known for their discretion.

The maître d' arrived with the Château d'Yquem. After popping the cork, he poured a small amount into the glass that sat in front of Smith.

Picking the wine glass up by its stem, Smith held it under his nose for a brief moment before taking a small amount into his mouth. He briefly allowed the wine to cover his palate before swallowing it. Smith nodded his approval at the maître d' who poured half a glass before setting the bottle down on the table.

As the maître d' stepped back, Smith noticed the redheaded prostitute was coming towards him. He decided involving Baldwin was not going to be necessary. As she arrived at his table, Smith motioned with his hand to the empty seat across from him. The maître d' pulled the chair out and held it as the woman sat down. The maître d' then stepped a short distance away. Smith, not one for small talk, began the negotiations.

"So, tell me, young lady, how much is this evening going to cost me?" Smith said with a knowing grin as he picked up the wine glass.

"A lot more than you are probably willing to pay," Susan Parker said as she removed the red mask covering her face. "Keep both your hands visible," she directed.

Smith froze. Not only was Susan's presence at his dinner table unnerving, he saw she held a pistol in her right hand. Quickly, she took the monogramed napkin off the table and covered the small Glock 43. Though now concealed from the rest of the establishment, Smith knew the 9mm pistol was still pointed directly at his chest. Regaining his composure, Smith smiled.

"Ms. Parker, I see you decided to join me for dinner. I must say you and the late Mr. Riley were definitely well suited for one another. You never seem to stop surprising me. I must ask, how did you find out about this restaurant?" Smith casually took a sip of wine.

If he could get her to drop her guard, Smith calculated, he could create a disturbance, which would draw the attention of his bodyguards. Alternatively, if he could drag out the conversation long enough, he could alert a member of the staff. Eventually, one of his agents would enter needing to use the restroom. It was all just a matter of timing.

"And though I respect the effort you are making; I am not sure what you are planning on doing, Ms. Parker?" Smith said arrogantly, as he motioned to the gun with his wine glass. "You can't just shoot me in front of all these witnesses."

"Well, you see, we have your personnel file," Susan answered. "Among other things, it provided us your home address. We initially considered taking you there, but after reviewing your security system, we discovered you had a safe room. We also determined your alarm system was hooked directly into the FBI's HRT at Quantico. We realized we would have a difficult time getting to you before the HRT arrived."

Smith nodded his appreciation for the work Susan had performed in her planning. He moved his left hand a little closer to the table knife.

"Fortunately for us, your file also mentioned your favorite restaurant," Susan said, motioning with her free hand to the interior of Le Bilboquet. "For that, we only needed to know when you would be coming. Do you remember my undergraduate student Josh Williams?" Susan asked.

As Susan mentioned Josh's name, the busboy, stopped what he was doing. He turned and looked at Smith and removed his face covering.

"Josh here took a job at Le Bilboquet a couple weeks ago," Susan continued. Smith suddenly did not like the direction the conversation was going. He watched as Josh lifted his shirt slightly to expose the handgun he had tucked in his waistline.

"Every day he checked the register for your reservation. We thought it might take a few more weeks, but we knew the call would eventually come. Once it did, the rest was relatively easy." Smith was becoming concerned.

"Josh canceled all the other reservations for tonight," Susan explained. "Then Derek's wealthy friend Michael King paid the owner and staff handsomely to close down for the evening, no questions asked." As Susan said this, Mike, who had been pretending to be the bartender, came around the counter. His muscular frame coming to stand not far from Smith's right. Panic began to come over Smith. He thought about yelling for Baldwin.

"You underestimated those loyal to Derek," Susan continued. "He had many friends." Though she kept her tone low, rage began to enter her voice. "Your men outside have already been detained by the two valets. You see they and the maître d' all served with Derek in the Marines."

Jackson and Skiers had assumed the role of the valets. Shortly after Smith entered the restaurant, they had gotten the drop on Smith's agents. Rios who pretended to be the maître d', had assumed a position near Smith's left side, opposite Mike.

"The couple sitting by the door?" Susan nodded in that direction with her head. "Well, that is Brian Hall and his wife Amy. Brian worked with Derek on Hanford's SRT. Do you remember when you threatened her life? I can assure you Brian does, especially since Amy was pregnant at the time," Susan reminded Smith.

The younger couple stood. Brian and Amy Hall turned towards Smith. Now paying more attention, Smith internally chastised himself for not recognizing the fit, clean-cut, young man as soon as he entered the restaurant.

The couple briefly looked at Smith before walking out the front door. Though they hated Smith, Brian was still a law enforcement officer. There was a line he was willing to walk up to, but he did not want to cross it.

Smith was not sure what he was going to do. He had to reason with Susan and the others.

"Listen, Ms. Parker," Smith began, "I am sorry about what we put you through."

"What you put us through!" Susan shouted, losing composure. "It wasn't like you 'put us through' a tax audit! You had Professor Wainwright murdered then tried to assassinate us! You had us framed for murder! Hell, you were going to have your people experiment on me! And, you shot Derek!" Susan yelled the last part.

"Yes." Smith was nodding his head, trying to get Susan to calm herself. "I did frame you both for murder. And I did send those men after you. Moreover, I regret having to shoot Mr. Riley. I had the utmost respect for him. But you must understand it was all done for national security. It wasn't personal." As Smith finished, he became more concerned when he saw Susan almost smile.

"Thank you," Susan replied. "Did you get all that?" Susan said as she glanced at the older gentleman in the white fedora. Smith had nearly forgotten about this man. Now that he scrutinized him closer there was an air of familiarity.

"Every word," John Winoski stated. He clicked off the small digital camera he had been using to record the conversation. Winoski had hidden the camera under one of the monogramed napkins similar to how Susan had the pistol concealed. He stood and tipped his hat towards Susan and proceeded to leave the restaurant.

"The fedora was my idea," Susan said, referring to her friend Professor Michael Wainwright. He was well known for wearing a white fedora. That was before Smith's assassins murdered him. "You see, Smith," Susan said as she stood, "we have you on camera admitting your culpability. We have your personnel file, we have John Winoski's testimony and nearly thirty years of evidence. We are going to burn it all to the ground."

Susan stood. Along with Josh, Mike, and Rios they triumphantly looked at Smith. For several long moments, he remained quiet.

"Is that it?" Smith finally asked. His tone now incredulous as he was no longer concerned Susan was going to shoot him.

"The video? Well shit, I was under duress because a crazy woman, wanted for murder, was pointing a gun at me," Smith began dismantling Susan's plan in front of her.

"Mr. Winoski and his information. When I am done with him, the disinformation campaign will paint him as nothing more than a disgruntled employee with good computer software and imagery manipulation skills.

"Hell, even if it goes sideways," Smith explained, "I've been a hundred different people over the years. I will just become one more. Besides, I am just a worker bee in this whole thing. In very short order, everything will be moved, rebranded, or otherwise altered, as we've done a dozen times before."

Smith picked up his glass and took a long sip of wine. Setting the glass back on the table, he looked at the four of them as he picked up the bottle and began refilling his glass.

"You're right," Susan said in an almost deflated tone. She raised the pistol and pointed it at his chest. Smith looked at her and smiled as he continued to fill his glass.

"Susan, don't," Mike said. "When you kill another person, it doesn't matter if he's a friend or an enemy, it changes you forever." The restaurant was quiet.

"Been there, done that," Susan said as she looked at Mike, a tear in her eye. Then her gaze fell back on Smith.

"This is for Professor Wainwright," she said as she pulled the trigger. The first shot struck Smith in the chest and took him by surprise. The wine bottle he held fell to the floor and shattered.

"This is for Marcus." Susan fired the second shot. It also struck Smith in the chest as he looked up in shock at Susan. A gasp came from his throat.

"And this is for Derek!" Susan raised the pistol six inches and fired the third shot striking Smith square in the forehead. He toppled over backwards in his chair, landing hard on the floor.

Everyone remained motionless for several moments. Susan, still with her arm extended, opened her fingers and dropped the pistol on the table. It knocked over several dishes as it landed. Not exactly sure what the next step should be, no one moved for a brief period. Then Mike took charge.

"It's over Susan," Mike began. "You and Josh get out of here." Mike squeezed her shoulders and gently pointed her towards the door. "Rios and I will clean this place up. When we are done it will be like he was never here," he said softly.

Several more moments passed before Susan turned and began walking towards the door.

"What about the two bodyguards?" Josh asked concerned about potential witnesses.

"They are already dead," Mike replied quietly. "I told Jackson and Skiers to take them out. I was planning on killing Smith myself after you and Susan left. He was too dangerous to let live and I didn't want you or Susan to have to do it. Don't worry, we got this. Their bodies will never be found. Go take care of our girl."

Rios had already picked up the pistol and was retrieving the industrial cleaning materials he and Mike had prepositioned.

As Susan stepped outside, she did not even notice the two bodyguards, Skiers and the limousine were gone. Jackson was standing there to meet her. He smiled in understanding as her emotions slowly consumed her. As Josh stepped alongside

Susan, a large thirty-eight-foot Thor-Miramar RV pulled up to front of the restaurant.

Purchased by Mike just two weeks earlier, the luxury RV was quickly converted to their use. Jackson walked over and opened the side door to the RV. Susan gave Jackson a hug then stepped into the motorhome. Josh shook Jackson's hand, then followed Susan inside. Once in the RV. Josh relieved the driver.

"Are you okay?" Derek asked as Susan stepped through the kitchenette toward the back living area.

Derek was laying on the king-sized bed in the back. He was still recovering from his injuries. The bed and living area had been turned into a makeshift hospital room. An IV was attached to Derek's right arm and his left arm had been put in a cast. The open collar of his shirt exposed large bandages crossing his chest. Susan smiled at him and wiped a tear from her eye.

"I am now," she said.

I was a miracle he was alive. During their escape, Smith had shot Derek twice. The first round entered through his back and exited his chest, collapsing a lung in the process. However, the second round had struck the MP5, slung across Derek's chest and did not penetrate.

Derek would have surely died as a result without Mike's forethought. Before attempting their rescue of Susan and Derek, Mike knew there could be casualties. So, he enlisted the help from his golfing buddy and Derek's former Corpsman, Dr. Jeffery Comfort.

The doctor just happened to be the head of surgery at UCSF. Over the last thirty years, Dr. Comfort developed many friendships, a number of former veterans who were now immersed in the medical field. They were as loyal to him as he was to Derek.

With their assistance and Mike's resources, he was able to set up an off-the-books trauma team. When they started the rescue attempt, the team was placed on standby.

Initially, it was touch and go. Dr. Comfort was not going to give up on his former team leader. Following nearly thirteen hours of surgery, Derek was out of the woods. He remained unconscious for two additional days. As he regained consciousness in the recovery room the others had already begun to hatch their plan to take care of Smith.

Derek protested when he learned of the plan. He did not want to endanger any of them further. However, he eventually agreed when they convinced him they would always be in danger so long as Smith was out there. Besides, they were going to proceed with or without his blessing.

As Josh relieved Dr. Comfort from the driver's seat of the RV, the doctor walked into the back and began a quick assessment of Derek.

"So how is our patient, Doctor?" Susan asked.

"Oh, he'll live," Comfort said with a smile, "and be all the more arrogant and a bigger pain in the ass because of it, I am sure."

Susan took a seat on the bed next to Derek as the RV began to pull away from the restaurant.

"So where are we off too now?" Derek asked. As he was still recovering, Dr. Comfort had been keeping him on some heavy pain medication. As such, Derek's mind remained a little cloudy.

"First, Mike has rented us a little house where we can crash until you are fully recovered," Susan replied.

"And then?" Derek pushed.

"And then we need to go rescue Scar and his troop," Susan replied. She leaned forward and kissed him.

"I love you," Derek said as she pulled away.

"I love you more!" Susan replied, for once getting the final word in. ◉

GLOSSARY

249 SAWs: A portable, belt-fed Squad Automatic Weapon. Commonly used throughout the military.

6.5 Creedmoor: An accurate, large caliber round used in sniper rifles.

A-10 Warthog: An Air Force airplane specifically designed for close air support and attacking ground targets.

ALARA: A term used in the Department of Energy to describe how to keep radiation exposure As Low As Reasonably Achievable.

ALICE Packs: All-Purpose Lightweight Individual Carrying Equipment. A backpack originally adopted by the US Military in 1973.

APCs: Armored Personnel Carriers. A softly armored vehicle used to transport troops from one location to another.

AMTRAC: Assault Amphibious Tracked Vehicle: Used extensively by the Marine Corps to bring troops from the ship to assault beaches. Used heavily during the Gulf War.

AN/PRC-77: Radio Set is a man pack, portable VHF FM combat-net radio transceiver manufactured by Associated Industries and used to provide short-range, two-way communication.

Blue Force Trackers: GPS satellite equipped computers and software that transmits a friendly unit's location on a battlefield.

Corpsman: A Navy medic assigned to Marine and SEAL units to perform emergency medical treatment to injured personnel in the field.

CPU: Central Processing Unit. The CPU is the primary component of a computer that processes instructions.

EBE: Extraterrestrial Biological Entity. Another term for alien.

FAST: The Marine Corps Fleet Anti-Terrorism and Security Teams. A unit with the specific mission of provided enhanced anti-terrorism capabilities to Naval Facilities.

FBI HRT: The Federal Bureau of Investigations Hostage Rescue Team. This is the premier tactical team in the FBI.

G-man: Government Man. This is a slang term used for decades to describe government agents.

Heckler and Koch 9mm MP5SD: A suppressed sub-machine gun made by Heckler and Koch, often called H&K and used by specialized tactical teams around the world.

IFF: Identify Friend or Foe. A variety of devices and techniques designed to help military units recognize other friendly military units to avoid accidental fratricide.

LaRue Optimized Battle Rifle or OBR: A semi-automatic modern Sniper Rifle manufactured by LaRue Tactical in Texas.

LCPL: Lance Corporal. A rank in the Marine Corps.

MARSOC: Marine Corps Special Operations Command. The Marine Corps equivalent to the Navy's Seal Team Six or Army Delta Force.

Minuteman: A nuclear equipped ICBM that could be ready on a moment's notice.

MOPP: Mission Orientated Protective Posture. The designation given to the clothing and gear designed to protect the wearer from chemical and biological threats.

Motherboard: A circuit board containing the principal components of a computer or other device.

NTS: Nevada Test Site. A Department of Energy Facility located North of Las Vegas.

OBR: Optimized Battle Rifle made by LaRue.

PFC: Private First Class. A rank in the Marine Corps.

Press-Check: A method of partially opening a weapon's slide to check whether the weapon is loaded or not.

RIP: Recon Indoctrination Platoon. Where Marines are placed before they attend the Basic Reconnaissance Course.

RPG: Rocket Propelled Grenade: A hand held rocket launcher used extensively throughout the Middle East.

SITREP: Situation Report

S-vest: Suicide Vest. A vest filled with explosives typically worn by suicide bombers.

TNT: Trinitrotoluene, a pale-yellow solid compound used as an explosive.

UCMJ: Uniform Code of Military Justice. Military laws and rules that when violated can lead to punishments to include imprisonment.

UCSF: The University of California, San Francisco Medical Center is a research and teaching hospital in San Francisco.,

Wachtmeister: This is a sergeant of the Swiss Guard, tasked with protecting the Vatican.

BOLO: Law enforcement acronym meaning BE ON the LOOK OUT.

COG: Continuity of Government. Plans developed by the government to protect senior government officials during disasters or events such as nuclear war.

FTCA: Federal Tort Claims Act: Is a 1946 federal statute that permits private parties to sue the United States in a federal court.

GAO: Government Accountability Office: The GAO provides fact-based, nonpartisan information to Congress. Often called the "congressional watchdog," the GAO investigates federal spending as well as fraud, waste and abuse.

GDP: Gross Domestic Product: The total value of goods produced and services provided by a country during a single year.

Global Hawk UAV: A large unmanned aerial vehicle designed for both surveillance or target acquisition.

GPS: The Global Positioning System (GPS) is a US-owned utility that provides users with positioning, navigation, and timing (PNT) services. This system consists of three segments: the space segment, the control segment, and the user segment. The US Air Force develops, maintains, and operates the space and control segments.

GSA: The General Services Administration is an independent agency of the United States government established in 1949 to help manage and support the basic functioning of federal agencies.

Heckler and Koch 9mm MP5SD: A suppressed sub-machine gun made by Heckler and Koch, often called H&K and used by specialized tactical teams around the world.

HVAC: Heating Ventilation and Air Conditioning.

LBV: Load Bearing Vest. Often ballistic, these vests typically are worn by tactical teams to carry the numerous items needed.

Nike Ajax: The Ajax was an anti-bomber missile designed to take down a high-altitude plane.

Nike Hercules: The Hercules was an improved anti-bomber missile. This missile contained a nuclear warhead. The theory behind the nuclear warhead was the missile, when fired, could destroy entire formations of Soviet aircraft.

Operator: Common term used to describe Special Operations Members who are "surgical" in their tactical abilities.

Phoneme: Any of the perceptually distinct units of sound in a specified language that distinguish one word from another.

PIV Badge / Credential: A standardized Identification card used by all branches of the United States Government.

PNNL: Pacific Northwest National Laboratory. One of the nation's premier research and development laboratories located in Richland, Washington and overseen by the Department of Energy.

POC: Patrol Operations Center, is Hanford Patrol's 9-1-1 center.

POG: People Other than Grunt. A derogatory military term to describe military personnel who are not in the "combat arms" fields (e.g. Cooks, Logistics, Motor Transport, etc.).

PsyOps: The cyber unit is the Counter Intelligence and Psychological Operation Section of the SRT, referred to as PsyOps.

RDD: The acronym stands for Research, Disinformation and Destruction. When the PsyOps Unit investigates a potential person of interest, they first conduct Research on that person. If it is decided the information is credible, if possible the

SCIF: Sensitive Compartmented Information Facility: United States National Security/National Defense and intelligence information is an enclosed area within a building that is used to process Sensitive Compartmented Information (SCI) types of classified information.

Shemagh: also called a keffiyeh and originated in the Middle East. They are a scarf-type wrap commonly found in arid regions to provide protection from direct sun exposure. Commonly used by military special operations units.

SRT: Special Response Team: A tactical team of the Department of Energy that is a hybrid of both a military Special Operations Team and police SWAT Team.

VIN: Vehicle Identification Number. Commonly placed on several locations of a vehicle, to include the engine, door panels and frame to identify the vehicle. ◉